The

BOOK

~ of ~

LIVING
SECRETS

The

BOOK

of

LIVING SECRETS

Madeleine Roux

Quill Tree Books
An Imprint of HarperCollinsPublishers

Quill Tree Books is an imprint of HarperCollins Publishers.

The Book of Living Secrets
Copyright © 2022 by Madeleine Roux
All rights reserved. Manufactured in Lithuania.
No part of this book may be used or reproduced in any manner whatsoever without written permission except in the case of brief quotations embodied in critical
articles and reviews. For information address HarperCollins Children's Books, a
division of HarperCollins Publishers, 195 Broadway, New York, NY 10007.
www.epicreads.com

ISBN 978-0-06-294142-8

Typography by Joel Tippie
21 22 23 24 25   SB   10 9 8 7 6 5 4 3 2 1
❖
First Edition

For Nini, Cici, and Mimi. Back then, we were goddesses.

Love is merely a madness.

—William Shakespeare, *As You Like It*

Moira Byrne did not believe in destiny, yet destiny found her in the public gardens, standing under a leafless tree, regarding an easel and a blank canvas. He was the most beautiful creature she had ever seen: trim and tall, with a wild mop of ebony hair and painterly fingers.

Destiny had brought them together.

How romantic, she thought. And how tragic. How could such a beautiful thing be all alone?

"Who is that boy?" she asked nobody. The others in her party at the picnic did not hear, but Moira asked the question again and again in her heart. Who was he? She had to have him.

Beside her on the picnic blanket, her fiancé, Kincaid Vaughn, remained buried in a book. He always had time for his books and science and experiments but never time for her. Moira stared at the boy painting, wondering what it would be like to hold his hand and kiss him. She held these two truths in her heart: that she could never marry her betrothed, and that she would do absolutely anything to have the handsome painter in the park.

Moira dispatched her maid, Greta, to approach him discreetly later, and Greta returned with a name and a token, for the boy had seen Moira, too. He had offered Greta a handkerchief to take back to the beautiful girl with the flaming red hair and green eyes: a square of cotton smudged with black paint.

"He's French," Greta had also said. "He has a funny accent."

Severin Sylvain, *Moira said silently, in her heart, repeating the name she had learned.* I will have him one day. I would give up anything to be his—my fortune, my family, my breath.

Moira Byrne did not believe in destiny, but she believed in true love, in a bond of souls. Souls not just married together but irrevocably intertwined, sewn together with the thread of Fate. Tear them apart and they would bleed. For love was pain, that could not be denied—her heart ached for the thing she wanted, the thing she would stop at nothing to have.

—Moira, *chapter 2*

Connie stood outside her date's house, swathed in orange tulle. Beside her, her best friend, Adelle, squeaked out a low "Eeeeee!" of anticipation. In all that puffy neon fabric, she felt like a sunset on an alien planet. She felt alien, too. Connie took a deep breath and raised her hand to knock on Julio's door.

Sadie Hawkins. *She* had asked *him.*

"I can't do this, Delly," she wheezed. It came out like a deflating balloon.

Adelle gasped and took a step toward her, practically glowing in the light of the glass sconces hanging outside Julio's front door. She had rented a Victorian-era ball gown from a theatrical supply store in Brookline. Sumptuous green velvet with black lace and a real bustle, chosen to match her favorite literary heroine's style.

Don't I look just like her? Just like Moira?

Adelle, blond and heavily freckled, didn't much resemble the scarlet-haired, porcelain-doll perfection of Moira, but she had looked so happy in the costume-supply dressing room, beaming with excitement, that Connie had told her yes, she looked just like Moira. It had made Adelle's day, and so it had made Connie's, too. Until Adelle reminded her that they needed dates, and didn't Julio always stare at Connie in class? And even Connie's strict Catholic parents liked Julio, which really was something.

"What's wrong?" Adelle asked, taking Connie by the wrist and dragging her away from Julio's front door. "It's okay to be nervous. Boys are terrifying."

"It's not that," Connie mumbled.

It was and it wasn't. She didn't feel afraid of Julio; she just didn't want to go with him to the dance. Take him on, 1v1 on the soccer pitch? Sure. Slow dance with him in a gymnasium under the flash of strobes and cheap purple gobos? No thanks. At night in bed, she lay beneath a ceiling plastered with posters of Megan Rapinoe, Layshia Clarendon, Serena, and Abby Wambach, and wondered if she could get up the courage to ask Gigi from the comic-book store on Commonwealth to the Sadie Hawkins dance. Gigi was a year older and went to private school, but she might say yes.

She *might* have, if only Connie had asked her.

"Can we go somewhere else?" Connie asked, putting her back to Julio's door. Adelle's stepdad, Greg, had dropped them off there, with the understanding that Julio's parents would drive them all to the school for the dance. Both girls had turned sixteen in September, but neither had made much progress toward a license, preferring their bikes and the T over summer driver's ed classes. "Typical Virgos," Adelle liked to say.

"Like where?" Adelle asked. Her lower lip wobbled, and Connie winced.

"Like anywhere else. Burger Buddies for a Pigmalion, or even the Emporium. I just . . . I don't think I can do this."

To her credit, Adelle did not cry. That didn't make the lance through Connie's heart land any softer. The disappointment was written all over her face—Adelle had been talking up the dance for weeks, obsessed with her dress, the way she would curl her hair, and the secret date she would only reveal the night of.

"S-sure," Adelle said. Her long green train dragged down the sidewalk, collecting leaves. "I knew this would happen. I pulled a tarot spread before getting dressed tonight, and right away the Five of Cups came up. Figures."

Connie nodded as if she knew what the Five of Cups signified. She didn't. Lately, Adelle had been submerged up to her eyeballs in the esoteric and the occult. She couldn't make a single decision without consulting a star chart or whipping out one of her growing collection of tarot decks.

"Delly? I'm sorry."

"No, it's okay. If you don't want to do it . . ."

Connie adjusted the backpack on her shoulder. Her normal, comfortable clothes were inside. She realized now that they had told on her the whole time—she'd had no intention of going through with Julio, with the dance, with Adelle's romantic notion of the perfect fairy-tale evening. The perfect *ball*. Connie knew that that was what Adelle wanted: to re-create the big dance from their favorite book, *Moira*. Everything was about Moira, if it wasn't about astrology, tarot, wizards, vampires, werewolves, or aliens. Adelle's imagination was as big as her heart, a heart that Connie could now see was clearly breaking.

"I'm sorry," she said again. At the end of the drive, she turned toward Adelle's house. It wasn't a far walk, but Greg had insisted on driving them, insisted on the formality. That was a point in his favor, at least in Connie's eyes: he knew how important the night was for Adelle. But Greg never really won points with Adelle no matter what he did; they were oil and water. Connie could already see rips forming in the tulle at the hem of her dress.

"I mean, I pulled the Three of Swords, too, so I should've known, but I'm curious . . . what made you change your mind?" Adelle asked, as they walked side by side under the occasional flash of streetlamps. Orange and yellow trees drooped over the lane; tumbleweeds of crunchy leaves were blown by a wind that they walked directly against.

I like girls, Connie didn't say. "Julio just gives me bad vibes."

They were quiet for a while. Connie took out her phone from

her backpack and texted Julio an excuse and an apology. Then she sighed. It would be all over school on Monday; he would tell his friends and they would tell everyone on the baseball team and then the baseball-team girlfriends would whisper about her. That wasn't really anything new; even Connie's own teammates had cornered her before, Caroline and Tonya in particular. Both girls were proudly out, and they were convinced Connie was gay too. "Look at you," Caroline had said once in the locker room, rolling her eyes and tossing her jersey away. "You're *sure* you're not gay?"

Shrugging them off just made it worse. But Connie wanted to come to that conclusion on her own, in her heart—she didn't want to come out just because she looked a certain way or dressed a certain way. *Nobody,* she had thought then, as she did now, *can make me something without my consent.* She knew the truth in her heart, she just didn't know if she was ready to say it aloud. It didn't help that she and Adelle were, well, *weird,* more interested in tracking down after-school D&D games and going to midnight book releases than finding a good house party for a clandestine make-out sesh.

Caroline and Tonya would have a field day with this.

"Hey!" Adelle nudged her, and when Connie glanced over at her friend, she was surprised to find her smiling. "I know what we can do."

"Yeah?"

"Let's grab our bikes and head to the Emporium. Look at this!" Adelle pulled her own slender smartphone out of the tasseled bag dangling from her left wrist. After navigating to her email, she showed Connie a newsletter from their favorite oddities shop, the Witch's Eye Emporium. A little creepy, she thought, that the email was personally addressed to Adelle, and sent only to her email.

"You gave Straven your email?" Connie asked.

"Sure, we both signed up for the newsletter."

"Yeah, but I didn't get this one," Connie pointed out. Her skin prickled and she shivered. Whenever that happened, her mother always said it was someone walking over her grave.

"Probably just a server hiccup or something," replied Adelle, who seemed completely unperturbed to be the sole recipient.

But Connie frowned. "Have you been hanging out there alone?"

"You mean more than usual?"

"Uh-huh."

Adelle was suddenly uninterested in eye contact. "Sure. When I have a free minute. He's teaching me advanced tarot techniques, and he gave me this book, *What the F*ck Is Tarot?* Oh man, Greg fliiiiipped out. He honest to God thinks I should be doing sudoku and SAT prep twenty-four hours a day." She pushed the phone screen closer to Connie's face.

NOV 13 ONLY—FULL MOON AFTER-HOURS TEATIME

"Mr. Straven wouldn't shut up about it when I stopped by this week," Adelle continued. "He says you should come by more often."

No thanks, Connie thought. She had plenty on her plate with practice and weight-room time and study groups, but maybe Adelle needed more on her plate. Maybe all this tarot and Straven stuff was a cry for help. Maybe, she thought, she should've noticed those changes in her friend. But they had been to the Emporium a million times; her paranoia was surely just that. She shivered again. *Someone walking over my grave.* A minivan flew down the road, blasting hip-hop, the six teenagers crammed inside laughing maniacally on their way to the dance.

Adelle tilted her head to the side, one curl brushing her round cheek. "He was disappointed when I told him we couldn't make it to the tea thing. Sadie Hawkins and all."

"All right—why not?" Connie managed a smile. If Adelle could turn around this quickly after a disappointment, then Connie knew it was only fair to bolster her spirits further. She would feel better anyway if Adelle went to the shop accompanied, unable to shake the feeling that this email sent directly to Adelle was suspicious. The old man had always been kind to them, but years of stranger-danger curriculum hadn't been lost on her. "All dressed up, might as well go out."

"Psh, I'm not biking downtown in this thing," Adelle said, fluffing out the tiered green skirts of her dress. "Greg would kill me. This rental wasn't cheap."

Greg turned out to be more interested in reruns of *Everwood*, posted up in his usual recliner, tucked behind a slew of bookshelves just to the left of the foyer. As the girls raced up the stairs of the spacious two-story colonial, Connie heard the TV cut out and the recliner squeak. Ahead of her, Adelle froze.

"Crap," she whispered.

"Girls?" Greg appeared at the foot of the stairs. He was tall and nondescript, the human embodiment of a thrifted cardigan. Adelle liked to call her stepdad "a nonplayable character." Adelle never knew what her mother, a world-famous death doula, saw in regular ol' unassuming Greg. "I thought you were going to the dance. Did you forget something?"

"Um . . ." Connie could hear Adelle conjuring a lie as she stalled for time. "Yeah. I forgot our copy of *Moira*. Can't forget that, not tonight!"

Greg blew out a frazzled breath and shook his head. "You could be reading *Rebecca* or *Emma* or, God, I don't know, *Catcher in the Rye*. Real books. Real *literature*. Why do you have to rot your brains with that bodice-ripping junk?"

"It's not junk, Greg!" Adelle shot back, heated. Bright points of red flooded her pale cheeks. "Why do you have to be so . . . so judgy? Mom says judgment is just unprocessed trauma being projected, remember?"

He rolled his eyes, adjusted his glasses, and returned to the recliner. "Do you need another ride?"

"No," Adelle called back, continuing up the stairs. "Forget we were even here." When they reached the upper landing and swerved toward her room, she muttered, "God, why does he have to suck so much?"

As soon as the door closed behind them, they were plunged into Adelle's fantasy world. Twinkling fairy lights covered the far wall, except for the window. The curtains were a dark, dramatic purple. Lately, the design choices had gone in a more macabre direction. Less Chip and Jojo and more Elvira, Mistress of the Dark. Adelle had stenciled alchemical designs on the walls in crimson and black, and her computer desk was pushed opposite the four-poster bed, partially concealed by scarlet mosquito netting. Their sanctuaries couldn't have been more different—Adelle's a darkly romantic, scatterbrained dream, and Connie's covered in pennants, posters, and hooks holding her collection of MLS jerseys, weight belts, and trophies.

A glittery black banner had been strung between two of the four posts of Adelle's bed, reading:

A BIT OF MADNESS IS KEY,

TO GIVE US NEW COLORS TO SEE

Adelle, Connie thought, a little uncharitably, was the only person in the world aside from the cast and crew who remained disappointed *La La Land* hadn't actually won the Oscar that year. Adelle began to strip out of her green ball gown with quick, peevish movements that Connie couldn't miss. While Connie pulled on her matching tracksuit bottoms and top, she felt her heart sink again. She looked at the banner hanging over the bed.

"Hey. I know I let you down tonight."

"It's totally okay."

"No, it isn't," Connie replied, sitting on the bed while Adelle changed into black ankle boots and a frothy black dress—what Connie teasingly called her Goth Lite Uniform™. "I know you were really looking forward to the dance. I messed up. I just . . . I can't explain it."

Not yet, at least.

"Just go with me to the Emporium," Adelle said seriously. She did, in fact, collect their shared, tattered copy of *Moira* and a lacy black mini backpack. "That will make up for it. Mr. Straven says the full moon is special, that he might even try casting spells tonight."

Connie's eyes opened wider. There was that warning shiver again. "Spells?"

"Mm-hmm." Adelle dropped down onto the bed next to her, the book landing on the duvet between them. Connie put her hand on the cover and felt the familiar thrill she always did when she touched her favorite book. She didn't love it nearly as much as Adelle did, but nobody loved the novel that much, probably not even the actual author. "I was thinking . . . even if we had gone to the dance, I was going to see if you wanted to go to the Emporium after," Adelle continued.

"Really?"

"Yeah. It's . . ." Adelle licked her lips, evidently nervous. Her mismatched blue and green eyes roamed to the book and Connie's hand. "He really wanted us to come by. There's a spell—a real spell—that he wants to cast for us. I know it sounds bizarre, and, like, I don't know if I believe it myself, but it might be cool, right? If anyone can perform magic, it's Mr. Straven. He's been teaching me so much, I think he might actually be . . . I don't know. Gifted. Touched by something magical."

They both loved the Witch's Eye Emporium specifically because it was the weirdest, creepiest, coolest place in Boston. But it had always seemed like a safe creepy, a make-believe creepy. Connie remembered the time two years ago when they had gone to Salem for Halloween with Adelle's mom. It was the first time she had believed that there truly were spirits and demons, and things that simply couldn't be neatly explained. She believed in science, but Salem had made her believe in . . . something else. Just something else, unnamed and ill-defined but real enough, and kept not in a corner of her brain, but deep in her gut. The town vibrated on a different frequency, one that was enchanting at first but gradually got under her skin. Adelle, of course, had loved it. That is, until they'd slipped into an unassuming candle shop, and the proprietor took one glance at Adelle, saw her heterochromatic eyes, and offered to give them free palm readings.

Connie's was perfunctory enough. She was pretty sure the goggle-eyed woman with her hair-sprayed tangle of yellow straw hair had just felt the weight-lifting calluses on Connie's fingers and run with that. But with Adelle? She took her time, hovering over Adelle's hand as if it were a cherished relic, made of glass, easily shattered.

"This line disappears into darkness," the woman had almost whined, shuddering. "You . . . you disappear into darkness, my dear."

Adelle's mother thought it was the funniest thing she had ever heard. Working in the funerary business, she had muttered a sarcastic "Hon, we all end in darkness, one way or the other, coffin or dust or ash."

But Adelle couldn't let it go. She hardly spoke for the rest of the trip, chewing her nails and staring out the window on the way back to Boston with big, haunted eyes.

"What kind of spell?" Connie finally asked, feeling as if the book beneath her hand had also shuddered.

Adelle twisted and waited until their eyes met, and then she gave the biggest, strangest smile. "He thinks he can send us into the book. Into *Moira*. Would you go if he can do it? Could we do this together?"

2

ADELLE SWALLOWED THE SHARP thorn of disappointment with a smile. At least her best friend had agreed to her harebrained idea—spending the night not at the Sadie Hawkins dance as planned, but at the Emporium. Now she just had to convince Connie to actually go through with the spell, but that wouldn't be so hard—Connie usually gave in and went along with whatever ridiculous scheme Adelle cooked up, like the time she'd made them leave out water for the full moon and then drink it the next morning, floating bugs, debris, and all. Or the time Adelle had convinced her to skip school so they could get their birth charts read by a visiting astrologer, or when, last summer, Adelle was convinced she could talk to her mother's cat and spent all afternoon meowing at the poor thing while Connie recorded them on her phone.

Luckily, *that* footage was long gone. Connie was her partner in crime; she would go along with the spell, especially after having dashed Adelle's dance dreams. That heady disappointment was still somewhat lodged in her throat, but it was time to wash it down.

If Mr. Straven really could perform magic, it would easily make her forget all about Sadie Hawkins.

First stop: Burger Buddies for two Pigmalions, cheeseburgers the size of a toddler's head, with all the toppings and a massive mountain of fries, a big middle finger to Adelle's stepdad, who'd made her family go vegan. It would probably make her puke the next morning, but the sense of rebellion was worth it. Little rebellions. Nothing big. The girls had pinky-promised two years ago, while freshmen, to not smoke or drink; they wanted to get into Yale together. Connie was a shoo-in for her athletics: soccer and track, swimming, and her true love, biathlon. Adelle, self-consciously book smart, would have to work harder.

"Big dreams," Connie would tell her whenever they heard about a kickass party they hadn't been invited to but had pretended to avoid, "big sacrifices."

They wolfed down their burgers too fast and then ordered milkshakes to go.

Back on their bikes, they cruised across Arlington, riding by the Ether Monument and slapping the base for good luck, then southeast toward the pond and the swan boats. They had picked a secret spot there beneath a shady tree: an outcropping of rock that jutted out over the pond and gave them a quiet, peaceful view of the swans. This was the site of their most furious debates: Who was the best March sister? Jo, of course, they agreed, although Adelle silently agonized, suspecting she was probably more of an

Amy. They ranked their favorite literary heroines (Laia, Elizabeth Bennet, Elisa, Katniss, Sierra Santiago, Jane Eyre, and, of course, Moira), and favorite books—Connie once outrageously placing *Jane Eyre* above *their* book, *Moira*, which felt like a betrayal. Nobody else seemed to care about *Moira* the way they did. It never got its sumptuous (and, in their opinion, much-deserved) costume-drama movie, never the *Bridgerton* treatment, never a BBC series.

No, *Moira* languished in the literary swamp where a million other books went to be forgotten.

That was why their guardianship of it mattered. They wouldn't forget *Moira*, or the author, Robin Amery. Almost no information existed about her online, no fan pages or social media, no interviews. After all their searching, Robin remained a brief biography in the back of the novel and a black-and-white photo of a serious-faced white woman with short gray hair smiling vaguely at something off camera.

> *A lover of all things romance, Robin Amery is the author of* Moira *and the award-winning short-story collection* Moberly's Adventure. *Born in Paris, Robin lives with her cat, Fentz, in Boston, Massachusetts.*

No amount of internet or library sleuthing turned up a copy of *Moberly's Adventure* or the award it might have won. Every so often, Connie asked her mother, who worked as a bookseller at a local chain, to try to arrange a signing or event and invite Robin Amery. Rosie would try, but nobody at the store could devise a way to contact her. The publisher, White-Jones, didn't prove to be much help either. *Moira* was long out of print, and they hadn't published anything new of hers in years. Nobody currently at

White-Jones even remembered working with her.

Robin and her book, it seemed, were in grave danger of disappearing altogether. They had to be preserved. Connie and Adelle were the founders, worshippers, and bishops in a church of two. The smallest literature-preservation society on earth.

The rock near the swans was also the place where they bared their souls.

Just a few weekends ago, Connie had confessed that she wasn't looking forward to Sadie Hawkins. Not even a little bit. All the dresses she had tried on had made her feel like Aaron Rodgers stuffed into five yards of tulle. She had been called pretty and cute as a little girl, but that tapered off as she grew up and kept growing. Up and up and up. Then a steady diet of sports and protein shakes gave her broad shoulders and a more angular face, one aunts and uncles called "healthy" and "strong." Strong, not pretty. Why not strong *and* pretty, she had always wondered, what made those things opposites to so many people? As she stood looking in that mirror while shopping for Sadie Hawkins dresses, those aunt and uncle voices boomed over a loudspeaker in her head. Adelle had sworn on every dead ancestor she could remember that Connie was an absolute vision, but her one voice couldn't drown out the others.

Adelle had had her own confession to make: at one of Connie's soccer matches, Adelle had started talking to a boy who'd reminded her of the male protagonist in *Moira*, Severin Sylvain— fair-skinned, with curly black hair, piercing gray eyes, a sleek, slender silhouette. He'd said he liked her weird eyes, and Adelle had blushed, telling him it was heterochromia iridis, and he nodded like he knew what that was. This boy's name was Brady or Grady; she couldn't hear well over the thunder of the crowd. They had made out behind the concession stand, but then he'd tried to put his hand up her shirt and Adelle had fled. That wasn't something Severin would do. Afterward, she hated herself a little bit for having kissed him at all.

It was a sacred place, so of course they had to bike by it on the park path and make sure nobody was there smoking cigarettes or mooning the swan boats. The little patch by the pond was clear, and the girls biked on, full of burgers and slurping their milkshakes, giddy from the sugar as they cruised toward the Witch's Eye Emporium. When Adelle glanced at her friend, Connie seemed calm, even content. She probably didn't believe that Mr. Straven's spell would work, but Adelle's hands felt electric—she was certain.

"So who was your mystery date?" Connie asked as they pedaled furiously through the park.

Adelle demurred, trying to pull ahead of her, but Connie was too strong on the bike, too fast. "It's stupid."

"Come on, tell me, Delly."

"No, it's really, really stupid. You'll think I'm crazy."

"But I already think that." Connie smirked.

"Ha. Ha."

Connie let it drop while they coasted down the path and out of the park, then turned left, weaving between tourists, passing by horse-drawn carriages and nighttime tours of haunted Boston via bus, the guide's voice flaring loud before vanishing as the girls dipped into an alley. When they finally reached the oddity shop, they parked their bikes in the usual spot, a cobwebbed nook just behind the brick stairwell that led to the double glass doors.

"So," Connie said, not even a little winded as they jogged up the stairs, "who was it going to be?"

Adelle dodged behind her friend, and by the light of the green gas lamps outside the shop, she pulled open Connie's backpack and withdrew *Moira*, anticipating the magic to come.

"Severin," she muttered. "From the book."

Connie snorted. "Like an imaginary friend?"

"I told you it was stupid."

Adelle's face felt hot with embarrassment as they entered the shop. She half expected a crowd of people dressed like her, all in black and lace, but there was nobody there for the big full-moon event. Weird. At least they wouldn't have to wait long to talk to Mr. Straven. That was a bonus, she thought.

The Witch's Eye Emporium was empty except for the girls, Mr. Straven, and one nondescript man dressed all in black, with a crisp felt fedora, who spent every day in the Emporium's window, drinking endless cups of coffee. No food or drinks were allowed in the curiosity shop, but he was exempt, apparently. Adelle led her best friend through the maze of tables, cabinets, and glass display cases to the counter. A huge grandfather clock with a carved wooden owl sat sentinel above the cash register. It ticked away silently, its pendulum broken since long before Adelle could remember. The shop burned incense that smelled like lavender, rosemary, and wonder. Six mice, frozen into various poses and professions, sat under bell jars beneath the grandfather clock. Connie found them gross, but Adelle loved them; her own mother's taxidermy collection had always been a fascination. A scientist in a tiny lab coat, a nurse wearing a white hat the size of a thumbnail, a professor with a patched and shabby jacket, a lumberjack with a tuft of beard, a cowboy with pistols drawn.

The sixth mouse was dressed like a witch in a flowing black robe, a matchstick of a wand glued into its right hand. Adelle stared at it while Connie leaned nonchalantly on the glass countertop.

Behind the tall counter, Mr. Straven struck a match and touched it to a beeswax candle impaled on an old-fashioned holder. He was an old, gnarled man, sallow and pale, with a bushy Santa beard and snowy hair, pockmarked cheeks, and very small, very black eyes. He always wore a shabby black coat and baggy trousers; a black hat, like the one the man who sat in the window wore, was propped jauntily on a peg near the taxidermied mice.

"Adelle!" he rasped, a deep sparkle in his black eyes. His gaze shifted briefly to Connie and then to the candle as he set it between them on the countertop. The wax of the candle was ebony, and it had been shaped into a kind of octopus figure, a mass of entwined tentacles, the tallest one holding the wick and flame. "And . . ."

"Constance," Connie reminded him. "Connie? I've been here a million times."

"Of course, of course!" He laughed and tapped the side of his head. "Bad with names."

Mr. Straven was incredibly absentminded, and sometimes called Adelle by what she assumed was his daughter's or wife's name: Ammie. Maybe Cammie. He had a mumbling voice, low and slurred. One of his eyes never quite seemed to focus correctly. Connie shifted uneasily and looked over the man's head at the clock.

"Bit early for you to be here, no? Thought you had that big dance tonight. You don't look dressed for a grand ball." He winked at Adelle, who laughed nervously.

"We decided to skip it and come here," Adelle said. "We had . . . Well, we . . ."

"I changed my mind," Connie chimed in, decisive. "And Delly said something about you having a full-moon event tonight. Are we the only ones here?"

He heaved a tremendous sigh, threatening the candle flame. The man near the window slurped his drink loudly, staring out at the sidewalk, as if to conspicuously not participate. "Things have been slow here lately. You girls are my most loyal customers. It's only fitting that you should have first crack at the real fun." Mr. Straven wiggled his eyebrows and ducked below the counter, producing a tray with a rock, a candle, a few sticks of incense, and a shallow stone dish filled with water.

"Real fun," Connie repeated, squinting. "You mean these so-called spells?"

As the man bellowed with laughter, the flame danced wildly on its wick again, and Adelle wondered how it managed to stay lit. The center of it looked almost green. A cold, slithering feeling wound through her as she stared into the flame.

"Don't sound so skeptical, young lady, or so proud." His black eyes glittered with . . . something. Adelle wanted to be charitable and call it mirth, but it reminded her more of ill mischief. "Or so hesitant. I thought you were keen to try this little experiment. Adelle here volunteered you."

"Did she?" Connie kicked Adelle's shin where Mr. Straven couldn't see.

"I thought it would be a bit of fun." Adelle pinched her lips together tightly, embarrassed. She'd thought Connie would be into it. They had done things like this before. On her last birthday, Adelle had become convinced she was psychic and tried to move a stack of homework papers with her mind. On a random sleepover night, Connie had tried to summon their favorite band with just the power of pure belief. They giggled about it all the time still, but that had been years ago, when Connie was ten, when anything seemed possible. As a joke, on a more recent Sunday, she'd tried again, this time hoping to conjure BTS tickets as a birthday gift for Adelle.

Of course, it hadn't worked. Magic never worked.

Until it did.

"Come on, Connie," Adelle said, hearing a whine enter her voice. She reached out and took hold of Connie's right wrist, giving a light squeeze. "If we can't be in a sweaty gymnasium having our first dance of the year, then we can do something even better. We can time-travel. We can conjure our own magic. Our own dance . . . Not a dance, a ball. A real ball with big gowns and gallant gentlemen and twinkling lights!"

Adelle bit down on her lip, telling herself to calm down. But she saw her friend smile and her shoulders slump in resignation. Connie was giving in.

She lowered her voice, almost conspiratorial. "Do you remember that palm reader in Salem?"

Connie went pale but nodded.

"She said one of my lines would end in darkness. That I would. Maybe this is what she meant, that we would go somewhere even she couldn't see."

But her friend didn't look quite convinced. If anything, she looked spooked. Adelle tried a different tactic. "Don't you want to meet Severin? And Moira? Don't you want to escape this dumb, dreary world for a little bit? It will be like a dream. Right, Mr. Straven?"

He had been nodding along with her every word, as if to encourage Connie to loosen up and go along for the ride. Adelle didn't know if she believed the unhinged stuff coming out of her mouth, but she wanted to. She wanted more than studying for the SATs and her parents' endless *Everwood* DVDs and gloopy vegan dinners that tasted like sand. She didn't want a Grady or a Brady; she wanted Severin. She just . . . wanted. It was an ache, and as she watched Connie chew her cheek and hesitate, she started to wonder—fear—that Connie didn't share that same wild and terrible ache.

"Connie?" she asked softly.

"I have shooting practice early tomorrow," her friend replied.

"Please."

Connie puffed out her cheeks. "I swear we're getting too old for this. Fine. I'm game. How do we make it work?"

Mr. Straven spread his hands wide, gesturing to the tray of items on the countertop. "Do you have the copy of the book I sold you?"

"Here." Adelle slapped it down next to the tray, sounding breathless.

"Perfect. We will orient these items in the cardinal directions around the book. You will find a passage where you would like to land in the novel, hold your hand over it, and recite an incantation, repeating after me."

Connie raised a thick, dark eyebrow. "Seems awfully simple."

"It is not *simple*, my dear." Mr. Straven fixed her with an eerily intense stare. Adelle didn't like it. "This incantation has been honed and perfected over hundreds of years. Perhaps thousands. It is the distillation of unknowable hours of research, sacrifice, and exploration. It can only be performed on a full moon; Mercury must be in retrograde. Mars, Jupiter, Saturn, Mercury, and Venus must be visible in the night sky."

"Aaand you're just going to tell it to the two of us?" Connie snickered. "I don't buy it."

"You don't have to, my dear. You just have to repeat after me and see for yourself."

The strange, slithering feeling wound through Adelle again. She took a small step back from the counter and realized for the first time that this whole endeavor was a bad idea.

She wanted wonder and magic, but not if it felt like this.

You disappear into darkness.

But now Connie wasn't backing down. Her competitive side had come out. In fact, she sounded downright defiant as she leaned toward Mr. Straven while he arranged the items around the book and lit the second candle. "If this works"—she gave a quick, glaring glance at Adelle—"and it won't, but let's say it does, how do I get back in time for practice tomorrow?"

"Easy," Mr. Straven purred. "You simply arrange the items around the book again, on the very last page, and repeat the incantation. That will return you to our world."

"And if we forget the incantation?" Adelle asked softly, finding her voice amid the doubt.

It was her turn to receive a cold, black-eyed stare from Mr. Straven. "Trust me, my dear. You won't ever forget this."

3

"WELL, I KNOW WHAT chapter I'm picking," Adelle said, reaching for the well-read, well-loved copy of *Moira*. A pit had opened in her stomach. Nerves, she told herself, not a warning sign. She turned to a page about halfway through the book and ran her palm fondly over the paper. In that chapter, their clandestine love firm but undeclared, the protagonist, Moira, and her poor beloved artist met in the park, the place where she had initially laid eyes on him, and vowed to make their first public appearance together. Sending him a secret message, she would sneak him into her home, into the fine evening planned by her wealthy family. That night, they would declare their love to the whole world. It would be a grand fete, the ball Adelle had hoped, in some small, silly way, to re-create at Sadie Hawkins—Connie with Julio and she with her imaginary Severin. Sometimes, when she imagined him, when she daydreamed in class, he felt as solid as the desk propping up her elbows.

"Here," Adelle murmured.

"What part did you pick?" Connie asked, craning her neck and trying to see, but Adelle's hand covered the spot.

"I guess you'll just have to see for yourself." Adelle closed her eyes, and like that image of Severin in her mind, the night of the glorious dance from the book was there—the house and the string music and the champagne flutes felt close enough for her to reach out and touch. Maybe it was, she thought; maybe this was really *real*.

She had always been a fanciful girl. Head in the clouds. Her mother, chronically serious, pragmatic, and grounded, had no idea how Adelle had come to be that way, more in love with the worlds she found in books than with the world going by all around her.

"Are you sure about this?" Connie asked. Adelle reached up to nervously tuck a piece of hair behind her ear, allowing Connie a peek at the page. It read: *I am a tired, haunted thing, flesh unmade, denied the one balm that could make and keep me whole: love. Give me love, and though now I be a moth all burned up by fire, I will grow new wings and fly.*

"It's just a bit of fun," Adelle reiterated, giving Connie a wide smile. But that pit was in her stomach, and it belched a cloud of nervous butterflies.

Mr. Straven loomed, seeming eager to be on with it. He turned toward the wall with the taxidermied mice and the hat on the peg and used a dimmer to lower the lights in the shop. The man in the window continued to sip his seemingly endless cup of coffee.

"Have . . . have you done this before?" Adelle asked, her voice wobbling as her palm began to sweat, the page clinging to her skin.

"Just once," he said.

"And it worked?" Connie pressed.

Mr. Straven squinted. "In a way." Before they could ask for clarification, he continued, "Now close your eyes, Adelle, and repeat after me: Split the world, coiled and curled, the curtain torn, the Old One born."

She waited to see if he was finished, and he nodded. As soon as the first shaky words left her mouth, Adelle felt the pit in her stomach widen, a biting cold from nowhere gripping her like a wintry fist.

But she closed her eyes and wondered if she was about to taste magic, and if it would make her feel warmer. "Split the world," she whispered. "Coiled and c-curled, the curtain torn, the Old One born."

Unseen, Connie gasped. Adelle smelled coiling smoke, as if the candles had suddenly gone out. She heard a voice then, bubbling up from the book, through her hand, and not into her ears but into her chest. It wasn't clearly male or female; it came from the cracks between the words that made up her thoughts. It came upon her like something always there but not yet seen, like a stranger standing in the corner, hidden by shadow, felt but not yet comprehended.

It wasn't her language. It wasn't any language, but the garbled sounds began to make a kind of sense. At first it only seemed like someone coughing, choking, desperate spittle bubbling up between babbling lips. But eventually she made out the words, and once she did, they rang clear as a coffin bell.

Yes, it is born. You will find it. Come. Come closer. Find it.

Adelle's eyes snapped open, and she felt herself tumbling freely forward, into something unnameable. A void. A tear. A place between places.

She clutched her stomach and screamed.

The conversation was exceptional, her friends told her, the dancing quite animated! Many fine young men had come! But none of this mattered. Moira waited to go down into her splendid ball with only one thought in her head: Had he kept his promise? Had he come?

He was danger and disobedience, a sin to covet, a poor fisherman's son so beneath her notice he ought to be underground. Yet she would not give up the dream of him. Her heart had made its choice, and that pain was hers to bear.

Had he received her message? Would he risk scandal and humiliation to attend the dance and declare their love to the whole of the city? Moira feared the answer but forced herself to leave her chamber and hasten to the ballroom, poised at the top of the stairs, searching the crowd for just one face.

There! Handsome as ever, smiling that incorrigible smile. Severin. Her soul's destiny.

Once she saw him again, the boy became her world. As she descended the carpeted stairs toward him in her decorated silk shoes, she felt the spell he had cast over her deepen. She dared not walk too quickly or breathe too deeply—for while Moira feared this new feeling overtaking her, far greater was her fear of breaking his hypnotic spell.

I knew I would have you, she thought. Or perhaps I knew you would make me yours.

—Moira, *chapter 15*

Connie stared in frozen, horrified wonderment—Adelle was gone. She had vanished, blinking out of existence as if someone had simply highlighted her and pressed delete.

It had worked. It had actually *worked*.

"We . . . we can't go together? I thought we would go together!" Connie cried.

"You'll meet on the other side."

"But—"

"Now you." Mr. Straven grinned. It wasn't a kind grin. "Put your hand on the book and say the words. Your friend is waiting."

Connie blinked. She couldn't move. Couldn't think. She felt suddenly in twelve places at once, torn between shock, excitement, and terror. Leaning hard against the counter, she felt the world spin, and then she toppled to the floor, sweating and panting as she tried to collect herself. A panic attack. She'd had them before, usually the night before a big game. Her heart raced, and she placed her hand there to try and steady it by sheer force of will.

How was it possible? How was the magic *real*?

"Constance?"

She couldn't look up at Mr. Straven. The world was spinning too fast for that. *Magic.* It was all Adelle ever talked about, but it always felt like just some stupid fun, like the time they went to King Richard's Faire for two days straight, a handsome jouster gave Adelle a ribbon, and for the rest of the semester they read her paperback copy of *A Knight in Shining Armor* by Jude Deveraux until the cover fell off.

"She falls through time in this," Adelle had said, dreamy sparkles in her mismatched eyes. "Maybe we could do it too."

"You're crazy," Connie had teased. "Nobody can do that."

This was what bonded them like two gems set in a single ring. Caroline and Tonya and Kathleen from her soccer team would be at Matt Tinniman's house getting drunk on schnapps and whatever else they could find in his dad's liquor cabinet. Kathleen even had a fake ID that she used to go clubbing downtown, not just to the "kiddie" nights that let in teens and handed out wristbands for booze. Breaking the rules always made Connie feel sick; even small infractions set her on edge, like her parents could see the guilt rising off her in visible waves.

Playing with Ouija boards and hanging out at the Emporium all the time felt like permissible trouble—it wasn't like they were buying weed and sneaking into college parties. Even if their brushes with the occult felt innocent, Connie always felt like when she touched their copy of *Moira*, the book touched back, somehow sticky. The girls only had one copy, the one sold to them by Mr. Straven, and they took turns holding on to it. When it was her turn with *Moira*, the novel called to her. Sometimes at night she would wake up for no reason and look at the book on her nightstand, watching it watch her back. It waited there, so obviously imprinted against the darkness of the room.

Adelle was always obsessed with the brooding, dark-haired love interest, Severin, but Connie wanted to meet the heroine, Moira. Moira with the long, dark red curls, Moira with her flashing green eyes and coy smile. Moira who loved fiercely and dangerously and with abandon.

Maybe Moira Byrne—the girl with the long red hair and flashing eyes—had always been her first crush. Okay, no maybes about it, she certainly had been, but it seemed like an Adelle thing to do, to fall in love with someone who had never existed at all. *No shade,* she thought, hating to have a bad thought about her best friend, *but you know it's true, Delly.*

What Connie wanted most of all was to kiss a pretty girl under a full moon with nobody there to whisper or judge.

That was what she had wanted, but now none of that mattered at all. Now she just had to get into the book because Adelle, impossibly, was in there. In there all alone. Stupid. Stupid, stupid.

Connie found her feet and slowly stood, her entire body shaking as she met Mr. Straven's steely gaze.

"Put your hand on the book, girl," he grunted.

"How did you d-do that?" she stammered. "Where did she go?"

"You know where she went," he replied. "And you can go too."

Connie drew in a thin breath, then reached for the novel. She looked at the softly bobbing flame of the black candle, and it went on burning with green fire. Then she closed her eyes and said the words.

"Split the world, coiled and curled, the curtain torn, the Old One born."

Behind her, she heard a sound like snapping bones, but she couldn't move—she was paralyzed with fear. A voice filled her head, smooth as velvet, icy as a lie. The words didn't sound like any language she had heard before, but that didn't matter. She knew what they meant, and she couldn't control her body long enough to change her mind and flee.

The garbled words spoke a promise, a warning. The thing she had come to do, the spell she had cast, it had worked.

Connie's eyes flew open just long enough to see that her hand was on an earlier section of the book, noticeably earlier. They would be separated, she knew, her mind a tangle. Separated and alone and far, far from home.

CONNIE SLEPT A DREAMLESS sleep and woke in a dusty room filled with shelves and crates. It took her a moment to remember the magic. The panic. The impossible reality of what they had just done. Crawling to her knees, she decided to try to leave some trace of herself. She wrote a message in the dust—her name, her age, and . . . and what else?

Please help. I don't know where I am, she wrote.

Ridiculous. Who would even find this place? It looked and smelled like it had been neglected for a long time. Hours passed; shock became numbness. She had to find something to eat, somewhere to go for answers. *At least I know this city,* she thought. *It's a start.*

Her first step outside into the night stole her breath clean away. The moon and stars could only occasionally be glimpsed behind the thick, unexplained miasma that enveloped the city. It was worse than fog, denser, carrying an unmistakable smell of rot. Standing on the stoop, she squinted into the darkness, sensing an unsettling, consuming silence punctuated only by the occasional moan of a fishy breeze off the harbor. She took a few steps down the shallow stairs leading to the street and then flailed, tripping over something heavy and soft at the bottom. Catching her balance with an athlete's reflexes, she spun around and found a body there, curled up against the first step. She could see it moving, just a little, the chest of a heavyset man in a gray suit rising and falling with shuddering breaths.

"A-are you okay?" she whispered. The silence over the city was so oppressive, library strict, she was afraid to break it. "Sir?"

Connie leaned down, preparing to poke him in the side to see if she could get an answer, when he lashed out suddenly, grabbing her by the wrist. She screamed.

His face was paler than death, his eyes wide and bloodshot, the whites glowing bright even in the darkness.

"The . . . dreams," he hissed, his nails biting into her skin as he tried to pull her down to him. A matted, gray-speckled beard flowed around his lips. "I . . . I can dream again. Do you dream? Do you hear the whispers? Calling . . . They're calling now. . . . I have to go."

As abruptly as he had grabbed her, he went limp. Connie stumbled back, watching as the man climbed to his feet, every slow movement a chore. When he stood, hunched, he turned his head toward the east, where Connie knew the piers and harbor would be. He smiled, slowly, and began to walk that way, to the east, his breathing suddenly calm, his steps not pained but purposeful. It reminded her, horribly, of how her father looked on the rare times they caught him sleepwalking.

The man reached the end of the block and turned the corner, disappearing. Connie shivered, holding back tears. His clothes. The shops. The silence. This wasn't her Boston. Where could she go? How would she ever get home, or find Adelle? Whatever happened, she wanted to get off the streets and somewhere safer where she could swallow her panic and collect her thoughts. From the abandoned shop she had woken up in, she tried to find landmarks, places that existed in 1885 and also in her time. Her phone was no help, no Wi-Fi signal at all, not even a roaming indication. . . .

She kept her phone use to a minimum, only occasionally using it as a light source or to jot down notes, but even so, the battery ran down and down. Her backpack had come with her and, even stranger, their copy of *Moira*. How had it made the trip? She'd assumed it would've stayed back in the Emporium. Maybe it had to come; otherwise, there would be no way to get back home. Connie clung to that idea, letting it be a small, flickering beacon of hope.

The safest place she could find was four blocks away, an old bakery that had probably once looked cheerful and welcoming but now sat dark and abandoned, foreboding as a moldering shipwreck. Connie managed to wedge open the shuttered servants' entrance and make a bed out of old flour bags in the pantry. Then she passed the interminable hours trying to think of an escape plan, trying to make sense of what plainly made no sense at all. She had to find Adelle, but nothing in the city looked right.

When she found Adelle, she was going to strangle her for getting them into this insane mess. A mess she refused to accept. It couldn't really be happening to her, and there was bound to be a scientific explanation. But as hours and then days passed, nothing changed. Either she wasn't waking up, or it was time to accept that it really was happening.

A few basic experiments in the bakery kept her busy. She made a shallow cut on her finger with the least rusty knife she could find. Blood welled up at once, and the wound stung. That answered that. She grew hungrier and hungrier, which answered another of her questions. Connie ate the one protein bar in her bag over a single day, then rationed stale bread from the owner's kitchen carefully, but it soon ran out. In the dusty apartment above the store, she found the remnants of a family's life, left behind in a panic.

More riddles. More confusion. She didn't remember this part of the book. What chapter had she put her hand on when she spoke the incantation? Connie tried to piece things together, but there was little there to find—a few tattered toys, a hairbrush, neatly kept ledgers for the business, and dozens upon dozens of empty tea canisters. Rummaging in a cupboard sandwiched between the only two beds, she found a journal written in a feminine hand. Most of the entries were mundane, just the day-to-day life of a young woman working the counter of the shop—the baker's daughter, she assumed. Connie skipped to the final pages.

June 2
The sea has turned black and the tea has run out. Mama says the Penny-Farthings will not bring more, as it is too dangerous to come here. I offered to

make the journey to the stone chapel, but she and Papa will not allow it. I do not know what will happen to us now that the tea is gone, but I can tell Mama is frightened. She tries to be strong, but I wish she would not. It hurts to see her strain so.

June 4

Papa was gone when we woke. I did not even hear him stir from the bed. Mama keeps saying he will return, but I know it is not true. Tomorrow I will go down to the Wall and his face will be there. He has walked into the sea and left us all behind. They say only the young remain now, and I fear it is so.

June 7

I am all alone now. Mother left in the night, and while I tried to stop her, it was as if Lucifer himself possessed her, and nothing I tried would make her listen. When I put my arms around her, her skin was like ice. Her eyes were open but I could tell she did not see me. I told her many times that I loved her, *but she could only say "He has called and I must go. He needs me. He has chosen me. He has called and I must go. Do you hear the whispers? Do you hear them?"*

I miss Mama. I miss everyone.

Without the dream tea I am doomed to die, too. There is nothing for it; I must try to reach the chapel. God protect me, I must try. I will not be called like they were, will not make the long and lonely walk to the sea. Please, Lord, please—the dead watch over me that I may live.

After that, Connie chose not to sleep in the family beds anymore.

There were cans of food but she couldn't get any of them open with just a set of old, blunt knives. She would have to find a new place to go, somewhere with more food and water. Connie used a scrap of charcoal and a flour sack to make a rudimentary map, knowing it was foolish to use her phone when it would soon die. She marked the bakery and the route back to the empty shop where she had first woken up. That was the way she had come (what was the word? *Arrived? Teleported?*), and she was afraid to stray too far.

She had to move, had to find Adelle. The accessible food had been picked clean by scavengers. At night she heard wailing and screams and, worse, the sounds of horrors she couldn't put a name to. Sometimes when she peered above the bakery counter and out the grimy windows, she spied a parade of oddly dressed men and women going by, their faces covered with leather masks, stained robes trailing from their shoulders to the ground, crude words that she couldn't read from that distance painted across the fabric. They carried lanterns that glowed with unnatural black fire, and they chanted what sounded like names, making their way slowly up and down the street, never tiring until dawn came and they drifted away.

Connie felt the hunger and fear gnaw at her belly, and at last decided it was time to go. She waited until the next morning, chucked a few battered tins of food into her backpack, and tip-toed out the way she had come, deeming the alleys safer and less conspicuous than the main roads. She would need the same items from Mr. Straven's tray to get home, but she had no idea where to find them.

One thing was sure—she did remember the incantation. She would never allow herself to forget it. She repeated it over and over, burning it into her brain.

The ugly fog draped over the city seemed thinner to the west and looked worst around the wharves. She struck out away from the water, mentally tabulating the blocks, trying to keep track of her distance from the bakery in case she needed to retreat. If she could bleed and feel hunger, then she wasn't going to risk asking for help from those masked weirdos chanting in the streets.

You have the book, she told herself. *You know Boston and you know the book; you should be able to survive anything.* But it wasn't like this in the book, was it? The story itself was all parties and teas, romance and intrigue, with just the occasional tense moment to keep things interesting—a duel, a prank, a kidnapping, a torn dress. Sometimes it seemed like Moira and Severin might not wind up together, and that was the worst of it. This was . . . this was a nightmare.

Had they really landed in their beloved book, or something much worse?

Hunger, a cruel beast, snarled in her stomach. It was getting harder to think. Even verging on starving, Connie could tell 1880s Boston did not look as it should. She was forced to leave the relative safety of the alley after traveling seven blocks, and she edged her way out onto what appeared to be a main thoroughfare. The bones of the city and its Federal architecture were there, but picked clean, as if by a scourge of vultures—the stark emptiness of it was like a carcass left to bleach in the sun. It was a ghost town, and she half expected to see a tumbleweed rolling down the road. Instead, she saw strange statues, effigies, erected in the middle of the street, heaps of stinking garbage rising all around them like moldering dunes. She picked her way toward the closest statue, constructed of driftwood, old bits of sails, and broken furniture. Four heavy boat chains had been draped over the "neck" of it, and large, splintered masts had been reconfigured into its body and arms. Curled paper streamers fell from the clumps of mud shaping its head, reminding her inexplicably of tentacles. What looked like a bucket of black paint had been dumped over the "head"; a sign nailed across the effigy's middle simply read: SPARE US.

It loomed ten feet tall, larger than a scarecrow but just as unsettling in the gloom.

Farther on she found tracks for horses to pull trains, and the avenue was wide enough to accommodate hundreds of carriages coming and going. The carriages were there, all right, but most were tipped over, ransacked, wheels broken or stolen altogether, everything down to the cushions destroyed. Abandoned horses, unfortunately, were there too, dead and picked clean by animals. Heaps of skeletons clogged the spaces between overturned carriages and pushcarts.

One of the horses, a black one, looked like it had only recently died, but as Connie made her way toward it, she realized it was moving. A mass of black rats had overtaken the body, and as she took another step toward it, the rats chittered and scurried, flowing like a dark river toward the gutter. She shivered. Could this be the book? Nothing but the horse's eyes remained, lids eaten away, the cold, frightened stare of death almost freezing her in place. Almost. Connie never froze.

Keep going. Don't stand still. Even if none of this is happening. Even if none of this is real. Don't stand still.

She heard the shuffle of footsteps in the distance, and the hum of the hooded figures chanting. Was daylight already waning? It was impossible to tell time reliably with the city enveloped in the stinking haze.

You can't let them catch you, Connie. It doesn't matter if you're hungry. Dig deep. Dig deep.

There were times on the trail, training for biathlon, when she was sure frostbite was creeping in on her fingers and toes, but she kept going anyway. It would feel like the ski poles had fused to her gloves and her feet had iced into her boots, but there were miles to log and targets to shoot. Her mentor, Coach Mindy, had told her: "The difference between you and the person you beat is how much you're willing to endure."

Hunger. Fear. Darkness. She would endure it.

Connie ran. She ran like she had never run before, not in training or in competition. Her feet ached and her lungs dragged on the air, but she didn't stop. *Track the blocks, count them, don't lose your bearings, look for landmarks . . .* The smog was thinner on the horizon, so that was where she would go. The chapel. That girl's diary had talked about a chapel. Connie kept her eyes up, but the signage on most of the buildings had been painted over, blacked out, things like *DO NOT LISTEN* and *THE VOICE LIES* covering anything relevant or useful. Not to mention, Boston had about a thousand churches that could qualify as said chapel.

Still, a building with a steeple would stand out, she thought, assuming the chapel had one, and she didn't see any of those as she pelted away from the carnage in the streets.

She realized she had zigzagged west, and she almost cried with relief when she paused to take a breath and found herself staring up at the statue of Benjamin Franklin. Even if most things looked different and the cars had vanished and the blue sky was long gone, she could orient herself with that. City Hall Plaza wasn't far. She was still in the thick of Boston, and she angled herself more or less toward Tremont so that if she kept her course, she'd find herself in Boston Common. From there, she reasoned, she might be able to navigate herself toward Moira's house, though in the novel it was located in a fictional neighborhood.

As she slowed to a jog and left Ben Franklin behind, Connie began to feel a pit widen in her stomach. She had run far, very far, but she hadn't seen a single soul since leaving the hooded chanters in the dust. Where was everybody?

Two possibilities occurred to her: one, that the chaos she had seen was just a taste of the chaos that had befallen the city, or two, that this really was the world of *Moira* the novel, and that meant there were only as many people as there were characters.

"God," she mumbled, her chest tight from exertion, "I hope that night at the shop didn't happen. I hope we're both in comas."

She slid into the cool, humid air of the trees clustered at the edge of the park. To her left, in the real world, burger joints and gyms and pubs overlooked the Common. Her stomach burbled, and she nearly doubled over from the pain of hunger. She'd just about kill for a Pigmalion from Burger Buddies. She angled herself toward where the Frog Pond would be in modern-day Boston, hoping that if she managed to make it there and press on, she could find the boundary of the city. Her understanding of the exact layout of Victorian Boston was foggy at best, but the bones of the city were old, and Connie surprised herself with how much she could recognize.

A dense, otherworldly silence filled the park. The fog above was mirrored on the ground, creeping toward her from the Frog Pond. Connie didn't hear any of those hooded chanters anymore, but she wondered if she might use the fog to her advantage. She ignored the persistent pangs in her stomach and dropped low, dashing from tree to tree and cluster of bushes, leaving the safety of ground cover only when necessary. St. Paul's Cathedral pierced through the pernicious fog to her left, covered in a film of dirt but still visibly bright through the trees. The Frog Pond couldn't be far, just one landmark, and if she could find *that*, then the small lake of the Boston Public Garden lay beyond, where in modern days people gathered to use the little boats and watch the swans.

The swans. Her and Adelle's meeting place. Someone had to have noticed them going there, since they made the trip all the time. Even if it was their secret, sacred spot, other people visited the park. The two girls tended to stand out—Adelle in her lacy Goth confections and Connie in her neon tracksuits. If missing posters went up, particularly in that park, their frequent visits there might just spark someone's memory.

Connie found the strength to run again, passing a murky depression in the ground that might one day be the Frog Pond. A few rudimentary trails cut through the grass, and her own nervous excitement made the trip seem short. Marshier, denser greenery and a smattering of cattails hugged the lake. It smelled boggy and disgusting, the surrounding reeds redolent with insects and the fog hanging over the water a sick, ugly gray color.

Holding her nose, she picked her way across the sludge to the future location of a gazebo and, not far from that, a handful of trees and the rocky outcropping hanging over the lake. That had to be the right spot. There were no swans, but Connie approximated the location where she and Adelle had gone to read together so many times. She dropped down on all fours and groped in the mist for a smooth spot of rock to use as a tablet. At the bakery she had grabbed the old tins of food and a dull knife, and now she used that knife to carve a message.

But what message should she choose?

The message had to be simple and clear, and lead their families or the police to the right place. They had fallen into a fictional world, but it was still a version of Boston— maybe any manipulation to the rock would appear in their timeline. It was a long shot, but even if her family never found it and only Adelle did, it would still be worth the effort.

If you're not dying in a hospital somewhere.

Connie banished the thought. She had to banish the thought. Grunting from the effort, she leaned into the knife, carving into the stubborn rock. It was harder work than she'd expected, and took six or eight goings-over to make even the slightest impression. She began to sweat, the humidity clinging to her like a hot film.

She leaned back on her haunches and examined her work.

ADELLE & CONNIE WITCH EYE STRAVEN

Maybe a few more passes and it would be legible. The ground beneath her began to rumble, the dust and flecks of stone she had dislodged dancing as the trees above her leaned and the earth quaked. Then everything went still and incredibly quiet. Something waited behind her. Something watched.

In her terror, she fell back on the words that had given her comfort as a child, the prayer she would whisper whenever she was afraid, back when she still went with her family to church every Sunday.

"Hail Mary, full of grace, the Lord is with thee," she whispered, trembling. She didn't know if she believed in heaven or hell, or in demons or Satan, but she was sensing something evil now. "Blessed art thou amongst women, and blessed is the fruit of thy womb, Jesus. Holy Mary, Mother of God, pray for us sinners, now and at the hour of our death. . . ."

For a moment, the rumbling stopped, and Connie braved opening one eye and twisting around to see what had come. A flap in reality hung, torn open, as if a page had been ripped in the middle, but instead of showing the following page, there was just an empty void. The gash had opened itself just off the edge of the stones jutting over the pond, positioned so that if she took a running jump, she might land inside it.

But Connie did not want to go near it. A humming sound emanated from behind the rip, and a growing pain in her head pulsed in time with it. She squinted, almost blind from the shattering in her mind, as if each second she stared at the tear, it clawed a little at her brain. It spoke in silken whispers, it enticed her to come closer. Connie bit her lip against the pain and stood, trembling, taking a single shuddering step toward it. She reached out and felt for the edge of the opening with her fingers, icy tendrils wrapping around her wrists as she found it.

A rip, as clear as if it were cloth or paper. A page. A torn book page . . . It seemed right and wrong at the same time. She didn't belong there, yet there she stood, pulling at the very fabric of what held the world together. Her hands, chilled and trembling, curled around the edges of the rip, and something grabbed back. A clawed hand closed over hers, digging deep and drawing blood.

A voice slithered into her mind, familiar yet unwelcome. The voice she had heard when the spell was cast.

You will serve, it said. *You will listen. Do you hear my whispers?*

"No!" Connie screamed, shuddering away from it and yanking her hand back. "No . . . Leave me alone!"

Do not resist. Serve.

The voice, it sounded . . . colder. Disappointed. Rejected, even.

"No," she managed to whisper again. "Whatever you are, leave me alone!"

Then a figure pulled itself free, entering from the rip and shoving her backward. Something big and oily, a creature with flashing teeth and wings, all of it covered in oozing black liquid. The smell stunned her, strong but not unpleasant, almost like . . . almost like *ink*. Fresh, wet ink. Connie gasped and tumbled back against the stones, clutching her injured hand, watching the slick monster emerge from the sliver of void, then spread its wings. It had the ugly, bulbous-eyed face of a gargoyle with an elongated mouth full of needlelike teeth. The inky black substance dripped from every inch of it. Shrieking, it took off into the night, swooping low before soaring up toward the hazy sky.

Women are, as a rule, physically smaller and weaker than men; their brain is much lighter; and they are in every way unfitted for the same amount of bodily or mental labour that men are able to undertake.

—*Anonymous*, Women's Work:
A Woman's Thoughts on Women's Rights (1876)

"Screamers! Watch your heads, boys!"

The riders burst through the mist, pistols flashing. Connie scrambled back against the trees, ducking with her hands over her head as another of the winged black creatures zipped down toward her, belched from the ragged opening hovering over the lake. Its claws cut through the tree branches, showering her with leaves. Whatever she had done by touching the rip, it had unleashed a flurry of the inky, flying devils.

The pistol fire was deafening. Huddled against the mangled

tree, Connie at last saw who had arrived in the pond clearing—a half dozen people riding tall, precarious bicycles. Not people—*kids*. They started to dismount in unison, but one of the freshly birthed creatures dropped out of the sky and took a young man by surprise, the dark and the dense fog swallowing his screams as he was carried off into the night.

"They got Alec! Goddamn screamers got Alec!" A young woman with a wild mane of red curls broke ahead of the others, her strange bicycle falling over as she dropped into a crouch. An embellished white cowboy hat swung around her neck on a chain. "Get low and spread out! Take cover—only take your shot if it's a sure one!"

A bullet zipped by the tree trunk and Connie's ear, close enough to make her scream. The cowgirl noticed, crawling toward her through the damp, tall grass until they were almost nose to nose.

"You hurt?" she asked.

Connie shook her head. "Wh-what are those things?"

"Dead is what they're going to be." The redhead pivoted, brandished a silver revolver, and cracked off three shots toward the monsters pouring out of the tear, using the heel of her hand to cock the hammer each time.

More figures approached the tree at the edge of the pond. One of the screamers swooped toward them so quickly it was nothing but a pale blur before it knocked the gun right out of the cowgirl's hand. She grunted and rolled into the grass, the revolver bouncing onto the rocky outcropping over the water where Connie had been carving her message. Up close, the creature was ugly, terrifying; its pointed muzzle glinted, full of tiny, dark teeth, and a crest of spines fluttered over its domed head.

It took a shot from one of the others in the clearing but simply shrieked in response, shaking out its wings and lurching for the redhead. If Connie had had her biathlon .22 rifle with her, she would've joined right in, but unarmed as she was, she hurried toward the rocks. It was better than looking at the screamer—her vision wobbled whenever she did, as if her brain didn't want to compute what she was looking at. Out of the corner of her eye, she saw a screamer diving straight toward her. Her heart stopped in her chest, but it wasn't the moment to freeze. Connie dove for the revolver, snatched it up, and spun around on her knees to fire into the back of the monster's head.

That did more than get its attention. With an earsplitting cry, it launched into the sky, black blood dripping from its wounds as it fled. The volleys of gunfire continued, one after another, the constant *pop-pop-pop* filling Connie with the buzzy hit of adrenaline she needed to shake off her fear. A screamer dropped dead out of the sky, then another, weighty enough to shake the ground when they hit.

"Everyone on the tear! Now! Fire on it now!" The cowgirl had popped up out of the grass, grabbing her hat and jamming it onto her head. "That means you too, stranger!"

Connie aimed the revolver toward the source of the monsters, watching five figures rear up out of the grass behind the cowgirl and aim their pistols or rifles toward the tear. She steadied her hands, took in a deep breath of the scummy pond air, and fired, but the gun just clicked.

"Toss it here!"

Adrenaline still coursing like fire through her veins, Connie threw the weapon to the redhead. She smoothly reloaded it and then, with the same agile grace, poured all the rounds toward the "tear." It wouldn't close, not completely, but it seemed to go dormant, just a barely visible seam torn vertically above the water, nothing coming out. Nobody moved. Nobody spoke. The smoke from the guns had dissipated when the cowgirl jumped to her feet, reloaded her revolver, and aimed it at Connie.

"Look here, fellas. We got ourselves a live one. Don't let her escape."

Connie didn't have time to react. Five pairs of hands descended on her. She tried to make heads or tails of the young men and women wrapping yards and yards of rope around her, but they were all dressed in similar dirty work shirts and patched trousers. They all wore matching black-and-white-checkered bandannas looped around their necks. Connie kicked and fought, but she was exhausted and starving, and soon she found herself fidgeting against the tight confines of the rope pressing her arms to her sides.

The redhead marched over to her, lowering her gun a little. She had thick dark eyebrows and close-set blue eyes. A deep scar ran across her left cheekbone, sweeping up toward her ear. She wasn't dressed like the others; her white western-style shirt was chased with fringe and smeared with dirt, grease, and blood. The brown skirt she wore was hitched up the sides with metal clips, revealing patterned trousers beneath.

"Not bad, Jacky-boy, you gave those things hell. Normally you couldn't hit a bull's rump with a handful of banjos," the girl drawled, smirking at a tall, strong boy looming over Connie. "Keep an eye on this girl—don't know if we can trust her yet."

"But I shot that thing! I tried to help!" She shook with rage. "I would've . . . I would've been just fine on my own. I don't need your help."

The cowgirl took a knee, staring Connie right in the eyes. "Yeah, sure, you had it all under control. Hmph, you don't look like a dirty Clacker, but it ain't easy to tell these days. One way or another, we'll sort this out. But not here, not here. Too dangerous."

Then she nodded toward that same tall young man, who took his checkered bandanna off and tied it across Connie's eyes.

"Hey!" Connie shrieked. "I'm not your enemy. Just let me go—I'm not a threat, I promise. I just want to find my friend and get somewhere safe. Maybe get some help. The police . . . or . . ."

In the darkness, she heard them all have a good laugh at that. The bandanna reeked of body odor.

"Well, she's dumb as a Clacker, but she isn't dressed like one, boss," a boy said.

Someone hauled Connie to her feet and prodded her to start walking.

"No place is safe anymore, and there ain't no police." She heard the western-style girl chuckle. "You know, you almost have to admire the gumption. If you weren't so big 'n' strong, I'd say you were born yesterday, sweetie."

"Don't call me that," Connie snarled.

"Right. Sometimes I forget my manners, but we can be real hospitable," the girl added to a chorus of dark laughter. "You'll see."

They walked and walked. Connie's feet ached. She smelled the air change, the humidity drop away, and the scent of coal dust and horse droppings return. They must have turned back toward downtown and marched her that way. She heard bells and the squeak of wheels. Only one of her captors walked with her, one hand steady on the rope; she heard the others scrambling onto their tall bicycles. Nobody talked, and when Connie tried to protest her treatment again, they shushed her. Even blindfolded, she sensed their giddy alarm.

Adelle sucked into the book. Monsters dropping out of the sky. A tear in the world itself. A gang of marauding cyclists . . . How could any of it be real? But Connie knew parts of the world were familiar and allowed herself to, just for the moment, indulge in the idea that she really was somehow living inside a novel. These characters existed in the world of *Moira*. The elite, uptown circle Moira ran in avoided the thugs and smugglers who inhabited the poorer parts of town. They spoke in hushed whispers about highwaymen prowling the streets, taking advantage of the darkness to rob unsuspecting ladies or take them hostage. Of all the people to run into in the book, she had bumped directly into the villains, the Penny-Farthings.

Her mind raced, piecing together what bits of their lore she could remember. They didn't feature much in the book, since

Moira didn't associate with their kind. They'd seemed more boogeymen under the bed than flesh-and-blood threat, but Connie was beginning to think they really were the scoundrels the hoity-toities thought them to be.

They stopped somewhere and Connie had nothing to do but listen. Someone gave an obviously codelike knock on a door, and then heavy hinges creaked and whined and a blast of warmer air rushed out to meet her, along with the smell of dust, burning candles, and unwashed bodies. She jumped as something fuzzy brushed her hand, then snuffled along her wrist. Just as quickly as the animal had come to sniff her, it was gone. They were inside now, and Connie tried to squish her cheeks around to make the blindfold inch up. It worked. The boys and girls escorting her must have been distracted, and she managed to see a slice of their destination. An old, abandoned church. They walked her down the rows of pews toward the altar, then paused. The cowgirl went ahead of them and pushed with her back and shoulders against the altar itself, shoving it out of the way until a hatch opened beneath it.

"Untie her," the cowgirl said, motioning for the others to bring Connie forward. "She's gonna need her hands. It's a long way down."

Connie gulped. She wasn't kidding about that. A ladder reached down into a cavern, dimly lit, at least twenty feet below. The cowgirl marched up to her while the boys unwound the rope holding Connie's arms to her sides, and then her blindfold was yanked down.

"Climb," the girl told her with a smirk. "Don't try anything cute; I'll have Slick Rose here trained on you the whole way."

The cowgirl spun the revolver barrel and nodded toward the hatch.

"You named your gun?"

Her smirk vanished. "I sure did. And Slick Rose says you ain't in a position to be casting judgment. Down you go, stranger."

Connie only hesitated for a moment. Part of her wanted to run, but the path back down the pews was choked with dirty-faced boys glaring at her. A big shaggy black dog sat watching her too, maybe the most intimidating sentinel among them. And then there was the redheaded cowgirl with the gun, and Connie relented with a furious sigh, starting down the ladder and into the unknown, into the villains' lair.

7

"There are young ladies who burn as bright as polished rubies," said Orla Beevers, without a trace of jealousy in her voice—Miss Beevers had the good grace to know when she was outdone. "And then there is you, Moira Byrne, and there is not a pearl in the sea that glitters as you do."

—Moira, *chapter 3*

Adelle opened her eyes with a jolt, reeling back, nearly plummeting into the murky pond water below.

"Oh my God," she whispered, blinking rapidly. "It worked. Mr. Straven . . . It really worked. I can't . . . I can't believe it!"

She rubbed her eyes, pinched herself. Nope. It was all real. She had landed in the park where Moira and Severin made their pact to dance at the ball, but more than that, Adelle had landed in the secret spot where she and Connie met so often to read and laugh and rank their favorite characters. A jagged, faint message was carved into the rock. Adelle scrambled forward and ran her hand across it, gasping. Connie must have come through too. She was somewhere in the book already, but at a different point in the story.

ADELLE & CONNIE WITCH EYE STRAVEN

Her eyes filled with tears. She was terrified, and so Connie must be too.

"I'll find you, Connie. I'm already on the right track," she whispered.

Yes, an unseen voice murmured back. *You are. We are so pleased you came.*

"Who's there?" Adelle spun, nauseous again. An eerie tear in the world, glittering, ragged and green, and filled with blurry lights, hovered over the water. Stars twinkled in the void there, tendrils of ebony smoke leaking through into this world, reaching for her. Her head exploded in pain. Clutching it, Adelle went down to her knees, shaking uncontrollably. Whatever it was, it watched her, and it felt terrifyingly near.

"Who are you?" she managed to ask. "What are you?"

Close. The word splintered through her head, not a voice but a searing brand. *So close now. You will serve.*

She had to find Connie, and the right materials, but how could they get back home without a copy of the book? Adelle pushed her fists into her eyes, trying not to cry. She spun and crawled back toward the grassy slope, away from the water and the tear and the voices. When she reached the grass, her hand touched something scaly, wet, and cold, but the weeds grew too high for her to see it properly. That was all right with her. From behind, from the shore of the pond, she heard voices, though these sounded different. Human. Adelle dragged herself to the tree that sheltered the reading spot. The trunk was riddled with holes, like someone had shot into it dozens of times.

Hazarding a glance over her shoulder, she noticed two figures lingering down at the water's edge, their attention clearly on her. They were close enough to the tear above the pond to suggest they might have come to see it.

"Hey! Hey there! Who are you?"

They wore dark masks and dirty white robes with words sloppily finger-painted all over. Adelle didn't trust anyone dressed that way. They looked like they belonged to some kind of cult, and she had gotten her fill of dark magic and the occult for the day. She picked herself up and ran, frantic, jerking up her skirt and sprinting as fast as she could through the park, trying desperately to orient herself despite being just about as disoriented as one could be. She didn't have Connie's athletic ability or strength, but she didn't let that stop her, pumping her one free arm and hurtling across the grass.

"She's getting away!" the man was screaming behind her. "Hurry! She's getting away!"

She ran and ran, through the park and into Boston Common, shocked to find it utterly still and silent. Sprinting wasn't exactly her forte, but the fear kept her going. Her chest began to ache, her feet screaming from trying to marathon in heeled shoes. She couldn't go much farther. Adelle spun slowly in a circle in the middle of the street, finding it strangely dim for early evening. A sickly yellowish haze had settled over the city, as if it could only be seen through a sepia filter.

Slowing to a jog, Adelle found herself before the famous Soldiers and Sailors Monument. That raised her spirits a little—at least she recognized this area. Flagstaff Hill. The pillar rose as tall as the surrounding trees, topped with a bronze woman with a sword representing America itself. Stopping to catch her breath, she checked over her shoulder. No sign of the robed figures. Either she had lost them or they were too slow. Adelle sheltered behind the monument, keeping it between her and her pursuers, nestled against the image of Edgar Allan Poe in stone.

Now she just had to find Connie, somehow, in all of Boston with no idea where she might be. Then a terrible idea came to her: What if those figures in robes had seen Connie when she was carving her message? Maybe she ought to go back and ask them. But what if they had taken her?

"This is impossible," she said.

Adelle closed her eyes tightly and sighed. What would Connie do? She had left the message, so she must be somewhere in the city. . . . Would she stay near the park? But for how long? Connie had been able to leave that message, so chronologically she had been in the book longer. Adelle had chosen a passage in the book at the halfway point, deep into the story. So much had already transpired—the betrothal, the first meeting in the park, the kidnapping plot, the whisper ball, and now the second meeting in the park . . . maybe that meant that in real time, Connie had been here longer too. She might try to find someone from the book and make friends—that's what Adelle would do.

"Yes," Adelle murmured. "That's what I would do."

But how to find them? Moira and her friends didn't live all that far from Boston Common or the gardens, often passing by as they zipped from social call to social call, the vast majority of the book taking place in candlelit ballrooms and rose-scented boudoirs. Maybe if she stayed near the park, she could follow someone who looked wealthy enough to lead her to Moira. At least it would be a start.

Rustling in the trees near the edge of the path drew her attention. Adelle peered around the edge of the monument, her stomach heavy with dread. No sign of Moira or Severin. Instead, the robed figures had come, searching through the bushes, peeking around trees. They had caught up. She had to move.

Adelle hurried on tiptoe down the street, listening hard for their footsteps, heart lodged in her throat, her attention not on where she was going but on what was coming after her.

Then the carriage struck.

The thing had raced up on her so quickly, and she had been so distracted, that she hadn't even noticed it coming. The wheel clipped her hip, sending her flying. Retching, Adelle flipped onto her stomach and let loose her burger and milkshake all over the street, feeling the hard scrape of stone against her cheek and the unforgiving chill of a deep, deep rain puddle soaking her dress. The horses driving the infernal thing stampeded back toward her, hooves heavy and glinting, beating the ground hard, hard, until the beasts' twin squeals of distress sang above the rhythm. They reared up, spitting white streamers, lips curled and eyes wide as they pawed at the air and then settled back down.

A door on the carriage flew open, and a girl with a face as bright as the moon appeared in the fog.

"Oh heavens! Oh heavens, oh heavens!" The girl catapulted herself artlessly from the step, nearly tumbling end over end into the street. She bustled toward Adelle with her hands covering her mouth, the frothy layers of her ball gown rippling around her like a silver tide.

"Are you dead? Did we kill you?" Her frantic panting reminded Adelle of a Pomeranian. "Please say we did not kill you! Oh, but if you are dead, then how will you speak?" She twisted, shouting back at the young man driving the carriage. "Hampton! Hampton, you beast, look what you have done!"

"I think I'm all right," Adelle grunted, managing to sit up. "My leg hurts, but I don't think anything is broken. . . ."

"You must let us escort you! Hampton! Hampton, come to me this instant!" The driver, a lanky redhead with painful-looking acne, hurried over to them, black coat flapping behind him.

"My apologies, miss, didn't see you there—what with you in that black dress, blended right in with the road!"

"Help her, Hampton, my God, help her!"

Their fussing and shrieking was almost worse than the physical pain. Voices echoed from the park. The hooded figures were looking for her. She let the boy help her up to her feet and she winced the moment she put pressure on her left leg.

"You are injured." The moon-faced girl sighed. "Where were you going? We will gladly take you the rest of the way."

The voices grew louder, and Adelle swallowed nervously, trying to hide herself behind the far narrower young man.

"I . . . I don't know."

"Lord, we knocked the sense out of you. Your head must be all a-jumble." The young woman gazed up and down at her. "Well, you are dressed very finely, I must say. Perhaps we have the same destination. Could it be Byrne House, for the summer-solstice fete?"

Adelle was maybe a little "a-jumble" as the girl said, but the words *Byrne House* and *solstice fete* snapped her back to her senses. The party at Byrne House—the solstice fete—was where Moira, in the novel, unveiled her true love for the first time. The climax of act 2. Byrne House, in fact, was Moira's family mansion. Adelle had landed in the correct day, time had passed, and now the ball was about to begin.

This isn't possible, she reminded herself. *This can't be happening. But it is. It is. Mr. Straven performed magic.*

The robed figures had noticed the accident and raced toward them, and Adelle decided she was safer off the streets, particularly if she really had managed to tumble through a wormhole into a fictional universe. Choosing this girl and her carriage seemed the obvious lesser of two evils.

"Um, y-yes," Adelle mumbled. "Yes, that was my destination too."

"Then it is decided! Hampton and I shall take you there

immediately, and I know we can find something to replace this frock of yours—you look positively drowned! But beautiful! Drowned but beautiful! Oh dear, I'm rambling. Come, Hampton, we mustn't be late."

Adelle walked to the carriage arm in arm with the strangers, limping, and then sighed with relief as they hoisted her into the warm back seat and the door shut, concealing her from the hooded figures. They had just passed the monument and reached the road, and Adelle sank down low, avoiding the window.

The girl settled across from her in a flounce of petticoats and silk, and then the carriage jerked forward, carrying them away from the square.

What am I doing? I have to find Connie. . . .

Adelle scrubbed her face with both hands, frustrated and confused. She couldn't believe what she was seeing and hearing, but the evidence was all around her.

"Where are my manners? First we practically run you down in the road and then we skip introductions! Moira would be scandalized; she's always telling me I'm coarse and unladylike, and I'm afraid I simply cannot stop proving her right." The girl produced a fan from a small satchel around her wrist and began fanning herself rapidly. "My name is Orla Beevers, and you are . . . ?"

Adelle froze, at a complete loss for words. Of course. Of course it was Orla—she was just like her description in the book. Orla Beevers, Moira's best friend in the world and hopeless dummy. Connie couldn't stand her in the book, but Adelle had developed a soft spot for the airheaded but well-meaning sidekick.

More than that, Orla had said the magic word. *Moira.* It was really happening, *had* really happened.

I've fallen through time and into my favorite book, and my best friend is here somewhere, just as lost.

The solstice fete. They were going to the ball, and Moira and Severin and all the characters she knew and obsessed over would be there. It was extraordinary, almost too much to take in, but Connie might have had the same brain wave and tried to find the main characters from the novel. If so, she would land in Moira's orbit, and perhaps someone at the ball would have seen her. Surely, Connie would stick out in her tracksuit.

"Adelle," she blurted out. At least, she thought, she could lean on the carriage accident as a crutch; it could explain away her confusion and ignorance. "Adelle Casey. It's a pleasure to meet you, Orla."

"I wish it were under more pleasant circumstances, obviously." The girl laughed nervously. Her teeth were quite brown and crooked, and she used the fan to hide that fact as much as possible. "But I feel much better that we have scooped you up off the streets; it is too dangerous for a lady to travel alone on foot these days. You never know what might be lurking in the shadows, my dear, or what fresh horrors have crawled out from the deep."

They danced. They danced until their sides ached and their feet burned, and Moira scintillated in his arms. A perfect night. A dozen times or more she glanced at her mother, convinced the disapproving old woman would try to separate them, but she abstained from the dance floor. They were free. They were, at last, together.

"I will never let you go," he whispered, his hand squeezing hers. "You are my beginning and my end."

Soon morning would come and they would be parted, and Moira dreaded it, painfully aware of every passing moment, every tick of the clock carrying them toward the inevitable end. But for a while longer, she could press her cheek to his and feel the welcome promise of his hand at her hip and his fingers wrapped in hers. She could not say when they would see each other again; he had taken such pains to be there, to slip unseen through the servants' entrance she had left unlocked.

"Severin, I do not want this night to end," she whispered back.

Tears welled in her eyes. "I cannot bear to see you go. Now that my parents know our secret, they will do everything they can to keep us apart."

"No, Moira," he said, holding her just a little tighter. "That is not our destiny, je te promets. You have been so brave, and together we have changed everything, you will see. Nothing is the same, Moira—we will be together, and whatever you desire will come to pass. Trust in the sacrifices we have made, mon cœur, and have faith."

—Moira, *chapter 15*

Byrne House sat back from the road, sandwiched between two smaller mansions, all afforded privacy by a tall hedge and decorative gate. Adelle recognized the area from descriptions in the novel and her own adventures around town in her timeline—it was a stone's throw from the Public Garden. All the homes there were stately, but most sat dark and almost hollow.

Only the windows of Byrne House glowed with any promise of life.

An orderly procession of carriages wound up to the gates of the mansion; passengers hurried out into the mist and then disappeared up the tidy cobbled path to the doors. The lower half of the house had been done in pale, smooth stone; the upper half, with protruding gabled windows, was a darker red brick. Clusters of ivy crawled high on either side of the entrance.

"Still on time!" Orla chirped, clapping her hands excitedly. "Excellent! And we shall clean you up and replace your frock even before the first waltz!"

Adelle leaned forward in her seat. Her left side still ached from where it had been struck, but the pain was soon forgotten. It was an arresting sight: a swarm of silk-clad ladies and top-hatted gentlemen streaming into the house, two imposing figures in leather hoods and long robes seemingly guarding the gate.

She gasped.

"Is something the matter? Oh! Is it your injury? We shall summon Mr. Vaughn; he is quite good with all manner of maladies. Just a hobby of his, of course, but Dr. Addleson is no longer with us, and if Mr. Vaughn cannot help us then certainly he will know better—"

Adelle wasn't listening.

"Who are those two?" she asked, pointing at the hooded figures. "Why are they dressed that way?"

She didn't remember anything like that from the book, and she had the damn thing nearly memorized—this ball was put down in the novel in painstaking detail. Every cucumber sandwich and gown was fit to include, apparently, but not people in what looked like bizarre ritualistic robes. Robes that matched those of the men from the pond. Their masks were hideous, patchwork brown leather that covered the entire face, leaving only two ragged holes for their eyes.

"Why, dear, how can you not know?" Orla narrowed her eyes.

"I'm . . . I'm new here."

That was clearly not the right thing to say. Orla covered her mouth with both gloved hands, reeling back against the seat as if she'd been struck. "I'm afraid your injury must be more severe than we thought. Did you thump your head? For many months now nobody comes or goes from the city, dear. The roads in and out are impassable, and the harbor is too dangerous for all but the keenest sailors to navigate. But *we* are safe! The rabble are not, of course, but you are clearly of good breeding, and so you mustn't fret."

Adelle nodded, biting her lip. "You're right. I must have hit my head. I'm sorry, everything is very, um, foggy right now."

"This is all Hampton's fault, obviously. He is a shameful driver, but without Simpson around, he is my only option. Your poor head! Your poor, poor head!" Orla almost sobbed, leaning forward to take Adelle's hands in hers. "Those are Chanters, dear; they protect us from the ruffians and criminals who want to rob us blind. And they preserve us from a grim fate in the sea. They make their sacrifices and provide us our protective elixirs and teas. I admit they look a tad . . ." She glanced out the window, observing the so-called Chanters. "A tad severe, but you need not fear them. You are with me, Miss Casey, and therefore a friend."

"How do you know?" Adelle asked cautiously, watching Orla's face closely for any signs of suspicion. "How do you know I'm not one of the rabble? And what do you mean about the sea? What's wrong with it?"

"Your cleanliness, for one thing," Orla said with a giggle. "That McClaren woman and her blighted Penny-Farthings always look like they've just fallen out of a chimney. And your fine dress, for another. The cloth is quite extraordinary! Do you really not remember anything? Not even the sea?"

The door opened and Hampton frantically lowered the step, then offered his arm.

"Hampton, you fool, you struck Miss Casey so hard she's lost half her wits! Shame on you! Shame!"

Hampton went pale. "M-my sincerest apologies, Miss Casey."

"We will get you inside and see to your injuries," Orla said to her, motioning for Adelle to leave the carriage. Then, to Hampton, she sighed. "Pray, Hampton, that she is not as unwell as she appears. I shall not feed you for a month, I swear it."

When they were both on the ground again, Adelle watched a third hooded, robed figure break through the crowd walking toward the front doors. He fell into conference with the other two, their dark heads bent together. She went rigid with fear. The third man held her little lacy backpack in his hand. Adelle felt the blood drain out of her body. She must have dropped it when she was flung into the road by the carriage. What was even in there? Her phone, her coin purse, her student ID . . .

Not good.

The last thing she wanted was to become suspicious and for those awful robed men to take her away. As Orla escorted her toward the house, Adelle heard snippets of their whispered conversation.

"Strange girl," she heard, and "sneaking around near the tear."

Adelle turned her head toward Orla, pressing herself close to the girl and feigning a huge smile. "You are being so kind to me. It was really my mistake, being right in the road like that. You shouldn't blame Hampton."

"Be on the lookout," she heard the third Chanter say as they passed. "Sharp eyes tonight."

"Nonsense!" Orla flipped her hair. "Hampton has always been incompetent, but I've really no choice in the matter. The rest of the staff either took the walk into the sea or ran off to join the Penny-Farthings. He is pitiful but loyal, and so I make do."

Walked into the sea? What on earth did she mean?

"Miss Beevers, a word."

Adelle winced; the Chanters had noticed and come to intervene. The one carrying her stolen bag loomed over them. She didn't care what Orla said about the robed ones; they didn't seem friendly to Adelle. How would she explain her phone to people from the Victorian era? And how would she explain why she was there, or how she had fallen into a novel with an old man's spell? Doubtless, recreational witchcraft was not a concept 1885 Bostonians would readily accept and forgive.

They were looking for her, and Adelle was determined not to be found.

"How can I help you, gentlemen?" Orla was steering them toward the Chanters. They smelled foul, like sardines and stale smoke.

"Ouch!" Adelle lurched dramatically toward the door, clutching her left thigh. "Oh, my leg! My leg! I really must sit down. . . . Did they find my bag? I, um, I simply cannot live without it!"

Orla gasped and, without another thought, ripped the backpack out of the tall Chanter's hand and thrust it toward Adelle.

"Miss Beevers—" The tall man made a grab for the bag, but it was too late.

"Not now, I'm afraid; my guest is injured and I must see to her. Thank heavens you found her belongings, what fine luck. Never mind, now, she is in my care. Do not worry, gentlemen—we shall find a moment to visit later. Perhaps after dessert. Come along, Miss Casey, lean on me if you must. . . ."

The man fell back, vanquished by Orla's enthusiasm. Adelle could imagine that many others had been defeated by the inability to get a single word in edgewise with Orla. She breathed a sigh of relief, clutching her bag to her chest and taking Orla's arm, pretending to limp, exaggerating the legitimate pain in her thigh. That had been a close call. Her heart thumped so loud she was sure everyone nearby could hear it, too. She could feel the Chanters watching them, their eyes burning into the back of her head as the girls disappeared into the throng of guests.

"There, there, we are nearly to the door," Orla told her gently. And they were. As soon as they passed inside, Adelle felt safer. While it wasn't home or even her time period, the house was lit and full, and soft, buoyant music from a string quartet flooded the foyer.

A serious-eyed boy in a dark suit checked names against faces from a list, but Orla simply told him, "This is my honored guest, Miss Casey."

He did not protest.

Of everything in this strange new world, this place seemed the most familiar to Adelle. She had lived in the book so many days of her life, dreamed of what Moira's family home looked like, and now she was inside the real thing. It far outshone even her imagination.

The music, the warmth, the sumptuous red wallpaper and heavy drapes, the stately wooden columns and oil paintings . . . it all gleamed, almost dreamlike, like a memory given new life by a word or scent.

The doors opened onto the red-walled and red-carpeted foyer, a striking room, almost like being inside the scarlet chambers of a heart. On the right, a curved staircase with wooden banisters led up to the family rooms—she remembered that detail from the book. The guests continued in a gossamer river of gossip and laughter to the left, bypassing the stairs and spreading out into the open corridor and, beyond that, through a wide arch, the dining room turned ballroom.

A petite young woman in full maid costume took coats and capes and disappeared with them into a side gallery.

By the dark wooden staircase, a tall young man hovered. The crowds near him parted, as if funneling her vision toward him, pointing like an arrow. Adelle knew him at once. The recognition didn't make the realization any easier to swallow—she was still, at the core of it, seeing a living, breathing version of what she had always considered fiction. But most of the main players in *Moira* attended this particular party, which meant she would be meeting them all, and soon—and here was the first.

You didn't do him justice, Robin Amery.

The author had glossed over Kincaid Vaughn's looks in the book. He was characterized as the less desirable bachelor, the soft-spoken, bookish boy Moira was supposed to marry but didn't, not wild and passionate and a little dangerous like Severin.

Kincaid, or Caid, as most of the characters called him, was the safe choice, from a good family. From the right side of the tracks.

Caid stood a head taller than the young men swarming the foyer, his shirtsleeves rolled up to his elbows, his fingers visibly stained with ink. A pair of owlish spectacles sat perched on his nose, softening his otherwise intense dark eyes. He adjusted those specs nervously, shifting from foot to foot in the throng of guests. He caught sight of them and a relieved smile lit up his face, bright as a lighthouse beacon in a storm. That smile, Adelle thought, was his best feature by far. With a few long-legged strides, he met them, giving Adelle a quick, curious glance before turning to Orla and shaking his head.

"You're tremendously late," he admonished, still smiling. "She has the entire house in an uproar. It's a battlefield up there, jewels and petticoats and all sorts flung to the far corners of the manor." Caid took a handkerchief out of his pocket and mopped his brow as if feverish, giving Adelle a sheepish frown. "N-not that I myself have seen a lady's petticoats. Of course not. It is just . . . just a figure of speech. Who is this, Orla?"

He spoke with nerdish formality, not something Adelle had expected or imagined, stumbling over his words just as any modern-day teenage geek would when discussing underwear with girls. His dark brown skin glistened with nervous sweat, almost enough to fog his spectacles. She couldn't believe she was looking at the Kincaid Vaughn from Robin Amery's *Moira*, a character who had seemed like a throwaway, just a boring impediment to Moira and Severin's happiness. But that damn smile. It was *radiant*.

Nothing about him said "impediment" to Adelle. Like Orla, he seemed oblivious to the strange robed men guarding the house. How could any of this be normal to them?

But it was, apparently, and Adelle wanted desperately to blend in, if only for her safety.

"This is my new friend," Orla told him lightly, taking him by the arm and steering him toward the stairs. "Hampton happened to strike her with the carriage on the way here."

"He what?" Caid's eyes swept up and down, and Adelle couldn't help but glance away.

"I'm fine," she insisted, mumbling. "Just . . . my leg is a little sore."

"And she is positively drenched from head to foot. Do not look at her that way, Caid, it is most bold, and a lady does not like to be seen so in public. I will not rest until she feels at ease among us, for I owe her at least that much. Moira's tantrums must be forgotten until we set Miss Casey here to rights!" Orla launched into another one of her speeches, dragging Adelle up the stairs, heedless of her leg.

"Ouch!" Maybe she really was more hurt than she thought. A sprain, or at least a temperamental bruise. Adelle grabbed blindly for the banister, and instead clamped her hand around the no less strong and steady forearm of Caid Vaughn.

"Goodness," he breathed, steadying her. His hands were so warm she could feel them through her soggy black dress. "Let me help, then, as you are now declared our friend."

Orla tittered, watching from behind her gloved fingers as Caid hoisted Adelle into his arms.

"What a picture you two make!" Orla sighed, then widened her eyes. "Oh, but that is wicked of me! What would your betrothed say, Caid?"

Adelle groaned inwardly. If this was the solstice fete from the novel, then Moira and Kincaid Vaughn were engaged to be married, despite Moira carrying on her secret, torrid affair with Severin.

And now here I am. Smack in the middle of it.

"I can manage," Adelle murmured. "You can put me down."

"Nonsense," Caid replied. He carried her without any hint of trouble, continuing up to the landing and then up another flight of narrow steps. "Miss Beevers will kindly keep her comments to herself. A gentleman always helps a l-lady in need, is that not right?"

"I'm simply teasing, Caid."

"I hate teasing," he said under his breath, too quiet for Orla, who had scurried on ahead, to hear. "Your teasing most of all."

"Thank you," Adelle told him when they reached the third floor. He did not put her down but kept following Orla through a candlelit corridor decorated in rich blue and white chintz, the carpets a stunning counterpoint in red.

"I cannot believe she struck you with the carriage. Her driver is a menace to society." At that, he managed a wry smile. He smelled wonderful, like old books and rosemary, but Adelle schooled herself not to think about that. After all, he wasn't real. None of this was. And yet his broad, steely shoulders certainly felt real under her hand. . . .

You're here to find Connie, you idiot.

"You're both being very kind," Adelle began, although Orla hardly seemed to be listening. "But I'm actually looking for a friend of mine. I . . ." *Think, damn it, think. You paid for that stupid improv camp last summer, now use it.* It was like when she and Connie had gone to the King Richard's Faire: she just had to play pretend and hope they didn't notice the zipper buried in the lace on her backpack or that her black dress was made of a polyester blend. *God help me if they find the phone.* "I . . . think she could be here. You see, we . . . we had a falling-out and I wanted to apologize. It's urgent that I find her."

There, was that so hard? Just tell fibs and blend in until you find her. . . .

"Orla knows everybody," Caid told her, gently setting Adelle down outside a closed lacquered door. "Certainly she can help you find this acquaintance."

"Of course I can! If you can help us see to Miss Casey's leg, or else find someone who can!"

"I am hardly qualified," Caid murmured. "But I will hunt down someone with a tad more experience than me. Does it hurt very badly?"

Adelle attempted a brave face. "Only a little."

Orla gave a few taps on the door, but nobody answered. "But after we dry you off and give you something warm to drink. I will not allow you to exist in this state of endampened distress for another moment!"

Definitely not a word.

"That is not a word, Orla," Caid said with a long-suffering sigh.

Adelle couldn't help but giggle, as if he had read her mind. They exchanged a look, and she saw a sparkle of something exciting and strange behind his spectacles. Orla hadn't noticed.

"What does that expensive governess of yours do all day?" Caid asked.

"Fiddlesticks, dear, I don't need an extensive vocabulary—just a husband with an extensive inheritance! Well! It appears that Miss Byrne, the Irish typhoon herself, is not in." Orla turned the knob and went inside, revealing a sumptuous bedchamber decorated in about a hundred different shades of green. "We can make ourselves at home until she appears; no doubt she is lording over Elsie as the poor girl sews her fingers to nubs somewhere. . . ."

"Green is her color," Adelle breathed, stunned to see the fantasy bedroom of her entire life there before her eyes. Next to her, Caid cleared his throat.

"I mean, what Irish girl doesn't love green?" Adelle scrambled.

"Do come in, Miss Casey, before you catch your death and the whole night is ruined!" Orla swept her arm dramatically toward the cozy armchair near the wardrobe. "Now, Caid, sweetest, fetch Elsie or Greta or whoever is about. Some chocolate for Miss Casey must be arranged, and we will tend to her leg, and of course then if she is well enough to stand, we shall dress her immaculately for the ball!"

9

"Boston in the spring! Boston in the spring! Is there anything more perfect?" Moira was all joy and exclamations, her arms thrown wide, her parasol behind her, exalting in the sun and in young love. At her side, Orla Beevers paused to lean down and inhale deeply of a blossom, the stem of a fat, blushing peony pinched between two fingers as she drank of its perfume. All was so well, and so bright, Moira could hardly remember a time before the fete. It seemed as if her life had begun the day she met Severin, but now her life flourished after she had passed the evening in his arms.

"The only thing more perfect is Severin," Moira sighed, taking her face away from the sun and going amongst the gardens on light feet, reaching out as if to playfully touch each and every flower that grew there. In her young heart, it was as if it all bloomed just for her.

"You must speak softly," said Orla, her tone rather too scolding for the sunlit day. "There is still an understanding with the Vaughns, and if your mother hears—"

"She will not hear," Moira assured her, laughing. *"She will not know! Not until she must. And she must. Our love will prevail, Orla, and I will be free of Kincaid Vaughn. It must be so. Oh, it must, it must, it must!"*

—Moira, *chapter 8*

A rat brushed against Connie's foot and she stifled a shriek. The caverns beneath the church reeked of sweat and damp and yeast.

A long, narrow passage had been carved into the stone, a single greasy torch on the wall giving enough light to show where the corridor intersected with a larger, wider tunnel. Connie winced whenever the cowgirl's gun poked into her back. She walked faster, eager to see these strange tunnels running beneath the church. They reached an impressively large thoroughfare through the earth, and she marveled at how a bunch of kids had managed it.

The start of subway tunnel digging, she thought, *or else catacombs they've expanded.*

At the fork, Connie realized the construction ended just to her right, but when they turned left, her wonder and curiosity were revived. It was like a miniature city hidden there beneath the church. In what was wide and tall enough to be a train tunnel, the Penny-Farthings had managed to construct a market of sorts, with stolen apple carts and crates. They had even built little huts and shacks out of uneven slats of wood. Some were labeled with chalk: *FOOD, MEDICINE, AMMNITION.*

What they lacked in spelling ability they more than made up for in ambition and scope. Children and teens began to appear, just rough shapes emerging from their hidey-holes. Here and there a lantern flared to life, illuminating more of the tunnel city. To the left, a ramshackle café had been set up, complete with bar.

It was like something from the Cour des Miracles in *The Hunchback of Notre-Dame*. Fitting, too, since the upper crust in *Moira* were convinced the Penny-Farthings only associated with thieves, murderers, and filth.

"Watch her," the cowgirl spat to her companion. The boy, his face smeared with dirt, half of it hidden behind his bandanna, sidled up to her with his own gun at the ready.

"They got Alec!" The girl raged forward, and the Penny-Farthings watching Connie followed at a distance that suggested it was better to stay out of her way. "The goddamn, cussed, no-good screamers got Alec! They were strong tonight, maybe the solstice makes 'em stronger, how the hell am I supposed to know anything about any of this? The world doesn't make sense no more. . . ."

More lanterns appeared, then more, a patchwork of light filling in the tunnel town section by section. Most of the onlookers held back, but Connie saw a handful of braver figures weaving their way through the rows of shacks and gawkers to meet the cowgirl. A cry went up somewhere, but Connie almost didn't hear it. Her mind had snagged on the word *solstice*. Several key events took place in the book on and around the solstice. It was the first real clue that felt concrete enough to orient her position in the story.

"Missi is back!" she heard. "They're back!"

"Wake up, Mississippi is here!"

"What did you bring us, Missi? Anything good?"

The crisp strike of a match drew Connie's attention to the bar.

She had to find a way out of the weird little warren, but for the moment she was relatively warm, and at least there were no monsters there. Not any that she could see, anyway.

Even villains can be reasoned with.

"Damn it!" The cowgirl marched to the bar, hoisted herself onto a stool, and slammed her hat down.

A voice boomed from behind the struck match, and a tall, furry man with the build of an old-timey boxer was bathed in the sudden yellow glow. He lit a row of candles melted into disfigured lumps on old, chipped porcelain dishes and placed two ham-hock fists on the bar.

"Mississippi McClaren, this is a house of God." The man, intimidatingly large and barrel-chested, sneered down at the far smaller young redhead. He was maybe sixty years old, and his hair had all gone to his face, his beard much thicker than his balding head. He spoke with a surprisingly refined British accent. "You will watch your tongue, young lady."

"Ha!" They both burst into laughter. "Shut up, you old son of a gun, and pour me something strong enough to shame the devil. We drink to Alec, and for all of us gone too soon."

"Amen." The man produced a bottle of spirits and a small wooden cup. His gaze drifted past the redhead to Connie and remained fixed there. "Now, what have we here?"

Mississippi McClaren shot a bleak look over her fringed shoulder. "Loose end. Found her at the new tear in the park. Not sure if she's a Clacker or just dumb as a stump."

"Hey!" Connie took a step forward, too fast, and felt the kid at her side jab her with the end of his rifle.

The barman twirled his oiled black mustache and beckoned for Connie to come closer. "Let me get a look at her. I know a Clacker at fifty paces, but not in this miserable dark."

Two young women joined Mississippi at the bar, one with a freckled brown complexion and long silver hair, the other with olive skin and two intricate black braids that trailed over her shoulders. How a girl her age had gone entirely gray, Connie couldn't guess. The ladies' checkered bandannas rested around their necks. Wordlessly, the barman poured them drinks.

The boy behind Connie nudged her forward until she was just a few feet from the bar stools and the audience now inspecting her closely. She squirmed. What would they see? A girl like them, or an outsider? There was no hiding her tracksuit or her nylon bag. She began to tremble. It all felt, suddenly, so real. Would they hurt her? Imprison her? That wasn't a fake gun at her back; she had watched it rip holes in the flying monsters, and after all her extensive biathlon training, she knew just how dangerous a firearm could be in sloppy hands.

"What on earth would make you think she was a Clacker?" the man asked with a snort. "This is excessive, even for you, Missi."

"Yeah? Then solve this puzzle for me real quick, stranger." Missi whirled on her stool, glaring at Connie. "What the hell were you doin' foolin' around by that tear? Nobody in their right mind goes near one of those things. Only fool Clackers who want to worship it."

Connie fidgeted. Last summer, Adelle had convinced her to waste a bunch of money on a dumb improv camp. Connie, never good at being put on the spot, had hated every minute of it. But

Connie, also bad at underachieving, had managed to win over the instructors and learn a few things. One of the little tidbits their fortysomething hippie teacher had told them repeatedly cut through the anxious noise in her head.

It doesn't matter what you're doing onstage as long as you sell it.

She had never been good at lying, but maybe, just maybe she could sell the truth.

"I was sending a message," Connie finally said. The tunnel had gone silent, everyone gathered there listening to the stranger—her—intently. A few dozen silhouettes watched from the shadows, and probably countless more, hidden in their shacks, listened. "That's a place I used to go a lot, so I went there to try and warn my family."

The barman stroked his mustache. "That sounds reasonable enough to me, Missi. You ought to give her a chance; we cannot exactly recruit in the streets."

"And she was a good shot, too!" blurted out the boy who, ironically, held her at riflepoint.

"You see?" The barman smiled.

"Why would you meet there?" Mississippi ignored all of them, tossing back her drink and glaring. "Why right there? That place is more dangerous 'n hell. Sounds like a place some fool Clackers would go."

"It wasn't always like that," Connie said, taking a chance. She had to believe that this world, even in the book, had not always been so terrible. After all, she had found the girl's journals in the bakery—it sounded like all the trouble and upheaval was something new, something recent. "I can't help that we picked that spot; that's just the way it is."

"Defiant!" The barman chuckled. "I like her."

"I don't," Mississippi muttered. "Not one bit. Y'all are too gullible—that's why we're losin'. Look at her!" She swung her leg around and pushed off the stool, swaggering back over to Connie. With a snort, she plucked at the standing collar on Connie's tracksuit. "What kinda clothing is this, huh? Some sorta newfangled armor straight from the deepest depths of hell? You and your friends pull this right out of the tear?"

Connie inhaled deeply, face-to-face with the cowgirl, so close she could feel the girl's breath on her chin. At that range, she could see the uneven depth to the angry scar running up her cheek. The barman was right—Connie *was* defiant. And angry. She had tried to help, after all, and now this stubborn, stupid girl wouldn't listen.

She had put up with enough, and now she was losing her temper.

"They're just my clothes," Connie bit out. "I'm not your enemy. I helped you fight off those monsters, right? I'm not looking for trouble. I'm just . . ." The anger burned out. She was so, so tired and so, so hungry. All she wanted was to lie down and eat something, anything. She sighed and looked at her feet. But her coaches said to never show defeat, so Connie lifted her chin and forced herself to meet Mississippi's eye.

A current as hot and crackling as lightning snapped between them. Connie knew how to spot a nemesis on the soccer field before the game even started; a troublemaker stood out. The cocky stance. The bored stare. The twitch beneath the muscles that belied their eagerness and aggression. If this Mississippi girl was to be her rival, then, at least she was pretty. Really pretty. In fact, with the red hair and lively eyes, she almost matched the description of Moira—

Don't go there. That's how you got into this mess in the first place. Adelle's fantasies and foolishness.

Connie rolled her shoulders back, signaling a truce. "I'm just trying to get home. I . . . just want to go home. I want to see my friends, my family. . . . I miss my mom and pops."

The redhead pursed her lips. She reminded Connie then of someone else. Her face looked softer, almost sweet. Her brow furrowed with sympathy. It was like the word *pops* had somehow cast a spell. Mississippi chewed her cheek, then shrugged and took a step back.

Under her breath, so only Connie could hear her, she said, "I'm watchin' you."

Connie didn't respond.

"So." The cowgirl turned and made her way back to her stool, then motioned for the barman to pour two more drinks. Connie wondered if that second one might be for her. "You want to go home, stranger. Hell, I don't even know what to call you!" She pointed to herself. "I'm Mississippi McClaren; you've probably heard of me. That's Sleepless Joe, and the corpse-lookin' fella behind him is Dreamless Dan." The barman was Joe, but Connie hadn't even noticed the man seated behind him, apparently fast asleep, with his head dropped back against the wall. Then Mississippi nodded toward the young women on either side of her. She motioned first to the girl with white hair and then to the one with braids. "This is Farai and that's Geo. We run this little band of misfits, but you probably heard of us too, in whispers and cusses. The Penny-Farthings." She had pronounced the name Geo like "Hay-oh."

Connie nodded. "I'm Constance Rollins, but you can call me Connie."

"All right, that's somethin'." Mississippi grabbed the extra drink, also in a tiny wooden cup, and brought it to Connie, waiting until she took it. She knew better than to refuse and knocked her cup against the cowgirl's. "This is Connie. Connie is just tryin' to get home, y'all. So, where's home?"

Connie took a deep breath, lifting the cup to her chin. It smelled like rubbing alcohol. "Here," she said. It was a risk, a huge one, but Coach Mindy had a saying for that, too. After a crappy biathlon meet, she would always tell her, "Don't seek your opponent's level, make your own."

So we play on my level.

Mississippi gave a confused laugh, cup poised before her lips. "Here?"

"Boston," Connie added. *Tell your story and sell it.* She drank the horrid alcohol down in one, forcing herself not to immediately vomit it up on her empty stomach. *Sell it. Sell your truth.* "Boston," she repeated. "I lied. When I said before that I wasn't a Clacker . . . I lied. I am one, but I don't want to be anymore. If you'll take me, I want to be a Penny-Farthing."

10

ADELLE FROWNED AT HER reflection in the tall mirror. Her face looked distorted, warped, like her skin wouldn't stay still. She reached out and tapped the glass, and the image only rippled more.

She gasped. Behind her, the young maid Orla had summoned yanked mercilessly on her corset laces. One more pull and the tiny sandwiches she had just bolted down would come flying back up.

"That's . . ." Adelle wheezed. "That's tight enough!"

"Nonsense!" Orla chirped. She was splayed across a cushioned fainting couch, a plate of miniature mincemeat tarts resting partially on her wrist and partially on her bosom. "A slim little waist is all the fashion; I can never get mine as tiny as Moira's."

The physician Caid had sent to inspect Adelle did not look old enough to be any sort of professional doctor, fresh-faced and hardly taller than her, with a desperate attempt at a beard that just looked like clippings glued to his face. Orla had lamented that all the truly superb physicians were gone. When Adelle asked what she meant by that, Orla had simply said they had walked into the sea with all the rest. Adelle knew with absolute certainty that such a thing never happened in the novel—Kincaid had lost a brother tragically, but that was to scarlet fever—and decided she needed to get some answers on that sooner rather than later.

"What do you mean about the sea?" Adelle had asked Orla softly while the physician dug through his leather bag.

"You know," Orla had murmured. "Or, well, I guess you mustn't. Your poor head! But of course many have walked into the sea. Before we had the Chanters' medicine, the dreams made so many go. Why, Kincaid lost his entire family to it. 'Tis a miracle he did not himself make the walk."

Adelle couldn't believe what she was hearing. Scarlet fever was not the same as his entire family walking off into the ocean. She already knew something was deeply amiss with this world, so much so that she wanted to believe Orla was just making it all up. The horror of it, if true, even in a fictional world, was hard to take. And Kincaid . . . Was he the only one of his family left? That must be awful.

Kincaid Vaughn's inner life was never explored in the book, but now that she had met him—or whatever one might call coming face-to-face with a fictional character—her heart ached at what he must have gone through.

He's not real, remember?

The "doctor" pronounced her leg unbroken, though Adelle didn't put much stock in his diagnosis. The bruising would fade, he declared, and she should rest. Then he left an alarmingly large bottle of laudanum for her to use "should the pain grow too unbearable."

Maybe she ought to be grateful he hadn't offered cocaine instead.

Adelle left the laudanum where it had landed on the delicate table near the fainting couch. Instead, she asked for some ice for her leg, but apparently all of it was being used at the party. Ice had become rare and dear, and the flavored ices for dessert mattered more than her bruises, apparently.

She decided to shove the discomfort way down deep and soldier on. An entire ballroom full of witnesses waited below, and one of them must have laid eyes on Connie. She hoped beyond hope that Connie herself would attend.

And then what? How will we ever get home? We need the book, but we're in the book.

Adelle wiped the deep grimace off her face. One step at a time. She had to find Connie first before worrying about what came after.

Greta, the maid dressing Orla, appeared skeletal with hunger but possessed ferociously strong hands. With a final, savage yank, Greta decided Adelle had been tortured enough and tied off the laces at the center of her corset. Then came a padded belt, and then a frothy contraption of embroidered cotton petticoats.

"What a stroke of luck that we are so similar! Moira had thought to cut up that old dress of mine to make something new, for she admired the pattern so, but I'm delighted she hadn't yet begun." Orla ate another tart, watching them at the mirror with a crumb-coated smile. She was glowing, happy, and Adelle tried to mimic her excitement with a nod. How could Orla chirp and flounce around when entire families were just up and walking into the sea? She didn't want to think unkind thoughts about a gentle soul like Orla, but it was hard not to wonder. "I would have worn this gown myself again, but Moira says I do not have the eyes for it. That violet will look so beguiling on you, dear!"

Greta fetched said violet frock, slipping it over Adelle's arms and pulling it snug before beginning on the endless round buttons going up the back. The violet silk gown combined with the bustle, petticoats, and corset felt like a suit of armor, and nearly as heavy. Her backside looked huge thanks to the bustle, but somehow it flattered her. Orla's tailor had embellished the front of the dress with black ribbons and beads and sewn clusters of purple and ebony fabric flowers to the narrow sleeves, which almost fell off the shoulder. At the waist, the violet silk was hitched up with more flowers, revealing a tiered underskirt and a waterfall of off-white lace.

Adelle stared at her reflection, watching Greta twist her yellow hair into what looked like fanciful little croissants and then pin them in place with jewels and ribbons. Pressing her hands firmly over her stomach, Adelle tried to picture where all her squishy insides had gone, for the gown made her look as sleek and curved as a vase.

The door crashed open. Adelle jumped, and Orla leaped to her feet, scattering crumbs and tarts.

"Orla! You wore that horrid silver monstrosity! Look at the state of you! A silver dollar in a beggar's pocket would shine brighter."

Adelle froze. In the looking glass she was seeing the heroine she had idolized for so long. How many times had she finished the novel and wished she could have the love, the hair, the life, the romance, the figure that Moira had? And now there she was, distorted by the ripple in the glass, her sea-green eyes flashing with anger as she stormed into her own bedroom. She matched it perfectly, clad in an emerald velvet confection of a gown that would put any modern wedding cake to shame.

Adelle's rental gown for the Sadie Hawkins dance would look like a tasseled rag next to it.

"I thought you liked this dress," Orla murmured, head bowed. It had taken only that one sharp outburst from Moira to dim her spirits.

Adelle gawked, wanting to jump to Orla's defense but aware— painfully, breathlessly aware—that she was staring at a celebrity. And Moira was every bit as beautiful as *the* Robin Amery had described her: perfectly proportioned, practically a porcelain doll with her milky skin and rosebud lips. Her bright hair had been swept up dramatically, leaving only two bouncy curls to frame her face. And those eyes . . . Men had died from blunter blades than those eyes.

"Ah. The interloper. Elsie mentioned you had hit a stray and dragged her inside." Moira smirked, brandishing a green lace fan in her gloved fingers and swaying toward Adelle. She inspected her from head to foot.

God, I'm getting tired of people looking at me that way.

"Orla, you little idiot, you should have left her facedown in that puddle—she's likely to steal your suitors and leave you an old, sad maid." Chuckling, Moira dipped into a quick, perfunctory curtsy.

Adelle tried to copy her, knowing she didn't match her grace.

"Moira Byrne," she said. Her voice was like smoke, sweetened with a light Irish lilt. "And you are?"

"A-Adelle Casey," she stammered, clumsy and afraid. This was *the* Moira. She hadn't expected her to be so intimidating, but then she hadn't expected to actually find her way into the book where the character lived. "Thank you for letting me attend your party. It's very kind."

"Oh, sweets, I am not kind; that was Orla. She did not ask me about any of this, did she?" Moira tossed her head back and laughed, then stalked over to Orla and hit her on the chin, quite hard, with the end of her fan. Orla winced, but the need to please Moira must have been harder, for she did not protest the strike. "No, Orla has naught but cotton in her fat head. She likes to presume, and presume, and think everyone shares her affinity for the less fortunate. Tell me, which Caseys are you affiliated with, exactly? Not the Haverhill Caseys, surely? Or I would have heard of you by now."

Adelle didn't miss the insult, and her anger at Orla being treated that way, after all the immense goodness she had shown, rankled her. More than that, Adelle knew Moira's dirty secret—she had fallen head over heels in love with a poor boy and had made plans to reveal him to the world at this very party.

"My family is from Back Bay," Adelle replied, giving a toothy grin. She challenged any dentist in 1885 to top the braces, retainer, and whitening routine her orthodontist, Dr. Laghari, had put her through. And Back Bay? Well, it was home, and she could only hope it meant something in 1885. Judging from Moira's stunned expression, it did. Her smug smile faded, replaced by an unreadable, doll-like mask.

"Well, that just shows you that appearances can be deceiving, does it not?" She tittered, and Adelle forced herself to stay quiet. "Let us all hold hands and be friends, yes? I am simply playing. Playing!" Moira shrugged her birdlike shoulders. "This is how we play, is it not, dove?" She tapped Orla with her fan again, this time gently. "Is it not?"

"It is!" Orla piped up, her lips stretched thin. "Moira has such a keen wit, I can never keep up."

"No, dove, you cannot, but you have many fine qualities, as I'm sure Miss Casey does too. Qualities that will surely win you the eye of every handsome beau in the place. Now! We are all dressed and perfumed and pinned and cinched." Moira turned in whimsical circles, her dress flaring out in a lovely swirl.

When she was still again, her pale green eyes sparkled with mischief. "Shall we not have some fun?"

"Miss Beevers?" Adelle asked, not certain where to put her hands or whether to lift her skirts or simply put all her energy into not limping like a pirate with a peg leg.

"Yes, dear?" Orla clung to her arm. Tightly. She got the distinct impression that Orla sensed she was a safe harbor from Moira's storm. They waited at the top of the stairs, sipping claret after Adelle had stupidly asked for beer and was told in no uncertain terms that a lady would not be seen sipping beer at a fete of this magnitude. For all the Victorian novels she had read, she was doing a poor job blending in.

Adelle didn't know if she liked the claret, so instead she just held the crystal glass and watched the dancers waltz below them. She leaned subtly against the railing at the top of the grand staircase, hoping to relieve some pressure in her leg.

"I wanted to ask you about my friend," Adelle said softly. She noticed all the young ladies were speaking in a tone just above a whisper and decided to mimic them. At this rate, if she took another improv camp she would certainly dominate. "The one I'm looking for? Mr. Vaughn said you know everybody. . . ."

"Dressing is so exhausting, I had forgotten all about it!" Orla, by contrast, drank her claret freely, snatching a third helping from a passing waiter. Adelle couldn't help but notice that the waitstaff, maids, and musicians were no older than she was. The musicians, in fact, looked like they were swimming in their formal wear, as if they were in costume and didn't belong. They were also not good, consistently and obnoxiously off-key.

In fact, she only saw a handful of adults in the entire ballroom, like homecoming but without the gymnasium, disco ball, and mocktails. *I'm at Sadie Hawkins after all.* The effect on her was strange. Here there should be beauty, overwhelming beauty, the glitter of candles and happy people drinking out of crystal champagne flutes, string music, a waltz, the giddy rustling of skirts and the promise of flirtatious glances across a crowded dance floor. But to Adelle it all felt somehow . . . gauzy. Blurred. All the elements were there—the dance and the music and the laughter—but it was like a bunch of precocious children playing dress-up, and she wondered if Orla or Caid saw it, or if she was imagining things.

"Dear? Dear? Miss Casey?"

Adelle shook off her distracted worry and turned back to Orla. Whatever Moira believed, Adelle thought Orla wore the silver dress just fine.

"My friend . . . Her name is Constance but we all just call her Connie. Connie Rollins," Adelle explained. She couldn't exactly describe a tracksuit to a bunch of Victorians, and so she stuck to the immutable facts. "She's very tall, and she has long black hair, wavy, usually in a braid or a tail. Hazel eyes that sometimes look green, and freckles. Freckles all over her nose and cheeks, even more than I have. And she looks strong, you know . . ." Adelle trailed off, trying to think of how a woman of that era might be described as athletic. She doubted Orla even knew what a barbell was. "Like she rides horses—active, and healthy."

Just describing her best friend made Adelle's heart heavy with sadness. She was leaving out so much, like Connie's thick, quizzical brows that always made her look as if she were working out the secrets of the universe. And her rosy cheeks. Connie's father lovingly called her Santa Cheeks. She hated it, and it made her flush, which only made her cheeks redder.

"I have to find her," Adelle confessed. Her eyes drifted to the dancers again, staring through them. "It's . . . it's been a long time since we were reunited."

It hadn't been, of course, but it already felt like an eternity. She just wanted to know her friend was safe, that this whole stupid situation she had gotten them into hadn't resulted in Connie being harmed somehow.

Orla tucked a bent finger under her chin, pursing her lips in thought.

"Perhaps she is one of the Quincy Rollins girls, though I believe they only have five sons. I suppose I could be mistaken, but I doubt it. There is a family with that name from Weymouth, too, but I doubt they could make it to town—the roads and sea are impossible just now. Oh!" Her face lit up, cheeks flaring pink. "Malachy Moulton had a brief engagement to a Rollins girl; perhaps he would know more, though I heard their engagement ended very badly."

She patted Adelle's hand excitedly. "I shall see if Mr. Moulton is in attendance, for I believe he is still among us. If so, then we may just have answers for you! Oh, I do love a puzzle!"

Before Adelle could interject and explain that Malachy Moulton being engaged to *her* Connie Rollins was extremely unlikely, Orla flitted away, leaving Adelle to frown and wonder and hope over her untouched claret. Speaking of Connie and now standing there with nobody to talk to, she felt hopelessly alone. Caid had never appeared again after Orla had herded her into Moira's bedchamber, and Moira herself had gone off to powder her nose a third time, convinced it was too shiny.

The clock in the ballroom struck nine. As the chimes sounded one by one, Adelle couldn't help but remember the scene from the novel. On that night, Moira made a grand entrance in her green velvet gown, and all her guests marveled at her beauty while she descended the grand staircase. Then she boldly threaded through the sea of admirers, her betrothed nowhere to be found. Instead, she chose to dance with a young man nobody recognized, a boy who didn't belong.

It was heart-stoppingly romantic to Adelle and Connie, but it couldn't happen if Moira kept attending to her shiny nose. Adelle sighed and decided to find Orla, tracking her through the busy dance floor. The silver dress made her easy to spot. Adelle took a step toward the staircase, hoping nobody would watch her clumsy entrance. Moira with her little dainty steps, she was not. Her dress had caught on the bottom of her heeled boot, and she tugged, hard, but one of the loose threads had looped itself all the way around the heel.

"Come on." Adelle jerked the hem of her dress harder with her left hand, stumbling into the center of the hallway. The waltz music swelled, dismally out of tune, speeding up and slowing down seemingly at random. She gave another yank and felt her elbow crunch against something soft and warm.

"My nose!"

Adelle spun, finding Moira there, blood gushing from her nostrils, her white satin gloves stained red as she clasped her hands over her face. It wasn't just shiny anymore but bloody and bruised.

"I'm so sorry!" Adelle shrieked, stumbling forward, trying to help.

Moira shook her head, ringlets bouncing, tears welling in her eyes. "You've spoiled it! You've spoiled my party! You've spoiled our—I hate you. I *hate* you."

"It was an accident, let me help, maybe it isn't so bad—"

Moira ignored her, whirling, skirts fanning out in a circle before she ran down the corridor, blood dripping in her wake.

Was this like time travel? Would something horrific happen now that Adelle had changed the course of the evening? Nobody seemed to notice—the music too loud, the drinks too plentiful. Adelle spun back to face the staircase and the dancers, but it was like nothing had happened. First the carriage, now this. . . . She couldn't seem to just keep her head down and find Connie.

She had to tell Orla; someone ought to go and comfort Moira, and Adelle hardly knew her. That, and she had just smashed her face in.

Adelle rushed down the stairs, holding her skirts up just enough to avoid another accident. The dancers enveloped her, dizzying and perfumed, and she fought through the crush, politely navigating the skirts and suit tails that brushed her as she tried desperately to find Orla. She had lost sight of the silver dress and now, adrift amid the sea of spinning, giggling couples, Adelle was too short to find much of anything. They began to carry her along, sweeping her up. Her leg throbbed. She caught snippets of conversation, gasps, apologies for stepping on a foot or hem . . .

"Do you not so prefer the Viennese waltz?"

"Did you see Arthur? He didn't even escort Vivienne to her seat after the quadrille!"

"Sir! Have a care for my shoes!"

"Please," Adelle pleaded, growing overheated. But she couldn't escape. Someone took her by the wrists and then the hands, a man she didn't recognize. "Please, I'm not trying to dance—"

When she looked up into the man's face, she recoiled. His skin was deathly pale, his eyes large and black. It seemed to her he had no nose or ears at all, just an empty mask staring down at her, smiling. They joined the waltz just as her stomach twisted with nauseated fear. She thought she might vomit if he spun her too fast, but he did, over and over, lifting her hand above her head and twirling her like a ballerina in a glass jar.

"Stop! Stop . . . I'm too dizzy, please . . ."

But the stranger just laughed at her, mouth wide open, with no teeth or tongue, a yawning black maw that threatened to swallow her up. Whispers poured from the hole of his mouth, and she felt sick in earnest, overcome by sudden trembling and a tightness in her head like her brain had grown too large and pulsing for her skull.

Close now. So close. I almost have you. You will serve.

The voice she had heard before, the one that had come to her just after Mr. Straven cast his spell and again when she'd landed in this strange world. Adelle reeled back, ripping her wrists out of the stranger's grasp. She pirouetted clumsily, holding out her hands for balance until the world stopped tilting. The vortex of dancers had deposited her on the other side of the ballroom, the grand staircase distant now, comically small, like something out of a doll's house. When she glanced over her shoulder, the man was gone, or rather, an ordinary gentleman with a pointed beard and a pained expression stood watcing her, the tilt of his eyebrow suggesting she was acting horribly uncouth.

The refreshment table lay before her; to her left and behind, the musicians played on. Rows of empty chairs awaited the dancers when the music ended. A single young man stood among the tables of food and drinks, frozen, his hands at his sides. He wore a dark suit and dark gloves, and his black hair had been combed back, slick as crude oil.

Maybe he could help her find Orla, or at least give her some idea of where she might have gone.

"Excuse me?" Adelle shuffled carefully over to him, cautious of her voluminous skirts. "Could you help me?"

He didn't respond. Or move. He remained perfectly still, facing away from her. The smell of the cakes and mousses and jellies might have otherwise been tantalizing, but their cloying sweetness only made her feel more ill. She approached the man carefully, asking again in a polite tone, "Would you mind if I asked you something, sir? I lost sight of my friend. . . ."

As she came closer, Adelle noticed that the black, oily texture of his hair did not stop at his temples, but rather continued around to his face. She gasped softly, inching around him, slowly, ever so slowly, finding that no matter how far she traveled around him in a circle, he remained back-turned, his head a perfectly glistening black orb, his hands curled into fists that never faced her, his feet ever pointed away.

Adelle stopped and backed up, light-headed again. She pressed her palms against the steel boning of her corset, clutching her stomach. Why couldn't she see straight? She glanced at the stranger again and watched as at last he tried to turn toward her. When his toes pointed in her direction, Adelle looked at where his face should have been and the ballroom collapsed around her.

There was nothing there. A hole. A hole like the tear, a window into a place between places. No stars twinkled there, just a void, the primordial pull of a nameless beyond. Nothing there, nothing there . . . No, not nothing, but something. Something cruel. The birthplace of horrors, the crucible of all nightmares.

She couldn't look any longer; it threatened to pull her forward like the dancer's wide-open, ugly mouth.

Closer still. Look inside. Look . . . See how it is born, see how it comes into your world.

The floor went out from under her feet. Adelle was falling, powerless to collect herself, utterly sapped of strength or the will even to command her own body. She blinked once, and when she opened her eyes again, the horrible stranger was gone. But that didn't stop the falling.

Someone moved behind her, lightning quick, and opened their arms to catch her. She felt the wall of a human chest at her back, and then two sure hands closing around the goose-pimpled flesh of her upper arms, the teasing gap of skin between sleeve and elbow-length glove. Her savior pulled her upright and Adelle breathed deeply, the tightness in her stomach gone, though the fear remained.

"Careful, mademoiselle, mm? Let us have no injured maidens this evening."

Adelle knew him before she even saw his face. It was a voice she had listened to in daydreams a thousand times, rich and tipped with humor, and embellished with a fading French accent.

Severin Sylvain. And there she was, held firmly in his arms.

She stood of her own power, but he didn't relinquish his grip on her arms. Instead, he gave her a crooked smile, one roguish lock of curly black hair tumbling over one eye. For a moment, she didn't know if she could speak, he was so beautiful. Unearthly.

"Are you looking for someone?" he asked. "You appear lost, at the ball or perhaps in dreams, and whichever it is, you must tell me. I am so desperately nosy."

Adelle glanced shyly at the floor. God, it was hard to breathe, hard to look at him. Was this what it was like, she wondered, to fall in love at first sight? There was a certain wintriness about him—the marble-white skin and softest of soft gray eyes, eyes the color of the sky before a snowfall. And that crooked smile . . . Now she knew why Moira wrote poems about him, why she risked disownment and worse to have him.

"I am looking for someone," Adelle murmured. "My friend, I . . . I can't find her."

Severin Sylvain extended his hand, bowing at the waist. He never looked at her except from behind that playful lock of black curls. "Perhaps we can look together, mademoiselle. I am yours to command."

11

"*And what shall you do while Severin and I are passing time together?*" *Moira asked. She had just finished dashing off a lie, leaving a card at the house for her mother and informing her that she and Orla should be returning late, as they had agreed to call on Mr. and Mrs. Anthony Harte. As the Hartes lived on the west side, Moira had explained eloquently and with profuse apologies, the journey back to Byrne House might detain them. But Mrs. Anthony Harte, Moira further elaborated, had only recently recovered from a childbirth-related bout of hysterics and was in need of sympathetic feminine company.*

Moira had no intention of calling on Orla's insipid sister or comforting her about anything. Instead, she had organized a generous bribe for Orla's driver Simpson, and he would take the girls to what he assumed was a luncheon on India Street. As soon as they arrived at the location, Moira would secretly rendezvous with Severin, and her family would be none the wiser.

"Orla? How shall you employ yourself?" Moira asked the question again, for her friend seemed quite out of sorts, staring out the window with glazed, strange eyes. Perhaps she was concerned for her sister; Orla had always been excessively sensitive.

"Oh." At last the girl spoke, soft among the clatter of horse hooves as Hampton carried them across town. "There appears to be a Western horse show not far from our destination." And here Orla produced a folded, tattered handbill from inside her fringed orange reticule. "You see, it says here it is a 'spine-tingling, rip-roaring sensation not to be missed.'"

"It sounds positively beastly," Moira gasped, staring anew at her companion.

"But you have all the excitement, I think," Orla continued, apparently unshaken by Moira's disgust. "I should very much like to have my spine tingled and my rip roared. Do you see? There is a young lady here with pistols! Can you believe it? Do you imagine it will be too loud and shocking for me?"

"I absolutely imagine that." But Moira smiled. "Could it be dangerous?"

"Oh no, I will make Simpson attend."

"Then I do not see the harm in it, as long as you keep it a secret," said Moira, feeling very magnanimous and reformist indeed. "After all, Orla, you are a young lady and unmarried. The West is said to build character in men, but I should not think it changes any women for the better."

—Moira, *chapter 8*

Wide-eyed and openmouthed, Mississippi McClaren signaled for another drink. "Well, knock me over and call me Susie, we got ourselves a spy!"

But Connie didn't smile. She needed a sanctuary to eat and sleep until she could find Adelle and get home, somewhere relatively safe, and the strange city the Penny-Farthings had carved out was as good a place as any. Those screamers had carried off a teenage boy with no trouble, and she wasn't going aboveground alone again unless she had a good reason to do it.

"I'm serious. I was trying to send a message because . . ." Connie sensed all of their eyes burning into her. Her lies had better be convincing and consistent. "Because the Clackers took a friend of mine. I'm done with them. For good. My family isn't associated with them and neither am I anymore. Let me join up."

"That is an extraordinary claim," the barman, Sleepless Joe, rumbled. He had taken up a pint glass and begun wiping it down, though he seemed to do it more out of habit than real utility. "Their loyalty is absolute. This has never happened before, so I hope you can understand our skepticism."

"Of course." Connie shrugged. "But you took me prisoner, and I want to go free, so I'm laying all my cards on the table. I just wanted to get away from them and get home, but if I can't do that, then I can at least fight for the right side."

"Prove it."

Or not.

Mississippi twirled her pistol and holstered it, leaning one elbow on her leg and smirking.

"Prove it?" Connie shifted.

"That's right. Can't be too hard. You should be able to prove a whopper like that no problem," she said. "If you wanna leave that Clacker life behind to steal and thieve and scrape out an existence with us down here, then you need to earn it. Show us somethin' incontroversible and I can be reasonable."

I doubt that.

Connie took the high road, choosing not to insult her or her vocabulary. "You said before that it's the solstice . . ."

"The twentieth of June," Sleepless Joe said, nodding. "Why would that matter?"

She blinked. Right. It was November in her reality, but of course they would have jumped to whatever season it currently was in the novel. Either way, she could use it. The solstice. Connie had survived long enough to see a busy time for the book's characters, and maybe—just maybe—she could use the novel's events to convince the Penny-Farthings of her spy's wisdom.

"There is a ball tonight," Connie said confidently. "Moira Byrne is hosting a party to celebrate the solstice."

"Huh." Missi leaned forward, squinting. "I'm listening. Give us more."

Steal and thieve and scrape out an existence . . . Just glancing around, Connie could tell the Penny-Farthings weren't exactly living comfortably. The parties in the book boasted tables a mile long heaped with all sorts of delicacies, more than enough food to feed a bunch of hungry, hiding children.

"They'll have supplies for the ball, to feed the guests," Connie explained, trying to sound like she wasn't just making it up on the fly.

"And it will be crawling with Clackers. You know they stick to the rich folks like flies to manure," Geo, the girl with the braids, pointed out. "It's no good."

"No, there's a hidden servants' entrance," Connie replied. The one that Moira used to sneak in her secret paramour, Severin. "It leads directly to the kitchens."

"This is good," Sleepless Joe murmured, rolling the end of his mustache around his pinky finger. "This could be very good for us."

"Only if we play it smart," Missi insisted, but she wouldn't tear her gaze away from Connie. "We lost Alec today, and most of our ground folk are spent. Would have to go in quick and quiet, just a few of us."

The girl on her other side, Farai, shook her head. "Can't carry much that way. If we risk something this big, then we need to make it count."

"Then we steal a carriage, pack it full of food, and take it south. There's a tunnel entrance there, but they will never track it back to us here," Geo suggested, speaking faster and faster, then jumping to her feet with sudden excitement. "And I am just the woman for the job. Horses listen to me—love me—they just trust me. I have a way with animals."

"Your granddaddy runs horses for Santa Anna at the Alamo one time and that makes you King Fisher, does it?" Mississippi chuckled, clapping Geo on the back.

Geo shrugged, but she looked smug and not willing to disagree.

"But I like that spirit," Missi continued. "And we could fit a lot of grub in a carriage. . . ."

"I feel the beginnings of a plan coming on." Sleepless Joe grinned, watching Farai, Geo, and Mississippi stumble over one another's words trying to come up with the best approach.

"But we have to hurry," Connie pointed out. "The ball won't go all night, and we should go while everyone inside is still distracted."

Mississippi grinned, striding forward, taking the hat that had fallen back on its string and plopping it on her head. "Then we ladies will get the job done. Farai? Geo? Get ready to ride. And you . . ." She stuck out one finger, beckoning Connie closer. "You come with me. There are a few things you need to understand."

"We use the penny-farthings because they're real quiet and they don't need feedin'. Horses are expensive and loud. Candles are tallow from all the dead horses and, well, other dead things scattered around. Food and ammunition is whatever we can scavenge, steal, or grow, which ain't much, but mushrooms like the damp, so I hope you ain't opposed to eatin' them." Mississippi walked a zigzag through the shacks and carts and tents of what she called "the Congregation" multiple times. She pointed out the sights as they went, though there wasn't much to see. The crypts beneath the church had been expanded into the tunnel, creating plenty of space for their ragtag town. Besides Sleepless Joe and the unconscious man behind him at the bar, Connie hadn't seen a single adult.

"Where are all the grown-ups?" Connie asked cautiously.

"You simple or somethin'?" Missi snorted. "They're in the sea. Like my daddy, like all our damn daddies and mommies and all the rest. They just got up out of their beds one day and left; now here we are, picking up the pieces, doing what we can. You're lucky yours ain't gone too."

She sighed and stopped outside a small, shallow room carved into the rock. It was at the far end of the Congregation, isolated from the other huts and tents.

"The dreams got to them first. That was before Farai and Geo figured out the tea. The Clackers got their magic and monsters, right? But we got our magic too. Geo learned from her father, and he learned from his father, and they were healers as far back as she can remember in Mexico. Farai apprenticed to a bonesetter lady, but she up and walked into the sea and never finished Farai's learnin'. Still, between the two of them they brewed up a tea that keeps us safe at night. Bitter as hell, just awful, but the dreams stop and we don't walk into the sea."

Connie didn't know what to say. It all sounded so sad and desperate, a terrible way to live. She didn't want to ask too many obvious questions and risk looking like a complete outsider—their willingness to work with her already felt tentative—but she wanted to know more. So much more. She thought of the bakery and the young girl's diary: apparently, when things had started to go wrong in the world of *Moira*, people must have been convinced to sleepwalk into the sea. If the Clackers could stop it somehow, maybe the wealthier folk of Boston were paying for protection of some kind. Maybe, she thought, that cold, slithering voice that had spoken to her was speaking to everybody. Maybe it was giving the Clackers instructions and luring people into the ocean.

But why?

The voice returned to her like a half-remembered nightmare. *You will serve.*

She hadn't heard the voice again since, and Connie could only hope her refusal to serve had somehow pissed it off enough to leave her alone for good.

In the alcove carved into the rock, behind a moth-eaten curtain, she watched three children, two boys and a girl, huddle together for warmth. An older teenager who reminded her of Adelle—blond, heavyset, and dressed all in black—offered them thin broth from a wooden bowl and a handful of dried strawberries.

The children were covered in what looked like deep, painful bruises. One bled from the scalp, red foam visible beneath his thin wisps of hair. Connie's stomach rumbled loudly at the sight of the food, even if none of it smelled remotely appetizing. She was starving.

"Agatha." Mississippi held her hand out and the older girl twisted. Her eyes were soft blue and worn like old velvet; she had seen too much for her age. "Some reprieve for our friend here, thank you kindly."

Agatha held out her palm, offering a few small, shriveled strawberries, but Connie shook her head.

"No, I'll be all right. Save it for those children—they need it more."

"Fine, but you're eatin' a mouthful of something before we leave. I need you sharp, and hunger makes you sloppy." Missi led her away. "Scurvy takes a lot of the young, if the dreams don't get them, or the monsters. But I'm sure you know all about that. Probably reveled in it with your Clacker friends before this miraculous change of heart."

"I'm not one of them," Connie assured her. "This is . . ." The children were so thin, so malnourished. . . . Connie finally tore her eyes away. "I didn't know about any of this."

And she hadn't. The author of *Moira* had chosen not to color in the lives of any of the Penny-Farthings, except for the convoluted kidnapping subplot in act 1 involving Moira's best friend. Most of it was resolved off the page, because none of it mattered next to Moira and Severin's love. Theoretically, it had already transpired, though Connie found it hard to reconcile the descriptions from the novel with this young, ragtag group. Down here were the forgettable characters, the ones who weren't glamorous or romantic, the ones just eking out a living in a big, churning city that could swallow anyone alive. She wondered if Robin Amery had given any of these characters a second thought, if she'd even considered them more than grimy set dressing. But they were real, and suffering—poor or dirty or criminal, they didn't deserve to starve in the deep, dark damp beneath Boston's monster-infested streets.

Connie felt suddenly oily all over, like someone had dunked her in grease.

"I'm sure we look pathetic to you. I mean, forget meat unless it's tinned. Fish if we can manage it, but most fish just wash up dead on the shore now, on account of that aberration in the harbor." She shrugged. "Nobody gets in or out of the city except for one boat. Your Clacker boat. One boat in, one boat out. How does it work? How can it sail when every other ship wrecks in the shallows?"

Connie realized she was accusing her specifically—or the people she had allegedly associated with—of causing it. "I don't know," she said, truthful. "I don't know how any of it works."

"Figures." Missi stopped next to an apple cart. No apples there, but a dozen or so cans of smoked clams and sardines, a stack of square, paper-wrapped packets next to them. She tossed one packet to Connie. "Your—their—horses eat better than our young."

"I'm sorry about those children, and I'm sorry about your friend," Connie murmured. "The one who got carried off. I'm sorry about all of this, but I'm trying to help. I want to help."

She watched the cowgirl hunch into a ball of fury, then relax. Her fist stayed tight, as if she might swing and slug Connie any second. "You are one of the good ones, and I will endeavor to remember that." Without warning, faster than any soccer opponent Connie had ever faced, Missi lashed out, grabbed her wrist, and pulled her close, close enough for their noses to touch. "But if this is a trap, if you get one of my girls killed? Then I will make it my personal business to end you."

Connie's lip twitched. *Rival, indeed.* "No, Mississippi, this is not a trap. End me if you have to. I'm not a liar."

And that was true, to an extent. She wasn't lying about the ball, or the servants' entrance, and she could only imagine how much food the kitchen must have in order to feed all of Moira's guests.

God. Moira. Her heart sank, or maybe it sighed. She wondered what Adelle was seeing; it certainly wasn't this. This wasn't romantic. Not the kind of thing Adelle would risk black magic for. This was the rotting foundation that propped up the glossy, gossamer world waltzing on top of it.

Mississippi let go, exhaling as if she had just run a race and taking three giant steps back. It was like some kind of madness or mania had overcome her and then she had broken free. She pressed both fists into her eyes and laughed dryly. "Lord, I hope you are telling the truth. It might break me if another pretty woman is nothin' but lies."

She stormed away, back toward the bar, leaving Connie to listen to the children slurping down broth, their protector, Agatha, cooing and fretting.

Connie stared numbly at the paper package in her hand, then tore it open, revealing a stack of dry, brittle crackers. As soon as she put one in her mouth, it turned to mush, hardly more than salted sawdust. Connie forced herself to swallow it down. She had to find Adelle, and soon—she was cut out for a lot of things, but not this. At least she still had her belongings. The Penny-Farthings had confiscated her backpack but returned it after a cursory search, when they realized it didn't contain any weapons or food. She counted herself lucky they hadn't bothered to inspect the novel there, just waiting to expose her. The spell supplies couldn't be too difficult to obtain, she thought, since candles burned all around her. A bowl or cup could be stolen from the bar, and a stone picked up from the ground outside. But incense? Where would she find that?

Chewing and chewing, her eyes traveled the long road back to the bar, where Missi fell into conference with her lieutenants, Farai and Geo.

The Clackers got their magic, right? But we got ours, too.

The thought gave Connie a glimmer of hope. If she survived the night, then the girls who dabbled in magic might know where to find incense. Connie closed her eyes and put another cracker in her mouth, imagining it was one of her mom's silver-dollar pancakes, sweet and fluffy, doused in maple syrup. Home was somewhere, locked behind a tall, dark door; she just had to survive long enough to find it.

"HERE, PLEASE SIT DOWN." Severin tugged Adelle lightly over to the rows of chairs. She sensed the strength in his grasp, but he didn't use it against her. His hold on her felt sure yet tender. This was what people meant when they said *gentleman*. He beamed at her, his smile dazzling. "You look as if someone gave you a fright. How may I help? Or perhaps it is my shocking manners that have horrified you." He curled his finger against his lip and chuckled. "May I have your name? Mine is Severin Sylvain."

I know.

"Adelle," she said. "Adelle Casey."

Her heart flip-flopped in her chest as she tried to sit down in the chair, managing her cumbersome bustle, pads, and skirts. She was, as Orla would say, completely a-jumble.

"And your friend, what was her name? Perhaps if we find her, it will calm you, Miss Casey."

"Orla . . ." *Connie. Connie Rollins. She disappeared! She's here somewhere, and I came here for you, but now I don't know what to do.* "Orla Beevers."

She almost added, "Do you know her?" But of course he did. Orla Beevers knew everything about Moira and did not at all approve of Moira's feelings for Severin. He came from a poor fisherman's family, not the high-society, moneyed clans that Moira was expected to marry into. Orla had no idea the lengths to which Moira would go, turning that crush into a proposal and then a secret marriage that would shock the entire city.

Could it scandalize the city more than monsters and cultists? She wondered if she would last long enough in the book to find out.

"She . . . she's wearing a silver dress." It was difficult to get a single word out. Adelle had suffered the jolt of being whisked violently through the dance by a hideous partner, then encountering a boy with no face, hearing whispers from nowhere, and finally falling directly into the arms of the most perfect young man in the world. It was enough to make her head spin like a merry-go-round, and she would have patted herself on the back if it wouldn't have made her look insane.

"The dancers swept me up. I feel . . . I'm sorry. I feel very dizzy."

"Worry not. I am here now to aid you." He pressed his fist to his heart theatrically, and it drew a weak laugh from Adelle. He was trying very, very hard. "If finding Miss Beevers is your desire, then it shall be done."

Adelle pressed her gloved fingers to her temple, feeling her head swim with confusion. She kept glancing at the place where the strange boy had been, like she couldn't trust that exact spot.

"Actually, I think . . ." *What do I think? I can't think—that's the problem.* "I think it would be better if I got some air."

Severin bowed at the waist, never returning her hand, and gestured to the front of the room, where the beautifully lacquered archway led to the door, and to the left of that lay the grand staircase.

"*Bien sûr.* You look quite pale, mademoiselle, and the air will set you to rights. Come with me—we will discover where all the fashionable ladies choose to faint."

Under any other circumstances, she would have been endeared, but this was frightening. All of it was frightening, even Severin. Together, they skirted the dance safely, Severin rather forceful about it, guiding dancers and drunken revelers out of their way until they had a clear path to the stairs. Moira had never appeared. Adelle couldn't help but wince. This was supposed to be their big night, and here she was, hand in hand with Moira's beloved, and he was leading her away from the festivities. If Moira showed, he would be nowhere to be found.

It was all wrong. She was rewriting her favorite book in real time. But when she glanced at Severin, when he gently pulled her this way or that to deftly avoid a collision, she couldn't bring herself to make it stop. How long had she wanted this? How long had this boy been just a dream?

And the dream, her dream, couldn't measure up to reality. He looked just as good in profile as he did straight on, with a fine, arched nose and shapely lips any modern-day beauty guru would envy. Poor as she knew him to be, he was the only one in the entire ballroom who wore his fancy suit with ease.

They traveled up and up, and Adelle pointed the toes on her injured leg, hoping to take pressure off without alerting Severin to her injury. She wasn't sure her pride could withstand being carried, fainting into a stranger's arms, and then being carried again all in one day. Besides, the petticoats, cage, and pillows strapped to her butt probably added twenty pounds, something his willowy frame might not be able to handle. Severin didn't comment on her subtle limp, but he did have plenty else to say.

"I find it hard to believe that we have never met, Miss Casey," Severin told her. They passed the fourth-floor landing, but Severin did not stop climbing. "I would remember such stunning eyes."

"Oh." Adelle bit her lip. "I have a way of blending in with the wallpaper."

As evidenced by her inability to get a date to any of the recent formal dances at school, leading her to bring him—or his imaginary counterpart—as her date. Usually Connie never wanted to go either, and they could spend the night giggling until dawn over movies, eating bowl upon bowl of microwave popcorn before falling asleep in a pile of sleeping bags.

"Impossible." Severin clucked his tongue. "Unless the quality of the wallpaper at Byrne House surpasses that of every other great manor."

"Then it's a mystery," Adelle suggested, hoping to avoid any pressing questions about her nonexistent Victorian lifestyle. Or manners. Or knowledge.

"Another mystery, how grand. I did not expect to end this evening in the company of a woman of mystery. Ah. *Nous sommes arrivés.* Let us see if this view is the cure for what ails you, Mademoiselle Mystère."

He seemed so casual, so at ease—he too must be perfectly comfortable with their version of Boston falling to pieces. Did the men in robes not bother him? Or the tear in the sky? Why did nobody at the party seem to notice any of it? Severin at last let go of her hand, and at once she missed the warmth of it. The staircase continued upward, but narrowed, giving the impression that only an attic lay above. In front of them, two tall doors with velvet-cord curtains and patterned glass led out onto a balcony that ran the length of the mansion. Sliding forward with a hop, Sylvain unlatched the golden door handle and let the cold, galvanizing air pour in.

"After you." He smiled.

Adelle paused. If her mother could see her going off from a large party alone with a boy she didn't know, onto a balcony where nobody could find her, late at night, she would have a heart attack. This was stranger danger, definition of.

But I do know him. He's not a stranger to me, not really.

Outside, the same dense, pea soup fog blotted out the stars. The front of Moira's house faced south, and most of Boston was in a blackout, though a single lantern glowed timidly here or there in the sea of darkened brick buildings, markets, churches, and roads. Only the surrounding blocks housed the expected candles in the windows, though the street below lay empty. Straight down, in the grassy turnaround outside the house, Adelle watched the hooded Chanters patrol back and forth, their pale robes making them look like ghosts drifting to and fro in the mist.

To the east, the waves sloshed rhythmically in the harbor. Adelle was amazed she could hear them at that distance, but the city itself was as silent as a mausoleum. Following the sound of the waves, she tiptoe-limped toward the far end of the balcony, leaning most of her weight on the railing. Something odd in the water had caught her eye, and it gripped her with magnetic force, pulling.

She ought to have known better, with all that she had seen and felt since arriving, but she couldn't help herself. It called out to her, seething and bright, the only point of light in the water other than the Deer Island Light, which glowed eerily green.

"What is that?" Adelle breathed. Her chest felt tight.

"Is it not marvelous?" Severin had appeared beside her, leaning casually against the railing and admiring the horror in the water.

"Marvelous? It's . . ." Adelle was at a loss. She didn't know what it was, or how to describe it. Why was he okay with it? "It's awful."

"Tell me," he murmured, his back to the sea, his eyes fixed on her. "Tell me what you see."

It is born.

The voice from before, from the Emporium and the tear, returned, slicing through her brain like an icy blade.

"A . . . monster, I think. But it isn't moving, is it? Or maybe it's breathing. It looks like it's fleshy, alive, like an organ, like giant organs pulled out and arranged in a circle, organs without any blood. Or . . . or a huge squid, but open in the middle." Adelle shivered. She couldn't look away. "How can you call it marvelous? What *is* it?"

She felt terribly afraid then, like she had woken up from a deep sleep in a bed she didn't recognize. This *couldn't* be in the book. She would certainly have remembered a writhing mass of darkly bruised tentacles opening like a swollen mouth in the harbor.

Once, she'd gotten an ingrown hair in her armpit, and she remembered it stinging like a wasp when she shaved in the shower. Just a bump, but it grew, and when she finally got up the courage to dig out the hair with tweezers, it just kept coming and coming, unspooling from a bloody welt. At the moment of pulling it out she had almost gagged with surprise, and she felt that same shivering revulsion in her stomach at the sight of the thing in the water, a cosmically ugly behemoth docked beside the pier.

Her eyes flew to Severin. Maybe she didn't *know* him. Or any of this. Maybe she didn't know a single thing about this place.

Adelle gripped the railing harder, worrying she was in free fall.

"Most people call it the Wound," Severin told her, his words filled with religious awe. "The Chanters are trying to appease it, thinking that if it takes enough people, it will be satisfied and leave. That's how they make sense of it, how they make sense of everyone sleepwalking into the sea."

Orla had mentioned the sea taking people, taking Caid's family. Had they been some kind of *sacrifice*? She stared hard at him. "But that's not what you think."

"No," Severin admitted, tossing the hair out of his face. He turned away from her to gaze at the pulsating horror of the

Wound. "I do not think it will ever be satisfied. It is not a pit with an end; it is a door."

"And all those people you mentioned, the ones who walk into it," Adelle replied slowly. "You think they're going through that door?"

Severin waved off her question. "No, no. The people going out mean nothing. What matters is what might come through the door from the other side."

Adelle didn't like the way he said it, with such wonder, such excitement, like he couldn't wait to see what it would be. "How can you bear it? How can you just go on with your life? Why aren't you afraid?"

"At first we did not go on with our lives," Severin explained. "There were riots, and whoever was willing—the navy, militiamen, volunteers—went to attack it, but their guns and swords did nothing to it, and every ship they sent against it sank." For the first time, he looked worn, sad. "Then the fog descended, encased us, and nobody could find their way through it. At last we were all alone, and it seems there is nothing to be done about it. It will stay until it wants to go. Fear dissipates, and this, all of this, becomes life."

"That must have been so scary," she whispered. He seemed awfully forthcoming, even effusive on subjects she should have known. Did he suspect her secret? Adelle's stomach churned. Maybe he had already realized she didn't belong. But if so, why be so friendly? So solicitous? Terrified she had already grown too suspicious, Adelle added, "You must think me so stupid and ignorant. My memory is completely addled. That carriage must have struck me harder than I thought. . . ."

"Oh, it does not bother me to speak of these things to you," Severin replied, with what struck her as great pity. "Even if it is a kind of sadness. Would we know joy, Miss Casey, if we did not also know fear and malaise? No, we could not live in terror every day," Severin replied with quiet resignation. "So now we simply live how we must. It takes fewer now, and the Chanters claim that they can control who stays and who goes. I don't know if that's true, but Boston's high-and-mighty believe it, so it's as good as law. The rich are safe and content, so I suppose the world continues on, yes?"

Adelle could feel his palpable regret. She wanted to give him some kind of consolation, to say, *At least you have Moira and you two are together,* but she was not supposed to know about his love story or his poverty, or anything about them. She almost wished she didn't.

"Can you hear it?" he asked softly. "The Wound?"

She swayed, the tightness in her chest expanding, her head throbbing in time with her heart. "Whispers," she said. "A thousand whispers all at once. I can't make out what any of them are saying, but it's calling to me."

"Yes, it sings. Beautiful, haunting night music. Promises. Temptations." Severin shook his head and sighed. "I often stop and think: it is amazing that I am alive in this time to see this."

They were quiet for a moment, and that moment stretched on until she lost track of herself, of time.

"Adelle? Miss Casey?"

Close. So close, now. Closer . . . Take us. Take us . . .

Adelle couldn't hear him or perceive him. Her focus had narrowed to the Wound itself, bright and grotesque, gleaming with its own internal light, its writhing tentacles beckoning like long, moist fingers. She had to go. The instructions were written in white lightning across her eyelids, burned into her, searing with insistence. How would she get there? Walking. Steady walking. However she could. But she knew only one thing: she had to go. It demanded that she go.

Those tentacles were not fingers at all but hooks, and they had dug in deep.

Adelle lifted her knee, propping it against the cool, slick railing while hoisting herself up. There was a bit of flat roof beyond, and then the sheer drop to the yard. That was all right—she would just keep walking, and if her legs snapped, then she would drag herself to the shore. The whispers were inside her, spreading out to fill every corner, cramming themselves into the tip of her nose, into her toes. They all said the same thing: that it was time to go.

Someone pulled on her. Someone called her name. They may as well have been on another planet, for all it mattered. The hooks yanked her forward, and she freed herself from the puller, swinging her legs around and landing with a thud on the roof.

Ouch, she thought, distantly, *that hurt. Oh well.*

Adelle put one foot in front of the other, heading east. A voice behind her, muted, said something she didn't understand, in a language she couldn't decipher or care about. Then there was a flash of red and a hand on her shoulder, and all at once the whispers were gone.

When it was quiet in her head again, she felt empty. Bereft.

Adelle crumpled to her knees, and then someone—no, Severin— spun her around and helped her back up again. She didn't care that he was a stranger; she leaned hard against him.

"I don't like it," Adelle told him, cold all over. "I want to go back inside. Orla . . . I need to find her. She's helping me look for a friend. I . . . I need to get away from that thing. Can we go back inside, please?"

"You must take care, Miss Casey," he said sternly, guiding her back over the railing with trembling hands. "Do not look at the Wound if you can avoid it. You gave me a fright."

"I gave *myself* a fright," she murmured. "Please, can we hurry?"

"To the kitchens," Severin proclaimed, taking her arm and stroking her hand. "Some warm chocolate will set you to rights. It always makes me feel better, yes? When I had a bad scrape, Maman always took me on her knee near the fire and gave me a cup of chocolate, and whatever was troubling me melted away."

"That's fine." Adelle shivered. "That sounds nice. Anything. I just need to be away from it."

As they returned to the doors, Adelle couldn't help but look back. The Wound. *What matters is what might come through the door from the other side.* Adelle thought of the tear she had seen in the park, the one hovering over their beloved reading spot, and she thought of the scaly dead thing she had accidentally brushed in the grass.

Severin thought the Wound was a door, and that something might use that door. *But something has already come through,* she thought, clinging to Severin. *Something is already here.*

"Do you have any rifles?" Connie asked, watching Mississippi load her pistol, Slick Rose, and then shove another six-shooter into her waistband. "I'm better with a rifle."

"Farai? Oblige her." Mississippi pulled the checkered bandanna up over her nose and mouth. They stood upstairs again in the church proper, pulling weapons and ammunition from a hidden door in the bottom of the priest's lectern. While Farai fished out an old hunting rifle, Geo unlocked the confessional nearby. It had been hollowed out, the chairs and divider removed to make space for their tall-wheeled penny-farthing bicycles. All of the women wore wide-legged trousers under their hitched-up skirts. Geo returned with a bike for Connie, and smoothed her two tight braids back over her shoulders before adjusting her bandanna. She wore an old men's coat, baggy, and a sleek black blouse with a cravat underneath. None of the women were as flashy as Mississippi, but she spotted a Virgin of Guadalupe necklace on Geo, easy to recognize for a Catholic.

Farai's wrists and neck were adorned with strands of dark blue beads, but her clothes were all black, stained from work, sturdy and practical, tall leather boots rising to the edge of her shortened skirt.

"What's the story with all of this?" Connie asked, nodding toward Mississippi. "This cowgirl thing."

Farai and Geo shared a look, smirking.

"Oh, please. Don't pretend like you ain't heard of me," Missi replied, huffy. She took her bicycle by the handles and began walking it down the center aisle of the church.

"I'm not pretending. I haven't heard of you. Honest."

Behind her, also leading her bike, Geo vented a whistle, the universal sign for *This is about to get awkward.*

Or ugly.

"My daddy was *the* Tulsa McClaren, and I was his assistant. We ran the most popular trick-shot show this side of New York City." Missi doffed her cowboy hat and held it to her heart.

"Which side?" Connie couldn't help but ask.

Farther down the line, Farai snorted.

"This side, damn it!" Missi snapped. "North side!"

"I can't imagine there's a lot of competition between here and Canada . . ."

"I think I like this Clacker," Geo added. "She's brassy."

"Would you two hush up? I'm tryin' to tell a story!" They reached the front of the church, where a young boy was crouched with the big shaggy black dog Connie had seen on the way in. He looked them up and down, his gaze lingering on Connie, before he opened the doors and let them out.

Missi dropped her voice to a whisper as they lined up outside on the silent street and climbed onto their bicycles. It took Connie a few tries, but she was a quick study when it came to anything remotely athletic. The wobbles were out of her system after just a block or two.

"We did this one trick where Daddy stacked three cans on his head and I shot 'em off one by one. Blindfolded. We came all the way from Kansas to give them somethin' they ain't never seen before. A Wild West horse show just like Bill Hickok's! But better, obviously. Spine-tingling and rip-roaring!" Missi sat back on her bike, not even holding the handles as she pedaled, gazing up at the sky and sighing wistfully. "We called it the William Tell-Your-Friends. Ha! That show sold out for a month straight, and we would've taken the act all the way to California if everything hadn't gone to hell."

"I'd like to see that trick some time," Connie said. "Sounds impressive."

"Sadly, you won't be seein' it tonight, girlie. We don't pull our weapons unless a monster shows up or those Clackers get real ornery with us."

"Just for defense," Farai underscored. "It will cause too much attention."

"The servants' entrance is an old smugglers' tunnel that runs under the neighbor's house," Connie said, using a stage whisper.

"And there's a chicken coop on top of the hatch, but it's empty."

Geo nodded along to every word and swore under her breath. "Feh. Tunnels. If we get caught down there, it will be a bloodbath, nowhere to hide."

Mississippi led them, turning right down a side street three blocks north of the church. "Then we don't get caught."

"While you ladies are inside, I will find us a ride back," Geo said, mimicking cracking a whip and flashing Connie a devilish smile. "Tonight we steal in style!"

Connie stuck as close to Missi's bike as she could. The streets were unlit, and with the stars veiled behind fog it was almost pitch-black in the street. Missi's white fringe at least made her easy to follow, and soon they had pedaled out of the church neighborhood, north and slightly east. The homes gradually grew larger, the roads smoother and with flatter cobbles. Connie had biked, run, bused, driven, and trained all over Boston, and she tried to use that knowledge to place herself in the city. Her money was on the Congregation hiding out under King's Chapel, but she wouldn't know for sure until she saw it again in the daylight.

More and more, the brick row houses sprouted towers, balconies, and grassy turnarounds for carriages. They shied away from the light, the occasional home vibrant with candles and lanterns, the glow spilling out onto the street. Slowing, Missi brought them to a stop at an intersection, and down the road to their left, Connie could hear music and laughter. A row of black carriages with stamping, nervous horses lined the block; some of the drivers lingered in groups on the sidewalk, smoking and chatting in low tones. Ahead, a pair of darkened mansions flanked the bright, merry atmosphere of the Byrne household, and to the right of the last house lay a modest yard protected by an iron fence.

The white-trimmed chicken coop was right where Connie had hoped it would be.

"Not bad, Clacker," she heard Geo whisper.

Come by the secret way I have described, my love. I do not care if my family forbids it—I will have you there, and under the solstice moon we will kiss, and all our pretty declarations of love can be made, ratified by starlight.

That meant Moira and Severin were somewhere inside, doing all their ratifying. She knew it was stupid and dangerous to want a glimpse of them, but she dared to stupidly and dangerously hope. The spell that had carried her far from home had been made because of Moira's book, and now she would be in her actual house. It was so ridiculous, so absurd, Connie couldn't help but laugh.

Missi dismounted and nudged Connie's leg with her elbow. "Somethin' funny?"

"No, just something in my throat."

"Fine, cough it out. Pull yourself together, would you? It's showtime." Missi wheeled her bicycle across the street at a run and the others hurried after her. Connie joined in, watching Missi vault over the fence and motion for Farai to pass her the bike. One by one, they handed the unwieldy contraptions across, and Missi hid them against the side of the empty town house, somewhat sheltered by crawling ivy and overgrown bushes.

Missi huddled the girls together near the coop, speaking in less than a whisper. "We go down and have a look around, get the lay of the land. Then we bring out whatever we can, leave it here, go back for more, and let Geo try for the carriage. Not worth riskin' a third trip."

"You three go down without me," Geo replied, moving back toward the fence. "I want to see if I can snatch a carriage on Hawkins—gives me a chance to lose them before I return here."

Missi clapped her on the shoulder and ducked back toward the coop. "Then it's decided."

There was no sentimental speech, no fussing, just a general deploying her troops, a coach sending her team out onto the field. Connie understood that energy, thrived in it. This was a familiar tension, second-nature focus and determination. Missi went first into the coop, then Connie, with Farai guarding the rear. The door squeaked, the bushes rustled, and they scampered inside while Geo disappeared into the night.

"How can it be empty and still smell like chickens?" Farai grumbled.

"Some smells are forever," Connie replied.

"No more discussion—we go through this tunnel silent as can be." Missi knelt and ran her hands around the flat surface of the wooden hatch, feeling for the edges. Someone had already scattered the concealing hay to the corners of the coop. Severin. Connie shifted from foot to foot, licking her lips. Back home— back in her real life—she didn't normally break rules, but now she had found herself wrapped up in a heist. A heist that was her idea, no less.

Missi cracked the hatch open and slid onto the ladder, sticking her tongue out in disgust. "It don't smell no better down here, ladies," she hissed.

They followed her into the secret passage. It wasn't anything glamorous, and it stank with the wet, wormy smell of post-rain pavement. None of them were short girls, and the ceiling only just accommodated their height. Missi paused, brow furrowed. Then she pointed to the candles dropped at intervals down the tunnel, melting against the stones, just pale, glowing puddles.

"Someone came this way," she whispered. "Keep your eyes open."

Connie tried to swallow without gulping and giving herself away. She knew exactly who had come through, and why. It didn't matter, she told herself; Severin would be enjoying himself at the party, dancing the night away with Moira while her mother stewed in the corner, plotting a way to separate her daughter from the common boy masquerading in fine clothes.

They scurried down the length of about a half block, the slope of the ground gradually trending upward. At the end, another ladder waited, leading up to a closed hatch. Connie just hoped it was open; it never said in the book if the doors could be latched.

Mississippi climbed up and prodded at the hatch with her fist, and after a few nudges it dislodged, not square and hinged like the coop hatch, but round and slotted into grooves like a manhole. After sliding it quietly aside, Missi pulled herself up. Connie glanced at Farai, reading the deep lines etched into her forehead. Farai smoothed her silver-white hair back from her forehead, blowing out a breath. This was the moment of truth.

A hand waved from above, signaling them to climb up. The hatch led them into a dark larder, cold and silent. The shelves were stocked floor to ceiling with crates of fruits and vegetables. An entire smoked ham leg hung from a hook near the door that led, Connie guessed, to the kitchens. Missi pressed her forefinger to her lips—that door was cracked open, a dangerous shard of light falling diagonally across the larder floor.

Farai immediately began opening crates with utmost care, rummaging without a sound, but Missi went at once to the tied-up bunches of herbs hanging next to the ham, as fresh and pretty as bouquets. She snatched as many bundles as she could carry, then scooped a box of potatoes into her arms.

The plums, Missi mouthed, a few times until Connie understood.

They had all that they could carry for that trip, and Farai descended back into the tunnel, a sack of potatoes the size of a toddler swung over her shoulder. The way back was more cumbersome, laden as they were with loot, but Connie made it back to the chicken coop first, her athleticism paying off. She pulled herself up the ladder and then motioned for the others to hand her the goods. Once everything was piled in the back corner of the coop, Connie joined Farai and Mississippi back in the passage.

"I hope Geo hasn't gotten herself into too much trouble," Farai murmured.

"No time to worry. If she doesn't make it with the carriage, then we find our own way back," Missi replied, marching down the tunnel.

"You would leave her behind?" Connie asked.

"She would do the same to me, to any of us. That food will save lives, lots of 'em. Those plums are worth their weight in gold."

Connie pictured the bone-thin children eating their broth and black bread, and wondered if this stolen stuff would be the difference between their recovery and death. She knew then that the stolen goods had to get back to those starving children, no matter what.

When they emerged into the larder on their second trip, something was different. Before, nothing had emanated from the room beyond but the soft crackle of a fire, but now there were voices. Mississippi didn't seem to care, bolting immediately for the leg of ham and grunting under the weight of it before passing it off to Connie, who cradled it like a baby. The thing must have weighed at least twenty pounds, and given her ravenous stomach, it smelled like pure meaty heaven. It would feed the Congregation for days.

It's not a Pigmalion, but it will do.

Farai filched another sack of vegetables—turnips this time—and Mississippi chose a crate of canned sardines. It was hard to believe they were going to get away with it. Missi was already nodding her head frantically toward the hatch, urging them to plunge back into the tunnel. She didn't need to ask twice; Connie's heart hadn't stopped thudding in her chest long enough for her to catch a satisfying breath since they found the coop.

But the larder had been well and truly raided. They had pulled it off. Connie shuffled toward the hatch with her massive pig leg, already dreaming of ham and potatoes before bed, when she heard it.

A laugh. No, a giggle.

She knew that giggle.

Connie froze, paralyzed by the impossibility of that giggle. More paralyzed by the possibility of it. And yet she would know it anywhere, in any reality, hers or this messed-up literary dimension. She whirled, unable to conjure a single coherent thought, hypnotized by hope, curiosity pulling her marionette strings, bringing her to the door.

She had to know. Had they run into each other? Of course. Of course she would have picked that place and that time to land in the book. . . .

"Constance! Hey! Hey, Clacker! What the hell are you doin'? Get over here—it's time to run! Don't make me leave you behind."

The voices next door stopped. Then came the footsteps, angry ones. The door to the larder burst open, bringing Connie face-to-face with a slight, dark-haired, angelic-faced young man.

"Constance, you damn fool!" she heard Missi shout.

"What is the meaning of this?" the young man demanded. His eyes raged from hers to the girls behind her, crouched around the secret hatch. "My God, you've come to rob them!"

She had to know.

Connie pushed him aside with her shoulder, and there, behind him, dressed in violet frills and lace, stood her best friend. Gasping, Adelle dropped her teacup, the china shattering at her feet.

"Connie!"

The young man's fist slammed into her cheek, but it didn't matter. Now she knew.

14

This was no ordinary menu but one of pure extravagance, not just the generosity of a host to one's guests, but a celebration, and that celebration, Moira knew, was for her. Her engagement. She had no love for Kincaid Vaughn in her heart, nor, she was sure, could she ever dredge up more than feelings of mildest friendship for him. But her mother refused to believe that it was true, or, if it was true, that it mattered.

So the solstice-fete menu would reflect Mrs. Byrne's joy at her daughter's upcoming nuptials. The vastness of this bliss included oyster and terrapin stews, pickled oysters, roast beef, beef à l'anglais, leg of veal, veal Malakoff, grouse (boned and roasted), smoked ham, smoked beef tongue, a variety of pâtés, and salads of chicken and lobster, and then, for dessert, ices, naturally, and sponge cakes—almond sponges and vanilla—lady cake, pound cake, dame blanche, jellies, and creams, and no mean assortment of wines and champagne.

Such a meal might encompass her feelings for Severin. For Kincaid

Vaughn, however, Moira's passion was not even an old, half-eaten potato croquette.

"Bon appétit," she thought, feeling hungry and in love, a most dangerous combination.

—Moira, *chapter 14*

Adelle slid to her knees next to Connie, throwing her arms protectively over her, hugging her tightly.

"This is my friend!" she shrieked at Severin, watching Connie rub her jaw, down on the floor but propped up on one arm. An enormous smoked ham leg rested against her waist. "I can't believe it, Connie. I can't believe I actually found you!" She pulled her into a hug, and Connie sank against her with palpable relief.

Adelle leaned back, studying Connie intently, examining her face, her clothes, her hair. It was Connie, yet it was so hard to believe. Tears spilled down Adelle's cheeks, hysterical, giggling hiccups gathering in her throat. "But why are you carrying a ham?"

"Who is this?" Severin demanded, looming.

"My friend Connie. Please don't hit her again; she's like a sister to me." Adelle scowled at him. The Severin she knew would never strike a woman. It didn't comfort her much to think that he had done it to protect her. This was *her best friend, her partner in crime, her platonic soul mate.* Then she noticed the two other girls who skulked in the shadows behind Connie.

"I do not think these ruffians are here for a social call," Severin growled, refusing to step back.

"Look at the brains on Frenchie," a redheaded girl in a ridiculous cowboy costume said. Less ridiculous were the two pistols she had drawn on them. "Ain't nothin' gets past you. Now, if you will excuse us, we were in the middle of robbing you blind."

"You see!" Severin fumed. "Adelle, these are not the sort of women you should associate with, and no friend of yours should either."

The redhead rolled her eyes, scoffing. "Oh please, Severin. Just because you traded in your fishhooks for silk tails doesn't mean you're better than us."

"Let it go, Missi," the other girl said. She was tall and narrow, with brown skin and striking silver-white hair. "This is not the time. We need to get topside."

"Give me one good reason why I should not rouse the whole house," Severin warned.

At that, Adelle pushed herself to her feet, ignoring the shooting pain in her leg. "Because . . . Because I won't let you! Connie wouldn't associate with bad people, Severin; you have to believe me. You have to trust that I know her."

"*We're* the bad people?" the cowgirl snorted. "Connie here says *you're* the one being held against your will."

"I'm not," Adelle promised her. She turned back to Severin. "Everyone just be calm, please."

Connie has a 4.25 grade point average. She'll be valedictorian if we ever get out of this mess. Soccer team co-captain, biathlon state qualifier, never touched a cigarette or beer in her life . . . Adelle heaved an exasperated sigh, furious with all the things she couldn't yell at him.

"I am sorry," Severin muttered, shaking his head and storming back into the kitchen. "But I cannot stand by while a blatant crime is committed."

The cowgirl cocked her pistols.

"Wait!" Adelle limped as quickly as she could to Severin, wrapped herself around his right arm, and tugged. There had to be a way to stall him. *You know him; you know all about him.* "You said you were at my disposal. That you were coming to my aid. Was that just a lie?"

Severin slowed, then stopped altogether, easing around on his heel to study her. Recovering from the punch, Connie got to her feet, helped by the redhead, who had relinquished her hold on a crate of canned food.

"Mademoiselle," he whispered, gazing down into her eyes, "I really must protest."

"No, *I* must. This is my best friend in the whole world," Adelle pleaded. "And if you are at my disposal, if you want to solve my mystery, then you will let her go. You brought me down here for chocolate, to make me feel better. Seeing her, knowing she is safe? That is more powerful than all the chocolate in the world."

He raised a single dark brow. "You play the blushing ingenue yet find a most diabolical way to cut me." Severin glanced over her shoulder at the girls in the pantry. "I confess, it is both frustrating and intriguing." Then, louder, he addressed the others. "Very well, little rats, scuttle back into your hole. I will not summon the cat, but only if you"—he turned to Adelle again—"stay at my side."

Adelle's head felt like it might explode. How could she stay when Connie was right there? She glanced at the cocked pistols and remembered how much it had hurt when Orla's carriage slammed into her. If they could be injured in this world, then they could die in it. She couldn't let that happen to either of them.

"Adelle!" Connie was being pulled back toward the round hatch in the larder floor by the other two girls. Breaking free, Connie stumbled forward, and Adelle rushed over to her friend, taking her hands and squeezing them tightly. She could feel the live wire crackling between the redhead and Severin; any moment it would start a blaze. The last thing she wanted was for that girl to pull her pistol and fire; in the cramped quarters, any one of them could go down.

"I have the book," Connie whispered. "But I have to help these people. Just for tonight. They need me, Delly. Come with us now—I'll explain some other time."

"I can't go. Please, just . . . Pigmalion," Adelle told Connie seriously, locking eyes. None of the others would decipher it, but Connie would know. "Noon."

Connie nodded slowly, as aware as Adelle was that they were being watched closely.

Be safe, Connie mouthed. They squeezed hands one more time, and Adelle told herself—promised herself—that they would find each other the next day.

Then the cowgirl darted forward, grabbed Connie by the back of her track jacket, and yanked.

"Pick up your ham and get," the cowgirl snarled. "Much obliged, Severin, you son of a strumpet."

Adelle watched Connie return to the shadows, their eyes glued together, while Severin had a long chuckle.

"Always a pleasure, Miss McClaren." He stuck his hands into his trouser pockets and rocked back on his polished shoes as the girls disappeared into the secret tunnel below. As soon as the round hatch was put in place, Adelle's heart broke a little.

Run after her. Go. What are you waiting for?

Severin's arm slid through hers, and Adelle repeated her promise—this was just a temporary setback. A necessary detour. Tomorrow she would find Connie at the location of their favorite burger joint and then nothing would tear them apart. Connie had the book, after all, and that meant they were going home. She just had to wait and hold on a little longer. What Connie had meant about the cowgirl and the others needing her, she couldn't guess. . . .

"Thank you for staying. I know she is your friend, but I'm afraid, my dear, that she has fallen in with sordid company. It wounds me to think of you sharing that fate. Ah, but still, I let them steal—how shall I punish you for making me do such a wicked thing?"

Adelle ducked her head, finding that his grip on her arm was stronger than she expected. "It's only a bit of ham—surely Moira can spare it. The guests upstairs certainly did not look hungry."

"Oh, she can spare it," Severin assured her, placing his thumb under her chin and pushing until she looked up at him. "But she *would* not. You have a generous heart, Miss Casey, rare in these times."

She didn't know how she could recover from the shock of

finding Connie, losing her again, and then having Severin Sylvain regard her so sweetly, like he had just spotted the first robin after a harsh winter. *Snap out of it—he hit your friend. He's not who you think he is. None of this is what you thought it would be.*

"It . . . It wasn't my ham," Adelle managed to say. "So is it really so generous?"

"And if it were yours?" he asked. "If it were your larder they were raiding?"

Despite his softly curious tone and warm hand on her face, she had to keep it together, had to remember that he wasn't real and wasn't a perfect gentleman, and this was all just a part she was playing until they could find a way home. Now that she thought about it, the cowgirl had been wearing a black-and-white-checkered bandanna, and a villain of her description was in the book: a thief and kidnapper. The Penny-Farthings—rats, as Severin called them in the novel. They were mostly forgotten amid the grand highs and lows of Severin and Moira's love story, but she did at least know that they were poor and liked to kidnap people.

"Everyone deserves kindness," she finally answered.

At that, he smiled. "Indeed. It is a marvel you have survived this long in a cruel, cold world." Severin sighed. "A world gone mad. Small wonder you are a friend of Miss Beevers; she too possesses an unhardened soul."

There came a flurry of footsteps on the stairs behind them, then Orla's high-pitched shriek as she bustled breathlessly into the kitchen. "There you are! Lord! The house is in an uproar. Someone has stolen a carriage, the dance has dissolved, and Moira never even made an appearance! It's a complete fiasco!"

"Speak of the devil," he murmured. Severin let go of Adelle's chin and cleared his throat. "Stolen? How strange!"

It seemed that for a little while at least, they would both be playing a part. She had almost forgotten all about Moira's big declaration to the world. Severin had spent most of the night with Adelle, completely rewriting the entire evening.

That can't be good.

"I suppose I should bid farewell to Miss Byrne and her mother before departing, then." Severin strode away from her and toward the stairs.

"Oh no." Orla wrung her hands. Her eyes slid between them quickly, and Adelle felt herself grow hot with confusion. "She does not want to see anyone. All guests are to leave at once."

"Ah, then I will escort Miss Casey home, if she has no objections."

Adelle glanced toward the pantry. What she really wanted to do was run after her best friend and forget this stupid charade altogether. But Severin's eyes were so imploring, as were Orla's, and their concern touched her genuinely. Besides, she would never track down Connie by herself at night, and it sounded like her friend truly had unfinished business.

She has the book, Adelle. You're going home soon.

But where, exactly, would she tell Severin to take her?

"I—"

But Orla came swiftly to her rescue, bustling over to Adelle's side and taking her arm. "I have asked that Miss Casey remain here with us for the evening. She had such a fright after the collision, and with a carriage thief on the loose I would feel better knowing she was safely inside with us."

Severin merely shrugged and swaggered to the bottom of the stairs, where he leaned against the arch. "*À votre guise.* Then I bid you both a good evening. It has been . . . disappointing, but not altogether uneventful."

With that, he bowed at the waist and disappeared up into the shadows. Adelle had to wonder how he would exit the house, since he had come by the secret passage. Perhaps in all the chaos, he would slip out the front door unnoticed.

Orla whirled to her, taking Adelle's hands and squeezing. "I could ask how you came to be in the kitchen with Severin unchaperoned. I could ask, but I will not."

"I saw something outside that startled me," Adelle quickly explained. "Severin thought some chocolate would make me feel better. It was all innocent, I promise."

Orla's brow furrowed. "I am not the one you may need to convince, dear. Come now. Moira requires all the feminine gentility and care we can muster. She has had a dreadful evening, misfortune after misfortune. We will all have some tea and shuck these silks, and gossip it all to rights."

Adelle blanched, knowing she was to blame for the vast majority of those misfortunes Moira had experienced.

They wound their way back through the house. Adelle's leg had lost some of its dragging soreness, and she kept pace with Orla while she led her past the foyer—still crammed with guests milling, gawking, and trying to shove their way out the door—to the third floor, and then down the corridor to Moira's mystically green bower. Stepping into the saturated color still felt strange, like entering a polished emerald.

When Adelle had last seen Moira, she'd been proclaiming her hatred for Adelle. The intervening hours had calmed her somewhat, and she sat perched on a bench at the end of her four-poster bed, wearing a pale pink nightgown with delicate puffs of lace at the sleeves, as light and sweet as cotton candy. She stared out the window, a purple bruise laid across her nose and upper cheeks.

Adelle winced.

"Are they gone?" Moira asked, exasperated. She cradled a teacup on a saucer, sipping it noiselessly, not even making a sound when cup met plate.

"Elsie and the others will see that the house is emptied and locked up, I am sure," Orla told her, releasing Adelle and at once hurrying to her friend's side. "I did not see your mother."

"She is undoubtedly having an elegant faint somewhere," Moira replied, then shifted her gaze to Adelle. Only her head turned as she brought her eyes to Adelle's. It was such a slow, mechanical movement, like her skull had detached from the rest of her body. Regan from *The Exorcist* could take notes.

"Is everyone gone?" Moira arched one beautifully slender red brow.

No, but that look does make me want to disappear.

"All the . . ." Moira struggled for a moment, and Adelle looked on in contrite silence. "All the gentlemen?"

"Mr. Vaughn never even braved the dance floor," Orla informed her, mopping at her face with the end of her silver sleeve. "And . . . And I briefly spied Mr. Sylvain, but he has also gone. I told him you wanted the house emptied, that everyone, even he, was to leave."

Moira nodded, taking another dainty sip from her blue floral cup. "And how did he seem when you told him I did not wish to see him?"

She was not asking Orla, clearly, but Adelle, snatching Orla's words out of the air before she managed to answer. Adelle knew she wasn't any good at lying, but she cast about for something to say that was at least half true. "He . . . He said he was disappointed."

Over Moira's shoulder, Orla gave her a puckered smile.

"Disappointed!" Moira scoffed and bit her knuckle, then stood, pacing imperiously from window to mirror and back again. "But not disappointed enough to insist on seeing me."

"Orla *did* tell him to go," Adelle pointed out.

Moira's eyes were green fire when she spun away from the window, clacking her cup down on the saucer. "How clear it is that you know nothing of the love games young folk play." She tossed her loosened abundance of dark red curls over one shoulder. "He should have fought for the right to see me. He should have made a gallant scene! Everything is ruined. *Everything.*"

"Too true," Orla murmured, plucking silk flowers and feathers from her hair, turning to regard herself in the mirror.

"I think it shows respect," Adelle blurted. She regretted it the moment the words left her mouth. Moira drew closer, stalking her like a panther, one pointed foot in front of the other, her chin lowered, her eyes predatory and keen.

"A-any boy who listens to what you say . . . I mean, that's rare, isn't it? It's good that he listens to you," Adelle said, hoping she was digging toward the light and not deeper into the earth. "It means he takes you seriously."

Moira stopped in her tracks, her face suddenly blank, panther to house cat. "I failed to think of that. Kincaid shows me nothing but respect, and it is rather a bore. But this *is* new for Severin. So unpredictable . . . And unpredictable is exciting." She sashayed to the bed, depositing her tea on the narrow table beside it before draping herself across the fluffy green blankets. "I must say, Miss Casey, you have given me food for thought, and I wish to forgive you. A little."

"It was an accident." Adelle looked at her feet. "I didn't mean to hit you in the nose. My hem was caught on my heel and I stumbled."

"If I keep you around, then I will be interested to see if you do anything besides stumble, fall, and faint, Miss Casey."

Adelle recognized a fake smile when she saw one, and Moira's had that sour new plasticky smell. The fluttered eyelashes only added to the petty veneer.

The lady's maid, Elsie, entered with a full tea tray. Adelle had no interest in any of it, but Orla rose to let Elsie unbutton the back of her gown and gestured to the refreshments. The maid handed Orla a steaming-hot cup to sip while she was undressed.

"I really am sorry, Miss Byrne," Adelle said. It still felt bizarre to say her name. "I didn't mean to ruin your ball."

"Pish-posh, there will be more of them." Moira waved her hand. "And we will do it bigger! And grander! Do not think yourself so important, Miss Casey; it was a minor inconvenience, that is all. We can arrange something for my birthday, and it can stupefy the town, and all of this silliness will be forgotten."

Orla choked quietly on her tea.

Adelle didn't believe Moira either. After all, she had stormed off after being elbowed in the face, told Adelle she hated her, and sulked in her chamber for the rest of the evening. This was supposed to be the climax of the act, with Moira and Severin making their love public, risking everything. How could she get over it so quickly? How could she be so fickle? Even with that bruise on her nose, Moira was still the most beautiful girl in any room. It seemed ridiculous to sit out the entire evening. Adelle could remember her twelfth birthday party with a mixture of shame and admiration, although she couldn't recall whose idea it had been to sled down the carpeted stairs to the landing in sleeping bags. It ended with her in the emergency room, a sprained ankle, and a very exasperated Mrs. Casey, but she and Connie had been back at her house for cake and a movie marathon a few hours later, laughing it off together.

But Moira wasn't a shake-it-off kind of girl, clearly. If she found out that Adelle had spent most of the night alone with Severin, Moira might not be able to paste on another rigid grin to mentally plan her birthday bash.

Orla slid out of her gown and disappeared behind a decorative paper screen beside the mirror, then reemerged in a simple buttercup-yellow sleeping gown. It was Adelle's turn to transform back into a pumpkin, and Elsie herded her to the screen, where she unbuttoned her with incredible speed while Orla and Moira chatted quietly on the bed. Who had made a scandal of themselves with leaden-footed dancing? Who had come to steal the carriage? Wasn't it exciting? But also terrible! Did Severin look perfect or angelic or both in his silk tails?

Both, Adelle thought, feeling slightly superior. That feeling was quickly dashed as she was pushed and shoved, turned and tilted, prodded and manhandled until at last she had been freed from all six hundred pounds of feminine frills and thereafter stuffed into a light white shift, one flouncy and shapeless enough to fit practically any young woman.

Elsie swished out the door, her arms heaped high with discarded gowns, her face fixed eternally in an absolutely neutral expression that any robot would envy. As soon as Adelle rounded the screen, Orla was there, forcing a cup of tea into her hands.

"Thank you," Adelle murmured. "I thought I would just go right to bed," she added, going to put the tea and saucer on the tray Elsie had left for them. "I'm exhausted. Sometimes tea keeps me awake at night."

Moira climbed beneath her covers, wiggling down into them while slapping her fluffy pillows into shape.

"No, no, you must have some." Orla wouldn't drop it, fetching the tea and holding it out until Adelle resigned herself to letting the bitter concoction just touch her lips. She decided not to drink it after that, but just pretend. It tasted vaguely of . . . She smacked her lips, trying to place the flavor. It was bizarre, and like no tea she had tried before. Was this what they drank in Victorian times? It was *intense*. It tasted . . . There! She had it. The memory flooded back from one of the times her stepfather, Greg, had tried to cook a vegan dinner for her and her mother, making sushi that just tasted like stale rice and nori. That was the culprit. Nori. The tea was just like seaweed steeped in scalding-hot water.

Adelle sat on the edge of the fainting couch with her tea, taking more "sips" until Orla wandered away, climbing into the empty half of Moira's bed. When it seemed she had fallen asleep, Adelle poured the tea out into the potted fern near the window and curled up on the soft velvet couch. A thin, doily-like blanket had been draped over the end of it, and she used that for meager cover.

A single candle burned low on Moira's bedside table.

I'm sleeping in Moira's bedroom. She's right there. It can't be happening, but I saw Connie. We're both here, and soon we'll be back together.

While she felt the inevitable tug of sleep grow stronger and stronger, she watched Moira and Orla, curled up side by side. How many times had she and Connie done the same, passing out after watching the 1995 BBC *Pride and Prejudice* miniseries again, all six hours, talking along with every line, falling asleep under Connie's fleece Red Sox blanket with Austen's poetry on their lips.

Before her was a screwed-up, fun-house mirror of their friendship, though she wouldn't dare assign Moira's role to either one of them. How strange, to come all this way, to finally meet their heroine, and find she was mean and shallow. It would be like air-dropping into Pemberley only to find out Elizabeth Bennet was a dead-eyed bimbo who hated books.

But Orla was nice. Orla, she liked. And Severin . . . Adelle clamped her eyes shut. She didn't know what to think of him. One moment he was everything she'd dreamed him to be, and the next he was odd and cold and violent.

The candle burned down, leaving her with her thoughts in the dark.

I'll see you tomorrow, Connie. I promise. I found you once, I can do it again.

THE CARRIAGE RATTLED DOWN the hill at breakneck speed, the horses rampaging across the cobbles with foam flying from their lips.

Geo giggled with mad delight, steering them around a corner to the right, into a dark neighborhood, taking them into what looked like nothing but endless shadow. Inside, crammed into a corner with her ham, sharing the bench with boxes and sacks, Connie stared out the window, while Mississippi glared continuously, hardly even blinking as the horses shrieked and the carriage skidded to a stop, sending them—and the ham, and several potatoes—flying around the box.

Farai hammered her fist against the wall separating them from the outdoor driver's chair. "A little warning next time, ya hellion!"

"Where's the fun in that?" came Geo's muffled reply. Then

she slid a small door like a mail slot open between them, her big brown eyes appearing in the gap. "Any casualties? Tell me the ham made it."

"I'm gonna be walking funny for weeks," Missi grunted. She kicked open the door and jumped out into the cold night, Farai leaping down after her. Connie came last, gently replacing the ill-gotten pig leg on the cushioned seat she had been occupying.

Missi wasn't finished glaring at her. They had stopped outside a fenced-in churchyard, and Connie made out a quaint chapel sitting back from the road under the muted starlight, its windows boarded up, its patchwork stone path choked with weeds.

"Help me with the penny-farthings," Missi said.

Connie had watched her pull a pistol and aim it in the direction of Adelle and Severin, and she wasn't about to push her any further that night. With a pang, she glanced back the way they had come. The carriage had taken so many sudden twists and turns, she knew it would be impossible to find Moira's house again easily. That was where she wanted to be, not climbing up onto a carriage to fetch down heavy, awkward bicycles that had been lashed to the top of their stolen means of getaway.

Even in the chilly air, it was difficult, sweaty work, and while she and Missi took down the bikes, Farai and Geo transferred the food into the abandoned church.

They worked in silence, but Connie sensed that Mississippi had plenty on her mind.

She didn't care. As soon as the food was delivered and she saw her chance, she was leaving the Penny-Farthings behind and making her way to her meeting spot with Adelle. Connie's plan built itself piece by piece, minute by minute. Her instincts had been right—she needed to get her hands on the incense that would allow them to cast the spell and go home. One missing ingredient, but Connie wouldn't rest until she found it.

"The carriage is empty," Geo told them, hopping the fence with Farai, coming to reclaim their bicycles. "The runners were waiting in the tunnels below. Now we can go home and enjoy the fruits of our labor."

"I pray the ride home will be smoother," Farai teased.

"You two go on ahead," Missi instructed them. "Connie and I will be right behind you."

Farai's silver hair glowed faintly in the dark. "No, you should not be alone with her, Missi. She almost got us captured tonight."

Mississippi chuckled, patting Farai on the shoulder. "Exactly. That's why I need to have a heart-to-heart with our new friend. Just . . . make sure we're all on the same page, mm?"

Even without light, Connie saw Farai's gaze flick to the guns holstered on Missi's belt. She could take care of herself.

"Tell Sleepless Joe to wait up," Missi added. She strode to the head of the carriage and slapped the nearest horse on the rear, sending the team into action and the carriage barreling away. "We won't be long."

Farai and Geo grabbed their bicycles and swung up into the high seats, each sparing a single glance over the shoulder as they pedaled away into the swallowing void of the unlit neighborhood.

"Let's you and I take a walk," Missi suggested, or rather ordered.

She nodded toward the chapel. "We need to get a few ideas straight between us."

If Farai wasn't comfortable with the idea of Mississippi being alone with Connie, Connie certainly wasn't thrilled at the thought of being alone with *Mississippi*. The church waited behind them, a silent sentinel shrouded in mist. Farai and Geo had left the last two bicycles leaning against the iron fence.

Connie glanced at the bikes, but Missi didn't miss anything.

"Running will only make me more suspicious. Come on." She started toward the fence, swinging open a low, busted gate and letting herself in. "It isn't safe for us out here."

Connie reluctantly joined her in the yard, then followed her into the chapel. She was doing a lot of that lately, following hesitantly, but she remembered the recent misery of scraping by on her own, hiding away in the bakery and eating crumbs. Putting up with Mississippi for another night, having a place to sleep and eat, that was preferable to trying her luck alone on the street. And anyway, she still needed something from her.

Ten minutes left in the match, she thought. *Tied. Just need to hold out until the clock runs down, and fight to be up by one when it does.*

Inside, the Penny-Farthing runners who'd arrived to transfer the food back to the Congregation had left behind a few stubby candles in the skeletal candelabras dotting the chapel. It was dusty and cool, unsettling in the way a place meant for gathering could feel when it lay empty. The unheard prayers of the lost and the desperate lingered in the space between the pews.

Mississippi said nothing until they reached the back of the

chapel. After dodging around an open archway, she started up a series of narrow steps that doubled back and up again, then again, leading to a white door with a broken handle. She nudged the door open and brought them into the bell tower. Connie ran her hand over the massive brass bell, feeling it hum like a gong that had been struck a moment before. It resonated with power, like just a rap of the knuckle would fill the whole world with sound.

Missi rounded the bell and sat in the frame of a tall window, one that had long ago lost its glass. She reached into her white fringe coat and pulled out a slender cigar and matchbook, then lit the cigar and puffed a sigh toward the clouds. "I'm of two minds, Rollins. Either your skull is emptier than this church, or you ain't turned on the Clackers at all, and you're here to spy."

"On you?" Connie leaned against the adjoining window, the smell of tobacco richly bitter on the air.

"On us," Missi replied. She blew out the flame on the match, but her blue eyes retained the fire. "I realize your friend is still with the enemy, but you need to come to a decision."

Connie shook her head. "You pointed a gun at my friend, you realize that, don't you?"

"No." Mississippi pushed the hat on her head back, letting the cord catch it and keep it resting around her neck. "I pointed a pistol I had no intention of firing at that loudmouth, upstart fishy French boy who gave you that shiner on your cheek. If he'd raised the alarm, we would all have been cooked, you included. You realize *that*, don't you?"

Adelle had somehow managed to find Connie, and in that

moment of shock and elation she had forgotten her cover story. Forgotten everything. A piece of home had floated through time and reality to reach her, and she had lunged for it with everything she had.

She stared at her feet, biting down hard on her lower lip. Like Missi would understand her situation, or even a small part of it.

"Frenchie didn't know you from Adam," Missi stated flatly. "And your friend says she isn't being held against her will. You weren't no Clacker. Not ever. The lies just keep piling up."

Connie jerked her head up in surprise, giving herself away.

Blowing out another swirl of smoke, Missi rubbed her forehead with her thumb and forefinger. "Gee, girlie, I ain't stupid. Look, I am trying my very damn best to trust you. You got spirit, you got smarts, and you're tall as a country smokehouse and just as hot, admittedly a weakness of mine."

Connie's cheeks caught on fire. Was she . . . Was Missi *flirting* with her?

She rushed on. "But that stunt you pulled in the pantry put us all in danger, and I know you are telling me lies. Give me something here, Rollins, let out just a little bit of rope so I got somethin' to pull me to shore. I've got too many folks to look after to waste my time on a liability."

Connie scratched the back of her neck, weighing her options. She didn't know where to start with any of what Missi had said, especially the smokehouse part, but she did know that she was tired of lying. More than that, she was just plain *tired*.

"I can't tell you who I really am."

Mississippi sat up straighter, resting her cigar hand on one knee. "And why not?"

"Because . . ." *What are you doing? There's tired and then there's crazy. . . .* "Because I don't know how to explain it to you in a way that doesn't make me sound completely insane."

"Take a glance around," Missi said with a sigh, gesturing with the lit end of her cigar to darkened Boston. "Insane is all we got."

Connie inhaled loudly. This was a big gamble, but now that she had seen Adelle, getting home felt like a real possibility. She just needed the materials, and they were one crucial ingredient shy.

"If I tell you the truth," Connie said carefully, "then I want a favor."

Missi chewed the end of her cigar. "What sort of favor?"

"A small one," Connie replied. "Just information."

For a moment, Connie was sure Missi would deny her. Even she could admit it was a vague deal. But Mississippi spat and stomped her boot on the wooden floor. "Goddamn my curiosity to the ends of the earth, if it ain't worse than a starving cat's. You win, Rollins. Let's hear this truth of yours and I will do my best to oblige you."

Connie rested her rifle against the wall, then pulled the nylon bag off her shoulder. It was one of those lightweight gym sacks with two shoelace-like strings to pull through and hook around the arms. Then she fished out her phone, handed it to Missi, and waited for the reaction. She had no intention of showing her the book—there was blowing her mind and then there was unraveling her entire reality.

Missi scrambled to take it, speaking with the cigar dangling out of the corner of her mouth. "The hell is this?"

"It's a telephone," Connie told her, grateful that at least the technology in its most rudimentary state had been invented by then.

"No, it most certainly ain't."

Connie smirked, watching her tap and flip the thing around like a caveman bashing a coconut with a rock. "It is. Where I come from, it is."

"And that's where?" Missi chuckled. "The moon?"

"No, but in my time we've put people on the moon," she said, watching the girl's eyes go wide. "We've been to space, what you think of as heaven. We use those little things as telephones. You can access anything anywhere on them, information, music, movies . . ."

"Movies?"

"It's . . ." Connie rolled her eyes at her own stupidity. "It's like going to the theater, but you can watch the same performance as many times as you want. Like if you performed a trick just one time and someone could watch it on that thing a hundred times."

Missi examined the phone from every angle, even sniffed it. "So I'm supposed to believe you're from the future?"

"Yep."

"Just how far in the future?" Missi finally pressed the button to wake up the phone, the screen lighting up just enough to flash the low battery symbol and the brand name. And the date. "Sweet Jesus," she hissed. "Is that the day? It couldn't be!"

"It is. One hundred and thirty-three years," Connie murmured. "Give or take."

Laughing, Missi oh-so-gently handed the phone back to Connie. "Frenchie punched you harder than I thought."

"He's got a weak right hook," Connie said, rubbing her bruised cheek. "I'm as lucid as I can be, well, after falling back through time." Time and some other stuff, but Missi didn't need to know that yet.

"I suppose that should come as some comfort to me." Mississippi puffed thoughtfully on her cigar. "That means this city survives. Even if I will be long gone, it survives. Tell me it does."

Connie nodded. "I grew up not far from here. Boston is bigger, much bigger, and modern, and it's just fine."

"The stupid accent hasn't changed much either," Missi teased.

"That's rich coming from Annie Oakley."

That almost knocked Missi off her perch and into the open air beyond. "Folks still know about her? Future can't be half bad, then."

"So you believe me?" Connie asked, shocked. She stuffed her phone back in her bag.

"I don't know yet. It sure is farfetched," Missi admitted. "Wild and farfetched. But I want to believe. I want to believe a fancy future lady might just know how to fight this darkness taking over the city. You might just be our savior, and boy, is that a temptin' thought."

Connie closed her eyes, suddenly guilty. So much here seemed different from the novel, she didn't have any answers for Mississippi. "I'll do what I can to help, like I tried to tonight, but I need that favor and I can't stay forever."

"Wish I could've seen the whoopin' and hollerin' when all that food came strolling into the Congregation tonight." Missi turned a far-off smile toward the harbor. "So. While I digest that mouthful of medicine you just handed me, why don't you tell me what information you need."

"I'm sure you can imagine that I'd like to go home," Connie said, settling against the broken window, joining her in staring out into the pitch black. "I have no idea if time is passing back in my world. I mean, I hope it isn't, but if it is then my family must be worried sick, so I need to get back as quickly as I can, and I think I know how to do it. First, I need some incense."

"Like the stuff priests use during mass?" Missi asked. She scratched at her chin with her free hand. "Farai goes to a woman sometimes. She don't like it, though; she gives Farai the shivers. She sells all manner of odd things, and Farai swears she has the Sight."

"The Sight?"

"Anything she predicts for you?" Missi said in a low, hushed tone. "It comes true. Geo used to go too, but she's too scared to go back. Them two know where she peddles her wares, and they can tell you where to go, but I doubt if they'll be willing to take you even half the way. Geo got spooked. Bad."

Connie shrugged. She had seen plenty of spooky stuff already. "I can go on my own. I'm not afraid."

"Didn't think you would be." Missi grinned. "If anyone in this city has what you need, it's her. But after you get that incense, can you do somethin' for me?"

Connie watched her stub out her cigar, the loose ash floating away like gray snow into the darkness.

Standing, Missi crossed to her, her left hand falling lightly on the big church bell, the silent third presence in the tower. Her eyes grew hooded and distant, and it was hard to tell in the night, but Connie could swear the rough cowgirl was about to cry.

"If you know a way out of this cursed place, if there's even a small chance, please, Rollins, I'm beggin': take me with you."

16

ADELLE KNEW IT WAS a dream when the pages began turning to ash in her hands. For a while it was hypnotizing, even in sleep—each page she tore out of the book another note in the rhythmic song. *Rip—teeeeear—rip—teeeear.* As soon as she let go of the paper, a small flame began at the bottom, then spread, a hungry red mouth that devoured the words, leaving nothing but more fuzzy matter to settle near her feet.

When he appeared, she paused, her hand a fist around the crumpled top edge of the next page. She had been sitting cross-legged in a round pool of light, and Severin encroached with a single step, watching her with his head canted to the side, a playful smile curling his lips.

She ripped one more page and he flinched, so Adelle stopped and stood, the book hanging loosely in her left hand. The kiss announced itself in the swift, sure strides he took toward her, in the hands he raised that cupped her jaw, in the way he stared at her mouth before coming quickly to claim it. His hands were cool on her skin, stained with paint. She remembered the way Moira had described his fingers in the book—painterly.

Severin kissed the corner of her lips, just once, then embraced her in earnest. It didn't feel real until she heard the slightly pained groan at the back of his throat, one she wanted to match and answer. Adelle opened her eyes, just a little, and watched the pages from the book tear themselves out. They had risen up one at a time, floating around them, catching fire and surrounding them in flame. Severin stepped back, still smiling, and pressed two fingers to his lower lip, then disappeared from the circle of light before Adelle could call out to him.

He had left something behind on her own lips, a stain that felt hot and then dangerously cold, a dollop of dry ice left to dissolve and burn. Adelle gasped, swatting at her face, but the feeling only spread, searing its way across her tongue, filling her throat with choking heat.

Suffocating. Oh God, I'm suffocating.

A black mass tumbled out of her mouth but wouldn't come free, wriggling, jellied black tentacles splatting against the floor, the weight of them tugging her down. Whatever he had given her, whatever had been planted against her lips, consumed her, cramming itself into every space, pushing against the roof of her mouth until she wished for unconsciousness. It slipped out of her nose. It wore her like a sock.

"Severin, come here," she tried to say. "Help me."

Her eyes rolled back. The book exploded in sparks.

So close now.

She couldn't see. The tentacles punched their way through her eye sockets. Everything was darkness when there was no space inside her to simply *be.* A lone soft shearing noise seesawed back and forth, the only thing in the numb blankness to hold on to.

Shhk—shhk—shhk—

A feather landed in her palm and Adelle felt her leg kick, jerking her awake.

It wasn't a feather sitting in her hand but a square tuft of hair, yellow like her own. Like her own . . .

Adelle blinked rapidly, still disoriented by the nightmare. She closed her fist around the hair clipping and heard a gasp that, in her groggy state, seemed as loud as a scream.

"Moira! No! What have you done?"

Murky gray light filled the bedroom. Adelle sat up abruptly, knocking someone's hand away. Moira's. She gazed down again at the hair in her palm. *Her* hair. It was all around her, stuck to her eyelashes and the front of her nightgown.

Moira stood over her, her eyes strangely black in the dim light, a pair of shears held aloft in one hand.

Orla climbed onto the fainting couch next to Adelle, sending long tendrils of blond hair scattering to the floor. "Oh no. Oh dear! Oh dear, just be calm, just be calm and perhaps there is a way to . . . To help or . . . Or to fix . . ."

Adelle said the first thing that came to mind. "What is *wrong* with you?"

It was a disaster. Adelle reached for her head, felt how much of her hair was missing, tears welling in her eyes. Moira hadn't done a kind job, hacking unevenly away.

Leaning down, Moira snipped the shears cruelly in front of Adelle's nose. "I heard all about your adventures last night. I heard you call his name in your sleep! Orla told me everything!"

"Please!" Orla petted Adelle like a fretful puppy. "You must forgive me, you must! She heard you whisper his name in your sleep and she cornered me, demanded that I tell her everything I knew about last night. She threatened to put my toes in the fireplace if I did not!"

Adelle absolutely believed that. What she couldn't believe was that she had managed to sleep through the whole debacle. She sprang to her feet and pushed Moira away, dashing for the mirror. It was worse than she'd expected: her once-long hair had been lopped off in random chunks, leaving the rest to stick up awkwardly in every direction. There was no salvaging it, even if Moira let her try, but she didn't fancy trying to wrestle the sharp scissors out of a jealous girl's hands.

"Gather your things," Moira seethed, pacing at the foot of the bed, still squeezing the shears threateningly. "Orla! Assist her! I want her out of my sight!"

And here Adelle had worried she might have trouble getting free of the house to meet Connie. She tried to stuff back her tears, humiliated, loath to let Moira feel like she had won something. What an unbearable person.

Never meet your heroes, she thought, hurrying to find her backpack.

Greta or Elsie had brought her own clothes back, freshly laundered and folded near the paper screen. Adelle whipped the nightgown over her head, not caring what they saw, and scrambled to pull on her bra.

"Please do not hate me." Orla followed her, muttering and whimpering. "You do not know what she is like when she gets in these moods!"

"Now I do!" Adelle shouted back.

"Yes, take your things." Moira didn't seem to notice them speaking, fuming, arms crossed over her chest. "Take your things and get out!"

Adelle stormed up to her but checked when she saw the shears still dangling there in Moira's hand.

"I will, or are you going to stab me?"

"Awfully tempting," Moira laughed. But Adelle could see the pain in her gaze, the desperation. She was a wounded animal, wild and unhinged. "Certainly your features are not altogether ugly, and it cannot be denied that your eyes are somewhat enigmatic, but a young man of Severin's taste and sophistication could never find you the superior beauty! You must strike him from your mind! Do it! Tell me you will never even think his name again!"

Adelle just wanted to be rid of her and, happily enough, lied. "Think of who?"

Moira managed a thin, amused smile. "Good. *Good.* I will not see my happiness unmade by a . . ." Adelle shoved past her. Moira floundered, clumsy in her rage. "By a plump, scheming minx!"

Orla gasped. Adelle flung open the door hard enough to make it bang against the wall.

"Get out! Get out of my house at once!"

Adelle was halfway down the corridor with no idea of where she would go or what she would do until noon when Orla caught up to her. She had pulled a rose-colored knit shawl over herself for modesty, and she tugged Adelle to a stop.

"Please," she begged, tears pouring down her round cheeks. "Do not hate me."

"There's only one person in this house I could hate," Adelle told her, trying to steady her breathing. She wanted to scream. She wanted to sprint back into Moira's bedroom and set it on fire.

"You are too, too kind," Orla murmured. She pushed a gray wool shawl into Adelle's hands. At once she knew what it was for. Her strange, botched hair would draw attention. "Listen well, Miss Casey, for at any moment she will appear and fly at me with those shears. My home is not far from here—Seventy-Five Joy Street. For now I believe it would be best if Moira did not think we were companions. I would have Hampton take you, but that would lead her to believe we are conspiring against her in some way, and also he is very useless. I will hasten to dress and meet you there."

"Thank you, Orla," Adelle said quietly, pulling the shawl over her head and wrapping it twice around her neck to keep it in place.

"No, Miss Casey, thank *you*. Tell me we are still friends."

Adelle puffed out a breath through her nose. "We are still friends."

"Yes!" Orla's already bubbly face all but popped.

"ORLA."

Moira's voice practically shook the foundations. Clutching her shawl, Orla disappeared back into the bedchamber. Adelle let her-self out, hiding her face and backpack as best she could, knowing those creepy Chanters might be out front and ready to confront her now that Orla was not there to intervene.

Just as she feared, two of the Chanters in leather masks and white robes waited at the bottom of the shallow stairs leading down from the front doors. Adelle hesitated on the top step, watching them stand perfectly still, even as Moira's screams of frustration leaked out through the third-story window above.

Just another Monday for them, probably.

Time to think fast. Adelle could tell by the drawn light strug-gling against the fog over the city that it was still very early. She would need to take Orla up on her offer and kill time at her house until meeting up with Connie. The street outside Moira's mansion lay empty, desolate, the mist creeping up from the east.

Another harried shout came from above, and Adelle decided to use it.

"You must go quickly!" She rushed down the stairs to the masked men, trying not to show too much of her face. "Miss Byrne is in danger! She saw an intruder in the house!"

"Blast," the one on the right muttered. Now that they had turned, Adelle could see that they were both young men, pale, with dark circles under their eyes and bodies as thin as saplings. The one who had spoken was slightly taller, with a pronounced hunch to his posture.

"You do it," the other one muttered. She could all but hear his eyes rolling in his head.

"No, it's your turn to deal with her."

"Fine. Idiot."

The taller one charged up the stairs and through the doors. Adelle had hoped they would both leave, but she took her shot, running down the stairs and toward the road, telling herself not to stop no matter what.

"Wait a moment, miss! I must ask you about the intruder! Miss? Miss!"

She counted it a victory that he called her "miss" despite her hobbling on a bruised leg and swaddled under a giant scarf like a babushka with her backpack clutched to her chest. Holding the bag that way, she couldn't swing her arms to keep her balance and gain momentum, so she tucked it over her shoulder and hoped a head start would be enough to stay a few steps ahead of the Chanter.

No such luck. His booted footsteps thudded on the cobbled path behind her. No sooner had she reached the road than she heard his gasping breaths and felt him lunge. Adelle squeaked with fright, pumping her arms faster, the shawl slipping to her shoulders, freeing her mangled hair. Then she nearly tripped headfirst into a line of overgrown bushes, spun around by the momentum of the boy grabbing her pack and pulling, hard.

She didn't stop. The bag was gone. He had just enough time to see her face and her chopped hair, his eyes blowing wide and his mouth tightening into a grim line of recognition.

"You! The one from the park!"

Another shriek came from inside the mansion, Moira's tantrum reaching its crescendo. It distracted him long enough for Adelle to reach the road and turn left, then swiftly right, dodging into the narrow gap between two townhomes, less of an alley and more of a convenient place for trash, rats, and rainwater to pool.

Moira already hated her; whatever they found in the bag couldn't damage her reputation further. Besides, she had no intention of going back to that horrible house. In a few hours, she would reunite with Connie and they would find a way to escape the world of the book together. Phones and student ID cards could be replaced.

This time, her pursuer didn't give up so easily. Adelle heard the echo of his voice behind her at the entrance to the alleyway. She limped as quickly as she could, wondering if the throb in her leg had gotten worse from her cramped sleeping position. Or maybe it was the stress. It didn't help that she was starving and hadn't so much as smelled a whiff of coffee. She was useless without her coffee.

She staggered out into the cross street, then veered left, seeing more clusters of townhomes that might offer a small gap or alley for her to hide in. The Chanter's footsteps grew louder as she threw herself into the next lane, this one wider and cleaner. Up ahead, she noticed that the area past the road flattened out onto a larger thoroughfare. If that was Cambridge Street, then she might just be heading in the right direction.

Her breath came shorter and shorter, panic settling in. It wasn't easy to navigate Boston without a phone, particularly when nothing looked quite like it should. Still, Adelle trusted her instincts. She generally knew where Joy Street was, having frequented the area with Connie for great sushi and a popular Korean food joint.

Trust yourself. Go. No matter what, just go.

She couldn't bear the thought of being caught. She refused to go back to Moira's house, and if she never saw Moira again it would be far too soon.

The Chanter was gaining, turning down the lane she had just chosen. Adelle took a chance on left again, dashing through a tall, unlocked garden gate. She sank down against it, hoping the Chanter would run right by. Closing her eyes, she bit her lip and listened, hearing a door creak open well before the Chanter's footsteps followed. But it wasn't the garden gate.

Peeling open one eye, she found a stout woman in a somber, dark dress, cap, and apron peering at her from the stoop. It was a tall, slender house, but pretty, red brick trimmed with white, the door recessed and decorated with a low wrought-iron fence. The woman's resemblance to Orla couldn't be mistaken—they shared the same round, ruddy face and sparkling eyes, the same pert little mouth always turned up in a nervous smile.

"Nothing out here but shadows and cold, dear. Come inside. Quickly now!"

Adelle picked herself up and did as the woman asked. The Chanter burst through the gate just as she reached the door, and the woman bustled around her, blocking her from the boy's view.

"Did a girl come this way? Funny blond hair, black dress? She would have been in a hurry," the Chanter asked, out of breath.

"Begone from my stoop, boy. I do not entertain your kind here," the woman replied tartly.

"Careful, old woman. The Chanters decide who is spared and who takes the walk."

"You decide nothing," she bit back. "Not even what you wear! I cannot believe you chose to put that ugly thing on your head and run to and fro in a soiled nightgown. All that you should spare me is your presence. Shoo."

"If you see that girl," he warned, his voice getting softer as he stalked away, "know that she is wanted by the Chanters. We mean her no harm; we only want to question her."

"I said *shoo*."

The woman bumped Adelle into the house gently with her behind, then shuffled backward into the foyer, closing the door as she went. The home was almost as comfortable on the inside as Moira's, but far more understated, the interior looking as if it had hardly been touched since the colonial period. It was tasteful and cozy, though sadly silent, a spacious home with nobody in it.

"Are you Mrs. Beevers?" Adelle asked, trying to hide her hair under the shawl. "Your daughter told me to meet her here."

"I am her mother, yes. And you are?"

"Adelle," she said, remembering to curtsy. "Adelle Casey. I met your daughter at the ball last night. We both stayed the night with Miss Byrne."

Mrs. Beevers straightened. She had graying dark hair that curled abundantly behind her ears, the rest of it hidden under the pinned black cap. Her hands were cracked and shaking, but she held herself with dignity. She also had a sharp eye, raising her brow and staring outright at Adelle's sloppily cut hair.

"Ah. And is this the work of Miss Byrne? She has threatened to do as much and worse to my Orla many times." She came forward and touched one shorn lock.

Adelle blushed and glanced at her boots. "We . . . didn't get off to a good start."

"Nobody ever does with her." Mrs. Beevers sighed. "What sense can ripen, beauty often spoils. She has never wanted for anything, and so has never learned to be kind. Have you eaten?"

Adelle knew her eyes sparkled at that. She couldn't help but like the Beevers family more and more. "No, Moira turned me out right away."

"Then I will put the kettle on, and after breakfast we will see if we can address that hair of yours before my daughter joins us. Come!" she trilled, turning and sweeping her way deeper into the silent house. "Come along!"

Adelle followed her down a front hall with navy blue wallpaper. Rectangular impressions in the grime told her that a row of portraits had once hung there. At the very end of the hall, just after those voids in the dust, she saw a painting of Orla. Adelle counted the missing pictures: four. Her eyes drifted back to Mrs. Beevers and her solemn black dress, her heart sinking as she linked the pieces together. She was in mourning.

Adelle pushed herself to keep up, hoping that, even if only for a short while, she could help fill that empty house with more than family ghosts.

17

CONNIE FLAPPED THE EDGE of her borrowed blanket over the book nestled in her lap. She tried to get comfortable, her mind buzzing from the blistering round of nine hundred questions Mississippi had wanted to play on their ride back.

What sort of guns do they have in the future? Are there animals on the moon? Does Oklahoma ever become a state? How many lady presidents have there been? (That one hurt to answer, though hearing of a female vice president nearly knocked Missi out cold.) *Do people live in floating castles? If I live in a floating castle can I own it, too? How long does it take to cross the ocean? Do women get the vote?* (That one felt better to answer.)

Connie explained with all the detail a brain half-liquefied by exhaustion could manage, and the depth and ease with which she answered only seemed to convince Missi more that she really was telling the truth. Although she insisted they really ought to have floating castles figured out. By the time they reached their destination, Connie felt like she had given an introductory course in modern politics, science, and culture.

The Congregation's underground lair reminded her of a somewhat cheerier series of catacombs. The homey touches they had tried to add seemed like tossing glitter on an open coffin. Mississippi had offered her a place to sleep not far from the makeshift bar, now emptied out. It was late by the time they returned, and Missi couldn't stop yawning as she showed her to what was little more than a handful of rough-hewn boards nailed together. Even most dogs would have turned their noses up at it, though Connie did spy a few mutts wandering around, finding warm bodies to snuggle up to for the night.

Sapped to the bone, Connie still couldn't sleep. Once Sleepless Joe shut down the bar for the night, the candles burning there were snuffed out. A few torches burned at the entrance, where kids took shifts to keep the watch. Connie had dug in her bag, finding her copy of *Moira*. She had to see if they had been wrong. How could the book be so different from the reality?

Geo approached with a wooden cup and a stub of candle skewered onto a holder, which sent Connie scrambling to hide the novel under her blanket.

"Trouble sleeping?" the girl asked, kneeling. She had taken her two sleek black braids and twisted them together, tying them off with a trailing scrap of fabric.

"Not used to so many people around while I do," Connie replied, and it was true.

Geo smirked and handed her the cup. "I hardly managed a wink myself the first month," she said. "Now the snores and sounds are like a lullaby, make me feel less alone."

Her eyes roamed to the partially hidden book on Connie's lap. She put the candleholder down and nudged it close.

"Here. Maybe you can read yourself to sleep. But make sure you drink the tea, yes? It keeps the dreams away. Keeps you safe." She glanced over her shoulder to where Farai leaned against the bar, surveying the quietly sleeping charges under their care. "Farai and I make it ourselves. Clove and oak apple, and maybe a secret ingredient or two. Tastes like death, but helps you live. The Clackers think we're witches for making it—let them think that, the fools. Our survival must indeed look like magic to them, after all the ways they've tried to end us."

Connie nodded and took the warm bowl, lifting it to her lips. She tried not to taste the intensely bitter brew as it scalded her throat. "I know," she sputtered. "I found a diary in a bakery, some girl whose family all sleepwalked away. She was trying to get here. Get to safety."

Scrunching up her nose, Geo giggled. "The Wallace Bakery down by the market?"

"I think so."

"That was probably Sonja's diary," Geo said. "She made it. Thin as a reed—scared, too, real scared—but she made it."

Connie didn't expect to feel so relieved, but their abandoned bakery and home had kept her safe for days, and she was grateful for the unwitting hospitality. "I'm glad."

"Drink it all," Geo cautioned. "Tomorrow . . . Listen to me

close. Missi says you want to see the oracle tomorrow. I will tell you how to find her, but I do not think it is wise to go."

"It's too important," Connie insisted. "I need her help."

Geo tugged nervously on the end of her twisted braids, glancing around and licking her lips. "I hear you, I do. But medicine runs in my family. It is in my blood. My father taught me how to find a malady in the body just with touch, just with a tap, with experience and knowledge. I know good medicine when I see it. This woman does not make helpful medicine. She is dangerous, you hear me? Touched by dark things."

"Will it make you feel better if I say I'll be careful?"

Geo smirked. "It does. But listen once more—she will ask to read your cards, to do her magic for you. Do not let her, yes?"

Connie crooked her head to the side, curious. "Why not?"

"She read my future once in her cards," Geo said. "And all that she predicted came true. That is no way to live—to see the path before you. You live your life moment to moment or else you spend it traveling by another man's map. She is a strange, strange woman—she did not want me to leave. I think she is very lonely or very dangerous, perhaps both."

Geo touched Connie on the shoulder and stood. "Tomorrow I will tell you how to find her. Enjoy your book, my friend, and sleep a dreamless sleep."

"Before you go," Connie asked, clearing her throat softly. "Where do we, um, you know . . . go to the toilet?"

Pointing to the darkened, cavelike back of the tunnel, Geo said, "There's a pit dug in the back." Reading Connie's blank expression, she shrugged and added, "It's not the Parker House, but what did you expect? Nobody will empty your chamber pot around here."

With that, she returned to the bar.

Thanks, I think I'll just hold it until everyone's asleep.

Choking down the last of the wretched, bitter tea, Connie watched her go. When she was sure she was alone again, she slid the book out from under her blanket and studied it near the weak candlelight. The first line of the novel would never leave her, cemented into her mind from the many rereads she and Adelle had embarked upon over the years. It seemed wrong to be reading the book there, huddled under her blanket, existing in the world of *Moira* without Adelle to experience this moment with her, but she had to know.

I know this book cover to cover, don't I?

More and more she mistrusted her memory of it. But without a doubt she remembered the first line: *Moira Byrne did not believe in destiny.*

Connie cracked the book, and there it was, the sentence she expected. But then, as she watched, before her very eyes, the words began to blur and rearrange themselves. She dropped the book in shock, mouth twisted open, a chill sweeping through her as a new opening passage took the place of the original.

It started with the ill omens—the fall of one great house, then another, and another. The eldest of the Kennaruck family sprang from his bed, suffered a strange malady of the heart, and died. The following day, every son and daughter—indeed, every person of his bloodline— dropped where they stood. The servants wandered out into the streets, dumbstruck and screaming, and when the coroner was called, he put his hat over his mouth to keep from weeping. He opened up the bodies in his cold crypt beneath the city hospital and found the hearts blackened and imploded, just a spidery pulp of dark veins.

The Vaughn family fell next to a new and unfathomable plague, this time of the mind. All but the eldest son left their beds one unseasonably warm winter night and, with slow and orderly determination, walked one by one into the sea. Their bodies never washed ashore. Later, a number of needles were found by the door, and it appeared that they had sewn stones into their pockets before marching down to the waves. That same week of incredible sadness, mounds of fish as high as children washed up on the shore. Some observant sailor found them there, multitudinously reeking, and did what the coroner had done to the Kennarucks and the Vaughns. He sliced open some of the fish, a dozen perhaps, and inside discovered that their insides were naught but eyes.

Connie shook, passing a trembling hand over her face. The book felt warm in her hands, like it had blood running through it and a life of its own.

How can this be happening? she thought, slamming the book shut. *What have we done?*

Though Moira Byrne may be the undisputed heroine of our story, one cannot describe the lady without also describing her ever-present companion, one Miss Orla Beevers. The youngest of four, Orla Beevers was a lady born of a not particularly memorable or well-bred family. One could consider Orla Beevers to be the barnacle clinging desperately to the bow of Moira's ship, but Orla might hardly begrudge one the comparison. While not particularly clever, she was, at the very least, sensible of her own qualities, of which she had many—a girl of no ambition and no talent, she was nonetheless an amiable sort, and always a welcome addition to any party, being so fortunately imbued with the buoyancy and temperament of a Gordon setter. And, like a dog, she followed loyally at Moira's side, as she must, as Moira's penchant for mischief and romance led her down many a crooked path. No meaner friend would dare venture alongside Moira in these things, but Orla Beevers proved steadfast and true, and might reasonably qualify

"No need to flinch, dear. I would cut my sons' hair every month, and I dare say anything would be an improvement."

Sipping tea and full of porridge, Adelle tried not to squirm. Just the metallic sound of the shears snipping away at her hair set her teeth on edge. She didn't know why, but she couldn't stop crying.

"Get it all out," Mrs. Beevers encouraged, standing behind her. She had directed Adelle to a chair in the mudroom off the kitchen, then draped a folded sheet around her shoulders and gone to work salvaging her awful haircut. "It made you feel safe and pretty; it is all right to mourn its loss."

"I'm not this shallow," Adelle murmured, wiping her tears with her sleeve. "I don't think I would care so much if she hadn't done it while I slept. It feels like she stole something from me."

"She did." Mrs. Beevers sighed. "I wish Orla would recognize Moira for the spoiled chit she is, but my daughter sees the good in everyone. Ordinarily, I would be proud of that, but anything unmanaged can become a fault."

Adelle didn't want to think about her dreadful hair anymore. She held the teacup against her chin, letting it warm her. Just like Orla's, Mrs. Beevers's kindness was disarming, and given Moira's coldness, she didn't understand it.

"Why did you yell at the Chanters like that on my behalf?"

Adelle asked. "Orla told me they protect you. Us. Aren't they . . . aren't they on our side?"

After a while, the light touches of the woman's hands on her head felt soothing. It reminded her of the long-ago days when her own mother would sit her down on the floor in front of the couch, put in an *Everwood* DVD, and brush out the snarls in Adelle's blond hair.

Mrs. Beevers clucked her tongue. "You tell me, dove. They were chasing *you*."

"I don't know what I did to get on their bad side," Adelle replied truthfully.

"And there is the answer to your question." Orla's mother brushed a bit of blond fluff off Adelle's shoulder. "They protect themselves, no one else. And how could I or you or anybody trust folk who worship that thing in the harbor? That is the test of all men: God and the devil are unseen, but how many godly men would jump to Satan's side if he appeared to them?"

Adelle frowned. "You think they worship it just because it's there? What if they're helping it?"

"I think they are weak," Mrs. Beevers stated flatly. "They seek to appease it because they are afraid, and so they cower and kneel, because it is easier to kneel than to fight. They give it what it wants, lest it punish them, too. My husband did not lose his arm at the Battle of the Crater because it was easy; he did because fighting in the war was right."

They both fell silent. Adelle could only imagine the pain she must be carrying around, having a husband maimed in the war and then losing so many of her family to the Wound. She didn't have the heart to ask if they had all gone that way, or if some had fallen to natural causes. Her tears welled again, and her voice shook when she spoke.

"Thank you, Mrs. Beevers. Since I have . . . I mean, you and your daughter have been so kind."

"This is a world full of outright evil now." Mrs. Beevers sighed. "Which makes choosing kindness all the harder, and all the more crucial. There, now. I think that is vastly better. Come and see."

Mrs. Beevers offered her hand and Adelle took it, rising to follow her back through the kitchens to the foyer, then right, through an archway, and into the downstairs sitting room. A piano and a blue velvet sofa dominated the room, poised below an impressive crystal chandelier frosted with cobwebs. Near the piano and the windows, a full-length mirror on a stand had been set up. Adelle pulled the sheet off her shoulders and balled it up, reaching to run her fingers through her twice-shorn locks. It did look much better, even and softer, more Audrey Hepburn and less He-Man.

"Everyone will think I'm a boy," Adelle grumbled.

Mrs. Beevers put her hands on both of her shoulders, smiling at her in the reflection. "It is hair, dear. It grows back."

Adelle managed a laugh and sniffled. "Small potatoes."

Mrs. Beevers lifted an eyebrow.

"It's, um . . . it's a saying in my family."

"I like it." Mrs. Beevers took her hands back, folding them elegantly in front of her waist. "Small potatoes indeed."

The front door opened and banged shut, and Orla floated into the room a moment later, dressed in a subdued mauve day dress. She unpinned a hat from her hair as she trundled toward them, her mouth drawn down with concern.

"Did you take care of her, Mama?" Orla asked, holding Adelle at arm's length.

"The best," Adelle told her. "But what is it? Why do you look so worried?"

"There is a crowd outside, all around the house," she said, dragging both Adelle and her mother to the windows. Just as she'd said, Chanters waited outside, densely packed, ringing the property. "Mama, tell me you did not scold them again! They protect us, but there is a limit to what they will endure."

Mrs. Beevers glared out the window, her jaw firmly set. "This is brash, even for them."

"There is nobody to oppose them now, Mama, you know that." Orla threw herself into her mother's arms. "I *told* you not to be cross with them. I *told* you. This is their town now."

Stroking her back, Mrs. Beevers simply said calmly, "I hope the two of you will do something about that when I am gone. And that is why you must get upstairs now, and quickly."

"Mama . . ."

The dark-haired woman all in black drew the curtains and then spun away from the window, taking Orla and Adelle by the hand. "Orla, do not be foolish. I have been lenient with you, too lenient, and now you must learn to banish this foolishness all on your own. You know why they are here, Orla; you know what this means. No. No crying. I will not allow it."

Mrs. Beevers pressed her lips together, then tugged her daughter closer, hugging her with one arm. Adelle just tried to keep up. Something thumped against the front door. Through the drawn curtains, Adelle heard the chanting begin. She couldn't make out the words, as they were speaking something she had never heard before, guttural and phlegmy, more like a sickness than a language.

"Go upstairs now, girls. Orla, listen to your mother." Mrs. Beevers strode to the hearth behind the blue sofa, took a fire poker, and brandished it like a club.

Orla remained frozen in place. Adelle's mind spun. The chanting grew louder outside.

"But what does it mean?" Adelle begged Mrs. Beevers.

The older woman inhaled deeply, her eyes ever on her daughter. "It means that our acquaintance will be cut tragically short. It means you must now look after Orla; you must help her to be strong." She turned away from Adelle and joined her daughter at the center of the room. "Here . . ." Her mother folded her into an embrace again, this time with both arms, rocking her back and forth, smoothing the hair away from her forehead. She whispered something to Orla and then pushed her gently away. "Now go. Go!"

A stone smashed through the window behind them, glass showering them like jagged rain. Adelle grabbed Orla by the wrist and together they raced toward the foyer and the stairwell. Through the narrow windows on either side of the door, Adelle saw more white-robed figures out on the stoop.

"I cannot leave her," Orla whispered, stumbling on the stairs.

"You heard what she said," Adelle replied. Her limp was slowing them down, but Orla was refusing to climb higher. Another window shattered downstairs. "Come on," she encouraged, sliding her arm through Orla's, taking the stairs one at a time.

When they reached the second-floor landing, the Chanters breached the house, and at once, Adelle heard someone come charging up the stairs after them. She pulled Orla harder, faster, forcing her up and up, ignoring the tight breathlessness that made her chest throb.

Far below, on the main floor, a man shouted in pain, and Adelle silently and fiercely hoped that Mrs. Beevers had taken down the lot of them with her fire poker. Orla nearly collapsed, sobbing louder with each labored step. On the top floor, Adelle looked to Orla for help.

"Where do we go now?" Adelle asked, gaze glued to the stairs. They were running out of time. "Orla!"

"The . . . the servants' pantry at the end of the hall. The window there is hard to see from outside."

Adelle didn't know what was worse, the agonized screams coming from the first floor or the moment they stopped. Through the silence, the angry footsteps on the stairs leading to their level continued, and that was enough to shut out any thought of retreat. There had been at least four Chanters visible through the garden window, just as many through the front door, and if they'd surrounded the house, then at least a dozen Chanters could easily overpower them.

It was Orla who led her to the correct door, flung it open, and then shut them inside. She caught her breath, leaning back against the door while Adelle waded through empty flour sacks, cobwebs, and mouse droppings to reach the broken window. The room was little more than a closet with two tall, barren shelving units against each wall. Adelle flicked open the catch and shoved her hand through one of the missing panes, slamming her palm up. It wouldn't budge.

Orla shrieked as the door behind her bounced with the force of a kick.

"Lock it!" Adelle cried, trying the window again.

"The lock is missing! What do we do? Heavens, what do we do?"

"The shelf! Help me push it!" Adelle sprang back from the window. Orla waited until she was in position to leave the door, dash forward, and join Adelle on the far side of the shelf. Together they pulled, groaning from the strain. The door exploded inward just as the wood at the base of the shelf creaked and splintered, the whole dusty contraption coming free and crashing into the opposite wall. The Chanter who had caught up to them stumbled back, blocked by the debris, at least for a little while.

"Submit," he said, grabbing hold of the shelf's edge and rattling it menacingly. "We have seen your faces. We know who must be called next."

"Oh . . . the devil take you!" Orla screamed, grabbing a handful of mouse crap and flinging it at him.

Adelle returned to the window, putting more force behind her push. At last the casement shook free, cooler air rushing in to meet her relieved sigh.

"Out you go," Adelle told Orla. "Quickly!"

"You have only but to dream," the Chanter warned, his eyes gray and piercing behind the hideous leather mask, "and we will claim you."

The rest of his words were lost to the wind as Orla climbed gingerly out onto the narrow strip of wooden trim and Adelle followed, just as unsteadily. She kicked the window down for good measure, then inched along to the right, where Orla had found a decorative bit of stonework to climb.

When they were both on the roof, Adelle ran to the eastern edge, toward the harbor, and discovered that the next roof over was close, but not comfortably so.

"The Gardeners' place has sat empty for a month," Orla told her. "They are all gone."

"We have to jump," Adelle breathed, her heart lodging painfully in her throat. The knot in her stomach tightened, a noose around her guts. "That shelf won't hold them for long."

"That observatory is our way in." The Gardeners' roof featured a decorative miniature glass house. Stone flowerpots in a Grecian style were huddled around each corner. The dirty panes of the observatory were intact, but that could easily change.

"The gap is too wide," Orla murmured. "I could never leap that far!"

"You have to." Adelle felt her second wind come with unexpected force. From the roof, they could see to the water, and in the early light, Adelle found the sight of the Wound even more unsettling. Somehow it had seemed like a thing only for night—that once the sobering light of day came, it would disappear like a nightmare you laughed off the next morning. But no, it sat pale and wriggling, larger than a sinkhole, pulsating at the end of the wharf, poised to catch anyone who walked off the edge. Inky clouds clustered over it for extra Mount Doomian effect.

Seeing it horrified her, but it also gave her an idea. Just like Frodo, she would force herself toward the point of greatest danger.

She took Orla's hand, clasped it. "If we make it to the road, we can try to reach the sea before your mother does."

Orla's round eyes lit up. "Yes . . . They will make her drink something to go to sleep, and as soon as she dreams, she will hear the call and take the walk. We could try to intercept her!"

"Surely we must try."

"But it will not work." Orla tried to snatch her hand back, but Adelle wouldn't let go. "Other folk have tried to stop their family and their friends from going to the sea. Nothing works! They cannot be stopped. . . ."

"But we *must* try."

"Yes. Yes, Miss Casey, you are right. My mother told us to fight, did she not? I will fight, but first I will take the leap."

"Orla!"

But she had already gone, winding up with tiny steps, the run of a girl who had never played or thought about a sport in her life. Yet she gave it her all, flinging her arms wide and sailing across the four-foot gap, landing with a thump, her elegant heeled boots hanging over the edge, then kicking wildly until she managed to drag herself to safety. Orla flipped onto her back and let loose a delighted cry.

"I did it! Miss Casey, did you see? I did it!"

Connie would probably laugh if she saw the distance they were trying to cross, but Adelle had never been one for athletic feats, and definitely not those that potentially came with a sheer drop down five floors.

We must try.

Adelle knew that if it were her own mother on the line, she would do anything to help, and so she ran as fast as she could, kicking off from the very edge of the stone lip on the roof and landing with about the same clumsy elation as Orla. She skipped the celebration, hobbling along to join Orla at the observatory, where the Victorian girl had clearly found her sense of spirit and determination, picking up a chunk of fallen flowerpot and hurling it through the nearest glass pane.

Orla cried joyfully at that, too, though she was also just crying.

Helping Orla through the jagged space left by the crumbling glass, Adelle tried to soothe her with low, solemn words. "We're going to find her, Orla. We're going to fight."

19

"Here. Rustled these up for you."

Connie glanced up from her breakfast of gritty bread and cheese funky enough to clear a room. A heap of yellowed clothing fell onto the empty stool beside her. Mississippi crossed her arms and leaned against one of the uneven posts sketching out the shape of the bar.

At least there was coffee, even if it was weaker than her will to stay awake. The tea had done its job, banishing dreams but giving her restless sleep. She rubbed her knuckle into one tired eye and picked up the top garment from the pile: a rumpled cotton skirt dyed navy blue.

"To help you, ya know, walk among us," Mississippi added in an undertone, punctuating it with a wink.

Connie smirked, but her smile soon faded. The night before, she had made Missi a promise she probably couldn't keep. Her stomach twisted into a knot, and she shot a furtive glance at her new friend. "Thank you. I really appreciate it; I appreciate all of this."

"You ain't home yet—don't thank me until we're free of this pit."

Speaking of . . .

Connie stood, wolfing down the last of her bread and picking up the rest of the clothes. "I should use the toilet and change."

"After you do, meet me topside. There's somethin' I want to show you."

They left in opposite directions, Missi heading back out toward the tunnel and Connie returning to her tiny sleeping den. She packed up her things and changed into her borrowed clothing, which felt more like a costume than anything she would wear normally. Nobody really noticed she had stripped down to her underwear, and Connie was used to wandering around almost naked in the locker rooms before soccer practice. In addition to the blue skirt, which rose high on the waist, Missi had provided a pair of wide-legged black trousers, a high-necked ivory woman's blouse, and a trim blazer that had once been a lush periwinkle corduroy but now had elbows and collar faded to white from use.

At the very bottom, the sharpshooter had left a black-and-white-checkered bandanna. Connie held it for a moment, rubbing her thumb over the worn fabric. It was a touching gesture, one that said: *You're still one of us.*

Connie shoved her tracksuit into her nylon gym bag, leaving the novel and her phone at the bottom. Before trotting off to the toilet, she slyly returned to the bar and asked Sleepless Joe for more coffee. While he was distracted, she drained the coffee, wincing from the bitterness, then shoved the cup in her bag along with the sad nub of a candle waiting to be burned on the edge of the bar top.

Just a stone from outside and the incense and she would be ready to cast the spell to return home. While she braved the toilet pit, she distracted herself with formulating a plan. She wasn't sure yet if they could all travel with one spell. She and Adelle had arrived separately, and Connie had decided they ought to try to go at once the next time, to avoid the jumbled arrival they had suffered when entering the book.

And her promise to Missi . . . well, that was something else altogether.

She isn't real. Even if she feels real, even if she seems like a friend, she's just a character in a book, nothing more.

Connie wove her way back through the Congregation and away from the foul-smelling toilet ditch. Now that she had the checkered handkerchief tied around her neck, nobody bothered her or stopped her when she backtracked through the tunnel that led to the ladder and the chapel above.

Makeshift potato-sack curtains had been hung over the windows, the ill fit allowing meager morning light to filter into the chapel. Connie had visited King's Chapel once on a field trip, and she remembered it being lush and formal, two stories, with a balcony and Roman-style white columns. Bright red pews lent it a regal air, while golden chandeliers cast a warm, holy glow over the marble walkway leading to the front. Now the pews were dirty and torn, the chandeliers lowered and ransacked for candles.

"Took you long enough," Missi teased, waiting near one of the pews and picking at a nail in it with her forefinger. "Thought you might have fallen in. You afraid of heights?"

"No."

"Good." Missi turned, fringe flying, and brought Connie through the chapel and to a recessed series of stairs. "You told me your escape plan; now I'll show you mine."

They traveled up a few flights of perilously steep stairs, then up yet another flight of steeper, dirtier stairs curving claustrophobically higher into the bell tower. Connie remembered some kids on her field trip refusing to go up, terrified of the cramped little stairwell.

At the top they stood inside the King's Chapel bell tower. Missi dodged right around the massive bell, modern for them but ancient for Connie, to a potato sack covering a window. The slats had been kicked out, so it opened onto a rickety platform and scaffolding someone had built onto the side of the bell tower, anchored to the narrow stone balcony fifteen or so feet below.

Connie felt the platform wobble as she crawled out onto it and winced, her breakfast swimming dangerously close to her throat.

"Just up the ladder. Almost there." Missi scrambled up with acrobatic ease, then sat on the edge of the roof and dangled her legs over it.

The chapel didn't have a steeple, though the roof over the main part of the building was sharply pointed. The roof of the bell tower, however, had barely any incline at all, enough so that someone, presumably Missi, had plonked something on the roof and covered it with a massive "tarp" of blankets and sacks stitched together haphazardly.

Connie breathed a sigh of relief once she was up the ladder and more firmly on the roof, kneeling and frowning at the covered object centered on top of the bell tower. In the swimming, foggy light of the morning, Connie could better see their location, and better see Missi.

"Are you wearing makeup?" Connie blurted.

She could swear the girl had rubbed pink paste on her cheeks, in almost comically perfect circles, like a doll's symmetrical red dots.

Missi wiped hard at her face. "What? No. Is it stupid? You said last night ladies in the future wear all kinds of stuff on their faces! Anyway, I wouldn't do that. You're crazy. Here, look at this. . . .'"

Connie grinned. Missi's face was redder than ever as she blushed from her neck to the roots of her curling red hair.

After pulling the massive blanket off with a magician's flair, Missi balled up some of the fabric and held it to her chest, waiting for Connie's reaction with wide, glittering eyes.

"It's . . ." Connie scratched the end of her nose. "It's a basket?"

Missi rolled her eyes. "It's a balloon. Don't you dummies have those in the future?"

Connie smacked her forehead. "Yes, we do. You seem to be missing the balloon part, though."

"Still finishing that," Missi explained, dropping the covering blanket and running her hand reverently over the large and somewhat uneven weave of the square basket. "Joe and I work away at it at nights, bribe some of the children to do it with us.

Their little fingers are better for stitchin' anyway."

"This is your escape plan?" Connie asked. She had to admit, it was imaginative. Borderline ridiculous, but also brave.

"We have tried every damn way out of this city except the air," Missi replied, steel in her voice. "My daddy was in London before he had me—I got the idea from him. He met the great James Glaisher, the man who flew over London." She heaved a dreamy sigh and looked to the sky. "Daddy would tell me all kinds of stories about him. About what a genius he was. Gave me a whole book full of his ideas about travel and balloons. Glaisher saw the streets of London from above, and he said the road 'appeared like a line of brilliant fire.'"

Missi closed her eyes, a sweet, sad smile softening her face. "A line of brilliant fire. A dumb old road looking that way . . . I want to see the world that way too. I want to think one last nice and pretty thing about this city before I leave it behind for good."

"Do you think it will work?" Connie asked. It wasn't any crazier than a magic spell.

"Joe thinks we can manage, but it won't carry much weight," she replied, and with a grunt began covering the basket again. Connie rose to her feet to help, taking hold of one damp edge. "I said I would go first, and Farai isn't scared to try neither. That way, it's just two of us that go if . . . well, if the worst happens."

Missi fell silent, looking more at Connie than at the blanket they were rearranging. "You think it's stupid, don't you?"

"I think it's bold," Connie said. *Just like you.*

It was Connie's turn to blush, but Missi didn't notice; she

busied herself with soaking up the compliment.

"Just for that," the sharpshooter said, digging in her pocket when the basket was once again covered and hidden, "you can have this now."

Missi handed her a folded square of stained paper. When Connie flattened it out, she realized it was a crude map of Boston, primarily the streets surrounding the chapel and the relevant ones that would take her and Adelle to the seer woman.

"You were going to keep it from me if I thought your balloon was stupid?" Connie asked, glancing up from the map.

"Nah, but I might have made you squirm for a bit. . . ." Mississippi nodded toward the ladder. "Before you go, just . . . be careful, all right? I don't trust that woman, not one bit. Farai and Geo are the bravest we got, and anything that scares them scares me, you hear?"

Connie nodded.

"Good. Go, get what you need to get, then come back here safely."

"You're worried about me," Connie observed, finding that she didn't so much mind when Missi blushed and smacked her playfully on the shoulder.

"I can take that map back," the cowgirl warned, tilting her head to the side and raising a finger.

"Then how will I get you out of here?" It came out without Connie thinking. She regretted it immediately. Mississippi's smile skewered her through the heart.

Don't get her hopes up, you monster—you don't know if she can come with you.

"I . . . I, um, I should go," Connie mumbled, wrenching herself away and scrambling down the ladder. She couldn't stand to look at the other girl for one more minute, not when her face was full of hope, and Connie had nothing but broken promises to offer.

20

ADELLE COULDN'T GET OUT of the Gardeners' home fast enough.

Orla clung to her, the girls arm in arm, both of them keeping away from the walls. Whatever had happened to the family had not been peaceful. As soon as they reached the third floor, the corridors and rooms devolved into controlled chaos. The house lay in shadow, but here and there uncovered windows let in shafts of dreary light. Adelle almost wished for the full dark. Chairs were arranged in strange configurations in the middle of hallways; doors had had their knobs removed, and those knobs were found elsewhere, placed in a circle; words written in ink, feces, and blood covered the wallpaper.

Worse, Adelle recognized snatches of phrases, bits of sentences that twigged her memory and made her spine go rigid with panic.

Souls not just married together but irrevocably intertwined, sewn

together with the thread of Fate. Tear them apart and they would bleed.
For love was pain, that could not be denied—her heart ached for the
thing she wanted, the thing she would stop at nothing to have.

As they traveled in a glued pair down the third-floor stairs, Adelle's eyes remained fixed to the wall. Cold sweat gathered at her temples. The flowery descriptions in the novel no longer seemed so charming when they were written with scratching fingers in hardened, black blood.

Tear them apart and they would bleed. BLEED. Tear them apart. Tear.

TEAR AND BLEED. TEAR IT OUT OF ME.

TEAR IT OUT OF ME AND I BLEED.

"Poor Mrs. Gardener," Orla whispered shakily. "Poor Mr. Gardener."

"Did they have children?" Adelle asked, swallowing a sick, sour mouthful of fear.

"Y-yes. Two young sons and . . ." Orla glanced at her, pale as a cadaver. "And a baby."

"I thought people walked into the sea," Adelle said. She didn't want to see any more of the writings, but something compelled her to look. As they rounded the landing, the scrawling on the wallpaper grew ever more frantic, the "paint" some unimaginable mixture as thick as paste. "Everyone keeps saying that, that they just walk . . ."

This doesn't look like walking.

"Sometimes—sometimes people resist," Orla stammered. "They try not to listen to the dreams, but it becomes worse and worse for them until they relent. It breaks my heart that they tried not to go. God in heaven, they were a lovely family."

Adelle quickened her pace. She wanted out of the house. The words blurred as they made their way down toward the main level.

sewn together with the thread of Fate

SEW THEM SEW THEM I HAVE SEWN THEM TOGETHER

ANSWER ME FATE

ANSWER

YOU CALL AND I ANSWER

IT IS BORN

IT COMES

IT IS HERE

"We have to get out of here," Adelle murmured. She didn't feel well. It wasn't just the smell or the palpable sense of dread and wrong and death that lingered in the house—when she looked away from the walls, she could swear the words were peeling off, following them, slithering like black snakes toward her. They wanted to infiltrate her mind, she was sure of it; they wanted to choke her like the vision from her dream. . . .

"We have to go, go now," she whispered, breaking into a run. She knew the words were coming for her, *hunting* her.

Yes, so close, you feel it.

The voice. Adelle kept only the slightest grasp on Orla's fingers, yanking her through the house until they stumbled into the front room. Something strange and yellow and taut like leather hung over the windows there. Adelle threw open the door, refusing to look any longer, refusing to acknowledge what those curtains might be.

Outside, the air obliterated the black snakes of words trying to infiltrate her. The door was shut and they were gone, but before she could think a single grateful thought, Orla gasped and flattened herself back against the door.

A Chanter standing in the road caught sight of them at once.

"What do we do?" Orla whispered.

He drew a weapon hanging from his belt, a club wrapped in newspaper, painted with paint or blood, Adelle didn't care to know.

"We can't go back in there," Adelle replied. "We . . . we have to run, or fight him, or . . ." She couldn't think. "Or . . . Or . . ."

A rumbling, grumbling thunder shook the ground beneath them. Orla screamed, huddling against Adelle's side. But then the source of the noise made itself known—from down the road, to their right, back toward the Beevers' house, a carriage shot along the cobbles, as unstoppable and swift as a runaway train.

The Chanter jerked to the side, club raised over his head, a muffled cry of surprise leaving him before the team of horses drove into his back, sending him flying across the road to land facedown in the gutter. The carriage pulled up short, the horses stamping and tossing.

The driver had protected his face from the dust with a black scarf, but he whipped it off to call out to them.

"Hampton!" Orla teetered forward on shaky feet, then found her footing and trotted to the box, taking his hand and wringing it. "You useful, beautiful idiot! You have saved us!"

"From now on," he said with a nervous chuckle, wiping at his spot-covered face, "I promise only to hit the right folk."

The door of the carriage swung open, surprising both of them, Orla bumping into Adelle. A pair of spectacles came first, then a handsome face, and finally a hand held out to help them.

"Caid! What are you doing here?" Orla's surprise was forgotten, and she rushed to him.

"When I saw those men surrounding the house, I went for help," Hampton said. "Found Mr. Vaughn on his way to Byrne House."

"I was going to call on Moira," Caid said, offering his hand to Adelle after Orla had climbed in. She took it, and at once felt a little safer. "But this is more important. If we hurry, there may still be time to help your mother, Orla."

"You saw Mama? Thank heavens!" Orla dug her nails into the seat cushion as Hampton started off down the road again.

Adelle took the place next to Kincaid, the sudden jostling of the carriage making the choice for her, sending her falling into the open space, her hand perilously close to grazing on his knee.

"Yes, miss. I kept watch from down the road," Hampton called back. "If you two hadn't come out I was going to go after Mrs. Beevers myself."

"That is very heroic of you, Hampton, and after how abominably we have treated you. . . ."

"'Tis all right, miss. I did run down the young lady there."

"Yes, and it was awful, but an accident! Obviously an accident. And now we must cherish you forever and ever. Please, drive on; I only hope we are not too late."

Though he said nothing, Caid exuded the same kind of reassuring calm as a mug of tea held in the hands, just the right temperature. Or a duvet fresh from the laundry. His outer left thigh pressed against Adelle's right, and she looked resolutely at Orla's skirt.

Caid didn't seem to notice they were touching, but Adelle very much noticed.

"Thank you for coming," Orla said, leaning forward and clasping Caid's hands, though they dwarfed hers. Tiny splotches of ink dotted the edges of his shirt and camel-colored suit jacket. "It is so good to feel that we are not alone."

"Of course," he replied. "I know how you must feel."

Adelle's heart twinged. He had lost so many family members. . . . It must be awfully triggering to now be racing to stop someone else's mother from throwing herself into the sea.

"What if there are Chanters with her?" Adelle wondered aloud.

"Then Hampton runs them down," Caid said without a hitch.

She glanced at Orla. "I thought they were supposed to protect people. That's what you told me last night, Orla, when they tried to stop us outside the party."

"They did not protect my family," Caid muttered. "Why anyone in this town trusts them is beyond me."

"They *did* help." Orla fiddled nervously with her skirt, sounding pleading. "They *have* helped. Fewer of our people have gone missing lately. . . ."

Adelle puzzled over "our people." With the streets empty and only a glimpse of Connie with the Penny-Farthings, it appeared that most of the city had vanished. Yet the soiree the night before had been quite lively. Perhaps what she really meant was the rich and privileged living in Moira's neighborhood.

"But Mama . . . She has never been one to hold her tongue, and she has never liked the Chanters." Orla glanced up, her eyes glazed with tears. "You were there, Adelle—did she provoke them?"

"There were some harsh words used," Adelle admitted. She swallowed around a thumbtack. "She was trying to keep them away from me. This is all my fault."

"And what did you do to anger them?" Caid asked.

"Nothing!" Adelle had run from them, of course, but they had not been friendly at all. Their outfits didn't exactly say "welcome party."

"Then the punishment hardly fits the crime," Caid concluded. "They protect only themselves."

Hampton steered them down the road carefully, nosing southeast, the lanes becoming more and more choked with overturned carts, carriages, bicycles, and ankle-deep muck. Adelle covered her nose and gagged. The stench was overwhelming, prickling at the back of the throat, rot and waste and fetid water.

"She will go by the Wall," Hampton called back to them. "Most all of them go that way."

"The Wall?" Adelle asked. She had forgotten all about her quest to blend in. These were things she ought to know, but she decided that any questions they tossed back could be explained away by her accident.

"Yes, dear," Orla said solemnly, her eyes even wetter. "The Wall of a Hundred Faces, though I dare say it must be a thousand faces now. Maybe more. Whenever someone walks into the sea, their face appears on the wall of the old wharf storehouse. As if . . . as if they are forever trapped in the stones. It is truly an evil sight, and you must promise not to look. It is too, too horrible. I shan't look. I . . . I cannot."

Adelle stared numbly out the window. Orla and Kincaid must both have family members who might appear there, forcing them to relive the horror of losing them.

How had the Boston of *Moira* become so twisted and dangerous? She glanced at the sun, trying to estimate how much time she had before Connie would be expecting her. After they found Mrs. Beevers, she would have to make an excuse and slip away. Everything she had seen, everything she had witnessed, only made her want to go home all the more.

But she looked at Orla vibrating with fear on the seat across from her, reduced to chewing her fingernails bloody as they raced toward the wharves to intercept her mother. How could she leave Orla this way?

She has Caid and Hampton, a reasonable voice argued. *She has Moira. She has friends, and she does not need you. You, who got her mother into this mess in the first place. You, who is driving a wedge between her and Moira. You, who doesn't belong . . .*

The voice turned more vicious and less reasonable. Adelle pinched the bridge of her nose, panic rising in her throat, threatening to close it up completely. Panic attacks were nothing new, though the first time she'd experienced one at school, they had rushed her to the ER, afraid she was having a heart attack. Usually it took an immense amount of stress to bring about an attack, and they tended to coincide with when her mother traveled for her job. She always felt more vulnerable without her mother close; they had been practically fused at the hip before Greg came along.

Connie had suffered panic attacks before her, and she helped her now whenever one threatened to strike. But Connie wasn't there just then to soothe her.

Adelle started one of Connie's breathing exercises, but it was too late. Her thoughts, her anxieties, were already spinning up, one minuscule flicker roaring into a blaze before she could recognize and stop it. She would have given anything to have her own mother there in the carriage, to have her scratch the back of Adelle's neck lightly with her nails, the thing she did to calm her down whenever her anxiety threatened to turn her into a yarn ball of questions, every strand a worry, real or otherwise.

And what would her mother think? What if time was passing there just as it was in the novel? Or, if she could get home, would it feel to her family like no time had passed at all? If the girls had genuinely vanished from the real world, then her mother must have realized by now that something was wrong. Or, rather, Greg must have. He would have called her and said that Adelle hadn't come home after the dance, and then Brigitte Casey, sitting in a Phoenix, Arizona, hotel room, would get a series of texts on her cell from Greg. Adelle squeezed her eyes shut. She could just picture it—her mother, full blond hair up in a towel after a shower, sitting on the hotel bed in a white robe, her legs stretched out in front of her while she watched *Forensic Files* and sipped a minibar gin and tonic, would text Greg something to the tune of *That's not like Adelle.*

When the next morning came with still no sign of her, Brigitte would fly home from the conference, and everyone would be immensely disappointed that the preeminent death doula scheduled to speak had to cancel her big seminar to answer questions from the police about poor, missing Adelle.

What are you going to say to your mom and Greg? How are you going to explain any of this? That is, if you even see them again. What if you never get home and they have to cope with your disappearance for the rest of their lives?

"Miss Casey? Miss Casey . . ."

She had almost fallen prone against the carriage window. Adelle snapped her eyes open, hearing her own labored breathing. Caid's face was inches from hers as she clawed her way out of her attack.

"Are you all right?" he asked, his voice soft with concern.

"My nerves . . ." Adelle hoped that sounded Victorian enough.

Orla reached down under her seat, pulled out a small drawer, and extracted a glass vial. She uncorked it, then handed it across to Caid, who waved it under Adelle's nose.

"Smelling salts, dear," Orla told her. "Should set you to rights."

The blast of ammonia slapped her in the nose hard enough to make her see stars.

"I didn't mean to . . . ," Adelle trailed off. "This is all very overwhelming."

"Well, steel yourself, Miss Casey," Caid said with a sigh. "We are approaching the wharves. If you would prefer to stay in the carriage, I can accompany Miss Beevers and see to her safety."

Adelle smiled faintly. He really was like a warm mug of tea, a blanket for the spirit. A boy had never stared into her eyes with such concern, and it felt nice enough that she wanted to get used to it. "I'm okay now. I will go with you. Staying here alone sounds much worse."

"There!" Hampton's shout worked as keenly as the smelling salts. "I can take us no further, but I spy her coming down State, by the warehouse just there. . . ."

They gathered against the window, peering out into the thick haze that had settled over the city. It was worse here, far worse, a miasma tinged sickly green. Rats scuttled freely across the intersection. Gray stone buildings surrounded them on both sides, the road abandoned, as filthy and cluttered as the streets that had led them there. They had driven close to the water, and Adelle studied the buildings, looking for landmarks, placing them somewhere near the aquarium, probably Long Wharf. That proximity to the sea could be smelled through the air oozing in from the open window to the driver's seat. Dead fish and low tide, a nauseating combination.

Through the mist, Mrs. Beevers strode toward them, head held high, eyes straight ahead. As she came closer, Adelle saw her blank expression, her mouth slightly slack, her arms limp at her sides.

"Chanters," Caid growled. "Six of them."

"Maybe Hampton can distract them," Adelle suggested in a whisper. "The carriage is big and noisy."

"I concur," Caid said. "Logically, that may give us the best possible chance to intercept Mrs. Beevers, or redirect her. Go, Hampton." He unlatched the door quietly, nudging it open with his boot. "Make them run the wild-goose chase."

Adelle smirked and glanced at him, amazed that the phrase had been around for so long. Caid mirrored her bemused expression.

"What?" He slid out the door, then held up his arms to help the ladies down. "It's Shakespeare."

"Oh, Mr. Vaughn, you can dazzle Miss Casey with your literary prowess later, for now we must be sleek and silent as the midnight alley cat. Come!" Orla jumped down before Adelle, and then she and Caid helped Adelle out, mindful of her leg.

Hampton waited until they were safely away, then cracked his whip, not bothering to conceal his approach, driving the coach directly toward the procession, veering toward the left so as to avoid hitting Mrs. Beevers head-on.

The trio navigated the slowing muck with big, clumsy steps. Orla held her gown up almost to her thighs, her petticoats and bloomers immediately stained a troubling greenish black. Caid took the lead, guiding them to the far side of the street and then around the gray warehouse. Behind them, the water could just be seen under a film of fog. It was black, completely, as if all the water in the harbor had been replaced with ink.

Somewhere in the fog, Adelle sensed the Wound lurking. Waiting. *Close.*

"Look at my hem," Orla whispered frantically. "Six inches deep in filth!"

"Sleek and silent," Caid chided her, huddling close to the stones and watching the way they had come. "Remember?"

"There is no hope," Orla sighed, regarding her skirt. "I shall have to burn it."

They heard the whip crack again in the fog, and then gunfire.

"God protect him," Orla murmured, taking their hands as they waited in the deepening gloom. "God protect my mother. God protect us all."

"You have shaken me out of myself," Severin said, and clutched Moira to his chest. They did not have long. Orla's driver would soon worry if Moira did not reappear, and to be caught en flagrant délit *would ruin any hopes Moira had of their love one day becoming proper and right in the eyes of her family. For she must have him. The words had become the drumbeat of her heart as surely as she felt his heart pound into her cheek.* I must have him! I must, I must . . .

"Before, I had my painting," said Severin. He stroked her hair, and she felt a kind of calm settle over her. "A painting . . . it can be changed at any time. A dash of color here, or another shadow. Always it can come back to life, and shift into something new." Then he drew back and studied the intricacies of Moira's face. "Our love is not a painting; it is a book. It is written, and it is immutable, the words now chosen and set. If you cut me open, it would be printed on my heart, vital and bright, written in blood."

—Moira, *chapter 9*

"Look lively, Farthings—Clacker commotion down at the wharves."

Connie glanced up from the novel nestled in her lap, watching Farai trot up to the bar while tying a strip of fabric around her hair like a headband. After she banged her fist on the bar three times, Sleepless Joe relented and poured out a drink for her.

"This is our chance," she added, addressing Missi and Geo, though loud enough for Connie to hear, as well as the small group of kids the girls had been giving a demonstration to. They were showing the older children how to properly clean a rifle.

"Our chance for what?" Geo asked, propped on a bar stool, resting her arm playfully on the top of a blond boy's head.

Connie had at first tried to nap, and when that didn't work, had decided to see how many changes she could find in the novel. So far, almost the entire first half had rearranged itself, reflecting the darker, stranger world she now found herself in. Scarier still, she had noticed new characters popping up, referred to by names such as the Outlander and the Interloper.

It's us, she thought, forcing herself not to throw the book across the room and draw attention. *It's putting us in the book.*

The second half remained untouched, which told her approximately where they were in the events of the story. She wished she could cheat and skip to the end, see how it all wrapped up, but now she knew they couldn't rely on the novel. It was a loose guide, nothing more.

The end is still unwritten. Let's hope it's a happy one.

Connie stuffed the book back into her nylon sack and pulled the bag over her shoulders. She wasn't taking any chances leaving that novel lying around.

"Our chance to figure out how the Clackers get their boat in and out," Missi answered, her face screwed up in concentration. It was a look Connie was becoming familiar with. It meant she was cooking up a plan.

"Exactly," Farai said, clapping her hands, then rubbing them together. "They are probably hauling in a shipment right now. Even if we cannot steal their navigation secrets, we can make more of their supplies *our* supplies."

"Ain't quite noon yet." Connie realized Missi was staring through the crowd around the bar at her. "What do you say, recruit?"

Connie had looked over the map provided by Farai and Geo, preparing for the journey from the chapel to Burger Buddies, and then to the seer woman's location. She would need to go east anyway to meet Adelle, so a trip over to the wharves wouldn't be far out of the way. And she would rather keep busy; otherwise, the book would suck her back in, and that thought made her shiver. She didn't even like carrying the thing around. It felt alive, like a snake coiled in her bag, ready to slither out and strangle her.

"No mistakes this time," Connie said, standing at the back. Farai and Geo shot her skeptical glances. "I promise."

Safely so. She couldn't imagine running into Adelle again randomly at the wharves, unless she, like Connie, had joined a club in the last day.

"Excellent! Jacky? Eyes up—you're with us too," Missi said, scooting off her stool and elbowing a boy tucked against the bar, whittling. Connie remembered him from the screamer attack; he had been the one to escort her, blindfolded, to the hideout.

His ruddy face lit up at being picked.

"We need someone to keep watch over the bicycles."

He deflated.

"I thought this girl was the enemy—now you bring her on every run. How is that fair?" Jack stormed over to a child and snatched the gun out of his hands.

"It is fair because I say it is," Mississippi declared with her usual tact. "Besides, this is mainly just an observationalist operation. Scouting, if you will. But that is prime Clacker country, so we take precautions."

Taking precautions meant arming themselves to the teeth. Connie even saw Jack stick a hunting knife the size of a baguette in his belt.

"You better not let us down again," Geo said, falling into stride next to Connie as they left the tunnel and headed toward the surface. Farai materialized on her other side, boxing her in. "I got to steal a carriage, so I am in a very good mood, yes? But I do not forget errors like that."

Connie glanced around for Missi's support, but she had charged way ahead with Jack, leaving Connie to the mercy of her lieutenants.

"I thought we were rid of you," Farai added, looking her up and down. "Off to see the witch woman. Change of heart?"

"I'm still going," Connie replied, keeping her eyes straight ahead from then on. "Thank you for the map. I appreciate it."

Both of them laughed, quite noticeably at her expense. They walked faster, leaving her behind. A single square of light mingled with the torches burning down in the tunnel, cast from the hatch above with the ladder that led to the church. Farai climbed up first; then Geo put one foot on the bottom rung and turned to face Connie.

"Do not thank us yet, stranger. Nobody who goes to see that woman comes back the same."

Even as the morning wore on, the sky remained the same grayish green, encasing them in what felt like a grubby aquarium. Connie followed the weaving path taken by Farai and Geo on their penny-farthing bicycles. The roads were caked in mud and sewage, dotted with small carcasses of animals that had gotten stuck in the muck, some half upright, as if prehistorically encased in amber.

Connie inched her bandanna up over her nose, using it to dampen the stench. Piles of discarded coal and refuse rose like gray dunes, mounded highest on the street corners. The buildings on either side of them were all abandoned, but grew more ominously defaced and dirty as they pushed farther toward the water. Here and there, one of the paper-and-timber effigies she had seen before veered up out of the garbage mounds, their rain- and grime-soaked streamers fluttering back and forth.

"Does anyone live out this way?" Connie asked. Burger Buddies wasn't far, but she shivered at the thought of having to go there alone, wading through garbage, bones, and manure while empty-eyed windows, black as pits, watched from above.

"Down by the water? No. Too dangerous. The wharves and warehouses took the worst of it, the madness spreading from there." Mississippi glided next to her on her bike, sticking to the same narrow path cut through the waste. "Everyone thought it was just disease at first, but then it got . . . strange. Folk disappear in a city, it happens, but not like this."

"I know this area," Connie replied softly. The quiet made her afraid to raise her voice. "It's right downtown, clean and pretty, a lot of people out and about, going to eat or going to work. It actually hurts to see it like this."

"Well, it weren't never clean here." Missi gave a dark laugh. "But it were a damn sight nicer than this. We won't linger. Some of our foraging kids have caught glimpses of a creature they can't put a name to. If it were more than glimpses, they probably would not have come back."

Up ahead, Geo whistled, coasting to a stop. They joined her and Farai, Jack wheeling up behind them.

The mist gathered in the streets, funneled low by the buildings, obscuring their view of the water. Obscuring their view of everything.

"I saw something," Geo whispered, dismounting her bicycle. She pointed straight down the road. They had just passed the Old State House, with its redbrick facade and stepped roof. "There . . . Do you see it now?"

They abandoned the bikes, and Connie wouldn't have been surprised if hers had stayed upright just from the amount of mud stuck to the wheels.

"Stay here, Jack," Missi breathed. "Face all the pennies around; we may need to leave in a hurry."

He grumbled and pinched his lips together but did as she asked, while Geo, Farai, Missi, and Connie stepped carefully into the intersection, each of them silent as they stared ahead into the fog.

"Good God, what are they doing?" Geo wandered toward the big, dark shape in the mist.

Gradually, the pale shroud drifting through the street lessened, revealing a team of black horses and a carriage. The mist rolled across them like smoke, like they were the last remains of a devastating fire. The sleek black horses and the polished carriage didn't belong there, a jewel glittering in a dung heap. Their beauty, their intensity, made the rest of the world seem all the more lifeless.

The girls moved forward together, slowly, Missi pulling the pistol from her belt. Geo struck out as the lead, arms wide, approaching the animals carefully, clucking her tongue soothingly as the horses reared and stamped. Their hooves splattered mud in every direction, their eyes bulbous and terrified behind their blinders. The left one whickered, tossing its head left and right as it strained against the harness securing it to the carriage.

Connie hung back, a tight, sour feeling in her gut. She could smell the horses' panic from fifteen feet away. But Geo eased up to them fearlessly, murmuring gently, at last reaching for the bridle on the left animal, tugging its nose close, pressing her forehead to its foam-flecked face. She stroked its glistening neck, and the horse calmed.

"I do not like this," Missi hissed, glancing around. "What the hell are they doin' here? Where is their driver?"

"Or the passengers," Connie added. The door on the right side of the carriage had been flung open and left that way. It hung off at an odd angle, bent almost in half.

"Or that. Yes. Christ. Get away from there, Geo, we have to keep moving."

"Something spooked them," Geo said, looking at them over her shoulder.

Connie gestured vaguely in every direction. "Sure. Take your pick."

Farai had moved around to the other side of the carriage, kneeling and investigating the wheels. "They fell in a hole; wheel probably lodged too deep to keep driving."

"Geo," Mississippi gasped. "Your hands."

The girl flattened her hands, palms up, both of them slick with blood. Connie froze. They had to go back. The hairs on the nape of her neck stood on end.

"Ladies?" Farai had drifted away from the carriage, into the fog, her voice muffled as she pushed ahead. "That blood does not belong to the horses."

Geo and Missi charged off to see what Farai had found, and Connie followed reluctantly. The carriage, stuck out in the middle of the road, deliberate and strange, seemed an obvious trap. They were vulnerable, distracted, and now even more so. The carriage had left a trail of bodies in its wake, leather masks and white robes turning brown from the street muck they lay in.

"Did—did the horses do this?" Geo stammered.

"I certainly hope so," Missi breathed.

Connie turned away, sickened, pressing both hands to the bandanna covering her mouth. Through the concealing mist, back down State Street, Connie saw a shape lumber across the intersection. The ground beneath them trembled with the *tha-thump-tha-thump* rhythm of footsteps.

"Missi. *Missi.*"

She tugged savagely on the girl's coat, but by the time Mississippi turned around, the silhouette was gone. Connie would remember the size of it, the sense that it was not a coach or a person, but a creature as tall and wide as an elephant, moving with an upright gait.

"Something is here. We need to g-go . . . that way, toward the water," Connie whispered. She didn't wait for a response, trying to keep her eyes up and away from the bodies littering the ground as she leaped through the squelching mud.

"Connie! Wait!"

She wasn't sure which one of them had shouted it. Connie would not wait. The alarm bells rang loud and clear in her head. Whatever it was, she was not sticking around to find out. The ground shook again, but this time with the force of an earthquake. Connie paused, trying to calculate whether it was wiser to keep going toward the water or turn back. A sea-scented, blustering wind cleared the fog in the road ahead for just an instant. She could see nothing but an emptier cobblestone thoroughfare in the desolate gully of gray stone warehouses.

It all looked so familiar, and yet drenched in darkness and despair. Squint and one could imagine the kebab houses, the bars and grills, the historic properties converted into condos and bistros and coffee joints.

But all that was yet to be, or never to be. Connie took her chances with the road before her, keeping to the center, where the carriage had swiped through the fudge-thick goop coating the ground. Beneath her feet, the city rattled almost constantly, a low-level tremor that didn't sound or feel like footsteps, but an honest-to-God quake. She moved as swiftly as she could, legs burning from the effort of walking in what felt like a blizzard's worth of snowfall, sweaty, deliberate work that made her glad for her athletic training.

She pulled the rifle down from her shoulder, not aiming it, but keeping it at the ready. Another wind carried a puff of fog away and brought a distinctive breath of the ocean, tinged with the rot of old fish. Connie left behind McKinley Square, the buildings sparser as the waterfront opened up, piers jutting out into the harbor, their ends unknowable in the mist.

Her heart raced, not just from the effort of forcing herself through the sludge, but from the shivery ground beneath her feet. The fog obscured what lay down the end of each road, and what lay behind her, surrounding her in a confusing haze. Shadows seemed larger in the mist, as if projected by an unseen machine. Most proved to be only static, leafless trees or more of the creepy effigies. Behind her, a crumbling church managed to pierce the miasma settling over the city.

Once, she had left behind her copy of *Songs Before Sunrise* in her locker and realized after soccer practice that the school had already been completely locked up. She managed to flag a janitor leaving for the day and convinced him to let her back in. Emergency, obviously. Big paper due the next day. Mr. Dean smoked a cigarette and told her not to tell anyone while she ran back to the second floor.

Only the overhead emergency lights remained on, the floors shiny with polish, the halls echoing with kenopsic emptiness. The school felt wrong, haunted-house tense, every shadow and nook darker than it should be. She noticed things she hadn't before—the high-pitched squeak of her shoes, the subtle patterns of tiled walls she'd thought were uniformly blue. And, standing at her locker, utterly alone, she felt sure something stood right behind her, watching. Maybe just her imagination, maybe just the residue of a thousand students and teachers who had come and gone through the halls.

The bang of her locker closing sounded like a gunshot, and she sprinted back outside, grateful to be free of a familiar place that had gone suddenly cold.

That feeling returned to her as she stood, teeth chattering, in the bones of a broken and bleeding city. She didn't feel powerful, not like a courageous soul facing down the apocalyptic waste of a zombie outbreak or nuclear disaster. Just small. Just terribly small and lonely, exposed, as if she too could at any moment crumble and join the bodies scattered across the block.

A scream rang out, echoing over the water. It sounded like a girl. Connie heard the others finally catch up to her, slogging across the intersection to the slope leading down to Long Wharf.

"Someone is in trouble," Connie told them, grateful that at least the heaps of garbage and human waste eased as they broke away from the streets and edged out toward the waterfront. A tall, reddish building, long and sturdy, took up the bulk of the wharf.

"We running *toward* trouble now?" Missi asked, putting a hand on Connie's shoulder, trying to stop her.

"Those Clackers are dead," Geo added. "There is no more to see. We should free those horses and return to the Congregation."

Another voice carried toward them through the fog, distorted by the water. "Orla! Orla, wait!"

"Orla?" Missi's eyes snapped open wide. "Orla Beevers? Ah, hell, I guess we are running toward trouble. I am going to regret this, I just know it."

It was Mississippi's turn to run recklessly away from the group. Connie was hot on her heels, but as the mist closed them in, she couldn't be sure if Geo and Farai had come along. It didn't matter—Missi wasn't just going with any old purpose; she had put her head down as if fighting the wind, brow furrowed, lips pale from pursing so hard.

Connie recognized the name too. Orla Beevers was Moira's best friend in the novel, one of the high-society girls who spent her time bent over sewing hoops and pianos, always at tea or a ball, ever fashionable, ever dainty. What a girl like that was doing on a dangerous, dirty wharf, Connie couldn't guess.

"Now the carriage makes sense," Missi muttered, more to herself than to Connie. "Or at least a kind of sense. I thought it looked familiar."

"You know . . ." Connie cut herself off, remembering that she had no reason to be acquainted with Orla, given the story she had told Missi. Then again, she was shocked Missi knew her, too. "Who is Orla?"

"An old friend." Missi wiped at her sweat-damp temple. "An old flame."

22

THE OLDER WOMAN'S FINGERS slipped out of her grasp for the tenth time. Adelle wouldn't stop trying, reaching out again and again, taking the cool, limp hand, a hand that felt like it already belonged to a corpse.

"Please, Mama, stop! You must stop. . . . Please! Can you hear me? You must wake up and hear us!" Orla begged her mother, voice hoarse from the sobs stopping up her throat. She walked in mirror step, her back to the sea, driven inch by inch up the wharf by her mother's persistent, steady drive to go where she was called.

"What do we do?" Adelle stumbled to a halt. They had traveled half the length of the stone walkway jutting out into the black water. No matter what they tried, Mrs. Beevers would not relent. If they stood in front of her, she simply dug her feet in and continued pushing herself against the wall of their bodies. If Caid swiveled her around, she made a sharp turn and continued toward her destination. When they pulled, Mrs. Beevers resisted, until they had to give up for fear of breaking her arms.

Caid anchored himself beside her, breathing hard, his arms out, shoulders shrugged up helplessly. Behind them, facing the water and along the back of a long, gray brick storehouse, the Wall of a Hundred Faces seethed in silent agony. She was grateful for the fog that had rolled in to mask it, shuddering at the thought of seeing it again. Orla had made her promise not to look, but Adelle couldn't help herself, then wished immediately that she had kept that promise.

Low waves sloshed softly against the pilings—no gulls cried or cargo ships blasted their horns. Out somewhere beyond the end of the wharf, the Wound throbbed in the water. Adelle couldn't see it yet, but she knew it was there, sensed it waiting there with the same dark energy as a lie. The closer they came, the more her head swam. She could still connect thoughts, but she didn't know how much longer that would last—just making a coherent sentence felt like stacking sand.

Pick . . . pick her up. Pick her up and carry her away.

It should have been obvious, but Adelle understood why none of them had tried it—there was always the chance that they might harm Mrs. Beevers or themselves. But they were running out of options.

"Help me," she said to Caid. Her voice sounded thin and wispy, as if she were speaking from inside a dream. "Help me pick her up."

She started the job without waiting for him, stooping down and sweeping her arm under the woman's black skirt, finding her right leg among the bustle and petticoats and ruffles. Caid joined in, doing far more of the work, hoisting Mrs. Beevers into the air while Orla gave a cry of alarm.

Mrs. Beevers froze, rigor mortis stiff. For a moment, Adelle was sure it had worked—if she stayed still like that, then they could carry her off and stuff her in a locked closet until they figured out how to get her to stop walking. But her relief was short-lived. Almost the instant the woman went into the air, the stones below them shook. Adelle had never been in an earthquake, but she could imagine this was just as terrifying, her legs immediately liquid, her balance shot as she lost her footing. A strangled little shout came from Caid as he fell to his knees, and Adelle rolled onto her side. Mrs. Beevers landed with eerie, catlike precision and continued down the pier, not a hitch in her step.

"What now?" Adelle propped herself on her palms, skin rasped by the rough stones beneath her.

Caid picked up his fallen spectacles and rubbed away the smudges, turning to watch Mrs. Beevers go as he put his glasses back on, chest heaving.

"What else can we try?" he asked.

"Something!" Adelle pushed through her exhaustion, through her frustration, to stand on wobbly feet. The tremors subsided, just hiccups now compared to the quake that had floored them. "Anything!"

Orla had not given up, racing alongside her mother, taking up her place again in front of her, every inch fought for, then lost, her face finally falling onto her mother's shoulder as she sobbed and tried to hug her to a standstill.

Adelle held out her hand, though Caid hardly needed it. He took it anyway, gingerly, and broke into a run with her until they caught up to Orla. Caught up to Orla and found the mists thinning, the Wound there in the blackened sea, with sunken and run-aground ships surrounding it like a crown of thorns. It was bigger even than Adelle had first thought, wide as a public swimming pool but with no bottom. The fleshy fingers fringing it waved to and fro erratically, following a rhythm she couldn't catch.

Closer. Yes, closer. Now I see you. Now I have you. This world will be mine, and all the worlds after. I am born. I am come. You will serve.

Shaking her head against the voice, Adelle tried to tear her eyes away but couldn't. It was horrible. It was mesmerizing, and Mrs. Beevers was walking right toward it.

They had left behind most of the wharf, with no more than a few yards to the end of the line. No more chances. Orla was being pushed perilously close to the edge.

"We have to stop her," Adelle murmured, her thoughts even more tangled. Sometimes when she blinked, it hurt, as if even the murky light penetrating the clouds and fog was far too much to bear, a migraine-like jolt to the senses that made her jaw ache. "Orla, I mean. . . . We can't lose her too."

Caid took her by the arm, his dark eyes glazed, perhaps a sign that he too felt the symptoms of coming so close to the Wound. Did it speak to him? Did it taunt him? Adelle tried to focus, watching Mrs. Beevers process down the pier in her all-black gown, her gait as confident and proud as a bride's.

"No!" Orla saw them approaching, throwing up her arms. "I will not go. I cannot leave her!"

The Wound churned behind them. Long tendrils like curls of paper waved beside the hydrostatic arms, though those too were pale as parchment, and appeared wrapped in it, printed with words and all, the paper like wet, loose skin slipping over muscle. Beneath the lap of the water, Adelle heard an unsettling squelching. Trembling, she peered over the hard stone edge, watching holes beneath the tentacles release ink with each pulse, turning the sea completely black.

The sucking void at the center pulled like a tornado. Orla's hair whipped out of its pins and ribbons, dancing around her tear-streaked face. She was nose to nose with her mother as they came to the end. Orla's heel slipped over the edge and she flailed, screaming.

"Orla!" Adelle cried. "Orla, wait!"

Caid said something too, but Adelle didn't hear him. She threw herself forward, leaping with both arms out, found Orla's hand, and yanked it backward. It did nothing to slow Mrs. Beevers, who almost floated for an instant as she took a placid step into the void, her body suspended before plummeting straight down into the churning black heart of the Wound.

It happened all at once, but frame by frame Adelle's elation at pulling Orla back from the brink quickly extinguished. The momentum of yanking her to safety sent Adelle flying forward in Orla's place, her toes scraping across the rough stone ground briefly before there was nothing at all beneath her.

She glanced up to see Caid and Orla scrambling to catch her, but it was too late. Shapes darkened in the fog behind them. The sickening sensation of whiplash came next. At first she thought she had slammed her head against the end of the pier like a diver miscalculating a flip, but no, she was still in the air somehow, a vise-tight arm squeezing her middle.

Kicking her feet as if she could somehow fly, Adelle stared down at her own boots, then at the black, fathomless pit at the center of the Wound. Mrs. Beevers was already gone, swallowed by the dark. Adelle ceased flailing, and once her arms went down she felt what had caught her around the middle. Frantically, she beat at it, knowing before looking what it was.

One of the slick, strong arms of the Wound had grabbed her, and then, before she could even call out, it began to crush her.

The palm reader in Salem had been right. *You disappear into darkness.*

Oh God, she thought, all the air forced out of her lungs. *It has me.*

"DELLY!"

Connie watched the monster in the water grab her best friend and hold her in the air like a prize, the rifle already coming to her shoulder.

"Careful where you aim that thing!" Missi called, leveling her own pistol. "Even if you hit it, she might fall right in!"

"I won't miss." Connie's heart jumped to her head, filling it with adrenaline and thunder. "Let me take the shot."

She wouldn't miss. She couldn't. Instinct or coincidence had led her to the wharf at that moment, and she wouldn't mess it up. Two others stood at the end of the dock, but they looked harmless enough, and they were screaming in alarm, so that had to mean they wanted Adelle back safely.

Connie shut out everything. She shut out the shock of seeing the gross, undulating monster in the water. She shut out everyone's voices. She was alone on the wharf, just her, the rifle, and the target. There had been biathlon meets with worse conditions, but never higher stakes.

Control your breathing. Find the window. Easy pull, no sudden movements. Steady arms. Steady gaze. Find the window.

The squidlike arm holding Adelle was squeezing the life out of her. She could see her friend's skin going paler, her face turning blue. When her hands fluttered loose to her sides, Connie knew there was no more time to wait, or aim, or doubt. It wasn't the shot she wanted, but it was the one she had to take. There was a small chance that Adelle would fall safely into the sea, but only if Connie timed her shot perfectly.

"Missi?" Connie murmured. Luckily, she heard.

"Yes?"

"Get ready to dive in after her."

"On your word, Rollins."

Connie just barely nodded her head, breathed out, found the pause, and fired. The first bullet struck the base of the wriggling arm, and the second followed once she could reload, but by then the arm had gone stiff and still, perfectly upright. The ground quaked again, and Connie slid forward onto her knees.

"Missi!"

"I am ready, as soon as that thing—"

But *that thing* had let go. The tremors persisted, rattling Connie's teeth, her heart no longer in her head but stopped altogether. She couldn't breathe. Adelle slid free, her body dropping like a stone into the pit. Into the monster.

Connie shrieked, her face suddenly hot with tears, and reloaded, clumsily, but reloaded all the same, slammed the rifle to her shoulder, and fired again. Missi fired too. But it was over.

Adelle was gone, and Connie couldn't breathe.

Adelle couldn't breathe. In the weightless second between the arm crushing her and the fall, she heard a familiar voice. The shapes out in the fog sharpened.

Connie.

No, Connie didn't deserve to see this. She didn't deserve to watch her friend die. But Adelle couldn't fight gravity. She felt, strangely, the other arms of the creature brush her, pawing at her as if trying to rip her away before she could disappear into the maw. But it swallowed her.

Too close. But let us see . . .

Adelle wondered if this was dying. Being ripped from her world and transported into *Moira* had been frightening, jarring, but this was so much worse. So much slower.

The harsh impact she anticipated never came. Adelle slid into total darkness, held in a cocoon of jelly. It was neither warm nor hot, but exactly the temperature of her skin. She clawed at her throat, still short of breath. Her middle felt like it had been hit with a dozen hammers, bruised and tender, and she couldn't stop shaking. Blinking, Adelle wondered if this would be it, if she would stay there, sightless and sore and suspended, forever locked in limbo.

And Connie had been right there. They'd been so close to being reunited, and for good. She could only guess what had brought Connie to the piers, but whatever the reason, Adelle tried to remain calm, even if terror raked at her throat as surely as her lack of air.

At least I got to see her one more time. At least she knows she can try to go home without me.

Calm wasn't doing it. She cried, sagging against the Jell-O prison holding her. Her mother had always tried to prepare her for death. It was part of her job, after all.

"What are you so afraid of? We all do it!" her mom would always say after dropping a particularly gruesome death factoid at dinner or at the mall or in front of any friend Adelle tried to make. Their house was filled with taxidermy, the one hobby Adelle shared with her mother—though when she'd floated the idea of becoming a taxidermist after school, Brigitte Casey had exploded.

"But you're so squeamish, and besides, you're going to Yale!" Brigitte Casey would shriek. She had been named after the famous actress Brigitte Bardot, and even resembled her a little, but in those moments of temper she seemed horribly ugly to Adelle. "Connie wants to go to Yale—thought you two were inseparable."

That always worked, bringing Connie into it, so Adelle would hang her head sheepishly and drop the taxidermy thing. And, yes, Connie did want to go to Yale, and with her brains and athletic badassery would absolutely get accepted. Adelle had never told either of them that she hadn't even downloaded the application, thought about AP courses, or brainstormed for her admissions essay.

Not that it mattered, now that she was dying.

What did her mother always say? Adelle was having trouble thinking and remembering, like the goo was leaching her mental strength away.

"Life is pleasant. Death is peaceful. It's the transition that's troublesome."

That was what her mom repeated—all the time, in fact. Isaac Asimov had actually coined it, but people misattributed it to her mom in puff magazine pieces and blogs all the time. That was how much she liked it. And whenever she did say it, Adelle became irritated. It grated on her that her mom—and Asimov—were right. People could get so twisted up worrying about how they might die, or how long they might live, that it took all the joy out of just being. That was how Adelle felt during a panic attack, like joy wasn't just far away, but on the other side of a wall, that everything in every direction was pain, and it was closing in.

But now Adelle knew how it happened, how she died. She realized, the tears slowing, that she wasn't afraid. But she did have regrets. Many of them. Maybe that was how it always went when a young person left too soon.

So much potential, so much she still wanted to do, and the only thing she had to look forward to was this neutral darkness.

Until she began to slide.

Adelle shuddered, repulsed. *Is this what being born felt like? If so, yuck.* The gooeyness around her grew slick, the bottom fell out from under her, and then she was gliding downward at a slow, even pace. She wrapped her arms around herself, afraid. She had just come to grips with her fate, and now it was changing.

She entered a different chamber, where she floated, as if gravity didn't exist in the belly of the monster. For that was where it felt like she was: an organic chamber, a stomach or pouch or whatever octopi used to digest things. *Connie would know.*

"Did you know starfish can flop their stomachs out to eat something next to their bodies?" Connie had said one day at school over cardboard pizza lunch. Adelle had just stared at her, sickened, while a sausage rolled off her slice.

"That's the grossest thing I've ever heard," Adelle had murmured.

"Isn't it awesome?" Connie had seen it happen at the zoo, invited there to partake in a weekend camp for gifted biology students.

The stomach chamber shimmered faintly with red light, like the glow radiating from a slowly dying lantern. It was immense, almost difficult to fathom—*Doctor Who* it's-bigger-on-the-inside huge.

And she wasn't alone in there.

The faraway walls of the monster lit up sometimes, brighter, as if in time with the sleepy rhythm of a heartbeat, revealing a complicated map of veins, veins as thick as roads. The first body made her gasp with surprise. Then she saw how many were there, and she covered her mouth, aghast. They floated beside her, though none of them seemed conscious. Adelle tried moving her arms, finding that she could almost swim through the atmosphere inside the stomach, avoiding bumping into the limp, silent bodies that drifted by like napping astronauts in a living space station.

She spied Mrs. Beevers not far away and grunted, pushing

against nothing, swimming closer until she could gently pull the older woman around to face her. Adelle had no idea if she was alive or dead; the humans in there seemed to be in some kind of stasis, frozen in time. Preserved.

How am I breathing? she wondered. Or maybe she wasn't. Maybe she was dead, and this was all an illusion. If so, it was most certainly the Bad Place.

The chamber lit up again, coinciding with an almost soothing, amniotic *thud-thud, thud-thud* as the heart of the monster beat on. Adelle left Mrs. Beevers behind, dog-paddling toward one of the walls, avoiding bumping into the other people as best she could. As soon as she came near, Adelle wished she hadn't. She sensed it there. Sensed its presence, sensed that it had turned its attention toward her.

This is not where I wanted you.

The voice surrounded her, shook her, existed inside her. Adelle almost choked from the force of it jolting her body. She treaded in place, watching the veins spider across the red, pulpy flesh of the chamber, saw it glow with its own white light, illuminating not just its insides but something beyond. Something outside the body.

"Where . . ." Adelle struggled to form words. She didn't know if she was speaking aloud or just thinking. "Where do you want me?"

Not here. You are no good to me here, traveler. Or should I say, Harbinger. No matter, you will serve.

"Then I'm still alive? Being inside this thing didn't kill me . . . ?"

No, Harbinger. You are not dead. Not here. I see now that you must live. You must carry and thrive.

Adelle couldn't believe she was talking to *it*. Whatever it was.

"Then why did I keep hearing your voice?" she asked. "Why did you keep telling me to come closer if not to . . . swallow me? Kill me?"

A pause. She could feel it gathering its thoughts, considering her. The stomach went dark again, and she realized that was worse. She didn't like not knowing where the other bodies were, or where she was. Then the heart thumped again, a warning like a distant drum, and light seared across the walls, across her eyes.

She saw what lay beyond and froze, then felt despair like an icy hand gripping her heart before tearing it away.

"No . . . no . . . What is that? What is this?"

Beyond the chamber walls lay a cityscape, an ancient maze of tall towers and endless spires, stairs that led to nowhere, balconies that overlooked forever, oceans that reached through the earth and joined with space. She saw only the silhouette of this city, but that was enough. And then it—*it*—moved among the towers; she had mistaken it for one of the misshapen citadels. The shape was roughly that of a man with stooped shoulders, its body draped all in a shroud of black mist, a head like a squid, dripping tentacles. A pair of great wings unfurled on its back, and Adelle felt her mind revolt as it turned to find her, sought her out with eyes the red of some hell humans could not invent or dream.

Adelle knew it was not in Boston, not even on Earth, maybe, but wherever it was, it was too close. Even if it waited at the end of the universe itself, it was too close.

The way is decided. You will go, and you will return. Yes, Harbinger, you will return. The door will open.

Adelle shook her head, but she knew it was useless. Those red, red eyes flashed a little with each word, and Adelle whimpered, her mind withering, unable to withstand its gaze. She wept, and clutched herself, and wished she could slip away like the others in the chamber.

On her next breath, she felt something cold and soft and flavorless glide down her throat. A light turned on inside her, but it offered no warmth.

You will go. You will pass through the door, Harbinger. The Dreamer's City prepares.

24

Women have many traits in common with children; that their moral sense is deficient; that they are revengeful, jealous, inclined to vengeances of a refined cruelty. In ordinary cases, these defects are neutralized by piety, maternity, want of passion, sexual coldness, by weakness and an undeveloped intelligence.

—*Cesare Lombroso, 1835–1909*

CONNIE STOOD IN THE mist, waiting. She would wait as long as she had to. Adelle had crossed the boundaries of reality itself, and now she was gone.

"I lost people the same way," Mississippi said. The others waited too, sitting solemnly halfway down the wharf. The monster—which she now knew was called the Wound—could not reach them there. "Lots of folks. My daddy, my friends, Congregation kids . . ."

Orla Beevers and Kincaid Vaughn had been briefly and quickly introduced to her. Kincaid had taken off his coat and wrapped it around Orla's trembling shoulders. It was not particularly cold, but they all felt the chill.

"I know," Connie snapped at Mississippi. "But this is different. It just is."

Missi placed a hand on her shoulder, and Connie surprised herself by not pushing it away. She was never good with grief or loss. When she'd found her first cat dead in the road when she was nine, she had refused to eat for two days, holed up in her room praying, her rosary beads indented into her palm, promising God whatever he wanted, as long as Bella came back.

Geo and Farai kept watch behind them, silent. There was no sign of Jack or the carriage driver, who Orla had fussed over in between sobbing the word *Mama*.

"I know it seems different because she was your friend, but we can all help you," Missi told her. Then she made a strangled sound and her nails bit into Connie's shoulder. "Unless . . ."

They locked eyes. Missi nodded toward the black water. "Unless she was like you," she whispered.

Connie swallowed hard, not seeing why it mattered to keep secrets. Everything was a mess. She had failed. Failure, like death, was not something she coped with. "Yes," Connie gritted out. "She was. And she was my best friend. And now . . ."

"Lord help us," Missi murmured, closing her eyes and hanging her head.

Geo wandered over, chewing her cheek. "We hurt for you, but

we cannot stay. This is Clacker central. This is their god. This is their territory. I am very sorry, but we must go."

"You can go," Connie told them, numb. "But I'm staying."

"You want to die too?" Geo sighed. "What good will that do? You want revenge? Then you help us fight this thing."

Connie shrugged. "This is how I fight. I'm not leaving."

"Do not take a tone with her right now, Geo," Missi growled. "If it was Farai in there, nobody would be pesterin' you to leave!"

"And what about the Congregation?"

"Oh . . . just . . . just shove the Congregation in a sack and roll it down a hill, would you? She is trying to *grieve*. Let it be, Geo."

"You are not in your right mind, so I will forget you said that." Geo turned and joined Farai again. They fell into whispered conversation, but Connie didn't care what they said about her. She would stay until nightfall, or maybe even until the next morning, and then she would follow the map to the old witch woman's place, get her incense, and go home. At least she could give Adelle's parents an explanation. At least she could do that much.

Kincaid had just helped Orla to her feet, shivery under his tan coat, when the wharf shook again, this time hard enough to send a splintering crack across the middle.

"Not again!" Mississippi shouted, grabbing Connie. They held each other upright as the tremor redoubled; Orla screamed as she fell back down to her knees. Waves that had been gently undulating against the wharf grew temperamental, crashing against the stone hard enough to send up a spray.

Connie squinted into the cascading black water, the waves

arcing over the pier, wave after wave cresting from the quaking, splashing down and leaving behind a foamy carpet. After a particularly violent set of waves fell and cleared away, Connie noticed a lump at the end of the wharf. It moved. Shivered. It was a body.

The earthquake eased and the water receded, returning to the placid sloshing of a moment before. Connie raced down the wharf, arms pumping as she sprinted to the bundle of body and slid down beside it.

Blond hair. Shorter than it should be, but blond all the same. Sodden black dress and Goth Victorian boots. She rolled the person over, disbelief and shock making her clumsy. But it was her. It was real. Adelle had come back, alive, taking tiny, shallow breaths as she lay splayed against the ground.

"Are you hurt?" Connie wiped the inky beads of water from her friend's face. "Adelle? Can you hear me? Please be okay. . . ."

The others pounded down the wharf to join them.

"Holy Mother," Geo whispered, crossing herself. "It is a miracle. Nobody has ever returned. Nobody."

Adelle coughed, a spasm gripping her body as she lurched as if doing a crunch, her legs flailing out in front of her. Connie supported her head, drawing her upper torso onto her lap, sticking a finger into her mouth and trying to clear out any extra water or foam.

"I'm . . . I can breathe," Adelle wheezed, coughing again. "And your hand tastes terrible."

"Oh God, oh God, you're here. You're here." Connie pulled her into a suffocating hug, then remembered Adelle had been picked up by a giant tentacle arm and shot at and dropped into a pit, and she eased her grip.

"Please," Adelle murmured, racked by another shudder. "Just can we please go away from it."

Connie crouched, bearing most of Adelle's weight while helping her carefully to stand. Before she could say another word, Kincaid Vaughn was there, wiping black water from his spectacles and holding out his hands.

"Let me help her," he said softly. Connie stared up at him, at his faint smile, and then at his shirt. He had given his jacket to Orla without prompting, noticing she was cold. But she felt like Adelle was too precious a package to risk with just anybody. Now that she had her back, Connie wasn't letting go.

"You can trust him," Orla told her.

"It's all right," Adelle rasped, touching her forehead to Connie's cheek. "He's carried me before."

When she was safely in the boy's arms and they were halfway down the pier, Connie vented a relieved laugh, gazing up with tear-glazed eyes at her friend. "He carried you before? That's a story I need to hear."

"How did you do it?" Orla stutter-stepped to a stop, clutching the coat around her shoulders. "I . . . I think I should stay. What if my mother returns too?"

"Stop, Caid," Adelle told him. They turned, and Connie could tell Adelle was struggling with something. Her face looked drawn, even for a half-drowned person. "I don't think she's coming back,

Orla. When I was in there . . . I was awake. I could see everything, all the people who went into the Wound."

Orla's eyes widened with hope.

"But they were all asleep, I think, or . . . or gone. I couldn't wake them up. I saw your mother and . . . and I couldn't wake her up either. I'm sorry. I'm so sorry, Orla. I wish I could've brought her back with me. I don't know why it let me go, but it did. It just let me go."

Orla's lower lip quivered, and she cursed. "Then why did you not save her?"

She whirled and ran back down the wharf, only making it a few steps before she collapsed into sobs.

"Let me handle her." Mississippi tipped the hat back off her head, frowning. "Get your friend someplace warm."

"My workshop is not far from here," Kincaid suggested. "Just north and west a short distance, near the Old North Church."

Connie knew the place; it was the oldest church in Boston and hard to miss. That wasn't a bad walk, and definitely closer than the Congregation hideout. She glanced at Geo and Farai, who didn't offer any other solutions.

Mississippi, unsurprisingly, made the final call. "Good. Take them there, get something fortifying in their bellies. You feel all right going with Vaughn?"

Connie nodded. "I just need to stay with Adelle."

"Fine. That's fine." Missi blew out a whistling breath. "What. A. Day. After I get all this sorted with Orla, I can send her your way. I doubt she wants to go back to an empty house. Too many ugly memories."

"She is certainly welcome," Kincaid said, curiously formal.

Connie couldn't believe he was the same nerdy, pompous Kincaid Vaughn from the novel. From page one he'd seemed constructed to be the obviously bummer choice compared to Severin, but now she saw only a soft-spoken gentleman with charmingly crooked glasses and a knack for chivalry. She didn't remember him being Black in the book, but then he was hardly even in it. Adelle's stepfather had always railed against *Moira* for being anachronistic, but then the whole world of *Moira* wasn't what Connie had expected. Maybe the universe of *Moira* was more expansive and more inclusive than what the author intended. Maybe it had taken on a life of its own.

"You two get back to the Congregation; see if you can't rustle up Jack on the way. He is not the type to wander off."

Geo and Farai seemed only too relieved to be dismissed, and hurried away from the wharf. Not that Connie could blame them—she couldn't wait to get somewhere, anywhere else. Mississippi strode back toward Orla, leaving without so much as a goodbye.

Connie decided not to examine why that made her chest tighten up.

The walk to Kincaid Vaughn's workshop took just over twenty minutes. With empty streets and no sign of Clackers or monsters, Connie arrived at the four-story yellow-brick warehouse knowing she had walked less than a mile, but feeling like she had run twenty.

"I can make it the rest of the way," Adelle assured them when they reached the door.

"Are you certain, Miss Casey?"

Kincaid took an old-fashioned key from his pocket to unlock the door, but it was already open. That didn't seem to alarm him, so Connie ignored it.

"Yes, I should stretch my legs a little," Adelle replied. "My neck is sore, but that thing didn't kill me. I don't know why, but it didn't kill me."

She was deposited lightly on the floor, and steadied herself on Kincaid's arm before taking a few steps into the airy front room of the warehouse. It was cool and well-lit, with plenty of windows and a skylight high above. They turned down the first hallway to the right, Kincaid leading them to a locked door on the far side of the corridor. This one did require a key.

"Welcome," he said, stepping back and holding open the door. "It . . . well, it is not luxury and splendor, but I find it comfortable enough."

Adelle hobbled to safety, Connie instantly beside her, holding her arm for support. They both paused just inside, knocked dumb and silent by the mad-scientist intricacy of it all. It was like walking inside Kincaid Vaughn's mind: every taste, every interest, every passion put clearly on display.

The lofted space allowed for a bevy of windows along the wall facing the door. To the left, a narrow staircase that looked like it could be folded up led to a balcony overlooking the workspace. Directly ahead, two patched and scratched leather couches sat facing each other on a patterned rug. A traveling trunk had been repurposed as a table between them. To the right, Kincaid had constructed an indoor garden, almost a miniature greenhouse, with rows of plants clustered together on three long tables. Beyond the couches, Connie saw a telescope, a drafting table laden with charts and maps and, under the windows, an expansive library, though he clearly had a mind toward even further growth. The poor bookshelves were filled to overflowing, books stacked in tidy piles when the shelves proved impossible. Beside that was another table, this one stocked with cutting tools, scraps of fabric and leather, and piles of pristine paper.

There was more, of course, crammed into every corner and yet somehow eccentrically cluttered without being dirty—an eviscerated clock with all its innards pulled out, mid-fix, and sketchbooks, and under the balcony, next to a basin and woodstove, a number of wonderful dusty hutches.

Connie's fingers itched to explore, like she had just stumbled upon the greatest flea market in history. But Adelle came first. Relieved to just be dry and warm, Connie helped Adelle to one of the leather couches. Meanwhile, Kincaid disappeared up the narrow stairs and onto the balcony, then returned with a thick patchwork blanket, implying that whatever was up there might be some kind of sleeping area.

"This is amazing," Adelle murmured, gazing around even as Kincaid handed Connie the blanket, which was subsequently tucked around the girl's legs.

"No, Miss Casey, *you* are amazing," Kincaid replied. He stood beside the trunk table, hands loosely in his pockets. "How *did* you return?"

A weary look passed across Adelle's face, but she rallied, picking lightly at her fingernails as she studied everything but his face. "I have no idea."

Lying. Adelle was terrible at it. Connie glanced at Kincaid, but he only shifted.

"Forgive my rudeness, but you told Miss Beevers that you could see the inside of the Wound. What was it like?"

That same weariness returned, Adelle opening and closing her mouth a few times. Kincaid rubbed at his brow and strode off toward the woodstove beneath the balcony.

"What a host I am! Interrogating you without first offering tea. . . ."

Connie settled in on the same couch, sitting on the edge of the cushions, against Adelle's bent knees. "You don't have to tell him anything you don't want to."

"I won't," Adelle whispered back, keeping her eyes peeled for his return. They were out of earshot, but only just. "I can't tell him everything. When we're alone, I'll . . . Oh, Connie. I don't even know how to describe it."

She saw the clench in Adelle's jaw that came like the rumble before lightning. Trying not to cry, she found Adelle's hand and just held it.

"We're together now," Connie said. "And when you're feeling up to it, we can bounce out of here. I have a plan. We can get all the same ingredients Straven used for the magic that got us here and re-create the ritual to get home."

Connie grabbed her bag and pulled out the wrinkled, stained map she had been given, showing it to Adelle.

"This woman? She has all kinds of witchy stuff. Missi's friends think she'll have incense. I grabbed a cup and a candle, and we can scoop up a rock anywhere."

Adelle smiled, wiping weakly at her wet, splotchy cheeks. "You managed all this, and all I did was fall in a hole and get my hair chopped off by a nutcase."

God, it was good to have her back. Someone familiar and grounding in the midst of all the strange, dangerous things they had survived. Connie hadn't even let herself imagine what it would be like to try to get home alone. Behind them, the kettle whistled.

Connie folded up the map and tucked it away. "What's the story with that? It looks, um . . ."

"It's fine," Adelle groaned. "You can say it."

"Not the best look on you," Connie chuckled, and she was glad when Adelle dissolved into giggles too. "It's some Prince Valiant realness."

"Mrs. Beevers did her best to salvage it. Moira attacked me with scissors in my sleep because I dared whisper Severin's name. I was dreaming! It's not like I meant to. . . ."

Connie just tried to keep up. They had each had some wild adventures apart, but now it was time to go home, alive and well, and reminisce about their Victorian misadventure while decompressing at Burger Buddies or passing notes in study hall. Eventually they would need to decide on an Official Story for families and cops, but just then, getting home was all that mattered.

"Mrs. Beevers . . ." Adelle's face fell. "I saw her in there. Ugh, Connie. It was awful. The things I saw . . . I don't know why it let me go. Why me? Why not anyone else?"

She couldn't finish. Gently, Connie dropped her chin on Adelle's knee. "Take your time. You can rest first. Soon this will all be over, and we can go home."

"Mm." Adelle looked away, staring back toward the woodstove.

Kincaid had returned, carrying a silver tray with three delicate china cups and a steaming pot of tea.

"Earl Grey." Adelle closed her eyes dreamily. "My favorite."

"Mine too," Kincaid said, placing little metal baskets over the cups and then pouring the hot water over them. "I would ask about cream or sugar, but—"

"It's lucky you even have tea." Adelle cut him off. She lifted the cup to her chest and let the steam rise for a while, inhaling it. "How do you get the water?"

Kincaid settled on the couch across from them, his height and size making the sofa look comically small. Even so, he held the pretty cup with ease, a man born into the life of social graces and standards. "I collect rainwater. Even that is not fit for drinking, but I found a way to purify it, using a modified version of Charles Wilson's ingenious system. Did you know, his invention provided fresh water to an entire mining town in Chile? Absolutely brilliant . . ." He trailed off, seeming to hide behind his teacup. "Here I am blathering on about Wilson while Miss Casey has seen the inside of the Wound and lived to tell of it. I am practically the John Franklin to your Joseph Bellot!"

Adelle forced out a polite laugh, but not one good enough to fool Kincaid or make him think she at all understood the reference.

It flew completely over Connie's head, but his obvious zest for dunking on John Franklin made her wish she could whip out her phone to google it.

"You see, Franklin was an absolutely dreadful explorer, just shocking, really, and . . . Well. The point is that Miss Casey should have the floor."

Connie had never seen someone trip over their words with such flourish. She couldn't help but think he was flirting with Adelle, especially the way he kept glancing at her whenever he thought she wasn't going to notice.

Or maybe it was simply nervous energy, considering Adelle was now the local miracle and celebrity. Maybe the novel could be retitled *Adelle*. The novel. Connie's heart sank to her butt. She would have to show Adelle what was happening to their copy of *Moira*. After today, Connie couldn't even imagine what would shift and rearrange.

"It was . . . very dark at first."

Connie could hear Adelle choosing her words carefully, but Kincaid leaned in, riveted, tea steam fogging his spectacles. Admittedly, she was also eager to hear about what Adelle had seen. It didn't even seem real. She had gone into the Wound, disappeared for at least ten minutes. Any normal person would have drowned.

"But then I started to see bodies all around me, just floating there," Adelle continued, lowering her cup and resting it on her stomach. Her eyes fixed on a point over Connie's shoulder, glazed, or maybe unfocused, one blue and one green, misty with memory. "It was this giant chamber—I kept thinking I was inside a stomach or something. And I could think and breathe somehow, and swim around. But I couldn't make the other people wake up. It's like they were just . . . frozen."

"But not dead?" Kincaid asked quietly. Connie heard the note of hope in his voice, remembering the rearranged first passage of the novel—in this demented version, Kincaid Vaughn had lost his entire family to the Wound.

"I don't know, honestly." Adelle twisted, staring at him. "I tried to rouse Mrs. Beevers, but she wouldn't respond."

"You called it a stomach," he said, scratching thoughtfully at his chin. Connie could tell the moment he clicked into analytic, science mode. "Implying that these bodies would be food." He struggled with the word, for good reason. "But they were intact? No sign of degradation at all?"

Adelle shook her head. "They were fine. It's not like they had been, um, you know, digested or eaten away or anything. They even had their clothes on."

"Fascinating," Caid breathed, forgetting all about his tea. "Baffling."

"I . . . don't remember anything after that," she said. Connie had known Adelle long enough to sense there was more, a lot more. Adelle was leaving something out—to protect them, she wondered, or herself? Connie rubbed her knee soothingly; whatever the truth might be, Adelle had suffered a serious freaking ordeal. "The next thing I knew, I was on the wharf, and all of you were there shaking me."

Kincaid nodded along, buying the story that Connie sensed was riddled with holes. "And how did you feel, Miss Casey? Afraid? Confused?"

"Sad, at first," she said, sniffling loudly. At once, Kincaid produced a handkerchief and offered it. Adelle smiled and took it, wiping under her nose. "I thought I was going to die, and I panicked. But then I felt calm, because I wasn't in any pain, and my mom, well, she helps people deal with death. That's her . . ."

Adelle's eyes flared just the tiniest bit in alarm, and Connie suppressed a grin. Victorians were morbid, she remembered that much from history class, but even they might balk at the concept of a death doula.

"She's an undertaker," Adelle blurted, glancing at Connie.

Close enough, she mouthed back.

"An unusual role for a woman, to be sure," Kincaid replied. "But our strange times require us to stretch beyond the confinements of what society deems polite and proper. Go on."

Connie had to hand it to him—he was nerdy enough to give her and Adelle a run for their money.

"So I just tried to stay calm," Adelle picked up. "I told myself: If this is death, at least you're not in pain. And Constance saw it happen, so she won't wonder what happened. That will make it easier to . . ." She bit her lower lip, inhaling shakily. "To move on."

Just a knee rub wouldn't do. Connie reached for Adelle's hand and held it tight, hoping she could feel all the relief and fear and tumult tearing her up inside. They had narrowly avoided catastrophe, and Connie told herself not to go back to those ten minutes when she thought Adelle was really gone forever. So many thoughts had attacked at once. How would she ever tell Adelle's parents? How was any of it fair? How had she bungled that shot? How, how, how?

"She's like a sister to me," Adelle explained.

"Indeed, your bond is palpable to even a casual observer. You are fortunate to have found a friendship such as this."

Connie smirked, Kincaid winning her over a bit more every minute. *Where was this dorky, wholesome, too-pure-for-the-world boy in the book?* Or maybe he had always been there, just tucked away or forgotten. It was hard to know anything for sure anymore, and now even the novel that had created him was not reliable.

"When I was in the stomach thing, I felt afraid again, and then confused, obviously. I didn't know why I wasn't asleep like the others. Honestly? I thought maybe I really had died, and this was the afterlife, and it was just being alone forever, with people all around but no one to talk to." Adelle finished her story, sipping her tea and cleaning her face with the handkerchief.

"You have given me much to think about." Kincaid stood, clacking his teacup back down on its saucer and gazing toward the drafting table closer to the windows. "I need . . . time. Time to consider all you have said. You should rest, Miss Casey, Miss Rollins. There will be time to interrogate these mysteries when you are refreshed."

Adelle nodded, trying and failing to hide a massive yawn. She finished her tea and leaned across to place it back on the tray.

"I got it." Connie intercepted her, grabbing the cup and placing her own on the table, then turning and fluffing the blanket, making sure Adelle was snug while she shimmied down under the covers.

"Thank you," she said. "Will you stay next to me?"

Kincaid had gone back to the stove and the basin. She heard him rummaging; then Connie spied him stopping over in his cozy library before returning with a stack of books, *Gulliver's Travels*, *Vanity Fair*, *Middlemarch*, and *The Tenant of Wildfell Hall* among them. Connie picked out the only one in the pile she hadn't read: *Vanity Fair*.

"For your watch, sentinel," Kincaid told her with a bow.

Connie almost didn't want to touch the books, they were so beautifully bound and printed. Such treasures would be worth thousands in the real world. "These are incredible."

"I saved as many as I could from the local churches and universities. When the chaos began, there were looters everywhere. These books may not belong to me, but I like to think they are happy in their new home." Kincaid handed Adelle a small vial he had been keeping in his pocket, first uncorking it for her. "Before you sleep," he told her gently. "It's a tincture of clove and oak apple; it keeps the sleeper from dreaming."

Adelle took it with tremulous hands, wincing at the smell.

"Clove?" Connie asked. "That sounds like the tea the Penny-Farthings made me drink."

Kincaid collected the vial after Adelle had tossed back the medicine. "I would assume they employ a similar principle—they brew the ingredients for efficacy; I distill them. I tend to prefer this method, done quicker, as the taste is rather unpleasant."

"After everything I've seen," Adelle said sleepily, "I'd rather not dream."

After he had discreetly and attentively checked that the blanket covered Adelle's feet, he stuffed his hands in his pockets and marched with feverish excitement back to his drafting table. By his standards it was probably a slip of propriety, but Connie found it sweet.

By the time he got there, Adelle was having trouble keeping her eyes open. Connie sat on the carpet, back pressed to the sofa where Adelle lay, reverently resting *Vanity Fair* on her knees, mindful of every thumbprint and crease she might leave on the priceless book.

Adelle leaned over and sneaked in a one-armed hug.

"He likes you, by the way," Connie murmured.

"I don't know. I'm probably just a science experiment to him."

"Nah. He likes you, and he's superhot. His *library* is superhot."

She heard her friend chuckle and roll onto her back, the leather creaking under her. "So why aren't you interested?"

Connie's jaw hung open for a moment. How to answer? Adelle didn't know about her attraction to other girls, and this didn't seem like the time for a frank and honest conversation, not when she could hear Adelle yawning almost constantly. It also didn't seem like the time to examine the spike of jealousy that had lanced through her, crackling and undeniable, when Missi volunteered to stay behind with her "old flame."

She couldn't imagine Mississippi McClaren with Orla Beevers, the shrinking violet, but then Connie didn't feel fit to judge. And anyway, it was none of her business. And *anyway* anyway, none of these people were real, just constructs.

That didn't change the fact that she had felt a certain type of way when Missi hadn't come with them. Or when the sharpshooter had quite obviously been wearing makeup to impress her when she showed her the hot air balloon. . . . It also didn't change the fact that she missed that crazy redhead, with her temper and her swearing and her ridiculous fringe. Then it dawned on her that Missi and Orla might never turn up at Caid's, and that if she and Adelle managed to find the incense, she would never see Mississippi again. That hurt. It hurt a lot more than she expected.

Connie massaged the back of her neck, feeling a headache coming on.

"I . . . think there might be someone else," Connie finally said. "I don't know. It's complicated. My head is all twisted up. I'm sure you know what that's . . ." She swiveled to look at Adelle, who had fallen fast asleep. Turning back to her book, Connie shrugged.

"Another time," she murmured, or—if Missi didn't return— never.

Are not there little chapters in everybody's life, that seem to be nothing, and yet affect all the rest of the history?
—Vanity Fair, *William Makepeace Thackeray*

"Where is she? Where is Miss Casey? I demand to know!"

Adelle sprang awake, asleep and crumpled and then instantly upright, shot out of her dreamless slumber like a haunted-house dummy being catapulted out of a coffin, and with the same effect. Severin's arms windmilled as he saw her come flying out of the blanket, his hair and clothes rumpled, paint daubs absentmindedly decorating his cheeks and hands.

"Declare yourself before frightening our patient half to death, man." Kincaid appeared behind her. From the rows of plants near the door, Connie emerged, rifle at her side.

"I did not mean to startle you, Miss Casey; my concern got the better of my sense." Severin closed the door behind him, attempted to center his cravat, and bowed. *"Je suis désolé."*

Connie stormed over to the couches, placing herself between Adelle and Severin. Adelle watched her friend absorb who she was staring down, and wondered if Connie saw what she did. Severin wasn't one of Connie's favorites, though she'd never exactly articulated why. Even if this was a reunion of sorts, their interaction in the kitchens of Moira's house had been brief and tense.

"How did you hear about our patient?" Connie demanded.

"I would also like to know that," Caid added. He hadn't moved from his rather protective position behind her.

Severin peered around Connie's shoulder, provoking her to scoot a few inches to the right, blocking him again.

"The whole town is talking of it," Severin stated. "The girl who came back from the Wound! Is it true? Did you really go inside and return?"

"It's true." Connie wouldn't budge. "And she's been recuperating ever since."

"How long have I been asleep?" Adelle asked. She pushed the blanket down her legs and tried to stand, finding that she felt much better.

"Almost three hours," Caid informed her.

"Are we not friends? May I not see you?" asked Severin.

In response, Caid walked around Adelle, strode up to and beyond Connie, and glared down at Severin with his spectacles slipping down his nose, his jaw set. He looked like he wanted to projectile vomit, possibly all over Severin.

"We share this building, Severin, with the understanding that we respect one another's privacy and solitude."

Connie retreated to the couch, joining Adelle, slipping her arm through Adelle's as if anchoring her there and away from Severin. It all felt ridiculous; Adelle was recovering and fine, at least physically. She didn't know if or when her mind would recover from what she had seen.

"You see, Miss Casey, I am his neighbor. His *friendly* neighbor. I only came to inquire after your health. There was such a commotion, and then I heard your voices! A welcome surprise, to be sure, but it distracted me completely! I could not at all concentrate on my art knowing you had suffered such an ordeal."

"We would never dream of keeping you from your art," Caid replied.

Adelle did not miss the slight sarcastic emphasis Caid placed on *art*—or the general edge to his tone.

"We should go," Connie whispered. "While they're at each other's throats. Are you okay to walk?"

"How far is this woman's shop?" Adelle asked. Frankly, Caid's sanctuary was so welcoming, so precisely her type of place, that she dreaded leaving it. She knew that the second she left, she would miss it.

"Not far," Connie said. "Just north of here, out by the surplus shop and that baseball diamond, right on the water."

"All right. I'll follow your lead."

The boys continued bickering while Connie escorted Adelle toward the door. Severin and Kincaid fell silent as they noticed the girls maneuvering around, ignoring them completely as they opened up the door and stepped out into the hallway.

"Miss Casey needs some air," Connie told them lightly. "We won't go far."

"Let me join you, I insist." Severin bowed again, tousling his fall of curly black hair. "Even this neighborhood can be dangerous."

"I can manage," Connie assured him, tapping the rifle over her shoulder.

"But, ladies—"

"I said I can manage." She turned a politer smile to Caid before saying, "Thank you for the hospitality. Will you be here when we return?"

Caid leaned against the door, his brow furrowed with concern, yet he didn't fight Connie on her decision to guard Adelle alone. "Of course. I will leave the warehouse door open for you. Miss Casey, if you are not too tired, perhaps later you would be willing to answer more questions for me."

"I can do that," Adelle said, not knowing who to look at. They were both regarding her so intensely.

"Ah! So you will answer his questions but not mine." Severin pouted, crossing his arms over his paint-stained shirt. "How unjust—you have broken my heart."

Adelle could feel Connie rolling her eyes without seeing it. "I will be happy to tell you all about what happened when we get back."

At that, Severin brightened, sweeping up her free hand and dropping a kiss on the back of it.

"Mademoiselle Mystère, you will have my undying appreciation if you do. The name is even more fitting now—wouldn't you agree?"

Connie had clearly had enough, and jerked Adelle down the hallway and away from the two boys. Hurrying to keep up, Adelle found that her leg at last felt perfectly fine, still tender if touched directly on the bruise, but not sore enough to make her limp. Her midsection was another story, throbbing still from the force of the Wound's tentacle crushing her. If she lifted her dress, she knew she would be black-and-blue.

"You don't have to be so rude to him."

Outside, a light rain had begun to fall. They pushed into the drizzle, the afternoon sky as dark as if it were already dusk.

"He's annoying," Connie muttered, marching along at a quick clip. "And he punched me. Weak-ass punch, but still. Don't you dare get an *actual* crush on him."

Adelle yanked her arm out of Connie's grasp, wanting to walk all on her own. "What is that supposed to mean?"

"You know what it means. I know he's your number one book boyfriend, Adelle; I saw the way you were looking at him in that kitchen. And I'm not blaming you! I'm sure if I had run smack into Moira the second I got here, I'd be smitten or something." She pulled the map out of her backpack, one hand on that, the other securely on her rifle. Her eyes swept the way forward and behind as they turned left out of the warehouse.

"No, you wouldn't!" Adelle cried. "She's horrible. Just . . . the absolute worst—you would hate her! She's vain and selfish and cruel. Look what she did to my hair! You said it yourself, I look like Prince Valiant's ugly little brother."

Connie grumbled and shook her head.

"Wait a minute. Why would you have a crush on Moira, anyway?"

"It was just an example," Connie grunted.

"Fine, well, for another example, I don't have a crush on anyone!" Adelle wasn't sure that was totally true, but if she did, it wasn't meaningful enough to keep her from knowing what was important, not anymore. Not after . . . "How could I? All I want to do is rip my brain out and get a new one. You don't know what I saw, Connie!" She slowed down, nearly falling to her knees on the damp cobblestones at the memory of the creature, its wings spread. . . . "Oh God, what I've seen . . ."

"Jesus, I'm sorry. I'm the jerk." Connie pulled her into a hug, keeping her from falling down.

"No, I'm the jerk!" Adelle embraced her in return, grateful to end the fight. "And I'm sorry. When I saw you in the larder I should've dropped everything and gone with you, but your friend had a gun and I didn't know what to do. Everything is so twisted up; none of it makes any sense. This isn't even the right book! It's not a romance—it's a nightmare."

Connie pulled back, tugging her by the sleeve into the alcove of a random building, away from the rain. She took out her bag again, brought out their copy of *Moira*, opened it to the first page, and handed it to Adelle.

"Look at it," Connie said. "Read it."

Adelle scanned the lines, her lips parting on a gasp as she found them unrecognizable. The cover, the font, the whole look of the book remained the same, but the text was completely different.

"Is the whole thing like this?" She leafed through swiftly.

"No, just to where we've gotten in the story," Connie said. "The back half is still the same—waiting, I guess, for us to determine how it's written."

"How can this be happening? How can any of it be happening?"

"I don't know." Connie leaned back against the shuttered door of the alcove, coal dust puffing around her as she did. "What did you see, Adelle? What really happened in that thing? Does any of it make this make sense?"

Adelle slicked the wet hair back from her forehead. "Most of what I told you and Caid was true."

"So he's 'Caid' now?"

"Shut up." Adelle nudged her, but Connie was smirking, and nudged her back. "I fell into some kind of goop chute; it was disgusting, but then it got much worse. It pushed me into this huge chamber, so big it could hold all the people missing from the city."

"Jesus, that's bleak."

"They were all just . . . floating there, not dead, but not alive, either." Adelle hugged herself, all of it coming back to her, every detail branded into her brain. "For some reason I wasn't like them, maybe because I didn't sleepwalk into the Wound like Orla's mother did. I was awake."

"Sure, I mean, who would do it voluntarily?" Connie asked.

"I tried to wake up Mrs. Beevers, but nothing happened. . . ." Adelle steeled herself, already trembling before the words came out. She didn't want to think about that thing speaking to her, its voice so loud it felt like it might shake her bones apart. "Then I swam to the wall. It felt like being inside a huge heart; I could hear and feel the pulse. It would light up the whole chamber. Then I tried to talk to it, and it answered me back. I saw . . . I saw something behind the wall, a city somewhere, and a giant monster walking through it."

Connie stared, wide-eyed and unblinking.

"It didn't want me in the chamber. It probably wants me dead— that's why it let me go. This thing . . . it has a plan. It wants something." She could no longer distinguish truth from deception. Even trying to speak about what she had experienced inside the Wound made her want to vomit. The words were sticky, the truth even stickier. "Whatever it wants, whatever this plan is, Connie, I think we're part of it."

They had reached the large X on the map, leaving behind what Geo had helpfully labeled CLACKER MIERDA—BEWARE, but Connie didn't see any shops or houses, just an overgrown field that gradually grew sandy and rocky, turning from grass to sea. A barrier of fog as impenetrable and seemingly solid as any wall hemmed in the northern border of downtown. It was no wonder ships wrecked immediately—nobody could navigate waters like that.

"I don't get it." Connie checked the map again. "Did she lie?"

"Look," Adelle murmured. She pointed ahead, toward the end

of the field where the land met the fog barrier. "There's something in the water."

"I can go look first. You've had enough of weird crap in the water."

"No, it's all right." Adelle took a few gradual steps forward and into the tall grass, her skirt brushing it softly. "It looks like a boat."

Connie squinted, finding that she was right—an old steamboat ferry had washed up on the shore, its nose jutting up above the rocks, just visible in the mist. They set off across the field together, picking up their step to avoid the prickly, damp grass.

"Ow!" Adelle stumbled, holding her toe. She bent down and picked up something tarnished and metal, vaguely shaped like a rabbit. A brass rabbit. "What the . . . Is this a paperweight?"

"They're everywhere." They littered the field like mines. Connie scooped up a larger one shaped like a lion. She noticed other odd things hiding in the grass too: fountain-pen nibs—hundreds of them—distributed among the weeds like gold and silver seeds.

"Watch your step," Connie warned. "And keep your eyes open. The Penny-Farthing girls are pretty tough, and even they're afraid of this woman."

"Well, she definitely has eclectic taste in lawn ornaments."

"Guess they haven't invented the flamingo thing yet," Connie snorted.

Adelle brought the brass rabbit with them as they picked their way across the trash-riddled field, occasionally *oofing* when they didn't see a paperweight and stubbed a toe.

"Just think," Connie said as the steamship loomed larger ahead of them, a makeshift door cut into the hull. "If she has incense, then we could be back home in our own beds before nightfall."

Adelle frowned. "How will we buy it? We don't have any money."

"Barter, I guess. She can have my phone, for all I care."

"I don't have much to offer," Adelle added.

She sounded forlorn, tentative. Connie kept glancing over at her, worried. It shouldn't have been a surprise that Adelle didn't seem like her usual bubbly self. Falling into the Wound had changed her. Really changed her. Still, Connie couldn't help but think Adelle wasn't all in on their plan. She ought to sound more excited about going home.

"You feeling all right? I mean, given everything? You okay?"

Adelle puffed out her cheeks, eyes forward as she lifted up her skirt to walk more freely. The rain had eased, leaving them in the chilly remainder that followed. "You know how at the end of *Lord of the Rings*, when Frodo doesn't stay in the Shire? How he goes to the Grey Havens?"

"Yeah." Of course she knew; she had read and reread the series, and watched the films countless times. Knowing it like she did, her concern deepened.

"I never got that," Adelle murmured, leftover rain shimmering on her pink cheeks. "Like, why doesn't he want to be with his friends? He's been through so much—wouldn't he want to just veg out at home and smoke his pipe?"

Connie didn't answer.

"But I get it now. I feel strange. Wrong, somehow. Like I saw something I shouldn't have. Like I'm someone I shouldn't be.

Peeked behind the curtain, you know? If there was something like the Grey Havens, I'd like to go there."

"You don't mean that," Connie told her. "You're just upset."

"No, I do mean it." Adelle reached over and touched her friend's shoulder reassuringly. "Don't worry, okay? I'm still coming home with you. That hasn't changed. In fact, I want to get back more than ever. Not sure how that's possible—what's more than desperate wanting? Are there words for it?"

"Good, because I'll drag you out of here if I have to. Hey."

Adelle laughed, and stopped, facing her as the prow of the ship cast them both in shadow.

"I'm sorry about all this," Adelle murmured. "This is my fault."

"I agreed to do it," Connie said. "Neither of us would've told Straven to do it if we'd really thought it would happen."

Adelle blanched. "Yeah, you're right."

"You're a bad liar, Delly."

"I'm sorry, I just . . . I didn't think it would be like this. Even if the magic worked, I didn't expect this."

"Nobody could," Connie sighed. "I forgive you, even if I wanted to throttle you for a while there."

"That's fair," she simply replied. "Let's get inside—those clouds look ready to open up again."

The hole cut into the hull showed nothing beyond, no hint of what awaited them inside. Cans and bells had been hung over the door, alerting the woman to anyone who tried to trespass. Connie didn't try to be quiet, preferring to announce their presence, not skulk around like burglars.

"Hello?" Connie called as the cans and bells jingle-jangled around her. "Is anyone there?"

Nothing beyond the outer appearance of the boat would make one think they had stepped inside a steamship. The shadowy innards had been filled, floor to ceiling, with trinkets and salvage. The woman had an apparent obsession with mirrors: looking glasses of every size and shape leaned against the curved wooden interior. The occasional porthole let in light, just enough to see by, to make the heavy dust visible on the air.

The seer had mounted tattered curtains everywhere, creating a maze of draped fabric. A half-mad, half-impressive chandelier made of spoons, broken bits of glass, and mirror shards spun slowly above a sloped table laid with chipped porcelain dishes; lumps of grass-speckled mud and clay had been formed into what looked like misshapen food on the plates. They crept along, huddled together, Connie itching to reach for her rifle but knowing that wouldn't make them look all that friendly.

"Hello?" she called again. "We're not trying to surprise you. Is anyone home?"

"Connie," Adelle whispered. "The floor."

It was covered in handwriting, sloppy and predominantly illegible. Now that she looked more closely at the walls, she saw that those had been written upon too. In some places, the pen had gone so deep it had scored the wood. Adelle had the better eyesight, and she stooped to try to pick up some of the phrases that Connie had no chance of making out.

"'The clouds methought would o-open,'" Adelle read clumsily.

"'And show riches ready to crop'—no, '*drop* upon me, that when I waked...'"

Her voice died down. Connie felt it too. They weren't alone. A woman in a black gown peeled away from the shadows.

"I cried to dream again," the woman rasped, finishing Adelle's line. "*That* was Shakespeare, but you two are not poets, so who, pray tell, are you?"

26

SHE WORE AN ILL-FITTING, dowdy black gown, theatrical in its grandeur but torn and dirty with neglect. It almost made her resemble Queen Victoria herself, especially with the concealing black veil falling from the cracked and broken tiara pinned in her gray hair, hiding her face. Every single one of her fingers glittered with dirty rings.

"Hello, is this yours?" Adelle held up the rabbit paperweight. "We found, like, a hundred of them outside."

"And you should have left it there." The old woman came at them; she was faster than she appeared. She snatched the paperweight out of Adelle's hand and backed up, cradling it to her bosom. "Fool. You do not know anything. You do not know a single thing about this place."

Adelle detected a slight French accent, one worn down by years and years of English, but there all the same. "We didn't mean to upset you. My name is Adelle; this is Connie."

The woman studied them both closely for a moment, then tapped the paperweight thoughtfully with one gnarled finger. "Adelle . . . Adelle and *Connie*. That is an unusual name."

"Short for Constance," Connie hurried to explain. "Do you sell things here?"

"So eager. In such a hurry." The woman turned and shuffled deeper into the bowels of the ship. Adelle glanced at Connie, who shrugged and began to follow. A golden pool of light bled across the floor, revealing more of the handwriting beneath their feet. They had rounded the full tip of the steamship's nose, and along the far side, the woman in black had set up a table and four chairs, a lantern there providing the flickering light.

"Sit with me, girls; visitors are something of a treat. . . ." She swiveled to face them again, gesturing to the empty, mismatched chairs. "I long so for callers. The table is set!"

"She doesn't seem that scary," Adelle said out of the corner of her mouth.

"Give it time," Connie replied. "Big 'Hansel and Gretel' energy in here."

Adelle snickered, then struck out ahead of Connie and took the chair nearest the wall. After Connie had sat down, she set her rifle on the floor near her feet, then pulled off her bag and held it on her lap.

The old woman turned in a dramatic circle, her skirt's train trailing behind her, before she sat on the other side of the lantern, the candlelight making her veil utterly opaque. When she went still, it seemed as smooth and solid as black marble. Adelle shivered, remembering the terrifying boy from Moira's party.

She placed her gloved and jeweled hands on the table.

"We introduced ourselves," Adelle pointed out. "What do we call you?"

"I rarely give a name," she replied. Her accent was beginning to irritate Adelle. It slipped and slid all over the place. "Sometimes I am called the Seer; some see the boat and call me the Passenger. But you two may call me Chordalia."

And she thought Connie was a weird name. . . .

"What brings you to my humble den of oddities and honesty? Shall I read your palms? Or your cards? Or tell you the path your life lines will take you?" Chordalia traced her own forefinger across her palm.

This was going to take forever. If the boat hadn't been so dark, Adelle would have had a mind to rebel again and just snatch the incense and run.

"We are looking for incense," Connie told her bluntly. "We can trade you for it."

"And what would you have that I might want?"

"More oddities," Adelle ventured. "For your collection."

Chordalia tilted her head to the side, the veil rippling. "Intriguing. But more than whatever you might have, you yourselves are fascinating to me. I do indeed possess what you desire, and I am willing to make a simple exchange."

"What kind of exchange?" Connie sounded as dubious as Adelle felt.

The woman spread her open palms wide again. "I will state a set of truths about you, and in return, you will say whether I have told true. Once this is done, you may have your incense."

Adelle found it a more than fair bargain, even a little exciting, but she noticed Connie shifting nervously in her seat, hesitating.

"Fine," Connie spat out. "Who's first?"

"Well, *A* comes before *C*," Chordalia said, almost mocking her. "So I will begin with Adelle. Give me your hands, girl, so I may feel your past, your present, and your path."

Adelle tried not to let her hands shake as she produced them, but she couldn't help but feel odd. Now that she knew for a fact that certain kinds of magic existed, the old harmless feelings she'd had regarding mysticism and fortune-telling needed updating. The silence and the expressionless veil made her shrink.

Just get through this. She's only a lonely old woman in a run-down boat.

As soon as their hands touched, a jolt passed between them, Adelle was sure of it. She closed her eyes, suddenly afraid. The last time she had let someone read her fortune, she had been told she would disappear into darkness. She very nearly had.

"Do not hide your gaze from me," Chordalia murmured, her voice different now, more lyrical, rising and falling as she began her fortune-telling. "Those eyes . . . unusual. Yes. You are an unusual young woman, are you not? Special, or that is the way you would have it be. You have never found yourself among like-minded souls. A bird among fish, a flightless creature who longs to soar. You have always been apart, and so you shroud yourself in black, not a sign of mourning but a mask. A scratched-out word.

An actress tangled in the curtain, never to tread the boards. Do not look at me, you say, though ever your heart shatters, desperate to be *seen*."

Adelle ripped her hands away, cowering back against her chair. It was all true. How could she know so much after only meeting Adelle for less than five minutes? She shivered and looked to Connie, who had gone rigid with fear.

"I was not finished, girl, but I suppose the bit about your love of fairy tales and magic is not nearly as interesting. And now you." The veil rippled again, turning toward Connie. With even greater reluctance than Adelle, she pushed her hands across the table.

Adelle watched, transfixed, wondering if the woman would paint as clear a picture of Connie.

"Strong hands," Chordalia murmured. "Yes, sure hands. Yours is a path of stone, already set. You the leader, she the follower. A contradiction—you speak with your body, with your physical feats, but yours too is a romantic soul. And contradictions are full of secrets, as are you. You do not belong here, girl. You are far, far from home. No ocean separates you from your place of birth, but time . . ." She sounded almost wistful, gentle. *Sorry.* "And a veil. A veil that separates one plane from the next. You have crossed a barrier you should not have, and now you wander a world not your own."

Connie grimaced, yanking her fingers back and curling them into fists.

"How did you know that?" Connie demanded. "Everything you said . . ."

"Connie," Adelle said softly, cupping her hand over her friend's shoulder. She hoped that just saying her name spoke the volumes she wanted to say—that they needed to be careful, that this woman might be their only hope of getting home. They needed that incense.

"How?" Connie asked again. "How did you know all of that?"

Chordalia reached up, removing the pins holding her veil in place one by one, explaining as she did so. "Your words. Your hair." She pointed to Adelle. Then her face turned toward Connie. "And *your* mannerisms. Your accent. Your . . . Boston Red Sox bag."

Adelle froze. Connie clasped her arms across her nylon gym bag. It was only decorated with the stylized red B of the baseball team, a team that hadn't even existed in 1885. How could the woman possibly know what that was? Unless . . . *Unless.* As soon as the veil dropped, Adelle recognized her face. It was like seeing a long-lost friend, or a relative one had only heard about and never met.

"It's you," Adelle breathed.

"Who?" Connie demanded, spinning to her.

It was true, the image before them wasn't quite the same as the one in the book. But Adelle saw the resemblance. She had put on weight and her hair had grown out, but it was definitely her. Adelle reached into Connie's bag, fished out the novel, and pushed it slowly, like a death sentence on paper, across the table.

"Robin Amery," Adelle said, opening to the back of the book with the author's biography and headshot. "*Moira's* creator."

27

CONNIE FELT LIKE SHE could see the dust settling visibly between them. Someone could have pricked her in the arm and she wouldn't have been able to move. Robin Amery. How was it possible?

"I never thought I would see another one from our world here." Robin's eyes filled with tears. "I . . . I don't know what to say. Are you real? Are you . . . No. No. You are not real. None of this is real; I had forgotten. One must never forget. Never."

Robin Amery stood, pushing herself away from the table, head in hands as she paced in her heavy black gown.

"We're real," Adelle insisted, standing. She was taking it better than Connie. Maybe going into the Wound had loosened more than one screw. But perhaps Adelle had the right idea. If she and Connie could fall into the novel, then why not the author? After all, she had the closest relationship to the book, the most intimate tie.

"We're real," Adelle repeated. "I promise you. Show her your phone, Connie. Empty out your bag."

Connie moved as if through molasses, shocked into clumsiness. She stood, banging the chair back to the floor, then ignored that and dumped out her Red Sox bag. It had to be real and happening, because how else would a Victorian woman know a modern Boston baseball team?

"Here, look at this. And this. Look at everything." Connie came back to herself, snatching up the dead phone and bringing it to Robin, along with her student ID card.

At first, Robin refused to touch the things, recoiling. Fat, glossy tears rolled down her face, darkening the lacy bib of her dress as they fell.

"How long?" Adelle murmured gently. "How long have you been trapped here?"

Connie hadn't thought of that. In the brief time they had been there, Connie had felt ready to run in circles, driven insane. If Robin had had enough time to repurpose a shipwrecked steamship and fill it with junk, to get a reputation as a seer, and to cover the entire hull in writing, then she must have been there a long, long time.

"I . . . have no idea." Robin drifted to one of the standing mirrors, smoothing her hands down over the bodice of her gown. "When I arrived, the novel had just begun. Moira and Severin had only just found each other in the park." Her voice shook around the names of her characters. "Where are we now?"

Adelle wiped her thumb across her lips, a nervous gesture Connie had seen a thousand times before. "At least halfway through," she said. "But . . . but the book isn't following—"

"The right set of events, yes, that is clear," Robin interjected. She squeezed her eyes shut and almost choked. "Just after I arrived, you see, things went awry. Nobody behaved as they should. A horrible monster appeared in the water. It was chaos . . . chaos. I thought it would be lovely to see it all, to see this world I built, but I'm afraid my being here has torn it all to shreds." She sighed and pressed the backs of her hands to her eyes. "After I finished *Moira*, I never wrote anything like it again. The magic was gone, you see. All gone. I poured myself into that book, maybe too much. I couldn't capture it again. My one book, my own masterpiece. But now I've destroyed it, and so have you. Tears in the sky. Now there are more, more because of you two."

Connie and Adelle had the idea at the same time, but Connie got it out first. "The Wound. That happened after you got here? And the monsters? The tears? All those people walking into the sea? You think our arrival did that?"

Robin nodded frantically, her thick gray hair bobbing around her ears, hanging in loose, unpinned curls. "Yes, yes, all of it. These characters I thought I knew, all of them have gone off script. I made a beautiful world, a rich, sumptuous world. This is not my world."

"But how did you get here?" Adelle asked, approaching her carefully.

"No . . . no, this is a trick." Robin clutched her head, a sob escaping her like a shocked cry. "In my head again. The voice. It sent you. It . . . speaks through you! Not the voice again. Not the madness."

"It speaks to us, too," Adelle assured her. "And I've seen what it is. I've been inside the Wound."

Robin grew still, hunched over, hands clasped over her ears while she slowly turned to regard her. "What? That . . . that's not possible."

Connie came to stand beside Adelle, silently offering her support.

"It's true. And it spoke to me in there. It's . . . it's like something from another dimension. It knows we don't belong here, but if what you're saying is true, if you noticed the characters going off script and the monsters appearing after you came, then maybe . . . maybe . . ."

"That was how it got in," Connie suggested. "Robin coming here must have torn open some kind of tunnel between worlds. The magic bent reality."

"You're right," Adelle breathed. "It said something about a Dreamer's City preparing, and a door. Coming here, to this world or dimension or whatever it is, upset a kind of balance. That must be what opened the door for it to come here."

So close. The ant sees the boot before it falls and knows it only as a harmless cloud.

Connie gasped, stuttering back a few steps. At once, Adelle was there, holding her around the shoulders.

"What is it? What's wrong?"

"I heard it," Connie moaned. "It feels like it's breaking my skull apart, hammering from the inside out."

"The madness, the voice . . ." Robin swished her hands together, pacing furiously. "But this . . . this is sense. This is not madness. For once it is not madness. It grows worse and worse, yes. First with me, now with you two. A world sundered, a world poisoned by what doesn't belong. We poisoned my beautiful world."

"How did you get here?" Adelle asked again.

"The man. The shop. I just wanted to escape. . . . *Moira* was the one good thing I ever made." Tears glittered in Robin's eyes. "I loved that little shop, I would go there to write, and when I couldn't write anything else, I gave him my own copy of *Moira*. He saw my pain. He saw my sorrow. 'I can help you,' he said. 'I can send you through, into that world. But you must come back, you must come back and tell me what you saw.'"

"Straven?" Connie blurted. "Was the man's name Straven? The Witch's Eye Emporium?"

"That name! That name, no . . . NO!" Robin shrieked, and pounded her fists into her eyes, then bolted, rounding the ship, disappearing into an unseen back room.

"Do we follow?" Adelle asked.

"We need her," Connie replied. "We need that incense."

Before they could give chase, Robin returned, guiding a cup of warm tea into Connie's hands.

"I had the kettle on before you both came," she said, sounding slightly sheepish in the face of their twin expressions of surprise. She had gone suddenly calm. "It's mint. I grow it myself on the roof; I don't trust any of the food. You must forgive me. . . . I don't know how to do this anymore. How to be human."

Connie held the tea under her nose, watching Robin closely. She couldn't decide whether she felt pity or sadness, maybe both. This was by far the strangest celebrity encounter she had ever experienced. They had tried a dozen times to find Robin back home, to have her brought to a library or store, but nobody could ever find her. Now it was clear why.

"You said something before," Robin continued. "About a Dreamer's City?"

"I saw it," Adelle replied. "But I don't think it's here. It's too big to actually be here. But the creature . . . it wants it here. Now I'm sure of it."

"The Dreamer's City, the Dreamer's City . . ." Robin chewed it over, thinking aloud. "When I was trying to write the stories in *Moberly's Adventure*, I used a book to research it. Must have been Rudolph's. . . . Yes. Andrew Rudolph, *The Lands Between*. That man, Str—Str—" She tried several times to choke out Straven's name but couldn't. "That man at the shop, he gave it to me. We would never find a copy of it now, though it was written well before 1885."

"Robin, I need to know. How long?" Connie pressed, returning to her real curiosity. "How long have you been here?"

"Years, I think, though it sometimes feels shorter, sometimes longer," she said. "And you two?"

The girls shared a look. Years. It didn't seem possible, but then Robin had been absent from the real world for at least that span. Connie decided not to mention anything—it could only be a sore spot for the poor woman.

"Not long," Connie said, hedging.

"Time must move differently here," Robin concluded, her gray head bobbing again. "That would explain my state, why I feel suddenly so ancient. My mind, my mental powers . . . are not what they once were." She gestured to the floor, to the walls and ceiling. "What you see here is my attempt to remember, to write down all that I know. All that I knew. I wanted to be in this beautiful world, but it's ugly. It's all ugly. Did I make it that way? I cannot say. I do not know."

Connie could sense another one of Robin's fits coming on.

"The incense," she said, feeling more driven to get home than ever. Her parents . . . She didn't allow herself to picture her mother. She didn't want to end up like this, like Robin. "We need it to go back. It's the answer, isn't it? If you think all these monsters and problems are from us being here, then the solution is to go back. If we all leave, things will get better, right?"

Neither of them answered.

"Do you have it or not?" Connie demanded, growing impatient. "We held up our end of the deal."

"That was before I knew for sure you were travelers like me," Robin replied, steely. "But I will play fairly, Connie. You can have your incense. I salvaged it from a church, from a priest's trunk. But I must know more . . . more of what Adelle saw. More of this Dreamer's City. It is the key."

She tapped the edge of her right forefinger against her mouth, then returned to the hidden area behind the table and chairs. They heard her rummaging, and Connie set her tea down on a random shelf, choosing not to take a sip.

"We could just run," Connie whispered.

"No, we should try to help her," Adelle said. "If we're the problem, then she's part of the solution, too, like you said. I just . . ."

Out of sight, Robin dropped something, swearing.

"You just what?" Connie searched her friend's face, but Adelle pressed her lips together, avoiding her gaze.

"Can you leave? Can you leave their world this way? Those girls down at the wharf, they seemed like your friends. Don't you think we should help them? Even if we go, do you really think all this stuff will just disappear? Their loved ones will still be in the Wound; there will still be tears and monsters, and all of it will have been our fault." Adelle dropped her face into her hands.

"Yeah," Connie sighed. "My stomach has been in knots over the same thing. I promised Mississippi I would bring her back, help her escape all this. Man, we were dummies, making friends here."

"I keep telling myself they're not real," her friend added, leaning against her. "But that isn't how it feels."

Missi had been ready to dive into ink-black water to pull Adelle out if she had dropped into the sea. She was weird and funny, and probably did belong more in the twenty-first century than the nineteenth. And the thought of leaving her behind to fend for herself, well . . .

"Here, I've found it! Worried for a moment that it was lost." Robin hurried over, her skirts rustling as she held out three little green cones of incense. "Cheer up, you two. We may be going home. There's no reason to look so glum, girls. Who died?"

The steamer lurched, metal and wood groaning in concert, one high, the other low. It sounded like innumerable screws trying to pop out of place at once. The hollow base of the hold banged like a drum, something large slamming against it.

"What was *that*?" Adelle hurried back toward the door, stopped short by Robin venting a strange, hysterical laugh.

"Not to worry, girls. The ship settles sometimes—"

The bang came again, this time louder, this time noticeably shoving the ship. And them. Adelle slid back, the floor suddenly at an angle, and collided with Connie, sending them into one of the curiosity shelves. The whole thing spilled over, marbles and playing cards and tiny porcelain cat figurines scattering to the floor. The mirrors fell, shattering, covering the boards in glittering, broken shards.

"That doesn't sound settled to me!" Connie screamed. She stuffed the incense into her nylon Sox bag and steadied Adelle on her feet, then ran to the porthole facing the shore.

Her heart raced to keep up with her eyes. It was the thing from the streets, from the fog, the hulking monster she had seen dodge from one street to the next, caught for just a frame in her memory, like Bigfoot dragging itself through the forest. Only this was bigger, much, much bigger.

"We have to get off this ship," Connie whispered. "Is there another way out? It's too close to the door."

"The stairs to the deck are this way." Robin twirled her hand, guiding them back toward the table. They scurried down the hall after her and plunged into the gloomy living area she had set up behind a row of makeshift curtains. There was a bed and a heap of pillows and blankets, but not much else to make the place feel like home. A massive wheel appeared to their left, and beside it an open stairway that led to the decks above. Their shoes and boots clanged on the metal steps as they raced up to the first level, and then the second, with a view back onto land, a chipped, white-painted rail, and passenger seats arranged for open-air travel.

Connie didn't particularly want to see what was knocking itself senseless against the ship, but they had to find some way off, and the creature lay between them and the field. They stood at the bow of the steamship, the wider, also open wooden deck below, and below that the hull, with the hole where they had entered.

"Oh God," she heard Adelle gasp as she laid eyes on it. "I can't look."

It wasn't a Bigfoot but a patchwork of people and faces, smashed together and covered in a thick black slime. A dozen or so humans crammed and oozed into a Frankenstein's nightmare, not stitched but fused, the place where one body began and another ended indistinguishable. It seemed to generate its own never-ending supply of oil-slick, oil-black goop, leaving a trail behind it, a clear path marked through the trampled field.

Worse than the look was the sound. The whole thing moaned and wheezed and cried, individual voices rising from it now and then, a disjointed lament of a dozen broken and dying hearts.

"The Befouler."

Robin had said it, her knuckles bone-white with terror around the railing.

"It has a *name*?" Connie cried.

"A girl came to me the other day; she wanted to banish it. That's what she called it—the Befouler. I didn't believe her, the poor, sad thing." Robin turned away as Adelle had. "She said it had taken her brother. That it was hunting in the streets, looking for more to add to its number."

The Befouler raised the bulbous pile of flesh that formed its right arm and punched it directly into the nose of the ship. Bones crunched. The shrieking voices rose. Connie's mouth had gone sandpaper dry, her lips forming around wordless, senseless curses. A face right on top of the thing's head opened its mouth wide, and she recognized it at once.

Jacky-boy.

"We have to get around it somehow." Adelle scrubbed her face with both hands, still refusing to look. "If you die, that creature in the Wound wins."

But Connie didn't have a solution. She always had one. Always. She had to. *Think, think, think.* The rifle. She had left it downstairs. Without another thought, she charged off back toward the stairs.

"Where are you going?" Adelle cried.

"The rifle! Maybe I can scare it off," she called back.

But Adelle was hot on her heels, grabbing her by the elbow and digging in. "Listen, we don't have time for that. We don't have—"

The ship's beams and boards and bones squealed again, the meaty thud of the Befouler smashing itself against the hull and dislodging the ship entirely. Rocks and gravel skittered softly somewhere off the bow, and then Connie felt the abrupt weightlessness of a ship beginning to float.

At the railing, Robin had already put one foot over, beginning to climb down to the deck below. "We must jump, girls—the boat won't survive long, and we will be lost to the fog."

"Are you crazy?" Connie shouted back, joining Adelle, relenting, and sprinting back to the bow. "You'll never swim fast enough! That dress will weigh you down!"

But Robin wasn't listening, and before Connie could grab her, she slipped over the railing, wrapped herself around a support post, and shimmied down.

"We have to stop her." Adelle slapped her hand over her eyes in frustration. "Oh, I hate heights."

"I'll go first," Connie assured her, whipping her thigh over the railing and beginning her descent. "It's not so bad, and if you drop, it's not far. I'll be down there—I'll help you, catch you if you fall."

She was glad then that Missi had given her a pair of trousers under the navy skirt. The coarse fabric helped too, giving her better purchase as she shifted her hands from the bottom of the railing to the boards near Adelle's feet, wrapped her legs around the same post Robin had used, and traveled down it like a fireman's pole.

The Befouler must have waded into the water after them. The hull shivered again, the creature's full weight, hurled against the ship, pushing them farther out to sea.

"Hurry! Don't be scared!"

Adelle straddled the railing clumsily and just as artlessly rebalanced her weight, digging her knees into the floor of the upper deck, then sliding down too quickly, her legs flailing as she failed to find the post. At least her hands shot out to grab it at the last second, and Connie dove forward, her shoulder easing the landing as Adelle tumbled to their level on the ship.

"Quickly, girls! To shore!"

"Robin!" Adelle's scream tore across the deck, flying above Robin Amery's head, as the author of *Moira* disappeared over the railing and plunged into the sea.

28

Just as Connie had warned, Robin's layers and layers of gown ballooned out around her for an instant, blossoming like a splotch of watercolor paint, then grew sodden with seawater and vanished beneath the foaming waves, dragging her down with the heft of an anchor.

"Robin!" Adelle cried again, watching her head go under. The author fought, swimming hard, making her way slowly toward the shore. But she was too unwieldy, and the Befouler had seen her, drawn by the commotion of her splashing. Its gooey black abomination of a body lurched toward her, even the small act of turning drawing a chorus of agonized howls from the dead or deadish or undead humans comprising its body.

"She'll never make it," Adelle added, pressing herself to the railing and watching in helpless horror as the Befouler closed the distance. "What do we do, Connie? What even happens if she dies?

Does she really die? In this world *and* ours?"

"I don't want to find out."

Connie threw herself away from the railing and trotted back to the cabins in the middle of the deck. The windows into the rooms had been busted out, and Connie climbed through nimbly, then returned with a coil of dirty and fraying rope. She arced it over the boat, into the water, the end plopping into the waves a foot or so from Robin's left side.

"The rope!" Connie thundered. "Robin! Grab the rope! You won't make it!"

Robin was pulled under by the weight of her dress again. Disoriented, doing little more than treading, she finally noticed the rope floating next to her. She coiled it around her chest, under her armpits, and Connie braced her feet against the railing, pulling. Adelle did her best to help, not nearly as strong, but grabbing the tail of rope behind Connie and heaving back.

But the Befouler sloshed into the water beside Robin, up to its knees while she tossed and sputtered, spitting out black water while Connie and Adelle fought to hoist her back up to safety.

The rope flew out of their hands, stinging Adelle's palms, burning them raw, as the Befouler pressed its stump hand against Robin's head, forcing her back under the surface with enough force to tear the rope free altogether.

"No! Damn it!" Connie's hands flashed out to try to catch the end as it whipped away, but it was gone.

The boat had stalled, but free of the shore, it would soon be pushed out to the fog by the tide or the Befouler, whichever came first. Then the hole in the hull would gradually fill, dragging them under as surely as Robin's dress had pulled her down.

"Don't look," Connie told her, taking Adelle by the crook of her arm.

The wind shifted, carrying with it the stench of the Befouler, a wet, slaughterhouse smell. Adelle didn't need to look; she had ears.

And she knew the moment it was over—a new tear slashed itself open in the sky above the paperweight-littered field. The shreds of sky and cloud hung loose, an endless void visible within the gash.

"So that's what happens," Adelle murmured.

The clamor that came next she attributed to the tear, at first, and then to the Befouler, as it trudged out of the sea. But it was neither. Horses. Several of them. Several horses racing across the field toward them, sleek black steeds galloping loud enough to bring the thunder, their riders screaming and roaring, firing off pistols and rifles as they charged the shore.

"They came for us." Connie ran to the lower deck railing. "They all came for us."

Down the line, Mississippi, Caid, Severin, and the two Penny-Farthing girls Adelle had seen at the wharf ate up the ground, their gunfire drawing the Befouler away from the edge of the water, its long, disproportionate arms dragging along the sand, leaving a thick trail of blackish tar wherever it went.

"Get out of your dress."

"What?" Adelle swiveled, leaning just as far and hopefully and desperately off the railing as Connie.

"We have to jump and swim while it's distracted. Do you want to get slowed down like she was? It's the difference between drowning and making it to safety. You can worry about their Victorian sensibilities later!" Connie had already flung off her backpack and begun stripping down and out of her thick linen and cotton clothing. The only thing she kept on was her bandanna, a pair of navy bike shorts, and a sports bra.

"I hate this," Adelle hissed. "I hate all of this." Her eyes flicked to the sky, though she had no idea what she was even praying to. "I hate it, I hate it, I hate it."

She pulled the lacy dress over her head and tossed it to the floor, shivering in her white cotton underwear, bra, and high-heeled boots.

The riders were about to overtake the Befouler, and they began to curve away from it, still firing, slowing their pace, letting the creature get good and angry, angry enough to give chase.

"Wait," Connie warned. "Not yet—it has to move. We have to know it's falling for it."

Adelle hopped from foot to foot, already mortified.

The Befouler took the bait, groaning and shrieking as the bullets struck, and pulled itself along, its disgusting snail trail bleeding into the long grass and away from the boat.

"Now!" Connie shrieked, grabbing her bag and kicking her legs over the tall metal railing. "Jump!"

29

THERE WAS A POINT, after Adelle, soaking wet in her underpants, had sobbed at everyone not to look at her, worried more about her modesty than about the sludgy corpse monster hunting them, when Connie felt the hysteria become too much.

It was just too weird. Too ridiculous. They had crawled out of the surf, freezing and trembling, and were met on the sand by Mississippi, Geo, and Farai. The boys, it seemed, had let the women handle the mostly naked swimmers while they led the Befouler away. And immediately, Mississippi had shrugged off her white fringed coat and tossed it around Connie's shoulders. Because of the cold, or maybe that mounting hysteria, Connie's mind at once went to borrowing someone's letterman jacket.

Farai was generous enough to lend Adelle her patterned shawl, and Adelle made use of every meager inch of it, managing to conceal herself to the upper thigh after being pulled up into the saddle behind the silver-haired Penny-Farthing.

Mississippi probably thought Connie had completely lost it, the way she was laughing and laughing, sitting with her on the horse, head thrown back as they joined the boys again farther down the field, now pursued by not only the Befouler, but also a torrent of screamers falling from the tear above.

Robin Amery was lost, and this was the result—the world she had lovingly created was ripping itself apart. Somehow, Connie had expected much worse, but then she didn't want to jinx it. There was still time for greater horrors to appear.

While they rode back to the warehouse, Connie burrowed down into Missi's jacket and just concentrated on trying not to succumb to hypothermia. Then they all holed up together in Caid's workshop, where the girls tried to find something for Connie and Adelle to wear. Screamers circled and dove, glancing off the windows, reminding them occasionally that leaving was suicide.

Orla had met them at the door, throwing her arms around Adelle in relief. It was she who finally managed to clothe them, taking two of Kincaid's old nightshirts and belting them, creating a kind of shirt dress that wouldn't be totally out of fashion in the twenty-first century.

"How did you find us?" Adelle asked, tucked up on the couch, an astronomical number of blankets mounded over her, the combined effect of both Kincaid's and Orla's fussing.

Severin made tea, Earl Grey again, and everyone congregated in the living area, the boys on one couch and Missi, Adelle, Orla, Connie, and Geo on the other, while Farai stood by the windows, watching the screamers gather.

"Orla and I weren't particularly happy that you two had run off again so soon," Missi explained, with mother-hen crossness. She aimed this at Connie, of course, keeping an eye on her as if she might go missing again at any second. "But I had an inkling of where you might be goin', and that led to the trail that monster had left all through the city. I roused the others when I saw where it led."

"We would have died without your help," Connie said, the hysteria fading into a hollow sadness. There they were, planning to leave this world, while its inhabitants risked their lives to save them. Even if going might make things better, Connie still wasn't sure it was the right thing to do. It seemed too simple, or maybe that was just her brain cooking up excuses to stay.

"And don't you forget it," Mississippi replied with mock stern-ness, giving Connie a wink.

Excuses, she thought, *like that.*

"And the seer woman?" Geo asked. Her braids had gone frizzy from the rain and the fast ride to and from the shore.

"She tried to swim, but the Befouler—that's what she called the creature—it got her. I think she drowned," Adelle explained. She stared down into her tea, thinking, inevitably, what Connie was—that losing Robin Amery meant something they couldn't possibly explain to the woman's creations. They had lost a mother none of them knew they had.

"Seems like it came just for the three of you especially," Missi remarked.

Yes, all three of the people who didn't belong, all in the same place, ripe for the killing. It was a miracle only one of them hadn't made it out.

"When I was inside the Wound," Adelle told them, "it didn't say anything about killing me, but maybe that's really what it wants. I don't know. . . ." She winced, and dropped her head into her hands.

"It could have just kept you," Kincaid pointed out reasonably. "Unless being inside of it is not a state of death. Perhaps there is still something we can do to help those trapped inside."

"Like what? I mean, I am all for it, but that is a tall order right there," Missi replied.

"Oh, but think of how extraordinary that would be!" Orla's eyes grew wide with possibility and hope, which was always danger-ous. "Surely, if there is a chance, we must try. Right, Miss Casey?"

The way she said it, Connie could only assume it was some kind of inside thing between them.

Adelle set down her tea on the mountain of blankets heaped in her lap, staring at Connie for a long moment. She was thinking it too. If they were really going to stay and help, then they would all need to come up with a plan, and that plan must inevitably include Adelle and Connie departing from their world, or the tears and the Wound would never really heal.

And that meant coming clean.

"Could you excuse us for a minute?" Connie asked, standing and wrapping a blanket around her waist.

"*Bien sûr*, Miss Rollins," Severin said. "But please: do not run off again. Thrilling as it was to rescue you, we have all had our share of adventure for the day."

Connie nodded toward the makeshift garden to the right, and Adelle climbed out of her blanket fort, tea in hand, and followed her to where it smelled like thyme and rosemary and everything green.

"We have to tell them," Adelle whispered, staring past her at the bewildered and waiting people on the sofas.

"I know." Connie coughed lightly into her fist and blew on her tea. "Mississippi . . . she might already know." It wasn't worth lying, not when the stakes were so high. "Fine. She knows. She knows because I told her I was from the future."

Adelle gaped. "Oh. But why? How did she take it?"

"Better than I expected, to be honest." Connie gave a dry chuckle. "She was pretty pissed after that debacle in the kitchen, and she was getting suspicious. I blew our whole operation trying to steal from Moira, all because I heard your laugh on the other side of the door."

Adelle smiled and wrinkled her nose.

"She could tell I wasn't being truthful. It was a gamble, but I figured it would at least make her keep me around if I could get her to believe me." Connie shrugged. "I showed her my phone and she grilled me for a while, but she came around. Mostly she just had a bajillion questions."

"So would I," Adelle murmured. "So will they all."

"So we tell them?" Connie asked.

Adelle nodded. "Do we explain about the book?"

"I don't think so," Connie replied. "Reality here is messed up enough."

"Rock, paper, scissors?"

Connie shook her head. "I can do it. You've got enough on your plate, Grey Havens."

Adelle squeezed her eyes shut. "I shouldn't have told you that; now you're just going to worry."

"I'm your friend, Delly—I'm always worried."

They clasped hands and wandered back to the party, the conversation there dying down as they returned. Standing with her back to the door, facing everyone, Connie dragged in a deep, deep breath and prepared for the hardest speech of her life.

"There's something we need to tell you all," she began, glancing at Missi. The sharpshooter gave her a slow nod of approval, and for some reason, that made it much easier to press on. "Make sure you're all sitting down."

30

ADELLE FELT A TWINGE of regret while she waited for Connie to drop the bomb. She had begun friendships with Orla, Caid, and Severin, and now she knew they would never look at her the same way again. Selfishly, she wondered if this might make them hate her. She had, after all, lied. Repeatedly. Ardently.

Please understand, she begged them silently. *Please don't hate us.*

"Adelle and I aren't who you think we are." Connie launched into it without much preamble. Slowly, Adelle watched their faces contort into confusion, one by one. Only Missi remained the same, watching Connie with the intensity of a dance mom mentally coaching her kid onstage.

"We're not from here. Well, we are. It's confusing." Sighing, Connie put her tea down on the trunk table and rubbed her forehead. "Adelle and I are from Boston, but Boston a little more than a hundred years from now. We wound up here by playing with magic. The seer woman, her name was Robin Amery, and she was from our time too. When she came, that's when everything started getting bad for you. The Wound, the sleepwalking, everything else."

Adelle might have couched that a bit more sensitively, but it was all true. The responses varied. Orla gasped and covered her mouth with both hands, turtling under a blanket as if she could reflect the truth back to them and unlearn it. Caid stroked his chin, frowning thoughtfully. Geo and Farai didn't seem to believe it, wearing matching smirks.

And Severin . . . he just smiled, gently, as if everything were right in the world. Maybe, she thought, it was a relief to know that there was a reason behind the madness and chaos: something that had felt unexplainable now made sense, like knowing where lightning came from or what caused an eclipse. It wasn't an act of God, but something attributable to tangible events.

That was partially how she felt anyway, now that they had met Robin and heard part of her story. She was the heart of the cataclysm; Adelle and Connie were the aftershocks. Now they just had to pick up all those pieces and patch them back together.

Somehow.

"I'm sure you all have questions. Tons. But the important thing right now isn't whether in the future we can all fly with our shoes or whatever; the important thing is that we put our heads together and figure out how to fix this," Connie finished, to dense silence.

"You found remarkable ways to survive," Adelle added, trying to give a spoonful of sugar. "You're clever and resourceful, and we can all work together to end this."

"I see no reason to believe you," Geo said, snapping to her feet. "You went to that crazy woman today. She is dangerous, powerful. Who can say what witchcraft she used on you; she could have made you think anything, even this nonsense."

"This ain't no hypnotism, Geo," Missi shot back, also standing. "I know for a fact because Connie already told me all of this. Show 'em your . . . your . . . cell tone thing."

"Cell phone," Connie said, picking up the backpack from beside the sofa. "This bag. It's not fabric you have yet; we make it out of nylon. Synthetic fiber."

"Fascinating," Caid muttered, squinting behind his spectacles.

"And this? This *B* is for the Boston Red Sox, our baseball team," she added.

"What happened to the Boston Beaneaters?" Missi asked, crest-fallen.

"I don't know, but we're the Red Sox now, and we're good. We've won the World Series like, a bunch of times," Connie said.

Adelle nudged her. They were getting off track.

"World Series?" Farai asked. "What is that?"

"My friends, my friends . . ." Severin waved his hands in the air, addressing them with the sternness of a politician climbing on his soapbox. He joined the rest in standing and tugged on the end of his shirt. "We are veering from the point. As Miss Rollins so elegantly stated, our task is clear."

"Severin is correct," Caid said, though it clearly pained him to do so. He wiped off his glasses and tucked his fist under his chin. Judging by his workshop, he would have a genius idea by the time they all finished their tea. "I believe our most pressing question should be: How exactly did you come to be here among us, and can the process be reversed?"

"Thank you." Connie pointed to him. "That's the energy we need. And to answer your question, we used spell materials—a candle, a bowl, a stone, and incense."

"Placed in a specific pattern," Adelle continued, then fumbled. Obviously, they couldn't mention the book. "And then we . . . asked to travel."

"And your request was to visit our time?" Severin asked. "Why?"

"We . . . we both love history." Adelle stumbled again, the real reasons far more difficult to explain. "And the books of this time. And the fashion. Wouldn't you want to time travel too?"

"I certainly would," Caid interjected.

"It sounds terribly discombobulating to me," Orla said.

"And we have all the ingredients now to try and return," Connie told them, steering back to the point. "Only, we're not sure that if we go, everything will go back to how it was. So if anyone has a grand plan for how to get rid of the Wound for good, now is the time to speak up."

Silence. Adelle could see the shock wearing off, everyone in the room growing antsy. There was still one more avenue they could explore, she thought, before giving up and just going home.

"While we were on the boat with Robin," Adelle began softly, "she mentioned a book that might be useful. Caid? You said some of these books in your library were taken from the university, right? Maybe I could have a look and see if you have the right one."

"Of course," he said. "Let me retrieve the ledger."

"And in the meantime, will you tell us if there are shoes that make you fly?" Severin grinned, receiving a nasty look from Orla. "What? Now I am curious."

"No," Connie told him. "Our shoes don't make us fly."

Missi crossed in front of Connie and Adelle, her arms stretched out wide. "Hey. Hush. Everyone hush up. Flying. Maybe that is the answer. *Flight.*"

"You lost me," Connie replied.

Adelle admitted her confusion with a shrug. But at least somebody had an idea. She and Connie might be from the future, but they didn't know the lay of the land like the characters who had lived the chaos of this Boston for months and months.

"The navy tried to bombard the Wound at first, but the damn arms just took the blow, and nothin' hurt it. Connie's bullet startled it, but it never bled. What if we flew over it? Dropped . . . I don't know . . . dynamite or torches into it from above."

"Alas, their shoes do not fly," Orla said wistfully.

Connie perked up beside her. "The balloon."

"The balloon," Farai murmured.

"The balloon," Geo echoed, tugging on the ends of her two braids.

"I'm sorry?" Adelle vented a dry laugh. "What balloon?"

"My balloon," Missi said. "The kind that can fly. It ain't quite ready, but we could put all the children on it, make its maiden voyage one to remember."

Caid had returned from the library by the windows, intimidating and scholarly leather-bound books under one arm. Fingers pinching the edge of his spectacles, he cleared his throat for attention. "My own observations of the Wound phenomenon and what

Miss Casey experienced within it led me to the conclusion that the mortal weapons that might kill us would have no effect on it. As stated, cannons and rifles proved useless."

"Blast," Severin murmured, sitting down hard on the sofa. "The thought of soaring to victory in a *montgolfière* was so gallant, too."

"We can still take that ride," Geo said slowly, the idea forming in her head visibly as her eyes widened and she grabbed at something invisible in the air, excited. "How does that thing get us? Through dreams, yes?"

"Through dreams," Farai whispered, catching the tail of her thought.

"The tea we make stops all dreams," Geo went on. Adelle glanced at Caid, the obvious barometer for logic, and even he seemed riveted, hanging on to her every word. "Clove and oak gall, steeped in hot rainwater. The ingredients are precious, but if we could make a big, big cauldron of it . . ."

"We could dump it in the Wound. It might wake up the dreamers inside, and if it communicates *through* dreams, then maybe it will stop the Wound from doing that, too," Connie finished. "That's . . . that's brilliant, Geo."

"I know." She shrugged, but smiled, pleased with herself.

Caid joined them again on the sofas, all but forgetting the ledger, setting it down and joining their little brainstorming circle. "Miss Casey described the inside of the Wound as a kind of stomach. Perhaps those who walk into it are some manner of food."

"They were all intact, though," Adelle piped up, glad to finally be of use. "Even their clothes were untouched. They didn't look digested."

"Then perhaps they are not food at all," Caid replied. "Maybe our brethren are being kept for some other nourishment. If they are unharmed then might the monster feed off their dreams? Whatever their purpose there, they must be freed."

"Then it appears we have a plan, *mes amis*." Severin came to stand between Caid and Missi, clapping them both on the shoulder at once. Missi growled and flinched away. *Amis* they were not. "Allow me to contribute what I can. Gall and clove are used in the production of many inks; I use them myself for my art. Take what I have, ladies; use it to brew your potion."

Farai nodded, though she kept her distance. None of the Penny-Farthing girls seemed thrilled to be hanging around Severin. "We should return to the Congregation. The balloon needs to be finished, and Geo and I can begin mixing the cauldron," Farai said, starting for the door. Severin followed at a polite distance, perhaps aware of the tension, despite his bluster.

"Connie?" Mississippi collected her fringed jacket from the sofa and pulled it on. "Will you be joining us?"

Connie glanced at Adelle, brow knit with worry. She shook her head, inching closer to Adelle. "I should stay with her. I promised we wouldn't get separated again."

"That was before we had a plan like this," Adelle replied. It was obvious by the fidget in Connie's leg that she wanted to go with the others. "We might need all hands on deck with the balloon. I'll be safe here, and I can check Caid's ledger for the book."

"Are you sure?" Connie asked, taking Adelle lightly by the elbow.

"Go," she said. There was something else in Connie's face,

something in the way Missi watched their conversation with eagerness, the way she stood just a little bit close to Connie. Was there something going on between them? Adelle hadn't considered it possible, but now that she studied them, it was hard not to wonder. Maybe it wasn't just an example when Connie had mentioned crushing on Moira. *Oh*, she thought. *I'm so dense.*

"I'll be fine," Adelle added. "Just be careful. We don't know where the Befouler is, and there are still screamers outside."

"Perhaps wise to separate you," Geo said in passing, on her way to the door. "If the Wound wants you for some nefarious purpose, it will be easy work if you stay together."

"And on that cheerful note," Adelle chuckled, pulling Connie into a tight hug. "Just come back, okay?"

Before slinging her bag over one shoulder, Connie reached in, grabbed the incense, and handed it to Adelle.

"We each keep part of the magic ingredients," she said. "We're going back together or not at all."

Adelle almost refused, but there was comfort in the thought, so she closed her fingers around the tiny green cones and nodded. "How will we know when you're ready?"

"Watch for a signal fire to the south," Missi replied. "I can send a runner to our secondary outpost, light up that church's bell tower. Once you see that, we are ready. Ready, God willin', to fly."

31

It was with great fanfare and relief that Miss Orla Beevers was returned to the goodly flock of neighbors and friends on Joy Street. Her mother and father, parents of good humor but strict and Christian decrees, wept openly as they embraced her on their doorstep, an impoliteness that was excused due to the severity of their grief and the extremeness of the situation.

Moira regarded this reunion with veiled excitement—not only because her companion and friend had been brought back home safely, but because Severin had been the unlikely architect of the victory. It was his lowliness, his familiarity with the less savory aspects of Boston society, that had led to Orla's recovery.

And while Orla appeared unharmed, she described a nasty ordeal indeed, holding court during an evening of supper and piano performances hosted by the Beevers family. Her brothers appeared jealous that their sister had survived the equivalent of a bandit attack, something *they had only read about in their tawdry serials.*

"They were too, too horrible. Thieves and beggars, all of them crass and dirty, more encrusted in filth than a dust-yard doxy! Their leader was the worst—a girl, if you can believe it! A circus performer of no real renown, cursing and spitting; even a sailor would have blushed!" Orla exclaimed over excellent claret. She had not a bruise upon her, but perhaps the bruise was deep and upon her soul.

"The devils! Did they harm you? Oh, my dear, did they lay a finger upon you? I will see them all hanged," Mr. Beevers sternly said, nearly knocking over his wine in his anger.

"They did not," Orla replied, slightly sheepish. Her tale could not be embellished with violence, but she lifted her head high as if it were all supremely harrowing. "But I am sure that with enough time, their evil natures would have prevailed. Had Mr. Sylvain not negotiated the ransom so expertly, I might now be in heaven, visiting with angels and not here, alive and grateful with all of you."

—Moira, *chapter 10*

"Do you really think it will work?"

Connie watched two dozen nimble hands sewing the patches of silk together, huddled under the glow of lanterns held over them by the older children of the Congregation. Hours and hours had passed, candles shrinking from stems to stubs. Carts and shanties had been shoved aside, making room to lay out the massive balloon in the center of the catacombs, a rounded quilt in a riot of colors, the silk collected from skirts, cravats, gowns, handkerchiefs, whatever could be found and spared.

"I always knew one day I would try lighting this thing up, so now is as good a time as any to try," Mississippi replied. They stood near the rows and rows of busy children, handing out thread and needles, directing them to wherever there might be holes or weak seams. "It's in my nature. I surely do not understand it, but I do think it was put into my blood. Whether it soars or crashes, I will fly it. Whichever it may be, I am glad you will be here to see it."

Geo and Farai had their heads bent over a massive iron cauldron off to the side, mixing a large batch of the tea. It smelled awful, the bitter reek filling the cavern-like hideaway. They had lined the cauldron with a leather bladder, lighter than the metal, for the balloon still had to fly. With the bladder full of tea, flight would still be possible, and the contents would make it across town with only a bit of sloshing and spillage. It had not yet been decided who exactly would accompany Missi to fly the thing.

"Missi . . ." On the ride from the workshop back to the chapel, Connie had remained silent and preoccupied, hating that soon she would have to break it to Missi that she couldn't come back with them. They had already set aside so many lies; it didn't seem right to keep it from her.

"I know, Connie. I know." Missi sighed and rubbed the toe of her boot over nothing. "If your presence here is tearing up our world, me coming back with you would just do the same."

That made it easier. A little. Connie frowned, trading a hopelessly bent needle for a straight one when a blond-pigtailed dirty-faced girl trotted up to her.

"There's something else," Connie ventured.

"Oh?"

"When I told you in that bell tower that I would take you back, I was lying. I just wanted your help. But now . . . it's different now. If I could take you with me, I think I would try."

Mississippi honked with laughter, nearly dropping her spools of thread. "And why is that, Rollins? You soft on me?"

"Something like that." Connie snorted, turning away slightly. "This place, this era, it doesn't deserve you. You were born way, way before your time."

"Maybe," Missi said, staring into the side of Connie's face. "Or maybe not. Maybe it takes people like me to shake things up, mm? Why do I dress the way I do? Why do I cuss so loud and jump at the chance to brawl?"

"Because you're crazy?"

She laughed again, this time louder. "That, that. And 'cause I always knew deep down inside what I was—somethin' that just did not belong. But that was all right. I knew that I fancied girls and only girls. What's more, I knew folk would want me to shove that down inside, to make it small and nothin'. That would make me small and nothin' too. And Rollins? I simply could not abide that."

Connie looked down at the floor intently. Her cheeks burned. She thought of the posters on her wall, of changing her mind right outside Julio's door, of her well-meaning but ignorant mother piling up fashion magazines outside her bedroom. She didn't feel small or like nothing, but she did wonder if saying her truth aloud and accepting it would make her even bigger and even more of something.

That "aloud" part didn't have to be for everyone, but she was beginning to think that it was for her. Connie had been afraid of it before. She had balked at being told what she was before it felt hers. But she wanted Missi to be hers. She wanted it all—the truth of her love, of her identity—to be hers, and to share it with everyone. With everyone, but especially with Missi.

Missi, strange and loud and fiery, was for her.

"It might almost be worth it," Connie murmured, still unable to look her directly in the eye. "To take you back. Even if it made our world fall apart. It would be stupid and selfish, but it would be mine, and I'd like it."

"Listen, Future Girl, you ain't gone yet, and I happen to be right here."

Connie nodded, getting up the courage to glance her way. She felt the same electric pressure in her chest that she had felt when they'd first met, when Missi had gotten in her face, when Connie had thought of her as nothing more than a loudmouthed rival, someone to defeat.

"Time is what you make it," Missi added. "My daddy told me that. He was wrong about a lot of things, but not that."

Time is what you make it.

Connie leaned over, not knowing if anyone was watching or noticing, though suddenly she didn't care. Missi had given her a chance, believed her when it counted, listened and fought and come to her rescue. If that wasn't first-girlfriend material, even if only for a tiny while, then she didn't know what was.

The kiss was quick and chaste and more of just a flutter, but even that much was enough to light a consuming flame.

She had always supposed another girl's lips would be soft, but it still surprised her. Connie's burning cheeks exploded into pulsing red points, and she stutter-stepped back, blowing out a weak breath.

"That your first, I take it?" Missi asked softly.

"Definitely."

"Well, I am honored. Let it not be your last, Future Girl. Even if it ain't with me, that kiss is too sweet to keep all to yourself."

Everyone except the extremely ill had been put to work finishing the balloon, so it came as a surprise to hear several pairs of footsteps pounding across the cobbles behind them. Connie roused herself as if out of a lovely, realistic dream cut way too short.

"Joe, this is the first time I seen you run." Mississippi whirled as Sleepless Joe, the bearded bartender, ran up to them, two young lookouts following close behind.

He gasped for air, shaking his head. "Clackers. Seems like all of them. They have found us. They are mustering in force outside the chapel."

"They must have seen us comin' and goin'." Missi dropped the thread and stormed past him, already on her way to collect her pistols at the bar. "Unless . . ." She froze, right foot in midair. "You think someone ratted us out, Rollins?"

"Kincaid doesn't seem like the type," Connie replied. "And he's holed up with Adelle doing research."

"Orla already knows where we are," Missi added. "She ran with us until the grime of it got to her. She had plenty of chances to tell and never breathed a word. No, it was that weasel-faced traitor!"

Severin. Unfortunately, it wasn't that hard for Connie to believe.

"He helped us against the Befouler!" Missi took off again, running for her weapons. "He helped us rescue you! I thought we could trust him."

"We have to protect the balloon," Connie said. "And the kids. And . . . and crap, if Severin is out there trying to sabotage us, then he'll go for Adelle!"

Sleepless Joe dodged behind the bar, ducking down and taking out two massive butcher's knives. Farai and Geo had noticed the commotion and trotted up to the bar with furrowed brows. The dogs, previously lounging among the invalids, woke up and galloped over with tails wagging, ready for action.

"Clackers found us," Missi told them. "We'll hold them off; you two keep brewin' that tea."

"It needs to steep—we can fight," Farai told her. She rolled the beads on her wrist nervously, or maybe for luck.

"And you . . ." Missi almost charged right into Connie, making her take a few steps back toward the middle of the hideout. She lowered her voice so only Connie could hear and shoved a rifle into her hands. "They're here for you, darlin'. Us too, but mostly you. If getting you safely out of here will set things right, then their whole messed-up religion is sunk. Their power is gone. Take the gun, and take the tunnel at the back of the lair, behind the toilet pit; it will take you back to the church with the bell tower. Get to your friend—make sure she is safe."

"I want to stay," Connie told her, grabbing her hand. "You all have already done so much. If they're here for me, then I should be the one to fight."

"That's not how this works." Missi spun her by the shoulders and pushed her toward the opposite end of the Congregation. "Our survival depends on yours. Stay alive. Close the Wound. We might not have much time, Rollins, so you damn well better make the most of it."

32

"YOU MADE THIS ENTIRE ledger?" Adelle asked, amazed. The leather-bound book had to weigh at least five pounds, every tall page covered top to bottom in columns with each book's title, author, and brief description, along with where he had chosen to put it in his "hot" library, as Connie had so observantly put it.

She had to admit, it wasn't *not* hot.

"As you may see, there is little for me to do these days but busy myself with experiments and work. I endeavor to employ myself usefully, even if only I can see the utility in it," Caid replied. They sat close together on the left sofa, Orla a lump under blankets on the opposite one. Adelle was again reminded of his scent, parchment and herbs, a masculine scent that didn't overpower, but constantly made her thoughts wander.

He had such expressive, strong hands. Moira considered Severin's to be "painterly," and maybe that was so, but Caid's looked like they could fix a watch or write for hours or clasp with just the right pressure during a dance.

"I thought you were engaged to Moira," Adelle said, feeling foolish the moment she did. They had bigger things to worry about, but she couldn't help thinking she was sitting there, having dreamy thoughts about someone else's boyfriend.

Caid frowned, leaning back and away from her, propping his palms on his knees. "It was the last thing my parents asked of me before they were gone. I feel bound to their wishes, though in truth she and I are far, far too different. Marriage requires compatibility of finances and family, however, not pursuits and passions."

"No!" Adelle couldn't help herself. She knew it was just the way he had been raised and the pressures of the era, but it still stung to hear. Caid smirked, one dimple appearing as he stared at her, taken aback.

"No?"

"No! No, that is . . . That's awful. That's stupid and awful. Marriage, love, whatever, it should be exactly about pursuits and passions," Adelle argued, sounding as offended as she felt.

"One might safely assume that women in your time are emancipated?"

"They are. We can vote, and own our own houses. We run businesses and wear whatever we want, for the most part. We're politicians and doctors, scientists and astronauts—you don't know what that is, but trust me, it's cool. . . ." Adelle trailed off, realizing her shouting was going to wake Orla. She flipped the page on the ledger, and began searching again in earnest. They had a job to do, after all.

"Ah." Caid smiled a secret sort of smile. "That explains so much."

"Because I'm loud," Adelle replied. "And opinionated."

"Well, yes. But a woman of strong morals and even stronger opinions has always been my ideal, though I'm afraid it is not the fashion."

"It should be," Adelle muttered. "And fashions change."

"They do indeed, Miss Casey, they do indeed."

"There!" She gasped. "This is it! Andrew Rudolph's *The Lands Between*. I can't believe you have it!"

Caid jumped to his feet, striding swiftly to the library. "I can. Rudolph is something of a popular metaphysician. He lectured at Harvard two winters ago; I had wanted to see him, but a blizzard prevented it."

"Have you read his book?" Adelle followed him to the over-stuffed shelves. Outside, dusk turned gradually to greater dark. The screamers had mostly dissipated, probably drawn away by Connie and the Penny-Farthings departing for their chapel. Still, a few circled, diving with alarming, untelegraphed speed, making her jump whenever one tapped the glass.

"Not yet, but now I certainly will. Here." Caid slid a surprisingly slender tome from the bookshelf. It was worn, with a violet cover and faded gold embossing the title. "I wonder what Rudolph might tell us about our present trouble."

"Robin Amery was sure that her arrival started the tears and the Wound," Adelle explained, both of them returning to the better comfort and warmth of the sofas, while she opened the book, hearing the soft, pleasant crack of the spine. "And when she died?

That giant tear over the field opened up. I think it was a direct result of her death. But she swore that everything was normal when she arrived."

Then you all started acting bizarro and going off script and being way hotter than you ever were in the novel.

Concentrate, Adelle.

"What else do you know about Rudolph?" she asked, her voice suspiciously thin.

Caid settled down on the sofa again, his long legs stretched out in front of him, just behind the trunk table. He scratched idly at the tantalizing hollow just above the open neck of his shirt. Unlike Severin, he didn't wear a fussy cravat.

"He is an eccentric, not necessarily respected, but his ideas are novel, and that won him some interest from fellow academics and researchers," Caid explained. "What his theories actually are, I cannot say."

"Yikes. Some of these chapter titles . . . Rudolph sounds two eggs short of a dozen. Oh! But this one looks promising," Adelle said, her finger gliding down the index at the front. "'On Nglui, the Sleeping Gate.'"

"It certainly looks like something," Caid replied, dubious.

"Caid . . ." Well, they were coming clean about almost everything else, and if he was going to help her solve the mystery of the Wound, then he needed all the relevant information. "When I was inside that thing, it spoke to me. I saw where it comes from: a city somewhere else, a terrible place, with a nightmare lord presiding over it. It called it the Dreamer's City."

Caid went still, his hand on his chest trembling. "That . . . does change things. The Sleeping Gate. The Dreamer's City. That sounds like they could be related. But why did you not tell me this before?"

"I . . . didn't want to frighten all of you," Adelle murmured. She felt awful, almost sick, the bruises over her stomach pulsing as if just thinking of the incident could bring back the pain. "And I didn't know if we were going to tell you the truth about where we're from. The Wound, this creature, it knows we don't belong. I just wish I knew what it wanted."

She expected him to withdraw, or maybe go cold, but he simply nodded once. "What you experienced in there sounds truly tormenting."

"It was," Adelle said. "Which is why I want to stop it. I want to help you put things right before we go."

"Many would have simply left the same way they arrived," Caid pointed out.

"Not us," she replied. "Not me and Connie. We care about this place."

More than you know.

A quick flicker of a grin came and went, and then he gestured to the book open on her lap. "The chapter, Miss Casey?"

She found the correct page and laid the book flat between them, and their shoulders touched as they leaned over to read the fine, somewhat faded print. It was a miracle the book was still in readable condition, but it hadn't gone completely unmarred during its relocation to the workshop. Adelle had never held a book that old, and almost felt guilty touching it. Any finger oils could make the pages degrade more quickly, but they had bigger problems than worrying about it surviving to modern ages for modern collectors to find.

"He certainly likes a long introduction," Adelle mumbled, impatient.

"Here, the top of the following page, he finally comes to the heart of it," Caid told her, leaning closer, his hand brushing hers as he pointed to the relevant line. Her lips moved silently over the words, each one spurring her pulse a little faster.

Our journey to Machu Picchu was relatively without incident. On the final day, a wayward traveler joined us, dressed all in black and wearing a wide-brimmed black hat. I never saw his face clearly, but his demeanor was friendly enough. He claimed also to be studying the astrological alignments of the ruins, and he accompanied us as far as Ayacucho. Before we parted ways, he thanked us for the company and asked if I would like to "see something special."

I recount this only because it stayed with me long after details of the man faded from memory, and I remember thinking his phrasing very odd. The special thing he showed me I cannot recall, so indeed it must not have been remarkable after all.

Yet it was after I returned from my trek along the Urubamba River that the voices began. You will accuse me, dear reader, of fabricating the following events, but I assure you that all I have put down here is true and accurate.

My doctor suggested that the strange happenings that began upon my return to America are simply the result of dehydration or some jungle disease that attacks the brain. Neither of these suggestions satisfies me. In fact, I wrote to my guide, Ernesto, who had helped me navigate the rivers, and he had not heard of any such disease. I trust the man to know the region from which he hails, and while I place no blame on my physician, I do doubt his understanding of Peruvian medicine.

Within the first month of my return home, I slept no more than a dozen nights. When I did happen to sleep, I did not dream. I began putting down a detailed log of my symptoms, and you will find it in this book, to study and interrogate, and probably discard.

I barely knew sleep, I did not know dreams, and yet my waking hours felt exactly like the disorienting violence of a nightmare. On the twentieth of July, in the year 1868, I lost time for a considerable portion of the afternoon. I woke to rain, and to my office completely rearranged: the chair moved beneath the window, all of my papers and books scattered to the floor, the carpet askew. On the floor, I had written, in my own hand and unwittingly, the following:

THE DREAMER'S CITY WAITS
NGLUI THE SLEEPING GATE—
EXTINGUISH THE FLAMES
ONE WORLD ENDS FOR ANOTHER TO BEGIN
NGLUI THE GATE
FIND THE DOOR, MAKE PASSAGE,
AND THE DREAMERS WILL COME

As you might expect, after the initial shock wore down, I immediately set about researching these bizarre places. My search for understanding would take me back to the Urubamba River, where I found little, only a single cave with paintings that did, in a certain way, resemble a rudimentary city, with a figure in the shape of a crowned nautilus positioned as king.

A colleague in London was kind enough to send me copies of a transcript recovered from the ill-fated voyage of the Dunwich, sailing from Liverpool to the Hudson Bay. Before their disappearance, the captain recorded in his journal that his crew had discovered discolored ice in the water off the northern islands, and then they came upon a whaler's vessel in distress. One sailor remained: a man in all black, wearing a black chapeau.

He offered to join and work his fair share, and also to trade with them what he had salvaged from the ship. Shortly after, the captain noted that many of his crew had become ill, citing "fevers they claimed were cold rather than hot, a wildness to the eyes, incoherent mumbling, and general malaise." Several woke in the middle of the night, left their hammocks, and hurled themselves into the arctic waters, lost. Two officers reported a troubling sickness of the mind. They heard voices when they were alone, and eventually turned violent, claiming that their outbursts were to "usher the Elder One in" and to "give him his unending feast." That they attacked in his name, and served him.

The Dunwich was eventually found lodged in the ice, but none of the crew were ever discovered. Only their logs and possessions remained.

During the worst of my symptoms, I also heard intrusive voices. At quiet times, I sometimes heard a call from outside my mind, a dark and commanding voice telling me that he was close, and I was left to ponder and research before I lost the final vestiges of reason.

A month after the first incident, I again woke from an unplanned

nap, this time to the discovery that I had hideously disfigured myself,
carving into my belly an image that I will reproduce below.

Andrew Rudolph had himself illustrated what he had found scratched into his stomach—a thick, uneven circle around an eye, and three Xs below it.

"'I had carved Nglui and three extinguished flames on my own belly,'" Adelle read aloud, finishing the section. "'I was and remain sure of that. A voice compelled me to open this gate, but though I searched far and wide for clues as to how to do so, though I searched for the flames, I failed in my task. I failed, it seems, this mystery employer. Eventually, the voices and the strange occurrences ceased, and I slept normally once more, or would have, had I not been left haunted by all that had happened, all that I had seen. In recent years, I have found even more allusions to this Dreamer's City and Nglui, but spread across the world, fragments of a puzzle I long and dread to solve.'"

Adelle sat back, feeling winded. The Elder One. It sounded remarkably similar to the Old One Straven had referenced in the spell that sent them into the book. There had to be a connection.

"'Spread across the world,'" she repeated. "So this is bigger than Boston. It's something the creature has tried to do many times before, but maybe this is the only time it's gotten this far. There was a man, Straven, who helped us get here, and he always dressed in black, and had a black hat hanging in his shop. He sent Robin Amery through and nothing happened, and so he sent us, too. It had to be intentional—he had to be doing it to open this gate. The spell he used called on the Old One, maybe that's the same thing as this Elder thing."

Caid nodded, still glued to the book. "And the flames . . ."

"The three of us who don't belong," Adelle whispered. "What if that's how this gate opens? We are the three anomalies here—maybe our presence or our deaths open a path between here and that city I saw inside the Wound."

"'Usher the Elder One in,'" Caid reread. "I believe, Miss Casey, that your theory is sound. Sound and troubling. We cannot let anything happen to you or Miss Rollins."

"Sure, but we also have to actually close the Wound." She pointed to Rudolph's diagram again. "What if this is the Wound? What if the Wound is Nglui, the actual gate—it just isn't open yet? We can't just leave it there. What if . . . what if somehow more people return here, more people who don't belong? Then it will just start all over again."

"Then we mustn't fail," Caid said simply. "It is a pity that time is short, and that part of our success relies upon your departure. There are so very many things I would like to ask a woman of the future."

Adelle grinned, though she felt terribly tired. It seemed like they still had so much to do, such a long road to travel. She wished she could just curl up on the sofa there and talk all about the wonders that awaited them at the turn of the century, and beyond.

"Make a list," she told him, turning her face toward the door in response to a gentle knock. "I will answer as many as I can before we go."

Caid stood and handed her the Rudolph book, then went to the door and checked the peephole. "You may not like this."

"Why? Who is it?"

"Mr. Vaughn? Are you there?"

Moira.

Adelle stood, gathered a blanket around herself, and dropped the book on the table. She could only imagine what mean, vain Moira would think of her ridiculous outfit.

"I can turn her away," Caid said softly. "After what she did to your hair . . ."

"It's fine," Adelle said, shrugging. Orla still dozed peacefully on the opposite sofa. "I fell inside a monster's stomach and saw a city that might be in another dimension. The hair thing seems silly by comparison."

Caid unlatched the door and swung it forward, and Moira brushed past him in a flawless scarlet day dress with long, tight sleeves, a prim, patterned jacket buttoned to her chin, and a swooping gray hat pinned to her hair. At once, her eyes landed on Adelle, but she simply frowned and plucked off her kidskin gloves.

"Will you be staying long? I'm afraid we're rather busy," Caid said, apparently not quite sure where to stand. He finally chose the midpoint between her and Moira.

"What I have to say is this." Moira puffed out her chest, inhaling for a speech. "I treated you abominably, Miss Casey, and when I heard about what you endured today, I found myself further degraded by my own behavior. A lady does not act so, and I hope you can accept my apology."

Adelle stared. Moira sounded sincere enough, though also a bit self-serious. "Apology accepted," she replied. The awful things Moira had called her didn't matter. Her hair didn't matter. Moira could shave it all off, for all she cared, as long as Adelle and Connie fixed the Wound and returned home safely. "It's all forgotten."

"What a relief!" Moira rushed to her, tucking her gloves under her arm, and took Adelle's hands. She smelled like lilacs and mint. Adelle couldn't imagine she herself smelled any better than old pond water. "I never considered myself a jealous person. This is a fault you have brought to light in me, and I will endeavor to rectify it. Severin sent me to fetch you; he is practically obsessed with the idea of us reconciling. He will not be satisfied until he has proof of our accord." Then she took aim at Caid. "As for our . . . *understanding* . . ."

He smiled. "What understanding?"

Moira brightened at once. "You mean . . . you are releasing me from our engagement?"

"Yes," Caid replied. Adelle could tell he was fighting to keep a sarcastic edge from his tone. "I have found it in my heart to do so. I'm convinced you'll be much happier with Mr. Sylvain."

"Oh, thank you!" Moira wiped at an invisible tear. "I always knew you were a perfect gallant."

That's a lie, thought Adelle. Moira never had kind things to say about Caid in the novel. Adelle glanced at him, but he didn't seem out of sorts. Moira simply waited and paced, flicked away another false tear, then spun back toward the door, her bustle sweeping the floor like quiet bristles.

"I had thought to make amends with Orla, too, and collect her, but she seems quite happy here; perhaps when she is awake you will tell her I wish to speak," Moira said. "Will you join me, then, Miss Casey? Severin awaits."

"I . . ." She looked helplessly to Caid, but he appeared just as baffled. "I suppose I can. May I have a moment?"

"Of course, but do not tarry, please!" She glided out of the room, the door closing gently behind her.

"Do you think she was being genuine?" Adelle asked when she was gone.

"I find her devilishly difficult to read, but I do think she was genuine, yes. . . ." Caid drew out the last word, scratching the hollow in his neck again. "But. Must you go?"

"Is something wrong?" Adelle asked, searching his face. "Or are you just saving me from terrible art?"

"Therein lies my hesitation," he replied. "I have never seen his work, and nobody has ever accused him of being modest. I've long wondered why he's kept his work a secret."

"Maybe he's just insecure." Adelle didn't know why she felt a sudden urge to defend Severin. Her perfect opinion of him had changed. He was beautiful and captivating, but the reality didn't live up to her fantasy. Adelle had fallen for him at Byrne House, but that felt like a lifetime ago.

And now that memory of the party and first seeing Severin left her almost cold. Maybe, she thought, because there in Caid's dusty, cozy sanctuary, filled with books and plants and *him*, she felt nothing but warm.

"You don't like him," Adelle observed carefully.

"Severin?" He snorted and shook his head, almost growling. "He is a compass without a needle, and frankly, I find him to be an unsavory lunatic."

"So, an artist," she teased.

At that, Caid relaxed a little and took her by the arm, escorting her to the door. "How quickly I forget that you are a woman from the future. I should not doubt your judgment in these matters."

"Where I come from, we call that a 'smart cookie,'" she said. "I promise to be one. Besides . . ." Adelle stepped through the open door he offered, casting one last look over her shoulder. "When I get back, I can tell you all about his stupid paintings. I won't be gone long. Keep an eye out for the signal fire—knowing Connie, it will come any minute."

33

Connie caught her breath at the top of the church, leaning against one of the broken windows and gasping, staring back the way she had come, toward King's Chapel. Gunfire echoed through the empty streets, smoke rising thick enough to envelop the chapel, but none of it told her who had won.

There was no time to stick around and wait to find out. She turned toward the water, searching the shoreline until she found the massive, glowing Wound off the wharf. She traced the route to the workshop, taking note of as many landmarks as she could in the dark before running back down into the church. None of the Penny-Farthings had left bicycles behind, so she would have to go on foot.

Connie raced north, keeping the water on her right, the backpack and rifle thumping hard on her shoulder. Before the attack, the Penny-Farthings had been nice enough to lend her more worn clothes, and she was grateful for them now, finding the loose slacks and jacket easy to run in.

She had to reach Adelle. Had to warn her about Severin. He was the only one who could have betrayed them, and her rage fueled her speed. The little prick. They finally had at least a half-assed plan to do something about their situation, and he had to go and ruin it. She wouldn't even allow herself to think about the battle back at the Congregation.

It wasn't fair.

God, can you hear me? Not fair. I don't get my first kiss and then lose her!

Tears flew, scalding and galvanizing, down her cheeks. Even if Missi survived the ambush, Connie would be on her way back to her own time soon. No matter what, that was probably the only kiss she was getting. Connie pumped her arms, the sticky muck covering the city streets impeding her every step of the way.

She traveled along the empty warehouses lining the waterfront, then took the next left and the next, trying to ease away from the more cluttered blocks, the sidewalks and roads heaped with drifts of rubbish and dirt and manure. Stray cats scattered, hearing the puddles splash under her shoes and hissing before joining the cockroaches in the shadows. Skidding through the wet muck, she stopped herself against the corner of a squat yellow-brick building and peered around the corner toward the voices she had heard coming from that direction.

Clackers.

Connie flattened herself against the wall, counting the different voices. They sounded nervous. Afraid.

"Never getting the rats out of that place," one of them said. "Too entrenched."

"Retreat was a mistake—we had them outnumbered."

"Not there to wipe them out, there to find the girls," the first replied.

Just two? Maybe Missi and the others had put up a real fight. But no, a third voice joined the conversation then. They were marching into the intersection, torches flaring out in a circle around them. Connie inched back farther and into a window depression.

"Only the one," that voice chimed in, a woman. "The blond one is no longer a threat."

Connie winced. Had Severin already done something to Adelle?

On Caid's couch, while Adelle slept, she had chewed her way through *Vanity Fair*. She remembered the weird, sick shock in her stomach when one of the characters died halfway through, unceremoniously. Just there and then gone, with no fanfare, alive and then dead in a single, cold sentence at the very end of the chapter: *Darkness came down on the field and city: and Amelia was praying for George, who was lying on his face, dead, with a bullet through his heart.*

Would that be Adelle? Cut short like that?

She waited until the pool of torchlight moved farther down and away from the intersection. It was still risky to run while they were that close, but if they were headed to the workshop, then she had to beat them there. Maybe Severin was waiting for backup. Caid, Orla, and Adelle would certainly put up a fight; maybe he didn't feel confident taking them all on by himself. He wasn't exactly physically intimidating. Connie told herself that was the case, that there was still time to reach Adelle and save her. It would be even colder, even sadder, knowing that she might be killed by a boy she had crushed on for so long.

When she got her hands on that sniveling, arrogant—

Connie was halfway down the block when she heard it: the low, steady thump of heavy feet dropping into the street. She backtracked, throwing herself around the corner and kneeling, trying to smash herself into the wall, in between two bricks if she had to. The waves sighed, rolling against the shore just three blocks to the east. If her rough calculations were right, Caid's workshop was only five more blocks north.

The Clackers seemed to be moving toward the Wound itself, but if they took a left, they could easily swing up toward the workshop.

And now she had the Befouler to worry about. Connie hoped that its more or less even pace meant it hadn't seen her. She had no idea how or *if* it could see, or if it used some kind of otherworldly sense they didn't have a name for. The moaning grew louder, voices crying into the darkness, agonized shrieks piercing the silence every few crashing steps it took.

"Please," one of the voices groaned. "End this . . . end this . . ."

Connie pulled her knees closer to her chest, balled up against the wall, the sharp bricks digging into her shoulders, the puddle beneath her soaking the seat of her pants. The Befouler stumbled out into the intersection, close enough now that some of the faces were level with Connie's. She shut her eyes, then squinted just enough to see, wishing she hadn't.

Don't breathe. Don't move. Don't even think.

"Release meeeee," a male voice droned. "Where are my legs, where . . ."

It paused, so close. Close enough to reach out and touch. A skull dripping with inky black ooze stared unblinkingly at her. Did it see? Could it alert the creature to her presence? Connie shivered. Her heart stopped; even her pulse seemed too loud and noticeable. She shifted her hand up to her mouth and held it there until the Befouler and its unbearable stench drifted on, melting back into the shadows, following the Clackers to the water's edge, or to the workshop.

She stood, slowly, checking around the edge of the building again before darting across the street, careful not to step in the thick tar sludge the Befouler left in its wake.

Five more blocks. She could do it. She just had to run like she never had before. Biggest game of her life. Seconds left on the clock. Just five more blocks.

"Hold on, Adelle," she whispered, the words dissolving in the dark. "I'm coming for you."

34

ADELLE KNEW SOMETHING WAS wrong the moment she set foot in the studio. For one, it was incredibly dark: only a single small candelabra burned in the center of the room, on a folding chair.

For another, no matter how much she called out, nobody answered. It wasn't a space with many places to hide—there were canvases everywhere, that she could tell, and a few tables for mixing paints, and a strangely haphazard mattress stuffed into a corner.

No Severin or Moira, but plenty of paintings. Adelle approached the nearest one. There were at least two dozen easels set up around the room, which struck her as excessive, but then Severin was a strange boy. And also excessive. Adelle went to the chair and grabbed the candleholder, lifting it to inspect the painting. The light flashed across it, the candles leaping with almost accusatory zeal.

Adelle was looking at a pair of eyes. Her own, in fact.

There was no mistaking it—the piece was just a pair of eyes, a woman's, crudely expressed, as if he had finger-painted it. One was messily colored blue, the other green. Adelle took a step back, gooseflesh rising along her arms. She tiptoed to the next easel and found almost the exact same painting. Her eyes, badly, weirdly done. The huge swipe marks around the eyes made them almost look sleepless, marked with bruise-like exhaustion. The next easel was the same, and the next. She didn't know why she kept checking, because each time she knew what she would find.

Her breath became hysterical hiccups. She wanted to fall to the floor and tuck her head against her knees; her chest squeezed tighter and tighter, a fluttering pain over her heart telling her the panic attack was coming and nothing could stop it. Still, she tried, turning her back on the hideous paintings, which now only seemed to her the ravings of an obviously unwell person.

As soon as she spun toward the door, the trick became clear.

"Moira."

"Ugly *and* gullible," she drawled, taking long, slow steps toward her. "You and Orla really are made for each other."

"What do you want?" Adelle asked. She tried to place an easel between them, but Moira was blocking the door and there was nowhere to hide. "I—I don't have any interest in Severin," Adelle stammered. "If that's what this is about. I didn't even mean to say his name aloud in my sleep; it was just a dream. A bad one."

"Of course it was, dove," Moira chirped, rolling her eyes. "There are no good dreams here anymore."

In a single even stroke, she pulled the shears from her velvet bag, holding them up so Adelle could get a look.

"There's not much left to cut," Adelle told her, dodging around another easel. There had to be a way out. . . . There had to be a way . . .

"Oh? I had decided on a rather more permanent alteration."

She lunged, stabbing toward Adelle with the shears. The easels fell as Moira chased her through the maze of stands, Adelle pushing them over toward her, trying to trip up Moira's feet as Adelle circled back toward the door.

"Why are you *doing* this?" Adelle shrieked. "I don't want him! You can have him all to yourself!"

"But I cannot, not when you are here. I found your little bag, dove, the one the Chanters took?" Moira clucked her tongue and shook her head, trying to trap Adelle against the far wall. "He doesn't love you for your beauty or your wit; he loves you because you are odd. You are a freak, and you do not belong. Artists always love what they cannot understand!"

"Stop, Moira! I promise you . . . I don't love him. I won't take him from you!" Adelle tried to fall back on her memories of the novel. "You two are meant to be together—everyone knows that. I know that!"

"Lies! It would be just my ridiculous luck, to have done all that I have and lose my one and only love to . . . to . . . whatever you are!"

Moira cried out, slashing recklessly, blindly. She had the rage but not the accuracy. Adelle tried to use that to her advantage, shoving more easels toward her, but she would run out of obstacles soon.

"I can explain everything," Adelle assured her. "Please, you don't have to do this, Moira. I can explain the backpack, the phone, the ID. . . ."

"I. Do. Not. Know. What. Any of that. Means." She punctuated every syllable with a jab of the shears, shredding the paintings as they were knocked toward her. With an impatient scream, she charged, eyes wide and teary, as if she regretted her fury but was powerless to overcome it.

"I gave up everything! I will not lose him!" Moira threw herself toward Adelle.

The easel between them was her only barrier. Adelle kicked it toward Moira, hard, and the wooden edge slammed into the redhead's left hand, stunning her. Cursing, she flapped her hand around, testing the pain. But Adelle didn't give her time to recover, body-checking the easel into her, using it like a shield to bash her onto her back. They fell, both of them crying out in surprise, and landed with a thump, a crack, and a *shhlck* on the paint-flecked floor.

Adelle roused herself, slightly dazed, ready to run for the door. But Moira had gone completely still. Then she gave a tiny wheeze, and Adelle climbed to her feet and pulled the easel up slowly, carefully, to find her heroine flattened to the floor, the shears jammed back into her from the impact, sticking out directly from the center of her chest. She looked almost like a painting, gracefully askew, her hands palms up, resting by her shoulders, her dark red hair fanned around her, the blood soaking through her dress almost a perfect match for the velvet.

Adelle dropped down next to Moira, frightened, hands hovering helplessly as her mind raced. Did she scream for help? Did she pull the shears out?

"Moira . . ." Adelle hadn't meant to kill her, had only meant to protect herself. A shadow darkened the door, and with the last of her life, Moira's eyes rolled toward it, her lips parting around a strangled laugh.

"Severin? Darling . . . is that you?" she murmured, eyelids drooping. Her hand fell to her chest, gripping the base of the shears but never pulling them free. "Severin . . ."

It was indeed him. Overturned candles lay strewn around them, the spilled wax surrounding the girls like a salt circle. Severin took it all in, approaching with restrained steps.

"It's bad," Adelle told him as he came to kneel near Moira's head. Gently, he stroked the hair back from her forehead, and her lips curled into a dreamy expression. "Severin . . . what do we do?"

"Nothing, Adelle."

"Wh-what?" Adelle shook her head. "No . . . We have to try and help her. It was an accident! She charged at me with those shears; I was just defending myself."

Severin held Moira's fingers where they curled around the scissors. His brow tightened, but he wasn't staring at his dying love. He was staring at Adelle. His lips twitched, as if something amusing had just occurred to him.

"I am going to tell you a story," he said softly.

"A story? Severin, did you hear me? Look at her! We have to get her help!"

"There is no need; she is surely dead," Severin replied lightly. Adelle gulped for air, drowning. This wasn't right. Why was he so calm? "Now listen very carefully, because I can tell you are a tender soul, and so I want you to understand why I did all of this."

All of what? Adelle had been the one to accidentally shove the shears in. . . .

"My father wanted me to be a fisherman. Always, always, he never stopped talking about it. Annoying." Severin snorted at the memory, as if he weren't laying his hand on a dead girl bleeding out between them. "It was his passion, but not mine. I knew he would never let me be anything else, not an artist, not a painter, but I could not live that life."

"Moira was your way out," Adelle said, trying to hurry him along without letting him know she was aware of every meaningless detail of his life. "She helped you leave the family business behind."

"She might have been, but I doubt that. No, I found another way."

She glanced toward the door, ready to flee, but he held up his fingers to hold her. They dripped with blood.

"*Un moment*, please," he murmured, eyes burning into her. "I want you to understand, because we are both soft at heart, and I sense your soul is similar to mine. Would you do anything for love, Miss Casey?"

"I . . . I think so. I don't know. Yes?" Her mind spun. Now she wondered if she ought to just say what he wanted to hear, keep him talking until she could find a way to leave.

He smiled. "Yes, yes, I knew it. And for your passion? Would you do anything?"

Adelle had landed in a different reality because of her passions, so that answer was clear. Moira had gone so still between them, and she wanted to get away from the body. Her eyes flicked to the door again. Surely Caid would come looking for her. . . .

"I . . . Yes," she said, appeasing him. "Yes."

"And so would I, and so I did," Severin told her. "I was strolling the shore for inspiration one morning, when I came upon a man fishing. He was dressed all in black, and I cannot remember his face, which is rather strange because meeting him changed everything. He asked if I would like to see something special, and I agreed."

Yes, Adelle thought, *you would.* But the story sounded familiar. The man in all black. The asking if he wanted to see something special. . . . The phrasing, the description, it couldn't be a coincidence.

Oh God, oh no . . .

"He showed me a fish he had caught," Severin continued, unaware of her panic. He held the shears again, tighter, blood pouring around the heel of his hand. "It had only one eye, red, shiny, and hard, like a jewel. He told me to take it and swallow it, and then I would receive a letter. If I did these things, anything I wanted—everything I wanted—would come to pass. Wealth, love, power . . . all of it would be mine."

"And you did it," Adelle breathed. *You stupid idiot.* "You did it."

"*Bien sûr,*" he shrugged, casual. "The tear had already opened near the warehouses; your Robin Amery must have come, then.

This man and his promises felt like another omen. I felt the winds changing, and so I chose to shift them in my direction."

She leaned to her right, preparing to scramble to her feet and run, but his attention never strayed from her. Of course it wouldn't. She had seen the paintings. He knew. He knew even when they first met that she didn't belong. This wasn't art, or obsession—it was madness.

Somewhere, in another reality, a banner hung over her bed.

A bit of madness is key, to give us new colors to see.

Adelle wanted to scream. So that was how the Chanters picked who to protect and who to antagonize—Severin had helped bring about the fall of the city, so no doubt they listened to whatever he said, hurting whoever he wanted hurt, disposing of anyone he felt was getting in the way of his desires. And the life he'd left behind, the poor life with his father, had to go too. Anything that didn't fit his vision was chaff to be discarded.

"The Dreamer's City," Severin breathed. "Don't you like the sound of that? I do. Perhaps all artists and lovers are free there. All the ugliness and dreariness of this shit-infested world is washed away, and nothing mundane is left to flourish. No pain. No drudgery. No loneliness. Only dreams."

"Severin . . ." Adelle felt her entire body go rigid with alarm. "You don't want this—you don't even know what it is! None of us do. Please trust me: whatever this thing is telling you, whatever it promised, you can't listen." Her snarled thoughts unraveled, then led her on a breathless, winding path back to the novel. "Y-you did get everything you wanted in the end."

"What?" He tilted his head to the side, roguish black curls bouncing.

"You did get Moira, and money, and the life you wanted. A life of art and beauty and passion. . . . You didn't do it this way; you didn't have to. You just loved her with everything you had and things fell into place. You used your wits to get Orla back from the Penny-Farthings when she was kidnapped. You charmed her family. It was all possible without this, Severin. All of this pain and suffering was for nothing."

Silent, he no longer looked so intense and frightening, and his shoulders sagged as he listened to her.

"I did love you once, Severin," Adelle rushed on. She had to talk him down, no matter what; she had to get him to see how truly unhinged he had become. "I did. But I loved the you in that reality, the one who won his heart's desire without hurting anyone to do it. That Severin was a bold, beautiful artist who saw a girl in the park and decided he would love her forever, and then he did, and it was perfect."

"You speak from the heart—that much is clear, Adelle."

He seemed to consider what she said, reaching out with his clean hand to brush her chin and then her lips. She shivered and recoiled, and his mouth hardened into a hateful line.

"That Severin has lost his love, and no longer feels a thing when he paints. But he will return. He will, when all of the ugliness is wiped clean. This world belongs to the dreamers now, Adelle, and I truly believe you are one of us, which is why it pains me so to do this."

A single candle near her foot had escaped the chaos. It sputtered out suddenly, casting his face in shadow—and Adelle threw up her hands just a little too late to stop Severin Sylvain from shoving the shears through her.

35

BREATHLESS, CONNIE FOUND HIM standing over two nearly lifeless bodies, candles spilled at his feet, white wax soaked in blood, his back to her. Adelle, still dressed in Caid's night shirt, looked still and beautiful, like an impaled saint.

"Sweet Adelle," she heard him chuckle. "Are you surprised I could not be swayed? Perhaps I am too, a little. Ah, you should see the look on your face."

Connie raised the rifle to her shoulder, never surer of any shot she had taken in her entire life.

"No," she said. Severin froze, then turned, and when she had the whites of his eyes, she fired. "You should see the look on yours."

The bullet struck him in the knee, just as intended. No need to kill—just keep him from escaping or causing any more trouble. Severin grunted and fell down flat on his chest, pressing his hands into the floor, trying to crawl away, but so much blood had mingled on the tiles that he simply slipped and swam and rolled onto his side. Breathing hard, he spat at her, all eyes and bared teeth.

Connie crossed to him swiftly, knelt next to Adelle, and pulled her up into her lap and away from Moira and Severin.

"Too late," he told her. "The Dreamer's City will come; I will know it. I will see it."

But Adelle wasn't done breathing. She grabbed Connie's forearm, trying to sit up. Luckily, he hadn't aimed perfectly; the shears had lodged in the gap between Adelle's collarbone and shoulder.

"We need to get you downstairs," Connie said, trying to keep calm, trying not to look at how much blood had seeped through Caid's shirt. "Can you stand?"

"I think so," Adelle murmured. She looked stunned, as if she still wasn't convinced there was a pair of scissors sticking out of her. Together, they worked Adelle into a limp standing position, Connie supporting her weight, one hand around her waist, the other on the rifle. "Connie . . . Where are the others? Why are you back?"

"Dead!" Severin lazed onto his back and spread his arms wide. "I sent the Chanters for them. Your plan will never work now."

"Can it." Connie kicked him in the jaw as they passed.

The gunshot must have been loud enough to echo through the warehouse. Caid and Orla appeared in the doorway, then hurried over to help support Adelle. They both caught sight of the mess on the floor, and Orla peeled away, staring at the macabre tableau the two lovers made, one wounded, the other framed in a pool of her own blood.

"How . . ." Orla gasped. "Is there nothing we can do for her?"

"She's gone," Adelle murmured. "Orla . . . I'm so sorry. I was just trying to defend myself; she attacked me with the shears."

"I knew he was trouble, but her, too?" Connie asked.

Adelle sighed and winced, and walked stiffly, trying not to agitate the shears. "Moira thought she was losing him. I guess she already had, but not in the way she thought."

"Listen to me," Connie said, not caring if the others heard, as they left the studio behind and turned into the hall, Adelle's shoes dragging a trail of blood. "We are getting out of here. Now. You need a doctor, Adelle, and nobody here is going to be able to help you."

"Miss Rollins is correct," Caid added, taking Adelle's injured side gingerly, only steadying her when she reached for him. "What matters now is that you get the treatment you need. We will find a way to close the Wound."

"The Clackers ambushed us at the Congregation. I have no idea how many survived, if they can still get the balloon in the air," Connie said. "I saw what's left of them when I was headed here, but I'm not sure if they're coming for us or going to the water."

"Severin is behind all of this," Adelle murmured weakly. "No matter what. He wanted all of this to happen. He wants to open the gate and usher in the Dreamer's City. He's completely out of his mind. He thinks he can open a gate to that city, and I'm afraid he might be right."

Orla finally joined them in the corridor, slamming the door shut behind her.

"We should not linger here, then," Caid replied. "Severin has no doubt told the Chanters how to find you."

"Take your time with the stairs, Delly," Connie told her. A narrow, steep set of stairs zigzagged down from the third floor to the main level. Adelle struggled, hissing out her breaths with each tentative step as they began the descent.

The building shook. Solid and massive as it was, whatever had just hit was enough to send a fine mist of dust falling down on them from the ceiling.

"They have the Befouler," Connie hissed. "Change of plans—can't take your time, Delly."

"There is a secondary door," Caid explained swiftly. "End of the corridor, first floor, but we must reach it before they see us. I was locking the entrance just as I heard the gunshot—after Miss Byrne called, I thought it better to turn away more visitors. If the doors last, we can reach the servants' entrance. There is a memorial not far from here that should allow for some privacy." He paused, then said with some exasperation, "Oh, come, let me carry her."

Caid opened his arms to them, nervous sweat shining on his forehead.

"It's fine, Connie," Adelle said with a rasping chuckle. "He's practically a professional at this now."

She looked worryingly pale as Caid lifted her into his arms with extreme care, mindful of the shears impaling her, bringing her pain but also keeping more blood from escaping the puncture.

"These relentless monsters." Orla stalled on the landing, waiting for them, chewing her knuckles. "I wish it all to be over. I wish it all to be a very bad dream."

"Miss Rollins, please take Miss Beevers ahead to scout for the Chanters. Do you have all that you require to return to your time?" He took the stairs slowly, one at a time, while Connie swept up Orla's arm and yanked her down off the landing.

"I have the book, candle, and cup in my bag; we can find a stone outside. Delly?"

"I . . . Oh God!" she wheezed, coughing. "I—I lost it! I must have left it in the workshop—"

"Never fear, Miss Casey. I was not going to let you leave anything behind." Caid tipped Adelle against his chest, carefully extracting the incense from his coat pocket and laying it in Adelle's lap. It didn't stay there long, Connie immediately swiping it to stuff in her nylon bag.

"You're amazing," Adelle whispered. "Now we just need a place to do the spell and hope it doesn't somehow usher in another apocalypse."

That was all Connie needed to hear. She pulled Orla down the stairs as the building shook again and again. Orla grabbed up her skirts to run faster, huffing and puffing to keep up. On the first level, Connie watched the front doors shiver, blasted with another punishing blow from the Befouler. The doors were locked, but she had no idea how long they would hold. Flames crackled at the bottom, torches setting the doors ablaze.

"Fire!" Connie yelled up to them. "They're not inside, but we've got fire!"

The Befouler hurled itself against the door, and Orla shrieked as the wood visibly bowed, a shower of sparks cascading into the hall.

"Oh, Miss Rollins." Orla hid her face in Connie's shoulder. "I have never been more afraid in my entire life. I fear I shall combust."

"Me too," Connie told her, watching the fire spread. "Me too."

36

"WE REALLY NEED TO stop meeting this way." Adelle clung to Caid's neck, no longer worried about how desperate she seemed. Her hands were growing cold, and a strange vibrating sensation in her toes made her wonder if she was already losing too much blood. Light-headedness threatened, but she kept her eyes on Caid. She couldn't look at the path behind them, knowing that any second, the Befouler might darken the corridor at their backs.

He laughed, blinking the sweat out of his eyes, and walked as swiftly as he could toward the end of the hall, where Orla and Connie waited, huddled on either side of the life-saving door. Adelle removed his glasses with her right hand, carefully wiped the sweat out of his eyes with her sleeve, then placed his spectacles back.

"Thank you, Miss Casey, but I really must beg you to cease any unnecessary movements," he said quietly, out of breath.

Connie unlatched the door and opened it with utmost caution, probably paranoid of any alerting groan or squeak.

"You have to see where you're going," Adelle argued. "I'd rather not be dropped."

"Never," he said seriously, and it sounded like an oath. "I would never drop you, Miss Casey."

"Adelle," she corrected, her voice wobbly with fear. It felt, increasingly, like she might die. The only thing holding her together was the strength of Caid's arms, and her absolute confidence in Connie to somehow make it all right.

"Is that not awfully informal?"

"I'm bleeding to death, and after tonight we might never see each other again. So I think informal is where we are," she said.

"I happen to agree," Caid replied, ducking and bringing them out into the cool, bolstering air. "Adelle."

From the pain or from fear, she collapsed deeper into his grasp, and she didn't imagine the way he hugged her tighter to his chest. On paper it was so tragically romantic, but now she was living it and found it only to be pain. Everything she wanted to say felt dramatic and stupid, morbid, or too silly.

"I made my list, you know," Caid told her, following Orla and Connie, keeping to the edge of the road as they left the workshop behind. "Given the circumstances, I now realize it is optimistically long. If you are willing, and well enough, perhaps you will answer my most urgent queries."

"Yes," she said. "It will take my mind off . . . everything."

"Has science proved or disproved the existence of God?" he asked.

Adelle smirked, thrown. "No."

"Have we left Earth behind for the stars?"

"We've landed on the moon, and there are satellites orbiting Earth, and we've photographed the solar system, sent probes. . . . It's a lot to explain, and I'm not the science-y one." Adelle laughed through her nose.

"Fascinating. Yes. Of course. Moving on—"

"My God, look! It's the signal fire, look!" Orla had stopped on the sidewalk, pointing up above the rooftops to the southeast. Just as Missi had promised, a fire burned at the top of the church bell tower.

"The balloon . . ." Adelle watched Connie sprint back to them, her face an odd mixture of expressions. Happy, then afraid, then angry, then confused . . . Adelle hadn't realized her friend had such complicated feelings about the plan. She winced, her chest burning as if someone had shoved a hot pepper in her esophagus. The fire burned brighter, a glow so powerful and hopeful that Adelle couldn't help but simply stare and stare. Caid stood transfixed too.

"The beacons are lit," she heard Connie murmur.

"Gondor calls for aid." Adelle closed her eyes, finding a tiny, depleting well of strength deep inside. "I want to see it."

"The balloon?" Caid asked.

"Yes, I want to see it. I want to see the Wound close. I have to know it's done before we go."

"Delly . . ." Connie had her *putting my foot down* face on now, no longer confused at all. "We can't risk it. You need to go home. Now."

"I'll make it," Adelle promised her. "Please, I have to know it's gone. This thing is bigger than us, Connie. We found Andrew Rudolph's book. . . . This creature, the Dreamer's City, it's tried to break through before. I don't think it's ever gotten this close; I don't think it's ever had reality bend like this. We're part of it. We can't give up, not when we're this close."

Connie swore and tossed her hands in the air, then turned a full circle and wiped her thumb across her mouth. "All right. But the second you feel too weak, or if the balloon goes down . . ."

"Of course," Adelle murmured. "Deal."

Connie told herself not to hope, but a stubborn part of her insisted that nobody could get that balloon into the air but Mississippi McClaren.

They trundled along toward the water, while Connie listed in her head the approximately one million reasons it was a terrible idea. They had no idea how many Clackers there even were; a hundred of them could be waiting on Long Wharf to surprise them. They didn't even know if there were other Befoulers. And of course there were the screamers to consider, not to mention the Wound itself. But that same stubborn part of her that believed in Missi believed in what Adelle wanted too.

Her coaches always, always told the team sternly to leave a field better than they found it, to pick up whatever trash they brought in, and to even carry out what others carelessly left behind. She and Adelle were part of the destruction of this world, and it was only right to leave it better than they'd found it, or at least to do the most and best they could.

Robin Amery was dead. Moira was dead. Severin might easily bleed out from his wound or develop a bad infection and die. She didn't know if those things could be undone, but she kept a spark alive for the people trapped inside the Wound—Adelle had said they'd looked like they were just resting, or in stasis, untouched. If they could bring those people back, restore them to their families and loved ones, then the guilt of all of this might eventually become bearable.

Her mind leaped to remind her that this place was fake, just a construct, but Connie ignored that impulse. That didn't matter. The characters had become real to her, Missi most of all.

Missi.

Her first kiss. She glanced up toward the sky, desperate to see some glimpse of the balloon. How would they even get it airborne? Surely Missi had thought of that, planned for it. If they'd only had more time . . . Between Kincaid's smarts and Missi's determination, they would have made an unstoppable duo, and probably have had the balloon equipped with laser guns and self-heating showers and a tearoom.

A lumpy, soft shape moved against the fog churning against the cloudy night sky. Connie nudged Orla at her side, then turned to Adelle and Kincaid. He was picking his way through the garbage and potholes with Adelle curled up in his arms. She looked pale but animated, chatting with him in low tones every step of the way.

"I think that's them," Connie said in a stage whisper. "The balloon! It's actually working!"

It was moving fast, outpacing the stormy speed of the clouds roiling behind it. A puff of light illuminated it for a moment, and Connie gasped. A fire. They were kindling a fire in the basket to keep the balloon afloat, and the glow showed the dizzying patchwork of fabrics sewn too hastily and desperately together. The balloon gained on them quickly, disappearing now and then behind a steeple, always emerging, the bulk of it radiating a muted brilliance like a lantern.

"That thing sure can go," Adelle cried. "We have to hurry or they'll beat us to the shore!"

Though Connie could hear the constant rush of the waves, they were not yet in sight of the water. They followed the curving road they had taken from the wharf after Adelle's reemergence from the Wound. Behind them, distant but unmistakable, the ground trembled.

"I believe the Befouler has discovered our absence," Kincaid said, striding faster, joining Orla and Connie as they trotted down the sidewalk. "A bit of haste is indeed in order."

Connie could hear them all struggling for breath. She wasn't tired or taxed, but the nervous anticipation left her lungs aching. Weighted down by skirts and heeled boots, Orla began to fall behind, but Connie took her arm, encouraging her along. The balloon soared over the city, closer now, becoming almost level with them as they raced toward the wharf.

A chorus of shrieks shattered the silence: a dozen sleek black shapes speeding overhead and toward the balloon.

"Screamers," Connie whispered. Then she shouted it, louder and louder, waving her arms, trying to get the attention of the balloon riders. "SCREAMERS!"

She clumsily reloaded the rifle as they ran, making a mess of the little powder packet she kept in her trouser pocket. Still, she managed to get the shot in, and fired blindly toward the screamers, knowing she couldn't hit one but hoping to warn the ballooners.

"Those things will tear right through the fabric," she muttered. "They'll never make it to the Wound."

But answering fire surprised her, pistol rounds blasting off the balloon basket, followed by a familiar whoop, and the sound of Geo and Farai screaming curses at the creatures. The screamers made a pass, and they managed to knock into the basket, bumping it a little south, but the gunfire had clearly unsettled them, and they flew off, circling, preparing for another assault.

The road curved steeply, dumping them out onto a straighter avenue that ran parallel along the water's edge. Shadowy warehouse silhouettes, familiar now to Connie, rose ahead of them.

"Keep up!" she cried. "We're almost there!"

The screamers filled the city with their hideous song, near again as they came spearing toward the balloon. Gunfire met them, but they seemed bolder, dashing directly toward the basket.

Connie raced ahead, now running almost yard for yard with the balloon as it intersected their path. She couldn't quite see the girls inside, but she could hear them frantically calling to each other to reload, reload!

"No!" She heard Geo then, her voice shrill and panicked. "The tie! Look, we're sunk!"

The basket tipped precariously, one of the four ropes attaching it to the balloon having been sheared by a passing screamer.

"No, no, no," Connie whispered. "Not now, not when we're so close!"

But she hurried on, passing between two warehouses and making for the wharf, the old brick storehouse ahead stamped dark and foreboding against the glow of the Wound beyond.

"The Befouler!" she heard Adelle calling after her, and paused, waiting for the others to gain. "Connie, we're going to be trapped out on that wharf!"

"We must close the Wound, is that not right?" Orla asked, red-faced and sweating in her heavy gown. "That is our only priority. We must be brave now, even if it means being taken by the Befouler. No others have attempted this—no others have been able to close the Wound!"

"Well stated, Miss Beevers," Kincaid said, nodding. "Discretion is the better part of valor, but now valor must be the better part of valor. This is our last gambit—what will be left of Boston if we do not dedicate ourselves completely?"

Connie couldn't help but smile, impressed by a speech that would make any coach beam with pride. They had become fearless, and that might be exactly what the night required.

"Then we press forward," Connie said, leading them between the warehouses. The balloon soared on, just above them now and then beyond, and as it went, dazzling even while crooked and homemade, the fire climbed—higher and hungrier after the screamers' attack—and the whole beautiful mess went up in flames.

37

THEY STOOD AT THE end of the wharf, watching their hopes go up in smoke.

Adelle, still in Caid's grasp, reached for Connie's shoulder, trying somehow to comfort her.

"It could still work," Adelle told her. "It could."

The flames had receded somewhat, the balloon blown high, high above the Wound, from the sudden rush of hot air. Sounds like heavy wings beating came from the basket, no doubt the girls using their coats and whatever they had to beat back the roaring flames. The edge of the fabric itself had not yet caught fire, but they would also soon lose sight of it if it went any higher.

"This . . . may not be altogether bad," Caid said slowly, obviously working his thoughts out aloud. "The tea they plan to pour into the Wound is no doubt the majority of their ballast. Once that is gone, they would have nothing to help them lower the balloon. If they can survive the fire, it may actually get them back down to the ground."

"*If!*" Connie thundered. "*If!* Would *you* survive a fire in that tiny basket?"

"The alternative is that they blow out to sea, Miss Rollins." Caid kept his voice steady. "And are never seen again."

"They have their problems," Orla murmured shakily. "We have ours."

She tugged furiously on Connie's sleeve, and they all turned in unison to find that the Chanters had come, though not in numbers anywhere near what Connie had projected. Only eight remained, their robes stained far beyond white, muddied and covered in gunpowder, some of them singed, one or two badly bloodied. Their varying heights suggested they were of different genders and ages, though they all wore the same grotesque, mis-shapen leather masks.

The two on the ends carried torches, the rest pistols and rifles. They would be in range soon.

"Get behind me," Connie said in a dangerous whisper.

That meant moving closer to the Wound, but they were still nowhere near its writhing storm of tentacles. The balloon seemed gone for good, having disappeared somewhere among the clouds, leaving them outnumbered and outgunned and alone.

"We tried," Orla said, clinging to Caid's side. She gazed up at Adelle, her eyes swimming with tears. Adelle attempted to hug her as best she could, but her left arm wasn't working so well. They had to hurry, and it seemed like they would have to cast the spell without defeating the Wound, leaving their poor friends to fend for themselves.

It wasn't fair, it wasn't right, but what could they do?

The screamers flew overhead, pursuing the balloon. The dense wharf shook, the slow thunder of the Befouler's tread growing closer as it passed the warehouses. Caid, Adelle, and Orla backed away with tiny steps, Connie doing the same, but out ahead of them, her rifle now raised after a swift reload. They passed the Wall of a Hundred Faces, staring at them, a twisted mosaic of pleading mouths and bulging eyes. Adelle hadn't looked at it closely before, but now she watched the tormented faces protrude from the stones, clamoring wordlessly for relief.

Adelle watched Caid look for the faces of his loved ones, and felt tears to match Orla's well in her eyes.

"What do we do?" she asked him gently.

Caid drew in a shaky breath, the first sign of fear he had shown in front of her. The force of it made her feel all the more frightened and helpless.

"We send you home," he replied, equally gentle, fighting through what she knew must be sheer terror. Once she and Connie were gone, he and the others would be at the mercy of the Chanters and the monsters, who seemed willing to take their time. Adelle almost wished they would hurry it up, fire the rifles—at least she would be there when their friends mounted a defense. Why hesitate? "Then you will be well, and safe, and we here will be what we will be."

"I would take you with me, you know that, right? If I could. In a heartbeat."

"And if it would not tear your world apart, Adelle, I would gladly accept."

Adelle couldn't tell him about the novel, about her first introduction to him, but then, she realized, she didn't need to. He wasn't that character, not anymore. Or, if he was, then Robin Amery had never understood him at all. She had made a beautiful world, but its goodness was in the little details she had abandoned, the characters who had become wonderful all on their own.

Severin Sylvain wasn't a romantic hero; this young man was.

"Meeting you was nothing like I expected," she told him. "I'm sorry we couldn't do more. Couldn't fix this."

Caid scrunched his eyes shut and tossed his head. His spectacles had gotten dirty again. "It occurs to me now that I should like to kiss you. Would you oblige me?"

"Please," Adelle whispered, her lips already closing on his. "Yes."

It was light and sweet, and simple, and Adelle loved it more than every sloppy behind-the-bleachers fumble in the world. Their first and last kiss. She hoped the tears transferring from her face to his wouldn't bother him. When he craned his neck back to look at her, Adelle tried to smile, but found it was easy, even if her chin quivered.

"What are they waiting for?" Connie muttered out of one corner of her mouth, her rifle steadied to her shoulder. High above, the screamers called back and forth to each other as if in celebration. They had found their prey.

"The Befouler." Orla covered her mouth, flinching away from the sight of it. "They were waiting for it, and now it has come."

38

"Maybe I should shoot," Connie said, fidgeting. "I'd rather die from the Clackers than from that monstrosity."

"You will not be dying, Miss Rollins," Kincaid reminded her sternly. "You will please hand me the rifle, and you and Adelle will cast your spell. It is time to admit defeat and salvage what we can."

Orla sobbed.

"Courage, Orla," he told her, carefully setting Adelle down. She couldn't stand anymore, and had to immediately kneel, cradling the shears still sticking out of her body. The bloodstain had spread down to her belly. "Courage and valor."

"A lady is not taught those things," Orla wailed, wiping fiercely at her face.

Connie pressed the rifle into his hands with a nod. Then Caid turned to Orla and gathered her to his side. "A lady does not need to be taught those qualities," he said. "A lady naturally possesses them."

Connie dropped down next to Adelle, shoving her backpack between them and tearing open the nylon flap. "I told you, Delly, he's a catch."

"Catch and release," Adelle sighed, tears drying on her cheeks. "Just my luck."

"Mine too," Connie replied, fishing out the candle and cup; she had scooped up a rock along the way. Carefully, she set the book beside the ingredients.

"What are you talking about?"

"Missi . . ." Connie snorted shyly, the wharf shaking under them as the Befouler advanced. "We, um, we kissed. There's a lot we need to talk about when we get home."

"Apparently."

"You know," Connie mused. "It's wild—I never met her."

"Who?" Adelle added the incense from her pocket to the pile.

Connie grinned. "Moira. I never got to see her alive. She was always my book crush, and I never met her."

Adelle frowned and glanced down at the scissors jutting out of her shoulder. "Ah, so she wasn't just an example. Well, trust me, it's better that you didn't."

"It doesn't matter, anyway," Connie said, glancing up toward the screamers. "I met who I needed . . . to." Her words ground to a stuttering stop as her gaze lifted. "Uh, guys? Balloon is back."

Kincaid spared a single glance, though Orla twisted around and tilted her head, staring in openmouthed shock as the balloon, trailed by a streamer of screamers, barreled down toward them, flames roaring around the edges of the fabric, devouring it. What was more, a hole flapped open in the balloon, roughly the size and shape of a screamer.

"Look out below!" Mississippi's alarm sounded just above the crackle of flames, the shrieks of the screamers, and the deafening steps of the Befouler as it brought its bulk and stench down the wharf.

"Dump it!" she heard Missi call next. "NOW!"

Even the Befouler paused as the balloon basket suddenly became a pitcher. The weight of the tea being poured over the edge and into the Wound made it list precariously as it shot toward the waves.

"They did it!" Adelle laughed, incredulous.

The Wound's arms flapped, the air shocked dead by the roar that came from it—otherworldly, deafening. Adelle almost flattened herself against the ground from the blast; Connie, Orla, and Kincaid struggled to keep their feet. The wharf quaked, spidery cracks splitting it down the middle. Waves churned and crashed, spilling bile-black water over the edge.

Connie remembered herself and hurried to protect the spell ingredients. Scrambling, she shoved everything they needed into the nylon bag, watching the waterline begin to rise, the Wound thrashing, drowning in gallons of the dream-inhibiting tea.

The Befouler called to its master, their twining voices crying in outraged agony as the Befouler raged toward them. Connie could see Kincaid's arms shaking as he aimed the rifle at it and then fired. The bullet struck—a great shot, in fact, though it was simply absorbed by the gelatinous hulk.

The shot had hit center, in the forehead of a new face lurching from the writhing mass of mashed-together bodies.

Severin.

"Lord in heaven!" Orla covered her face and looked away. "It took him."

"They don't think we can pull this off," Adelle murmured, staring over her shoulder at him with steely ferocity. "That's why the Chanters didn't fire. They don't just want us to die; they want us to die horribly. But we won't. I *can't.*"

Connie could read that expression with absolute best-friend precision.

"Delly! If you take those shears out and try to stab him, I swear on my life I'll—"

"Connie!" Adelle waved her arm toward the sky. "Connie, look out!"

The Befouler had come, and Kincaid was stuck reloading while Severin's mangled body leaned out of its front, almost its own oozing appendage. No matter how quickly Kincaid worked or how much Connie helped him with the powder, they would never make it in time.

But the balloon, now freed of its ballast, engulfed in flames and torn to shreds, had other plans—its own wild plans. Adelle watched Mississippi appear over the edge, hanging off the basket, legs kicking as she hauled down on a rope, veering the balloon sharply toward them. The balloon was coming down, and fast, and it was headed right for them.

Connie shoved Kincaid down, all instinct, and together they

tackled Orla into a pile, settling just beside Adelle as the ground shook, the Wound thundered, and the water splashed over them in freezing torrents.

Severin had wanted to see the grand *montgolfière*, and now he would, as it crashed down into the Befouler and set the creature alight. Its chorus of screams blotted out even the Wound's protests, the slick black tar covering the Befouler igniting like fuel. Three figures jumped from the balloon, landing rough and somersaulting, as the basket all but flattened the monster from the speed of its descent.

The fire raged, and the Chanters called out to each other in confusion as their weapon and their god died.

"That was incredible!" Connie leaped to her feet. A moment later she was in Missi's arms. The cowgirl winced but hugged her right back. Connie held her at arm's length, noticing the loosened, busted sling around her shoulder and the grazing wound across her bicep.

"You're hurt." Connie checked her over for other bandages.

"Don't you fuss about that now." Missi waved her off. "Did it work? Is it gone?"

They all turned in silence to the Wound and watched its tentacles flap slower and slower, only wriggling before they flopped over uselessly into the water, somewhere below the line of the wharf. The waves raged on, dying down near the wharf's midpoint, though rising higher and higher above the Wound, crashing down onto it, spray and foam obscuring it entirely from view.

"The Wall...," Orla breathed, blinking fast. "The faces are gone."

One by one, appearing through the veil of seawater, figures emerged—with tentative steps and raised arms, but they came. Nothing stirred inside the Befouler. Those lost to it were gone, it seemed, its victims smashed by the balloon basket.

"Now," Kincaid reminded the girls, reaching toward them and opening and closing his hand. "Give me the candle."

"Lay out your spell now, while the Wound is dead, before you idiots cause more trouble!" Mississippi shouted. She softened her words by squeezing the back of Connie's neck affectionately. "Who put those darn scissors there, girl?" She pointed, befuddled, at Adelle's chest.

"Caid can tell you the whole story," Adelle whispered. "I don't think the culprit will be a problem now."

Adelle was growing paler by the minute. Connie bit down on her lip, frantically spreading out the ingredients, slapping open the book quickly before anyone could notice the title. She cast her gaze skyward, determining north and south, then ripped the incense out of her nylon bag. There was no shortage of seawater for the cup.

Heavy, wet splats made them jump as screamer bodies dropped out of the sky, some landing dead in splayed piles along the wharf, others disappearing into the sea.

Orla huddled closer to Kincaid as he returned with the candle, lit from the fire still turning the Befouler to greasy ash.

"Say your goodbyes now and then go and greet them," Kincaid told her with a smile. "They will be confused, and they will need reassurance."

Connie took the candle from Kincaid and poured out a little wax on the wharf, then ground the base of the candle down into it. Everyone gathered in a circle, protecting the weak but brave little flame.

"They got Joe, Rollins, and too many of the children," Missi said, shaking her head. Farai and Geo were covered in soot, singed and bruised but alive. "We didn't sacrifice all of this and break my beautiful balloon for you to fall down now. Cast your spell, darlin', and get on home."

She leaned down and kissed Connie on the top of the head, and Connie knew in her heart it was for luck. She took Adelle's hands, and they both nodded, as ready and unready as two people could ever be. Connie wanted to stay and look around, and see their friends reunite with the people making their way down the wharf, but there was no time, and if they waited too long, their presence might just create some new terrible chaos for their friends to suffer.

"I'll miss you," Adelle murmured, keeping her gaze on Caid as she added, "I'm going to miss you all so much."

"Don't forget us," he replied, her blood staining the white linen covering his heart. "But live. Live and live, and we will do the same."

Orla simply sobbed and dislodged herself from the group to drape her arms around Adelle's neck one last time. Then she backed away and inhaled, loud enough for them all to hear. "My heart cannot take any more of this!"

"Ready?" Connie took both of Adelle's hands again.

"No. You?"

"Nope."

"She'll be fine," Adelle promised her. "She will."

"I know," Connie said, worrying anyway. "She's Mississippi McClaren. She can do anything."

Adelle closed her eyes, and Connie did too, and surrounded by sad and hopeful faces, they both put their hands on the book, on the last page, and spoke the words: "Split the world, coiled and curled, the curtain torn, the Old One born."

Epilogue

ADELLE LOOKED UP INTO the audience. Only two dozen or so friends and family had come, but to her it felt like the crowd packing a two-story Times Square bookstore. She found Connie there in the front row, hand in hand with her new girlfriend, Gigi. Gigi had transferred midsemester and joined the biathlon club, and Connie had found the courage to ask her out just before classes ended for the summer.

Connie winked and gave her a thumbs-up.

Everything had been different since they came home.

The next day would mark the one-year anniversary of their return. Adelle had started to lose consciousness on the way to the hospital, but luckily Long Wharf had been crowded with tourists when they popped back into reality, and she was saved by an Italian couple with a working cell phone and snatches of English.

There were questions, too, of course. In the ambulance, the two girls tried to shore up their story. They decided, in the end, that they just wouldn't try to explain any of it. Rumors started. Stories were spun. Most people assumed some kind of suicide pact gone wrong, or that they had been drugged and kidnapped by a psychopath. The girls bit their tongues, and let their peers and friends and family speculate where they had been for those mysterious days. In their world, it had amounted to just over seventy-two hours.

"I don't remember," Adelle told her mother whenever she got up the courage to ask. Brigitte Casey was still in high demand, but she stayed home more. That would only last for a little while, Adelle knew; her mother was too in love with her job to curb it for long, and that was fine.

Adelle didn't mind being home alone with Greg as much anymore. She had found her path, and she was showing everyone, all two dozen or so in the audience, what that meant.

Yes, she had a path. She knew what she was meant to do now.

She opened the soft-covered, self-published book, ignored the coughs and squeaking chairs, and breathed in the coffee-scented air, then read aloud the first sentence of her first book.

"You don't know the meaning of a kiss until it becomes a memory."

The reading went about as well as it could. She made it through the first chapter of the book, and then everyone stood and clapped, and Adelle could see her mother beaming in the audience. Even Greg looked moved. She imagined Caid there next to them, dressed in a blazer and khaki pants, his glasses more modern, maybe tortoise-shell, but his wide, dimpled smile flashing as he cheered her on.

Sometimes she was sure he was around. Connie said the same thing—that every now and then she would catch sight of a pretty redhead at the mall or at a Sox game, and think: *That was her. I know that was her.*

It never hurt less, but Adelle found herself craving those glimpses all the same.

The store where Connie's mom, Rosie, worked, Country Shelf, had been kind enough to set up a signing space for her. They couldn't stock the book without a legitimate ISBN, something Rosie Rollins had warned her about, but Adelle didn't mind. It was more of a passion project anyway, and she was just grateful that they had indulged her, letting her give the reading and then sign all the copies that had come in a tightly packed box.

Giddy, she whipped out her Sharpie for Connie and Gigi. Shiny glitter stars decorated Gigi's cheeks, contrasting with her spotless brown complexion. She had a cute pixie cut but wore elaborate pink wigs when they went out. Her looks were already getting buzz online, and she had a flair for entertaining makeup and gossip streams, amassing more fans than Adelle's book ever would—Adelle was enamored; Connie rolled with it. They made quite a pair, Connie in her baggy yoga pants and oversized hoodie, and Gigi in her shiny pink bows, neon short shorts, and sky-high platform sneakers.

"Look at this," Connie squealed. "You're famous!"

"You're my first celebrity encounter," Gigi teased. "Will you sign my hand? I'll never wash it again."

"Very funny." Adelle rolled her eyes. "You're the celebrity,

Gigi—you have like five hundred followers. But seriously, was it okay? My voice kept cracking. I sounded like a rubber chicken."

"A cute rubber chicken, though." Connie watched her sign the book to her. "You know I'm playing. It was great, Delly. You should really go for this."

"Mom is letting me pick writing schools, at least," she said. Every message seemed trite, so she just signed her name. She could personalize it later, when they had more time. "She still won't give up on the college thing."

Connie was of course working on her application to Yale. Her admissions essay was going to be a doozy.

"I'm sure she loves this," Connie assured her. "You can both be acclaimed authors. Her dream come true."

"Yeah, somehow I think her stuff has more of a following, and it's about funerals. Thanks for coming." Adelle grinned up at them, flush with adrenaline and excitement. There were still at least eleven more books to sign. She could treasure every one of them. "Burger Buddies after?"

"Don't let Greg see us," Connie chuckled. "Yeah, of course. We'll be in the corner over there reading this hot, hot, hot soon-to-be bestseller."

The crowd thinned out. Her mother and Greg came and went, a little worried that she wanted to stay out. Curfews had become mandatory and enforced, which Adelle understood and respected. Home by nine, every time, no exceptions. Only Connie and Gigi were left in the store when the staff began to close up. Adelle was putting the cap back on her marker when a shadow fell across the table, and a copy of her book landed faceup, startling her.

"Love in the Abyss," a low, slurring male voice said. "Dramatic title."

"Thank you." Adelle got her marker ready again, then glanced up to see who had come to get it signed.

He had a snowy beard and pockmarked cheeks, and he wore all black, including his hat, which matched his small, intense eyes. Those eyes fixed on her, mean and cold, and a brittle smile split his face. *Predatory,* she thought, and then: *His mistake.*

Mr. Straven.

"You came back," he murmured, leaning down toward her. His breath reeked, but Adelle didn't recoil. She had been waiting for him. For a whole year, she had been waiting. "Robin never came back, but you did. Then the gate didn't open. The three of you went through, the three flames, but it didn't work, did it?"

Adelle stared.

Mr. Straven hissed through his teeth. "Stupid girl, you don't even know what I'm talking about, do you? Did you just play dress-up? Did I waste all that time for nothing?"

It was her turn to smile, calmly, steadily. "I know what you're talking about, Straven. *Servant.* The flames were lit, three out-landers went through, the gate was opened, and I . . ." She knew the others couldn't see her, not from their vantage and not with Straven standing in their way. Her eyes went black, her purpose clear. She had carried It back, and soon It would be born.

"And I? I walked through the door." There was nothing left inside her but what she had brought back. It was all there, waiting to unfurl.

Straven began to stumble away from the table, shaken, his hands curling into weak little claws as he tried and failed to scream.

Acknowledgments

As always, I want to thank Kate McKean for being the best agent an author could ask for—her guidance, enthusiasm, and belief have never wavered and here we are, fourteen books deep. I want to thank Andrew Eliopulos, not just for his editing work on this book, but on all the projects we did together. What an incredible adventure, and I was so fortunate to be the recipient of his wisdom, hard work, and creativity. His thoughts and help are all throughout this novel, helping shape something roughly bizarre into something coherently bizarre. Thank you, Andrew, for the years of creating together—it was my absolute privilege to work with you.

I also want to thank Alyssa Miele for picking up the baton and running with me. Thank you for giving me the hard notes and the fun ones; your insights have grown this story tremendously.

I'd like to acknowledge Chelsea Stinson and Anna Hildenbrand, who will know exactly what their contributions are when they read this. This whole thing may as well be nested inside that beat-up old Harry Potter journal.

It's crucial that I acknowledge the support of my family and friends, who support me through the journey of every novel-writing process. Thanks especially to Trevor for the brainstorm sessions, emotional support, and walking the boys when I'm too swamped to leave the desk.

Finally, to my readers who have followed me from the Asylum days and to those who are just finding me now—your support, outreach, and love make all of this possible.

Want more gothic horror
from Madeleine Roux?

Turn the page for
a sneak peek into

Chapter One

Malton, England
Autumn, 1809

The road to Coldthistle House was dark and dangerous. So said the woman taking me there, the English rain driving as slow and steady as the wagon.

She found me at the Malton market, where I told fortunes and read palms for pennies. It earned me clucked tongues and black looks from passersby, God-fearing folk who would alert the local parson and see me driven out of their town. But pennies, even ill-gotten ones, will feed you.

Telling a fortune is no easy thing. Indeed, it appears simple, but to tell the future convincingly, one must make the deed all feel as natural and wending as a river cutting its path. Truly, it comes down to reading what resides in people's eyes, how they breathe, how their glance shifts, how they dress and walk and hand over their coins.

I was on my last fortune of the morning when the old woman stumbled upon me. The market day would happen rain or shine, and this was another day of rain in a long, drizzly spell of dreary days. Nobody lingered. Nobody but me, it seemed, and I lacked the respectable reasons of the farmers and craftsmen selling their wares.

The girl in front of me blushed and kept her head down under a thick woolen scarf. It matched her plain, sturdy frock and the coat buttoned over it. Little bursts of tufted yellow-and-gray wool peeked through the weave. She had a fanciful streak. A dreamer. Her ruddy cheeks grew redder and redder still as I told her future.

"Ah, I see it now. There is a love in your life," I said softly, echoing her expression. An old, cheap trick, but it worked. She squeezed her eyes shut and nodded. The teachers at Pitney School had all but beaten the accent out of my voice, but now I let it come back, let the soft Irish lilt color the words the way this girl wanted them colored. Pinks and purples as vivid as her cheeks. "But 'tis not a sure thing, is it?"

"How did you know that?" she whispered, her eyes opening on a gasp.

I didn't.

A dreamer. A reacher. Truly girls of this age—my age—were as open to me as a map. I'd traded such fortunes for sweets and books at Pitney, risking the rod or worse.

"His family dislikes the match," I added, studying her closely.

Her expression fell, her gloved hands in mine clutching with a new desperation. "They think I'm low because of the pig farm. But we never go hungry! So much snobbery and over pigs!"

"But he is your true love, aye?" I could not help myself. Just as I needed the pennies to eat and that eating to live, I needed this, too. The power. Did it work every time? No. But when it did . . . The girl nodded, wetting her lips and searching out my gaze.

"I would do anything for him. Anything at all. Oh, if you could only see Peter. If you could see us together! He brings me apples at luncheon, apples he buys with his own coin. And he wrote me a poem, the sweetest poem."

"A poem?" Well, then they were practically married. I gave her a secretive smile. "I sense a future for you two, but it will not be easy."

"No?"

"No. 'Tis a hard road unfolding ahead, but if you take the greatest risk, you will reap the greatest reward." Her mouth fell open a little, the desperate thing, and I let my smile dwindle to deliver her fate. "An elopement is your only hope."

Running away. A choice that would likely end in the two lovers being disowned and shunned. He might get another chance at a life and a wife, but she would not. The words burned a little in my throat after the fact. *Why tell the girl such a thing, Louisa?* It felt different, even wrong, when in the past, tricking my snobby schoolmates at Pitney had felt like a personal victory.

The young woman's eyes widened at me in alarm. "E-Elope?"

It was as if it were a curse, so hesitantly did she say it.

"Or find another to love," I hastily added. There. Well enough. I had offered an alternative, and that made me feel less the cur for taking the girl's pennies. The casual way I offered the substitute made her grimace. She did not believe true love was a thing to throw away, as I do. "But you knew that already."

"Surely I did," the girl murmured. "I only needed to hear you say it." She placed two pocket-warmed pennies in my palm and looked up at the gray, sinister clouds. "You have the gift, do you not? You can see the future, tell fates. I see it in your eyes. So dark. Never have I seen eyes so dark or so wise."

"You're not the first to say it."

"I hope I'm the last," the girl said, frowning. "You should find yourself a better path. A God-fearing path. Maybe it would brighten those eyes."

How fear would brighten my eyes, I could not say. I doubted she could, either, really. I closed my fist around the money and took a step back. "I like my eyes just the way they are, thank you very much."

The girl shrugged. The bloom on her cheeks had faded. Sighing, she hunkered down into her scarf and fled the market, her well-worn boots splashing in the puddles between cobbles.

"She won't soon forget ye, and that's a fact."

The old woman's voice, thin as a reed, didn't have the intended effect. I had seen her lurking, after all, and expected her to pounce sooner or later. I turned slowly at the waist, watching the crone emerge from the soaked overhanging of a market stall. Fewer than a dozen yellow teeth and pale gums flashed at me, a pauper's smile. Her hair sprang out from under her tattered bonnet in dry bunches, as if it had been lightly scorched over a fire.

Still, there was the skeleton of beauty behind the sagging

flesh, an echo of wild loveliness that time or misfortune had tried to quiet. A complexion as dark as hers meant a laborer's life in the sun or else a foreign heritage. Whatever her birth, I doubted it was anywhere near North Yorkshire.

"Do you make a habit of following little girls?" I asked primly. My true accent vanished. I hoped my arch schoolroom voice sounded half as severe as those of the teachers who had forced it upon me.

"Thought you might need assistance," she said, lowering her head down and to the side. "A little cheer on this dreary day."

I might have known she would reach for my hand and the money in it; thieves were as common as merchants on market days. My hand snapped back and behind my skirts, to obscure the coin in the dampening fabric.

The crone sniggered at me and drew closer, staring up at me with one good eye. The other swam with milky rheum. Her clothes, such as they were, reeked of wood smoke. "I've no interest in robbing you."

"Leave me be," I muttered, eager to be rid of this nuisance. When I turned, her bony hand flashed so quickly toward me it seemed a trick of the eye. Her grip on my wrist was crushing as a blacksmith's.

"Would it not be better if that paltry sum was more? Not coin enough for scraps and a flea-ridden bed but a real day's earnings . . ." With that same unnaturally strong grip, she wrenched open my fingers and placed her hand over mine. The space between our palms grew suddenly hot, a lick of fire passing between us, and when she took her hand away it was not pennies but *gold* in my grasp.

How was it possible?

I sucked in a gasp of surprise, then remembered myself and remembered her, too. If she led a life on the road telling fortunes, then I should not be shocked at her penchant for sleight of hand. No doubt the coin had been hiding up her sleeve, ready for just such a dazzling purpose.

"You must want something from me," I said, narrowing my eyes. "Else you would not be so generous to a stranger."

"Just a gift," she said with a shrug, already wandering away. Such moments of luck never sat right with me—surely such riches came with a price. "Keep warm, girl," the crone added as she hobbled away. "And keep safe."

I watched her disappear behind a cheerfully painted fish stand, the tattered ends of her coat trailing behind her like a shroud. There was no reason to wait longer. If this fool of a woman was so interested in being parted from her money, then I would not refuse her the pleasure. At once, I ran with the hint of a merry skip to the shop window I had passed on my way into the town. Meat pies. The smell was intoxicating, dampened not a jot by the drizzling rain. Lamb, fish, liver, veal . . . With the coin in my fist, I could afford one of each and be spared the pain of choosing. It would be a feast the likes of which I had not tasted in, well . . . In truth, I had never been faced with such overabundance.

The man tending the shop window pulled up the rain shade

as I approached, leaning out and stacking his immense forearms like ham hocks on the sill. Ham. Yes, I'd have one of those as well. Beady blue eyes regarded me from under a cap. His must have been a profitable trade, for his clothes were new and not mended.

"One of each, please," I said, unable to keep the smile out of my voice.

Those eyes staring down at me shifted to the side. Then they slid over my face, my bedraggled hair and muddied frock. His fingers drummed on the sill.

"Beg your pardon, my girl?"

"One of each," I repeated, more insistent.

"'Tis five pence a pie."

"I can well read the sign, sir. One of each."

He simply grumbled in response and turned away, returning a moment later to face me and my growling stomach, handing across six kidney-shaped pies in piping-hot paper. They were released to me slowly, as if he were allowing me plenty of time to rethink my recklessness and run.

But I received the first pie and then the next, handing over the gold and feeling very satisfied with myself indeed.

The satisfaction did not last. The instant he set eyes on the gold, his demeanor changed from one of reluctant cooperation to rage. He snatched up the coin and kept behind the rest of my food, knocking most of it off the windowsill and back into the shop.

"What's this? Don't think a drowned rat like you would be

flashing around this kind of money. Where did you get it?" he shouted, turning the gold this way and that, trying to determine its authenticity.

"I earned it," I shot back. "Give that back! You have no right to keep it!"

"Where'd you get it?" He held it just above my reach, and like an idiot I tried to scramble for it, looking every bit the desperate urchin.

"Give it back! You can keep your bloody pies! I don't want them anymore!"

"Thief!" he thundered. From inside the shop, he produced a silver bell as big as his fist and began ringing it, screaming at me above the clanging din. "Ho, men, we have a thief here! Look lively!"

I ran, dropping pies and abandoning the gold. The bell rang hard in my ears as I pelted through the market square, feet splashing in puddles, skirts growing muddier and heavier by the second as I tried to vanish into the dissipating crowd. But all eyes turned to me. There was no escaping the mob I could sense forming in my wake, the ones who would come for me and throw me in the local jail or worse.

Up ahead, the buildings cut away to the left, and an alleyway sliced a narrow route toward the outskirts of the village. I had time, but only a little, and this might be my only chance for escape. It might also lead me toward more men who had heard the cry of "Thief!" but I dashed off a hope for the best and slid on mud-slicked feet into the alley.

I collided with a brick wall and paused, catching my breath, screaming when a hand closed around my shoulder and yanked.

Spinning around, I came face-to-face with the rheumy-eyed crone and her yellow grin.

"Changeling eyes, that's what the girl saw," the woman croaked, as if there had been not a hitch in our previous conversation. "But a sturdy good frock and boots only mended the one time. Soft hands. Not a maid's hands." That one eye focused to a slit. "A runaway, eh? An orphan on the run. I can see it. The life of a governess wouldn't be for you."

"What does that matter?" I spat out breathlessly. There was no time for idle chitchat. "So you do what I do—you're a traveler. You tell fortunes and the like, so what?"

"I do, and with more discretion than you, girl," the woman said with a croak of a laugh. The laughter made the echo of her lost beauty glimmer, almost truly visible. Still gripping my shoulder, she dragged me to the opposite end of the alley and pointed. I looked toward the church she indicated and the crowd meant to come for the thief, for me. A mob. By now the girl I had told the fortune to would have repeated the story, and they would be hunting not just a cutpurse but a witch, too. It would be her father and her brothers, the priest, and whoever else felt like driving a starving girl out of the village and into the menacing cold.

I had suffered and survived this banishment before. Perhaps this time they sought graver punishment.

"Repent," the old woman hissed.

"I beg your pardon?"

"That's what they want from you, surely. Oh, they'll take you in," she said, laughing again, the sound whistling through her broken teeth. "Show a little contrition. Works, doesn't it?"

The mob expanded. It wouldn't be long now before they felt bold enough for a confrontation. Thief. Witch. No, it wouldn't be long now. The crone had conjured gold to give me, and if she gave it so freely, then there was more where that came from. She might be clever, but I could be cleverer. I could make that gold mine.

"I know a place, girl," the crone said. She paid no heed to the riot forming just down the street. She only had eyes—one eye—for me. "Soft hands now can be hard hands soon. I can find you work. Dry. Safe. Plenty of food. Got a spot of pottage and a hunk or two of pork in my wagon. It will last us the ride, if you're keen to ride, that is."

Not the choice I had hoped to make that day. Rather, I simply wanted to decide where to spend a few coins for a hot meal and a bed for the night. But that dream was dashed for the moment. A new dream formed in its place—me with pockets full of gold and a way to start a new life. The crowd spilling out from the church, however, was a vastly different story.

She latched on to my fidgeting. "Hanging is no end for such a pretty, pale neck."

"How far?" I asked, but I had already turned to follow her, and she led me away from the view of the church, toward another muddy alley running between an alehouse and a butcher's.